'That is a copy of the Official [...]
you to think most carefully be[...]
afterwards, if you reveal anything that I am about to tell
you, or that you might learn in future, you could, not to
put too fine a point on it, be put up against a wall and
shot.'

'And suppose we refuse to sign?'

'Then you will leave this room at once and accept whatever duties your CO sees fit to assign you to. But – and
this is the crucial point – in doing so you will have
deprived your country of the full use of your not inconsiderable talents.'

Frankie's heart was beating fast. At last she could see
some point to the drudgery of the last weeks. Whatever
it was that they were not allowed to speak of, it must be
something very important. She sensed that she was on
the brink of the sort of adventure she had dreamed of
when she had immersed herself in the novels of John
Buchan. She scanned the page in front of her rapidly
and reached for her pen. 'Here you are, ma'am.'

About the author

Hilary Green is a trained actress and spent many years teaching drama and running a youth theatre company. She has also written scripts for BBC Schools Radio History programmes and won the Kythira prize for a short story. Hilary now lives in the Wirral and is a full-time writer. *We'll Meet Again* is her first novel.

Hilary Green

We'll Meet Again

HODDER

W

Copyright © 2005 by Hilary Green

First published in Great Britain in 2005 by Hodder and Stoughton
A division of Hodder Headline

A Hodder paperback

1

A CIP catalogue record for this title is available from the British Library

ISBN 0 340 83900 7

Typeset in Plantin Light by
Phoenix Typesetting, Auldgirth, Dumfriesshire

Printed and bound in Great Britain by
Clays Ltd, St Ives plc

Hodder Headline's policy is to use papers that are natural, renewable and recyclable
products and made from wood grown in sustainable forests. The logging and
manufacturing processes are expected to conform to the environmental regulations
of the country of origin.

Hodder and Stoughton Ltd
A division of Hodder Headline
338 Euston Road
London NW1 3BH

This story is dedicated to my tutors and fellow students on the MA Writing course at Liverpool John Moores University, in gratitude for their unfailing help and encouragement.

ACKNOWLEDGEMENTS

I should like to thank Vivien Green, my agent, and
Alex Bonham, my editor at Hodder and
Stoughton, for their invaluable help
and encouragement.

All the principal characters in this book are fictional but many of the people who appear in a subsidiary role really existed. I have remained faithful to the historical record as far as possible but their speech and actions are the product of my own imagination. I hope and believe that I have done them no disservice.

Chapter One

Frankie was ten minutes away from home when the air-raid warning siren began to wail. She quickened her step. Her mother had not wanted her to leave the house in the first place. She would be frantic now at the thought of her out on her own in the blackout, with a raid about to begin. Then there would be her father's cross-examination to cope with. Where had she been? Who had she met? Why was she late? Frankie felt the muscles between her shoulder blades tighten with frustration. She knew her father was only being protective, but it wasn't as if she had any secrets to conceal. She had wanted to get to the library before it closed – the thought of being without a book to read during the long dark evenings was insupportable – but she should not have lost track of time browsing the shelves. Now it was almost impossible to hurry. The street was filling with people scurrying towards the nearest shelter, some carrying babies or small children, others loaded with armfuls of blankets and thermoses of tea. In this bitter winter weather an hour or two in a damp underground shelter was enough to chill you to the bone. With no street lights and every window shrouded in blackout curtains the street was in total darkness and, dodging to avoid a large woman dragging a protesting toddler by the hand, Frankie walked straight into a lamp-post. The impact left her temporarily dizzy and as she paused and tried to pull herself together she felt her arm grabbed by a strong hand.

'Come on, luv. Down the shelter! Jerry'll be overhead in a minute.'

The ARP warden ignored her protestations that she must get home and marched her towards the entrance to the nearest shelter. Unable to resist both him and the flow of bodies heading in the same direction, Frankie gave in and followed the others down the steep flight of steps into the narrow, tunnel-like space. Already people were staking out their claims to stretches of the benches that ran along both sides, spreading rugs and pillows, settling in for a long night. Frankie squeezed herself into the last remaining space and pulled her coat closer around her, trying to convince herself that it was a false alarm and soon she would be able to slip out and head for home.

She looked around at the other occupants. They were mostly women and children but there were a few older men and a sprinkling of uniforms – boys home on leave or passing through on their way to the docks. Many of the troop ships heading for North Africa left from Liverpool. Immediately opposite Frankie was a young man in army uniform. Frankie had seen enough soldiers in recent months to recognise a captain's stripes on his sleeve, and his cap badge read 'Sussex Light Infantry'. He's a long way from home, Frankie thought, and at that moment he looked up and caught her eye. She lowered her gaze quickly and groped in her bag for one of the books she had collected from the library.

From above came a series of dull, thudding detonations. The anti-aircraft guns along the docks had opened up. It wasn't a false alarm, then. All along the shelter eyes were raised towards the invisible sky and women drew their children closer to them, as if to shield them with their own bodies. Not far away a small boy started to wail and his mother began to bounce him on her lap, singing 'Ride a cock horse to Banbury Cross'. Between the thuds Frankie could hear, or imagined she could hear, the throbbing drone of the bombers. She opened the book. It was *The Thirty-Nine Steps* by John Buchan and she had been waiting for it to become available for weeks, but now she read and reread the opening sentences without taking them in. She raised her eyes and found herself looking at the young officer again. He had taken off his cap and she could see that his hair was dark, crisply cut with a slight wave. Below it were a short, straight nose and a mouth that looked as if it would smile easily. She could not tell what colour his eyes were, because they were lowered to the newspaper he held on his knee. He had a pencil in one hand and was obviously doing the crossword. Unexpectedly he looked up again and she had just enough time to register that his eyes were neither blue nor dark before she dropped her own and felt herself flush with embarrassment.

'Good book?' The voice was low pitched, warm, educated – what her friends at school would term 'lah-di-dah' – but the tone was friendly.

'Yes – well, I don't know, really. I've only just started it.' She was furious with herself for not being able to think of anything more intelligent.

'What is it?'

Frankie hesitated. She knew from her family and friends that this was not the sort of book girls were supposed to enjoy. She wished she had chosen something a bit more highbrow – Dickens or Thackeray perhaps. Silently, she passed the book across to him.

'Buchan! Oh yes, it's a great story! I couldn't put it down.'

'You've read it?'

'Oh yes, rather! But don't worry. I won't spoil it by telling you the plot.' He was grinning at her, and his eyes were a bright hazel that sparkled in the reflected light of the dim electric bulbs that illuminated the shelter. 'You like adventure stories, do you?'

Frankie's reply was drowned by an explosion that made the ground beneath her feet shudder and sent a trickle of fine soil particles through the joins in the sheets of corrugated iron that lined the roof and walls. Two more followed immediately after. A child began to scream and one of the men swore and was quickly hushed by his wife. Farther down the shelter, someone began to recite the Twenty-third Psalm.

'The Lord is my shepherd. I shall not want. He maketh me to lie down in green pastures. He leadeth me beside still waters. He restoreth my soul. Yea, though I walk through the valley of the shadow of death, I shall fear no evil . . .'

The captain leaned across and handed the book back to Frankie.

'Hard to concentrate, in these conditions.'

'Yes.' She took the book and lowered her head to it, trying to hide the fear in her eyes.

'How are you at crosswords?' he asked.

Momentarily Frankie forgot her shyness. Crosswords were a favourite hobby of hers.

'Quite good, actually.' Then, afraid that this sounded presumptuous, she added, 'Well, sometimes.'

He folded the paper and passed it across to her. 'I'm stuck on four down. See if you can make any sense of it.'

She looked at the clue and felt an intense desire to be able to solve it. *Not found in the sea, on land or in the air. You could be on the wrong track here. 3-7.*

Frankie grinned and handed the paper back. 'It's red herring.'

He looked at the clue and struck himself on the forehead. 'Neither fish, flesh nor fowl. Of course! What an idiot!' He wrote in the answer and smiled at her. 'By the way, I'm Nick. Nick Harper.'

She hesitated. She had been brought up not to talk to strange men. Was this one trying to pick her up? But what harm could come of it, here in this crowded shelter?

She said, 'My name's Gina Franconi, but most people call me Frankie.'

'Franconi? That sounds like an Italian name.'

'My grandfather brought my grandma and my dad over from Naples when Dad was just a little boy.'

Nick held out his hand. *'Piacere,* Frankie.'

She put her cold hand into his warm one. 'Oh, you speak Italian?'

'I spent two years in Milan before the war. Have you ever been to Naples?'

'No. Dad's always talking about taking us, but we never managed to get there.' She paused. 'And now, I suppose we never shall.'

'Can't be easy, being an Italian family in this country right now,' he said sympathetically. 'Have you had any trouble?'

'We've had a few funny looks and snide remarks but it's not bad, really. Mum's from round here, so people know us. And Dad took out naturalisation papers years ago, so he hasn't been interned, like some of the men we know. He hates Mussolini and the Fascists. He's always said he won't go back to Italy, even for a visit, while they're in power.'

'They won't be there for ever,' Nick said reassuringly. 'I'm convinced most Italians don't want them.' He felt in his pocket and produced a bar of Cadbury's Dairy Milk. 'Have a piece of chocolate?'

Frankie looked at it longingly. She could smell it, even through the musty odour of the shelter, and it made her mouth water. 'No, I mustn't! I can't take your ration.'

'Go on! I can get as much as I want from the NAAFI.'

She took a piece and as she ate it he went on, 'Have you got a big family?'

'Not really. Just Mum and Dad and my younger sister. And Gran, of course. But she doesn't live with us. How about you? Have you got brothers and sisters?'

'No, I'm an only child. There's just me and my father. My mother died when I was quite small.'

'Oh, I'm sorry. That must have been hard for you.'

'I don't remember much about it.' Another bomb exploded, a little farther off this time. When the noise had died away he went on, 'And you? Do you speak Italian?'

'Oh yes. My gran's never really learned English. She always insists that I speak to her in Italian.'

He looked at her and there was something in his gaze that made her uneasy. She got the impression that he was no longer making casual conversation.

'So - what do you do?'

Frankie hesitated. She longed to be able to say she was doing something exciting, something that would impress him. Instead, she said in a small voice, 'Not much, at the moment. I only left school in the summer. For now I'm helping out in the shop, till I decide what to do next.'

'School!' He seemed surprised. 'I'm sorry. I didn't mean to be rude. You just seem . . . well, very grown up.'

'I'm seventeen. I'll be eighteen in May.'

'What sort of shop is it?'

'My father's. It's a barber's shop. He calls it Figaro's – you know, after the Barber of Seville.'

'Of course. Is he an opera fan? Silly question! All Italians are, aren't they?'

'I don't know. Dad is, anyway.'

'You said you were making up your mind what to do. What do you think that might be?'

Frankie hesitated. He seemed to be asking a lot of questions. She recalled the posters and the warnings on the wireless about not giving too much away to strangers. *Careless talk costs lives!* But what could she possibly tell anyone that could be useful to an enemy? She glanced at him and he smiled and raised his eyebrows.

'Sorry. Am I being too nosy?'

'No!' she said hastily. 'No, it's just that . . . I don't know. Dad wants me to train as a ladies' hairdresser, so he can open a salon alongside the barber's shop. My teachers were trying to persuade me to stay on at school and try for university, but that's only for the toffs, isn't it? My dad could never afford it.'

'There are scholarships, you know.'

'Yes, I know. But I wouldn't feel right, anyway – not while there's a war on. I want to do my bit, like everyone else. I thought of joining up, but Dad isn't keen on that idea. He says there's no knowing who I might be mixing with.'

He started to say something but his words were lost in an ear-splitting whistle. A woman screamed, 'Oh, my God! My God!' Then Frankie was thrown violently forward onto the ground between the benches. For a second or two she could neither see nor hear. When full consciousness returned she became aware that she was lying face down and her mouth and nose were full of earth. The darkness was total and there was a weight across her that prevented her from rising. In a panic, she began to struggle, and the weight resolved itself into a warm, living body.

Nick said, somewhere close to her ear, 'OK, OK. Lie still a minute. Are you hurt?'

She realised that he had thrown himself across her to protect her, but that the two of them were enclosed in a small, dark space. She spat to clear her mouth and managed to say, 'No, I don't think so.'

'Good. Just keep still and I'll see if I can get us out of here.'

She felt his muscles tense and he grunted with effort. For a moment there was no result, then there was a noise of grinding metal and falling debris as he forced aside the sheet of corrugated iron that had collapsed across them. A faint light penetrated the darkness and Frankie felt cold air on her face. Nick grunted again and his foot caught her in the ribs as he struggled to his knees. Then he grabbed her arm and the two of them scrambled to their feet. Frankie looked up. Above her was a jagged hole and beyond that the night sky, reddened with distant fires and criss-crossed by the beams of searchlights. She realised that the roof of the shelter had collapsed, burying all those within.

Already there was the sound of running feet heading in their direction and the clang of an ambulance's bell. Someone shone a torch down on them and a voice called, 'You OK down there?'

Nick called back, 'Yes, we're OK, but there are other people buried. Give this young lady a hand up, will you? I'll see if I can shift any of this.'

Frankie looked along the trench that had once been the shelter. All she could see was a tangle of metal sheets and wooden beams, the gaps between them filled up with bricks and loose earth. Nick was tugging at the edge of the nearest piece of iron.

The voice from above called, 'We're lowering a ladder to you, luv. Can you make it up on your own?'

Frankie called back, 'Don't worry. I'll stay here and see if I can help.'

She scrambled across to Nick and began heaving at the metal sheet with him.

'You get out,' he said. 'Leave this to me.'

'No!' She gritted her teeth. 'There are people under there. I want to do something.'

With a final shove the sheet of metal tilted, spilling a mini-landslide of soil to one side and opening up a dark cavity beneath it.

Nick grinned at her. *'Brava, signorina! Avanti!'*

For the next hour or more Frankie's field of consciousness narrowed to the width of the trench. Others had joined the effort now, hauling at the debris from above, but in spite of their urging she refused to leave Nick's side. Her hands were torn and bloody from pulling at the sharp edges of the metal and every muscle in her body ached, but she had no thought of giving up. They found the woman she had noticed earlier unconscious, with the terrified child clinging to her body. When Nick tried to lift him he struggled like a wild animal, but when Nick finally succeeded in detaching him and handed him to Frankie he burrowed against her, shivering, too shocked even to cry. She was wondering whether to climb out of the trench with him when a cry of pain stopped her. Nick had opened up a small gap in the debris clogging the trench and through it a man's voice sobbed, 'Help me! For God's sake, somebody help me! My bloody leg's trapped.'

Frankie handed the child up to one of the helpers above and moved back to where Nick was working. He shone a torch into the space and illuminated the man's face, ashen and contorted with pain.

'Help me! Help me!' the man begged again.

'Hang on, old chap,' Nick said. 'We've got to make this hole bigger to get to you, but we'll have to work carefully or the whole lot could come down on you.'

Another man climbed down to them and Frankie moved back to let the two of them have room to work. Above her she was dimly aware of voices calling out and the drone of aircraft overhead but her ears felt as if they were stuffed with cotton wool. The trench smelt of damp earth and brick dust and something more pungent. She wondered whether the explosion had damaged a sewer pipe. She felt the earth shake under her feet and knew that another bomb had dropped nearby. '

She heard Nick say '. . . looks in a bad way. Not sure how much time he has.'

The other man raised his head and shouted, 'Where's the fire brigade? We're working with our bare hands down here.'

There was a reply from above but Frankie could not make out the words. The two men scrabbled and heaved, passing back bricks and clods of earth, but then there was a creaking noise and the sound of metal grinding against metal.

Nick said, 'Stop! The whole lot will collapse if we go on like this. Look out!'

Frankie pressed herself against the side of the trench. Above her head a sheet of corrugated iron supported by a partly severed beam spilled a cascade of earth and concrete at her feet. Her heart pounded. If Nick's warning had come a second later the rubble would have fallen on top of her.

All the while the man had continued to moan and call out in a voice that wrenched at Frankie's heart. There was a brief consultation and she heard someone say something about 'heavy lifting gear' and another voice reply 'not for a while yet'. Then a new figure clambered down one of the ladders that had been propped against the side of the trench. He was an elderly man, his hair showing white in the light of the torches.

'I'm a doctor. I can give him something for the pain if I can get through to him.'

There was a general shuffling of positions and Frankie saw the doctor take a hypodermic syringe out of his bag and load it. Then he got down on his hands and knees and attempted to crawl into the hole. It was useless. She could see from where she stood that he was too big. He backed out and removed his overcoat, but he was still too bulky. Nick tried next and succeeded in working the top half of his body into the space. Then there was a creaking of timber and a shower of debris fell around him. He squirmed backward and stood up.

'It's no good. The hole's not big enough and if we try to enlarge it we could bury him completely.'

The wounded man's cries had faded to a low, sobbing moan. Frankie edged forward. 'I could get through.'

They all looked at her and the doctor said, 'No, no. Not a job for a young lady.'

Frankie looked at the narrow hole leading into darkness. Her skin crawled at the prospect of going into it but she insisted. 'I'm the only one who could do it. We can't just leave him like that.'

Nick looked at her and Frankie felt she was being assessed. 'She's right. Let her try, Doctor. Give her the syringe.'

Frankie's stomach lurched. 'But I've never given an injection. I don't know how!'

'It's not difficult,' the doctor said. 'It doesn't matter where this is administered. All you have to do is push the needle in. It's like puncturing an orange.'

Nick reached out and took hold of her arm. 'Look, all you need to do is wriggle into that gap until you can reach the poor fellow. Give him the jab and then we'll pull you out again. You can't get stuck, I promise you.'

Frankie looked up at him and took a deep breath. 'All right. I'll try.'

The doctor handed her the hypodermic and she lowered herself onto her stomach and began to squirm forward, using her elbows and knees to propel herself, while Nick shone a powerful torch from behind her.

'Hang on, old chap.' he called reassuringly 'This young lady's going to give you something to take the pain away 'til we can get you out. Keep going, Frankie. You're doing fine.'

The tunnel he had made was perhaps six feet long, but it seemed much farther. The hypodermic in her hand made movement harder so she put it between her teeth. Edges of metal and brick tore at her elbows and knees and ripped her clothes, and she was terrified that the whole pile would collapse on top of her before she could get out. Her movements dislodged stones and bits of brick and the sound sent spasms of fear through her intestines. Inch by inch she squirmed forward until at last she was close enough to the trapped man to reach him. His eyes were closed, his face rigid with the struggle against the pain. One of his sleeves was ripped and she could see bare skin beneath.

She panted, 'All right, I'm going to give you an injection. I'll try not to hurt you.'

She pulled at the fabric of his sleeve, exposing a larger area. It was difficult to bring her right arm forward in the confined space. She rolled onto her left side to free it, and pushed the plunger on the hypodermic to expel any air, as she had seen her own doctor do. The thought of sticking the needle into living flesh sent a new wave of nausea through her body but she held her breath and jabbed it into the man's arm. It went in more easily than she had expected and she felt a thrill of triumph. Slowly she depressed the plunger until the syringe was empty and withdrew the needle. Almost immediately the man's face began to relax.

He opened his eyes and breathed, 'Thanks, lass!'

She tried to smile at him. 'You'll be all right soon. They're going to get you out.'

From behind her Nick called, 'Have you done it?'

'Yes,' she called back.

'Good girl!' he called. 'Hold tight, I'm going to pull you back out.'

She felt his hands gripping her calves and tugging and had

a moment of panic in case her skirt rucked up as she was dragged back and exposed her knickers. He must have thought of that problem too, because he pulled the hem of her skirt with her, so that she was finally able to scramble to her feet without embarrassment. He helped her up and for a moment he put both arms round her and held her close.

'Well done, *piccina*! Well done!'

She huddled against him, aware of the trembling of her own body against the warm solidity of his. Then he detached himself and propelled her gently towards the ladder leading up to street level.

'Come on. We've done our bit. Let's get you home.'

As she reached the top of the ladder Frankie realised that the street was now full of people and the searchlights had gone out. At some time during the last hour, or perhaps even before that, the air raid must have finished. Some kind of pulley had been set up nearby and, as she watched, a sheet of corrugated iron was hauled up. The man trapped beneath it would be freed soon. Someone put a blanket round her shoulders and led her to a chair.

'Here you are, luv. Get that inside you.'

An enamel mug of sweet tea was pressed into her hand. Frankie looked around her. The street was dark no longer, illuminated by the pulsing glare from two burning buildings. Through the smoke she could see that the shelter was not the only thing that had been destroyed. On the opposite side of the street three or four houses had been reduced to rubble. She wondered briefly where the chair she was sitting on had come from. Out of one of those derelict shells, or donated by a neighbour whose home was still intact? A new thought struck her, like a hand grabbing her windpipe. She pushed the blanket aside.

'I must get back!'

Nick gripped her arm. He was sitting close by, nursing his own mug of tea.

'Take it easy. Drink your tea.'

'But my mum and dad!' she cried. 'I don't know what's happened. I must see if they're all right. I need to get home.'

'OK. OK. We'll go as soon as you've finished that.'

For a moment she resisted but her legs gave way and she sank back onto the chair. Now that the frantic activity was over she was shivering with exhaustion and shock.

Nick went on, 'Where is home, anyway?'

'Just round the corner. That is . . . if it still . . .'

He squeezed her arm. 'I expect it's all right. Anyway, your family will have taken shelter, won't they?'

'Not my dad. He always insists on staying in the shop. He reckons if an incendiary comes through the roof he'll be on hand to put it out that way.'

'Well, he could be right,' Nick said. 'He sounds like a very determined chap.' He swallowed the last of his tea. 'Come on, drink up. Let's get you home.'

When she got up he took her arm and tucked it under his own. She was glad of his support. Her legs felt like jelly. As they walked he said, 'You did a great job back there. Well done.'

Frankie said nothing. All her thoughts were concentrated on what she might find when they rounded the corner.

Nick went on, 'You know what you said about working in your father's shop?'

'Yes?'

He stopped and turned to her. 'Is that what you really want?'

'No, not really. That is . . . I don't know.' She scanned his face, confused.

He said, 'I know it's none of my business, but I must say I think it's a terrible waste.'

'Why?'

'You're obviously a very clever girl, and you've got guts, too. The country needs people like you.'

For a moment she looked up at him in silence. She wanted to ask him what he thought she should do, but he turned away and walked her on.

'Sorry, I shouldn't be interfering. It's nothing to do with me.'

As they turned the corner Frankie tightened her grip on his arm. The street was full of smoke. There was a fire engine parked right in front of her, blocking her view and the steam rising from a burning building mingled with the smoke. She let go of Nick's arm and plunged forward, stumbling across the cratered surface. Then she came to a halt with a small, choking sob.

'Which is your dad's shop?' Nick asked, catching up with her.

'That's it, over there. The plate-glass window's gone, but it's still there! Oh, thank God!'

Her mother flung the door open before Frankie could find her key and swept her into her arms, sobbing with relief. There followed a confused few minutes during which Frankie tried to embrace her sister and her father and introduce Nick, while Nick simultaneously explained where they had been and apologised for not bringing her home sooner. Then her mother noticed the state of Frankie's hands and carried her off to the back kitchen to have them washed and dressed. As they went, Frankie heard her father insisting that Nick must join him for a glass of the strega he hoarded for 'medicinal purposes' or very special occasions.

When she came back into the hallway, her hands swathed in bandages, Nick was just shrugging on his greatcoat.

Her mother exclaimed, 'Oh, Captain Harper! Won't you stay for a bite to eat, or a cup of tea at least? I've just put the kettle on.'

Nick shook his head. 'I'm sorry, Mrs Franconi. It's very kind of you but I should have reported hours ago. They'll be posting me AWOL if I don't show up soon.'

He held out his hand and took Frankie's bandaged paw. 'Thank you for what you did this evening. It's been a great pleasure making your acquaintance.' He lifted her hand and touched his lips to the skin of her wrist above the bandage. '*Ciao*, Frankie.' He turned to her parents and sister. '*Signore, signora, signorina! Arrivederci.*'

He came to attention, saluted smartly and opened the front door. Frankie felt a lurch in the pit of her stomach. He was going, and she would probably never see him again. Without pausing for thought, she jumped forward.

'I'll see you out.'

As she followed him out into the cold night air the harsh voice of the local ARP warden bellowed, 'Put that light out!'

It was a silly demand, considering the fact that the whole street was lit up by the flames from a burning building on the other side, but it gave Frankie the excuse she needed to pull the door to behind her. Nick turned to face her.

'I'm glad I've got a chance to speak to you in private. I had a word with your father. There's an outfit that would be glad to have your services. It's pretty exclusive and I told him you'd only be mixing with girls from very good families, but I'm afraid he wasn't very keen on the idea.'

'What sort of outfit?' Frankie asked. 'What would I be doing?'

Nick's eyes held her own. 'I'm sorry. I'd like to tell you more but I'm not allowed to. All I can say is that you would be doing something that would employ your courage and intelligence much more usefully than . . . well, than staying at home.' He reached into an inner pocket and produced a small rectangle of card. Frankie watched, her pulse quickening, as he scribbled something on the back of it. 'Of course, the final decision is up to you and your parents, but if you are interested – and if you can persuade your dad – go to this address and ask to speak to Mrs Phyllis Bingham. Tell her I sent you.'

Behind them the door opened again and her father called, 'Gina! Come inside. What are you doing?'

Nick gave her the card and squeezed her arm gently. 'Take care, Frankie. 'Bye.'

She watched him walk away in the glow of the burning buildings. He did not look back. She glanced at the piece of card in her hand. On one side was his name and an address in Sussex. On the other he had written '64, Baker Street, London'. London! It seemed to Frankie like the other end of the earth. She told herself that she would go to the dark side of the moon if it meant running into Nick Harper again and recognised, in the same breath, that her chances of getting to either were just about equal.

Frankie bided her time the next day, waiting for a propitious moment to broach the subject that had kept her awake most of the night. There was a lot of clearing up to do, for a start. She helped her father to sweep up the broken glass and made mugs of tea for the men who came to board up the window. Her mother was out helping at the WRVS kitchen that had been set up in a local church hall to cater for those who had been bombed out the night before, so it fell to Frankie to entertain the friends and neighbours who called in to make sure that she and her family were all right. Several of them stopped for a haircut, whether they needed it or not, so her father was kept busy. Frankie worked hard, performing menial tasks such as sweeping up and washing out towels without complaint. Her opportunity came late in the afternoon, when the shop was empty and she and her father retired to the little staff room at the back for a cup of tea.

She waited until her father had settled in his chair and lit a cigarette and then said, 'Dad, about what happened yesterday . . .'

He looked up at her, his brown eyes warm. 'You did well, Gina. Captain Harper told me how you helped those people. I was proud of you.'

Frankie glowed. Her father was not easily impressed and praise from him was something to be treasured. Encouraged, she pressed on.

'He said he'd talked to you about a job I might do.'

Her father exhaled with a small, dismissive 'pouff'. 'That crazy nonsense about some secret organisation that might need you? He must be out of his mind if he thinks I'd let you go off on a wild-goose chase like that.'

Frankie took a deep breath and forced herself to speak calmly. 'It probably isn't a wild-goose chase, Dad. I don't think Captain Harper is the sort of man to suggest something like that.'

'Then why couldn't he tell us what was involved? He can't expect us to take it on trust.'

'He said he wasn't allowed to. You know what it's like, these days. You've seen the posters telling us not to discuss anything that might be useful to a spy – "Walls have ears" and all that.'

'And he thinks we might be spies? Because your grandfather was Italian?'

'No, Dad! Of course not. He wouldn't be offering me a hush-hush job if he didn't trust us, would he? But don't you think it's important, particularly because we came from Italy, that we should show that we're prepared to do our bit?'

Her father looked at her, his brows drawing down. The smile

had gone out of his eyes. 'Are you telling me you want to take this crazy job?'

'I just thought it might be worth finding out a bit more about it, that's all.'

'Huh! And how are you going to do that?'

'He gave me an address to go to. In London.'

'So you want me to let you go running off to London now?'

'Yes, please! I'd really like to find out what it's all about. After all, I don't have to take the job if I don't like the sound of it – or if you don't approve.'

Her father stubbed out his cigarette and got up. 'Gina, you're only seventeen. If Captain Harper thinks I'm going to allow a daughter of mine to go gallivanting off to London in the middle of a war, then he's more of a fool than I thought. Forget the whole idea.'

'But, Dad . . .'

'Enough, Gina! Come along. We've got work to do.'

Frankie nursed her disappointment until the shop closed and they went up to the flat above for their tea. Her mother looked up from peeling potatoes at the sink.

'What's up with you? You look like you've lost half a crown and found sixpence.'

Her father answered before Frankie could speak. 'She wants me to let her go running off to London to join some mysterious organisation that Captain Harper mentioned.'

'And you've said no.'

'Of course. What does he think we are? Gina could end up anywhere. We've no idea what sort of people she'd be mixing with.'

'Dad, Captain Harper did say that it was very exclusive. He said I'd be with girls from very good families.'

'Yes. So what? You're not going.'

'No, of course not.' Mrs Franconi dropped the last potato into the pan with a plop. 'What would people like that, top-drawer types, want with someone like our Gina? She'd be out of her depth. Quite right, Father.'

Frankie saw her father's chin go up. His nostrils flared and his eyes gleamed. Suddenly he reminded her very much of her Italian grandfather.

'Are you saying our Gina's not good enough for them? She's a very bright girl and she's been well brought up. I'm telling you, she could hold her own with any of them!'

Ada Franconi caught her daughter's eye across the kitchen and winked and Frankie drew in a quick breath. But before either of them had a chance to speak again the door crashed open and her sister, Maria, threw herself into the room, sobbing.

Ada caught her in her arms. 'Maria, love! Whatever is it? What's happened?'

'It's not fair! It's not fair!' Maria sobbed.

'What's not fair? What's going on?' her father demanded. 'Speak up, girl!'

'Now then, give her a chance,' Ada said gently. 'Come along, love. Sit down here and tell us all about it.'

She coaxed Maria into a chair and the girl's sobs subsided into hiccups. 'It's the other girls at school, calling me names. Just because we're Italian.'

'Names? What sort of names?' her father asked.

'Wops! Eyeties! They say we're spies for Mussolini. They say we ought to be interned like the rest of them.'

'Oh, love!' Ada murmured helplessly.

Mr Franconi leaned over and took his daughter by the shoulders. 'You tell them you are as English as they are! You have nothing to be ashamed of. We hate Mussolini. Tell them about your cousin Eduardo, who went down with his ship trying to protect the convoys that bring food to fill their bellies!'

Maria looked up at him, her eyes red and swollen. 'I wish I was a man! I wish I could go and fight. I'd show them whose side we're on!'

'Now, now!' Her mother hugged her consolingly. 'We do our bit. We have to keep the home fires burning, don't we? Now, how about a nice cup of tea?'

Frankie watched as her mother filled the kettle and Maria dried her eyes. She was sorry to see her sister so upset and angry at the cruelty of the girls who had taunted her, but uppermost in her mind was the thought that if she had not interrupted at that point her father might have changed his mind about letting her go to London.

That night, just as they were getting ready for bed, the air-raid sirens sounded again. Wearily, Frankie and her mother and sister gathered up blankets and books and the flask of hot tea that Ada prepared every evening 'just in case' and headed for the shelter. Mr Franconi, as usual, refused to leave the shop. Frankie wanted to stay with him but he would not hear of it, so she trailed off to the shelter with the others. The bombs that night fell on a different part of the city, so they heard nothing more frightening than a few distant explosions, but the bombers came over in wave after wave and it was dawn before the all-clear sounded. Chilled and yawning, they trudged back through the scattered debris in the street to find Mr Franconi standing in front of the shop. His face was pale, his normally immaculate dark hair dishevelled and there was dried blood on his upper lip.

Ada ran to his side. 'Guido, what's happened? Did we get a hit? I thought nothing dropped this close.'

In answer her husband pointed to the front of the shop. Scrawled in large letters across the boarding that had replaced the window were the words 'EYETIE TRAITORS'.

'I heard them outside,' Mr Franconi said. His voice sounded to Frankie more weary and defeated than she had ever heard it. 'They must have thought I was in the shelter. I tried to stop them. I . . . lost my temper.' He touched his nose. 'That's how I got this.' He drew himself up. 'If I was ten years younger I'd be in uniform . . .'

'And we'd have no one to take care of us,' his wife said. 'Come on inside. We'll sort this lot out in the morning. It's not people from round here, that's for certain.'

All through a long day Frankie and her father worked in the shop as usual but trade was slack, although it was a Saturday. It had been thin for a long time, with so many men away at the war, but that day was worse than usual. Mr Franconi painted over the offensive words but Frankie could not get rid of the feeling that some of their regular customers had seen them and decided to keep away. And the friends who might have supported them had all had their hair cut the day before. She guessed her father thought as she did. He usually went about his work with enthusiasm, humming snatches of opera as he snipped and shaved, but that day there seemed to be nothing she could do to lift his mood. Because there was not enough work to keep her occupied she was bored, but when she escaped to the staff room and opened *The Thirty-Nine Steps* her father snarled at her to find something useful to do instead of skulking about with her nose in a book. So she mopped the already immaculate washbasins and swept the floor for the third time and allowed a cold fog of depression to envelop her.

She was relieved when, at four o'clock, her father bolted the shop door and turned the notice to 'Closed'. He took off his overall and put his coat on.

'I'm going out for a bit. Tell your mama that I'll be back for tea.'

It was after six and they were trying to decide whether to sit down to tea without him when he returned. He looked, Frankie thought, if not exactly cheerful then at least less defeated than earlier. He kissed Ada and nodded at the two girls.

'Well, it's settled. I've been to see Carlo Pacini up at Crosby. He'll take you on as an apprentice, Gina. You can start Monday week.'

There was a silence in the kitchen. Frankie was too shocked to speak.

After a moment her mother said, 'Well, this is a bit sudden.'

'There's not enough work for two people in the shop,' Mr Franconi said. Pacini's a good hairdresser. She'll get a good grounding with him. Now, what's for tea?'

'Sausages. The butcher called them pork but if you ask me there's more breadcrumbs in them than anything.'

And the conversation turned to the eternal subject of food and what they might have been eating before the days of rationing. Frankie chewed on mouthfuls of sausage that seemed to consist of sawdust rather than breadcrumbs. Her throat felt tight and she had to force the food down, but she knew that to leave it would be to incur a lecture on the wickedness of wasting what little the ration provided. It seemed incredible to her that her fate could have been decided in two or three sentences, as if it were no more important than a change in the weather. She felt the depression that had been gathering over her all day like a physical force pressing on her head.

That night, for once, there was no raid, but Frankie lay awake, thinking of Nick and the mysterious organisation that he wanted her to join. She had no idea what it might entail but she felt that she would do anything if only it allowed her to escape the future that lay ahead of her.

* * *

The next day being Sunday, the whole family went to mass. Frankie did not take communion. She had not been to confession for two weeks now and she was running out of excuses. The fact was that she could not face admitting to Father O'Reilly her growing discontent and rebelliousness. She knew he would palm her off with a few platitudes and a couple of Hail Marys, which would solve nothing. When she allowed herself to think seriously about it, she had to admit that in view of the destruction all round them the teachings of the Church seemed increasingly irrelevant. She even wondered whether she was beginning to lose her faith, and that frightened her.

After the service friends and neighbours from the Italian community gathered round, outraged by the words daubed on the Franconis' shop.

Signora Boschi from the photographer's shop round the corner sighed despairingly. 'I don't understand it. I've lived here all my life. My children were born here. Why should they think we would turn against the country where we've made our lives?'

'We should think ourselves lucky!' retorted Antonio Borelli, who owned the ironmonger's. 'Over the water in Birkenhead they have had riots. My brother-in-law's parents have had to leave their home. All the windows were smashed the other night.'

'Now, now, Tonio,' his wife reproved him. 'There's no need to start spreading panic. We're safe enough here. Everyone knows us. It's only a few hooligans from round Lime Street causing trouble.'

In the afternoon they all went, as they did every Sunday, to have tea with her grandmother. Frankie was very fond of Nonna Franconi, and when she was younger she looked forward to these Sunday afternoons, but recently she had begun to find them a trial. One of the attractions had been the magnificent feast that Nonna always put on, the table loaded with delicacies from Parisi's, the little Italian grocer round the corner. Now, rationing had reduced the spread to a pale shadow of its former glory, and they munched Spam sandwiches spread with margarine and bright yellow fairy cakes tasting of baking powder and dried egg.

As they entered the room Nonna sang out happily, '*Guarda,* Gina! See who is here? Enrico is home on leave.'

Frankie's heart sank. Enrico was the grandson of Nonna's greatest friend and they had grown up together. Frankie knew that it was Nonna's plan that they should eventually marry and the thought filled her with horror. Enrico had always been an unattractive boy with a bony face and ears that stuck out, and since puberty he had acquired a spectacular outbreak of acne. Frankie felt sorry for him but her aversion was founded on something more than physical repulsion. Because he was almost family they had been left alone together much more than her father would have thought suitable with anyone else, and Frankie had been twelve the first time Enrico tried to put his hand inside her knickers. She had told no one because she was embarrassed, but their every encounter since then had degenerated into a kind of wrestling match. When war broke out Enrico had volunteered for the navy and since then he had been at sea most of the time, but Frankie knew what to expect while he was home on leave.

As she anticipated, he asked her in front of everyone if she would like to go to the cinema with him the following evening.

'There, Gina!' Nonna said. 'You would like that, wouldn't you? It will make a nice change for you. Guido, you don't object, do you?'

Her father smiled and nodded at her. 'No, no. Of course not. You go and enjoy yourself. We can trust Enrico.'

Trust him to spend the whole evening trying to grope my breasts and stick his tongue down my throat, Frankie thought. Aloud she said, 'I don't know. Perhaps I ought to stay with Mum and Maria in case there's another raid.'

But her objections were brushed aside and Enrico leered at her across the tea table.

The evening turned out even worse than she had imagined. On the way home Enrico pulled her into an alleyway and thrust himself against her.

'Come on, Gina!' he muttered, his breath hot on the side of her neck. 'I'm only home for a few days. You wouldn't send a chap back to his ship without something to remember in his lonely bunk, would you?'

'I don't know what you mean,' Frankie gasped, trying to writhe away from him.

''Course you do.' His knee was pressed between her legs and one hand was gathering up her skirt. 'Come on, don't be a spoilsport.'

'Enrico, stop it!' She shoved at him. 'You know I'm not that sort of girl.'

'The other girls do it. The lads come back talking about what they've been up to on leave.'

'So you just want to be able to brag about me in the mess, is that it?'

'No!' He drew back a fraction and she could see the desperation in his eyes. 'I could be killed next trip and I've never had a woman. You wouldn't let me go to my death without knowing what it was like, would you?'

'Then pay some woman to do it with you!' Frankie whispered fiercely. 'Don't try to blackmail me.'

'But I love you! We're going to be married. It's OK if we're going to be married. Come on, relax! I won't hurt you.'

He thrust himself against her again, his mouth trying to find hers, one hand pinching her breast painfully. She gathered all her strength and managed to get her knee into his groin. 'Get off me!' she snarled as he jerked back and loosened his grip. 'We are not going to be married! And I do not want to have sex with you. Now get that into your head and leave me alone!'

The last words were almost a scream as she finally broke free of him and began to run. She ran all the way home and burst into the kitchen, where her mother was sewing. At the sight of her mother's calm face something snapped inside Frankie. She flung herself into a chair, laid her head on her arms and burst into hysterical sobs.

'Good heavens, girl! Whatever's the matter?' her mother exclaimed.

'Everything,' Frankie sobbed. 'Enrico, Dad, everything.'

'Enrico? What's he done to upset you?'

Frankie lifted her head. 'He tried to force me to have sex with him. Mum, I hate him. I don't want to be married to him.'

'Tried to force you! Wait till I tell your father. And who mentioned marriage?'

'He did. He seemed to take it for granted.'

'Well, he can forget that idea.' Her mother leaned across the table and took Frankie by the shoulders. 'Gina, love, nobody's going to force you to marry someone you don't love.'

'But you all take it for granted,' Frankie wept. 'If it's not Enrico, then it's got to be Franco or Giovanni or Patrick. Some good Catholic boy who lives round the corner. I don't want to be a ladies' hairdresser and marry a local boy and never go farther away than New Brighton. I can see myself in a few years' time with a tribe of snotty-nosed kids and a job I hate and it's not fair! I can do better than that.'

'Life's not fair,' her mother said tersely. 'And what do you mean by better?'

Frankie sniffed and controlled herself. 'I don't mean better, exactly. Different. I mean, there's nothing wrong with living here and having kids but I want to see a bit of the world first. I want to do something different, something exciting.'

Her mother studied her for a moment. Then she nodded. 'You're right. You can do better. You've a good head on your shoulders and it's a shame not to make use of it. You want to go down to London and find out about this outfit Captain Harper mentioned, don't you?'

Frankie could hardly breathe. 'Yes,' she whispered. 'Just find out. I mean, if I don't like the sound of it or if you and Dad don't approve I don't have to go any farther with it. But yes. That's what I really want.'

Mrs Franconi got up and crossed to where her apron hung on the back of the kitchen door. She took out her purse and withdrew a pound note.

'I've been putting a bit by for your birthday present but I guess you'd rather spend it this way. Here you are. This'll pay for your train fare and a bite to eat while you're there. You'd better go tomorrow.'

Frankie's hand shook as she took the money. 'What about Dad?'

Her mother gave a small, tight smile. 'I'll speak to your father.'

Frankie got up and threw her arms round her mother's plump waist and buried her face in her shoulder.

'Thanks, Mum! Thanks.'

Her mother stroked her hair. 'Love, you know your dad and I only want what's best for you, don't you? We'd never want to make you unhappy.'

'I know,' Frankie murmured. 'I know. And I love you, too. I don't want to make Dad angry. But I need to live my own life. You do understand that, don't you?'

Chapter Two

Sixty-four Baker Street was an anonymous building, distinguished only by the sentry on duty outside and the sandbags that guarded its entrance against bomb-blast. A brass plate declared it to be the headquarters of the Inter-Services Research Bureau, a title borne out by the variety of different uniforms worn by the men and women going in and out. Frankie's heart was hammering against her ribs as she approached the corporal behind the desk in the front hall. What would he make of a strange girl turning up unannounced and asking to speak to one of his superiors? She realised, too late, that she should have written and asked for an appointment, but she had been too anxious to get to London before her father changed his mind to think of that. She felt physically sick at the thought that she might have to return home and confess that the whole thing had been a waste of time. Her only hope was that Nick Harper's name carried some magic that would waft her through the barriers and into the presence of the mysterious Mrs Bingham.

She drew a deep breath, lifted her chin and said, as clearly and firmly as her quivering diaphragm would permit, 'Excuse me. My name's Gina Franconi. I'd like to see Mrs Phyllis Bingham. I've been sent by Captain Harper.'

The corporal seemed neither surprised nor impressed but picked up the telephone and conveyed her request to some higher authority. A few minutes later Frankie was following a girl in ATS uniform along a warren of corridors. The girl left her in an outer office, where a secretary seemed equally un-surprised by her sudden arrival. She looked up from her typewriter and raised one immaculately plucked eyebrow.

'Take a seat, please. Mrs Bingham will see you shortly.'

Frankie sat, her knees and feet pressed tightly together, hands clutching the bag she held in her lap. She was acutely aware of how she must look to the other woman, who was beautifully turned out in a dark grey jacket and skirt, with a cream blouse that had to be pure silk. Frankie was wearing her old navy school skirt and gabardine mac, brightened and, hopefully, made less like school uniform by a bright red scarf and the little navy-and-white hat that her mother wore to church on Sundays. With clothes rationing now in place, there was no chance of a new outfit, even if she had been prepared to take the time to buy one.

Frankie shifted in her chair and wished she had stopped for a cup of tea and a bite to eat. The train journey from Liverpool had taken half the day, with many unexplained hold-ups between stations, and the sandwiches her mother had packed for her had been eaten long ago. The carriage had been packed with servicemen going on leave or returning to their units, and several of them had tried to start a conversation. They meant well but she had not known how to respond and had felt awkward and ungracious. After a bit they gave up and left her alone, but she had been on edge all the way to London. Now she was beginning to wish she had never started on this adventure.

As the minutes passed her feeling of panic grew. What on earth had possessed her to come all this way, on the instruc-tions of a man she hardly knew, to sign up for . . . what? She began to wonder whether, if she made an excuse to leave the room, she would be able to find her way back to the front hall, and if she got there whether she would be allowed to leave the building. She was about to ask the way to the nearest Ladies Room when the phone on the secretary's desk buzzed and the woman looked across at her.

'Mrs Bingham will see you now. Just go through that door there.'

As she entered the inner office Frankie's knees were shaking so violently that she felt sure it must be visible to the woman behind the desk, but her first sight of Phyllis Bingham was reassuring. She was younger than Frankie had expected, in her mid-thirties at a guess, with a pleasant, kindly face. She was wearing a uniform that Frankie did not recognise.

'Come in, my dear. Don't be nervous. Come and sit down.' The voice had a light Scottish brogue.

Frankie sat, as instructed.

'So, you're Gina Franconi.'

'Yes, miss.'

'Captain Harper wrote me a note about you.'

Frankie's heart bounced like a rubber ball trapped in her chest. 'Did he?'

'Oh yes. You seem to have made quite an impression on him.'

'Does he . . .' She stopped and cleared her throat. 'Does he work here?'

She saw the look of amusement in Mrs Bingham's eyes. 'Not exactly. Let's just say he drops in, from time to time. But I doubt we'll be seeing much of him for a while now.'

The bouncing ball became a deflated balloon. 'Oh?'

Bingham's mouth twitched. 'Well, what do you suppose he was doing in Liverpool?'

'Of course – waiting for a ship. I should have realised.'

'Never mind,' Bingham consoled her. 'He'll reappear one of these days, like the proverbial bad penny. So, let's get down to business. You've come down specially, all the way from Liverpool?'

'Yes, miss.'

'Well, you're obviously keen. Tell me a bit about yourself. How old are you?'

'Seventeen, miss. Nearly eighteen.'

'And where did you go to school?'

'Convent of Notre Dame, miss.' Frankie fumbled in her bag and produced an envelope. "I've got my matriculation certificate here, and a testimonial from my headmistress.'

Bingham took the papers, glanced briefly at the certificate and spent considerably longer reading the testimonial. At length she said, 'Your headmistress speaks very highly of you, both as regards your academic ability and your character. So far, so good. What about your hobbies?'

'I like reading, and doing crossword puzzles.'

'Yes. Captain Harper mentioned that. Were you ever a Girl Guide?'

'Why?'

Bingham smiled gently. 'You know, if you're going to get on you will have to learn to answer questions instead of asking them.'

Frankie felt herself flush. 'Sorry, miss.'

'And you'll have to start calling superior officers "ma'am", not "miss"'

'Yes, miss – ma'am.'

'Good. Now, were you in the Guides?'

'Yes, ma'am.'

'Did you learn Morse Code with them?'

'Yes, ma'am. I've got my badge for it.'

'Good.' Bingham sat back in her chair and Frankie felt that she was being studied. 'So, what makes you want to join the FANYs?'

Frankie stared at her, feeling a blush rising to her cheeks. 'The what?'

Bingham seemed quite unaware of her embarrassment. 'The First Aid Nursing Yeomanry. What makes you think you would like to join?'

Frankie was gripped by a feeling of disappointment that amounted to a sense of betrayal. All this way, for this? Just because she'd given one injection.

'No, thanks. I wouldn't. I don't think I'd be any good at first aid and I don't fancy being a nurse.'

She had spoken brusquely but Bingham seemed not to be offended. Rather, the look of gentle amusement on her face deepened.

'You wouldn't be asked to do either. Let me explain. The FANYs were formed originally to care for wounded men in battle, and that is what our predecessors did, very largely, in the first war. Now, however, most people associate us with jobs involving motor vehicles – chauffeuring high-ranking officers, for example. In fact, one branch of the organisation now comes under the ATS, as the Women's Transport Corps. Some of us, however, have preferred to retain our independence.'

Frankie felt a stirring of new interest. 'Sorry, miss – ma'am. Is that what I'd be doing – driving officers?'

Bingham's gaze became more direct. 'No, what I have in mind is something that would make more use of your particular abilities.'

'How?'

'I'm afraid I'm not at liberty to divulge that at this point. All I can tell you is that you would be serving your country in a very important way. Once you have undergone your basic training, provided you complete it successfully, I shall be able to be more specific. Are your parents agreeable to you joining up?'

Frankie hesitated. 'It depends. What do I tell them I'm joining?'

'Tell them you are joining the FANYs.'

Frankie stared back at her. There was no trace of amusement on her face now. 'That's what I was afraid you were going to say.'

Bingham looked puzzled. 'It's a very exclusive organisation. I don't understand your objection.'

Frankie drew a deep breath and nodded slowly. 'No, of course. You wouldn't.'

Bingham leaned forward. 'If you like, I will write a personal letter to your parents, telling them about the corps and its history. I can't go into detail, as I've said, about exactly the kind of work you would be engaged on, but I can assure them that you would not be in any danger – or no more so than you would in Liverpool. I can also make it clear that you would be mixing with girls from very good families, and the brigadier insists on the very highest standards of behaviour. They need have no concern about your moral welfare.'

Frankie said nothing for a moment. Bingham's words might reassure her parents, but to Frankie's ears they sounded like an invitation to go back to school. On the other hand, it meant the chance to get away from home, away from the hairdresser's apprenticeship that her father had arranged for her.

Bingham said quietly, 'We need girls like you, Gina – intelligent, hard-working, strong-minded girls who like an intellectual challenge. And you would be doing really useful work, I can promise you that.'

Frankie straightened in her chair. 'OK – I mean, all right, ma'am. When do I start?'

'As soon as your parents have signed the papers agreeing to you joining up. Then you'll need to get yourself to Overthorpe Hall. It's in the country, near Banbury. I'll give you a rail warrant. That's where you'll do your basic training.' She smiled. 'It will probably all seem very strange at first, but I'm sure you'll soon make friends.'

'But it's true, Dad! I've been looking them up in the library. They've been going since before the last war and they don't belong to any of the other women's services. They're completely independent.'

The family was sitting round the kitchen table over the remains of their tea, and Mr Franconi had Phyllis Bingham's letter spread out in front of him.

'Well, I've never heard of them,' he said doggedly. 'And who in their right mind would give them a name like that?'

'But that's just it!' Frankie exclaimed. 'Women like that – ladies – they just don't use that expression. It doesn't mean anything to them.'

'What expression?' asked her younger sister, feigning innocence.

'Never you mind,' said her mother.

'You keep out of this. It's nothing to do with you,' said Frankie.

'Well, they sound a right snooty lot to me,' the younger girl asserted, sulkily.

'Gina's right, Maria,' their father put in sharply. 'This is not your business. Keep quiet, or go and do the washing up. Gina, what I want to know is, what do they want you for? What are you going to be doing?'

Frankie wriggled uncomfortably in her chair. 'I don't know, exactly. Mrs Bingham said she couldn't tell me until after I finished my training. But she said it would make use of my "particular talents".'

'And what might those be?'

'Fluttering her eyelashes at nice-looking officers.'

'Shut up, Maria!'

'I saw you with Captain Harper. That's why you want to go and join these fannies. You think you'll see him again.'

Her father fixed Frankie with a stern look. 'Is that true, Gina?'

'No!' Frankie paused just long enough to contemplate how easily the lie had come to her lips, and then to wonder whether it really was a lie. 'Anyway, he won't be there. He's gone overseas. He's probably in North Africa by now.'

'Never mind,' her sister said with mock sympathy. 'I expect there will be others.'

'There won't! It's an all-female corps. Don't listen to her, Dad.'

Her father grunted sceptically. 'The ATS is all women, as I understand it, but you know what people call them.'

'Officers' groundsheets.' Maria sniggered, evoking a shocked 'Maria!' from her mother.

'That's enough from you,' her father said. 'It's not a nice expression, which is why I don't want it applied to a daughter of mine.'

'But, Dad,' Frankie protested, 'that's what I'm trying to say. This is different. The ATS takes all sorts. The F-A-N-Y' she spelt it out to avoid any further double meanings – 'are much more selective. You have to be invited to join. When you read their history you can see why.'

'Go on, then,' her father challenged her, 'if you know so much about it, explain it to me.'

Frankie sat forward and pulled a notepad from her pocket. After an afternoon spent browsing in the library she was bubbling over with information that she wanted to share.

'OK. Apparently, it all started with a man called Baker, back at the end of the last century. He was a cavalryman in the Guards and he was wounded at the battle of Omdurman. He was left lying on the battlefield and he could see that all around him men were dying because there was no one on hand to give them basic first aid. He had this kind of vision of a troop of mounted nurses who could gallop onto the scene as soon as the fighting was over and take care of the wounded. He made up his mind that if he survived he would create a corps to do exactly that. Well, he did survive, but he couldn't do anything until he left the army a few years later. Then, in 1906, I think it was' – she consulted her notes – 'he advertised for "high-spirited and adventurous young ladies" to volunteer for his organisation and he called it the First Aid Nursing Yeomanry. They all had to be able to ride and they needed to have their own horses, or be able to pay for the hire of a horse and its upkeep. That's why it's a yeomanry.'

'What is a yeoman?' Maria demanded.

'It's those plump, elderly blokes in red tunics that look after the Tower of London, isn't it?' her mother asked.

'Ah yes, "Merry England" – Edward German,' her father said, and began to sing in his rich baritone, 'For we are the yeomen, the yeomen of England. No other land could bear us but our Mother Land Old England . . .'

'Dad, please!' Frankie clutched her head in frustration. She could feel tears catching at her throat. This was so important, and it seemed her family could not take it seriously.

'All right, love.' Her mother patted her knee. 'Go on, you tell us. What does it mean?'

'I didn't know, either,' Frankie confessed, 'so I looked it up in the dictionary. It means someone who owns his own land, rather than renting it. I suppose we'd call him a gentleman farmer these days. So you see why that would fit in with Captain Baker's idea. Girls who came from that background would be able to ride and likely to have their own horses.'

'Well, if that lot down in London think we're buying you a

horse, they've got another think coming,' her father growled.

'No, Dad! Listen a minute. That's how it all started, and to begin with it was just the way Captain Baker imagined it. They all learned first aid and camp cookery and signalling and how to get a wounded man up onto the back of a horse. But of course, there wasn't a war on back then so they never had a chance to do it for real, like. And then, by the time the Great War started, everything had changed. Motor cars and tanks were in and horses were out – and anyway, the fuddy-duddy old generals who were running the war wouldn't let them go anywhere near it. The idea of women – *ladies* – up at the front line was something they couldn't cope with at all.'

'I bet!' her father said, with a chuckle.

'So what did they do?' her mother asked.

Frankie looked around the table. At last she had captured the full attention of her audience. 'Well, they didn't let the generals stop them. They weren't part of any of the official armed forces, or even the Red Cross, so they didn't have to obey orders. They got themselves over to France and set up a hospital in an abandoned convent. Then they got hold of some motor vans, the sort used to deliver bread and such, and converted them into ambulances. They used to go right up to the front line and pick up the wounded, even when the shells were bursting all around them. They were the first women to drive motorised vehicles under fire anywhere in the world, and lots of them were decorated for bravery.'

'Is that what they want you to do?' her mother broke in. 'I thought that letter said you wouldn't be in any danger.'

Frankie sighed. 'No, Mum. That was the last war. Everything's different again now. The army have their own medical services, so they don't need the FANYs anymore.'

'So what do they do?' Her father was losing patience again.

Frankie hesitated. 'I'm not sure. I told you, Mrs Bingham

wouldn't say what I'd be doing. It must be a bit hush-hush, I suppose.'

'But you wouldn't be going overseas?' her mother prompted.

'I don't think so. I've got to go to Overthorpe Hall for my training. I suppose it's a stately home of some kind. And Mrs Bingham says the brigadier insists on the highest standards of behaviour.'

'She's got a shock coming when you turn up, then,' her sister said rudely.

Frankie ignored her and appealed to her father. 'I want to do something useful, Dad. And I want everyone to see that we're just as patriotic as the people who've lived here for generations.'

Mr Franconi was silent for a moment. Then he said, 'You girls get these dishes washed. I want to talk to your mother.'

Frankie collected the plates without further argument. Nothing had been settled but she knew her mother was on her side and was fairly confident that she could talk her father round. Getting ready for bed that night she pondered the lie that had come so easily when her sister accused her of only wanting to join up in order to see Nick Harper again. It was true that this had been her reason, initially, but now the quiver of excitement at the pit of her stomach was less about the prospect of romance and more to do with the beginning of a great adventure.

Overthorpe Hall was just as Frankie had imagined it, a fine old manor house set in its own extensive park. As she got out of the taxi that had brought her from the station she had a momentary vision of horse-drawn carriages disgorging elegant men in evening dress and beautiful women in furs and jewels. The image was immediately destroyed as she entered the hall by the familiar smells of floor polish and boiled cabbage. The faint feeling of nausea that she had been trying to ignore all day intensified. It was going to be just like going back to school, after all.

The young woman who had opened the door to her checked her name on a list and instructed her to take her luggage to Dormitory Four.

'Up the stairs, turn right and then up the back stairs to the top floor. And get a move on. Tea's in ten minutes.'

Frankie lugged her case up the grand staircase and turned right as instructed, but before long she was lost in a maze of passageways that made abrupt right-angle turns for no apparent reason and went up and down steps to different levels but never led to anything that looked like the back stairs. She was about to dump her case where she stood and head back to the front hall when she heard voices from beyond the next blind corner.

'So I said to her, clothes rationing or no clothes rationing, if you think I'm showing up at a ball in one of last season's frocks you must be mad! I don't care how many Spitfires you're trying to raise money for.'

The voice was a languid drawl and on the last words its owner came into view. She was as tall and lean as a racehorse, an impression enhanced by an immaculately cut uniform. Her platinum-blonde hair was drawn back in an elegant chignon, emphasising a prominent nose and eyebrows plucked to a severe arc. Her companion was shorter, sturdily built but not plump, with dark auburn hair coiled back in a neat roll on either side of an open, merry face. Seeing Frankie they both stopped and the first girl's immaculate eyebrows lifted languidly.

'Yes?'

It struck Frankie that she would have used the same tone to

a tradesman who had come to the front door by mistake. She swallowed and summoned up the vowel sounds she had been taught in elocution lessons at school. 'Excuse me. I'm looking for Dormitory Four.'

She saw the two girls exchange a fleeting glance and knew that her attempt at the language of their class had failed miserably. The tall one said, 'Are you sure you're in the right place?'

Frankie felt the blood rising to her face and anger rose with it. 'No,' she replied sharply and in her own accent, 'that's why I'm asking!'

The other girl spoke for the first time. Her speech was as refined as her companion's but her tone was friendly and accompanied by a sympathetic smile.

'Are you a new recruit? This place is a bit of a rabbit warren, isn't it? Dorm Four is where we sleep. It's just round the corner and up the stairs. You can't miss it.'

'Thanks,' Frankie responded curtly, picking up her case.

The blonde girl was already moving away but the other lingered. 'I'm Diana Escott-Stevens – Steve to everybody here – and my friend's Marjorie Granville. What's your name?'

'Gina,' Frankie said, taken by surprise.

'Gina what? We're not supposed to use first names. It's a rule of the corps.'

'Oh, sorry. Franconi. Most people call me Frankie.'

Steve smiled again and Frankie noticed that her eyes, which were somewhere between blue and green, smiled too. 'Welcome to Overthorpe, Frankie. And don't worry. We're all new here. Midge and I only arrived yesterday.'

From the far end of the corridor the blonde girl called irritably, 'Come on, Steve! There'll be nothing left to eat if we don't hurry.'

Steve winked at Frankie. 'Better go! Hurry up and dump

your things. Tea's about the only decent meal of the day, if yesterday's anything to go by.'

By the time Frankie found her way back to the dining hall there was nothing left but a few sad-looking scones. She saw Granville and Escott-Stevens with a little group at the far end of the room but was careful to avoid them. There was an empty place at another table.

'Excuse me. Is this seat taken?'

The four girls already at the table looked up and Frankie saw surprise and amusement on their faces. She wished that she could somehow get by without speaking at all.

'No, that's OK. Sit down.' The girl nearest to her nodded briefly and then turned away. 'I say, Benjy, pass some of that disgusting substitute for jam, will you?'

The four girls had obviously all been at boarding school together and they resumed their conversation as if Frankie were not present. It seemed to centre around reminiscences of various teachers and the exploits of some of their contemporaries, which sounded to Frankie rather childish but had her four companions in fits of giggles. She was annoyed by their bad manners. She waited for a break in the flow of chatter and said, 'By the way, my name's Gina Franconi. Everyone calls me Frankie.'

There was a silence. The four girls looked at her as if an empty chair had suddenly found a voice. Then the one nearest said, 'Oh, hello. I'm Beth Whitehead.' She reeled off the names of the other three and Frankie responded with a polite 'How do you do?'

'Franconi?' said one. 'What is that? Spanish?'

'Italian,' Frankie said.

They looked at her. 'Italian!' someone echoed. 'But aren't the Italians . . .'

'My grandfather was Italian,' Frankie cut in quickly. 'My

father has lived here all his life. He's a naturalised British citizen. I was born here.'

'Oh, right . . .'

'Do tell me,' another of the girls said, 'what part of the country do you come from? I don't recognise the accent.'

'Liverpool,' Frankie told her.

'Really? Poor you! It must be a terrible bore living in the provinces. What school did you go to?'

'Notre Dame.' As she spoke Frankie knew it was not the right answer.

'Oh? Where's that?'

'Scotland Road.'

'In Liverpool?'

'Yes.'

'Oh, right. Patty, darling, I've been meaning to ask, have you still got that nice little bay mare? The one who did so well in the Pony Club gymkhana.'

The conversation resumed and once again Frankie found herself excluded. She looked around her, covertly studying the other recruits, trying to make out whether any of them came from a similar background to her own. Since they were all in uniform there were no obvious visual clues and she could not pick out individual voices in the general hum of conversation. Her throat ached with the effort of suppressing a sob. What a fool she had been! She had been so keen to impress her parents with the good breeding of her future companions that she had not given any thought to what it would be like to live with them, or what they might make of her.

After tea they were summoned to the Assembly Hall to be addressed by the brigadier. Assuming what she hoped was an appearance of casual self-sufficiency, Frankie followed the other girls into the hall. She found a place at the end of a row and stood with the others as the officers entered. Brigadier

Gamwell was grey haired, with a weather-beaten complexion and a rigidly upright carriage. She viewed the ranks of recruits with a wintry smile.

'Be seated, please, ladies.' Chairs scraped as the girls resumed their seats. 'As your commanding officer I should like to welcome all you new recruits to the First Aid Nursing Yeomanry. You are joining an organisation with a long and proud history. I myself was one of the original members and served all through the Great War together with my sister Hope. When we left in 1918 to start a coffee plantation in Kenya we did not expect to be recalled to fight another war. But the call came, and here we are – myself as CO here, while Hope takes charge of operations in Scotland. I tell you this to illustrate an important point. Once a FANY, always a FANY. We are no longer needed in the role our founder envisaged for us. Instead, you may find yourselves called upon to perform a wide variety of duties. Flexibility has always been our great strength. But whatever form those duties take, however menial the tasks you are assigned may seem, I expect you to perform them with the same spirit of service and the same attention to detail that have always been our hallmark. We are not ATS, or Wrens or WAAFS. We do not answer to their High Command. But, in the words of a general in the last war who had reason to be grateful for our services, we may not be fish, flesh or fowl but we are very good red herrings!'

There was a ripple of laughter from the audience. Frankie was trying to grasp some fleeting association. Why did that phrase ring a bell?

Gamwell went on, 'One further thing – no FANY is ever anything less than a lady! From now on, the reputation of the brigade is in your hands. I shall expect all of you to maintain the highest standards of behaviour, both here and outside.

That is all. Your platoon commanders will assign your duties.'

Frankie did not relish the prospect of sharing a dormitory with the haughty Granville and Escott-Stevens and three others. She had never shared a room with anyone except, on rare occasions, with her sister, and even then she had jealously guarded her privacy. The thought of getting undressed in front of a lot of strangers made her squirm with embarrassment. The other girls appeared quite untroubled by the situation and, watching them as they wandered about in their underwear, cleaning their teeth at the washbasin in one corner or putting their hair in curlers, Frankie was not sure whether to be shocked or envious. It was obvious from the conversation that, like the four she had sat at tea with, they had all been at boarding school and most of them knew each other, either from there or from other social contacts.

Eventually, she scrambled hurriedly into her pyjamas, keeping her skirt on until the last possible minute, and slipped between the icy sheets on her narrow bed. After lights out she lay for a long time, listening to the others murmuring together and then to their deepening breathing and gentle snores. Only when she was quite certain that they were all asleep did she allow the unshed tears that had been threatening to choke her all evening to fall.

The new recruits soon discovered that Brigadier Gamwell's reference to 'menial' duties had not been fortuitous. Frankie was disappointed to learn that her daily routine would involve more sweeping and scrubbing than she had ever had to do in her father's shop. It seemed that their days were to be divided between drill and physical training on the one hand and cleaning and cooking on the other. Her only consolation was the recognition that this was as much of a shock to her companions as it was to her.

The physical training was the hardest part. Frankie had

never been much of an athlete. At school there had been gym lessons and they had played netball and rounders but it had never been seen as an important part of her education, and once in the sixth form she had succeeded in avoiding most games periods. It was clear from the start that the others had a very different attitude. Many of them had played hockey or tennis for their schools and they were fit and very competitive. Anyone who could not keep up was rapidly labelled a 'duffer', and when teams had to be picked, as they were with depressing frequency, Frankie got used to being one of the last to be chosen. Worst of all were the compulsory early morning runs. This was something Frankie had never encountered before and she panted and sweated after the others until she thought her lungs would burst.

She was not the only one to struggle. There was one pale, plump girl who was excused all such exercises after she had a severe asthma attack, and one or two others who simply shrugged off the exhortations of the instructor and the comments of their colleagues as if they were of no importance. Midge Granville was one of those who drifted casually through all the PT sessions, her whole demeanour stating as clearly as words that she had no intention of breaking sweat or disturbing her immaculate hairdo. Frankie wondered why she was allowed to get away with it and wished she could emulate her indifference, but she was driven on by a sense of insecurity. These other girls seemed to be here as of right, but she felt that she was only here under sufferance and could be expelled if she did not conform.

After PT came something even worse. The showers. If Frankie had felt embarrassed getting undressed in front of others, the idea of parading herself naked in public was mortifying. She watched the other girls drifting in and out of the shower cubicles, borrowing shampoo or talcum powder, and wondered how they could be so shameless. There was no way out of it, however. She pulled off her clothes and dashed into a cubicle, then wrapped herself in a towel before emerging.

Drill was not quite so bad. In spite of her lack of prowess in athletics Frankie had good coordination. She had always enjoyed dancing and her innate sense of rhythm made marching in step easy. If only her boots had fitted better she would almost have enjoyed the drill sessions.

On the first afternoon they were all given cleaning jobs to do around the house. To Frankie's disgust, she was in the same platoon as Midge, and that day the two of them were told to scrub the kitchen floor. It was a large room, floored with worn quarry tiles, and whoever had cooked there previously had not wiped up any spills. Frankie regarded the greasy expanse with weary resignation.

'Oh well, better get on with it, I suppose.'

Midge watched as she filled two buckets at the sink and added some washing soda. Frankie handed her one of them, together with a scrubbing brush.

'You start that side and I'll start this.'

Midge gazed into the bucket. 'You don't seriously expect me to put my hands in this, do you?'

A flash of anger broke through Frankie's depression like lightning through cloud. 'Unless you know a fairy godmother who will come down and wave a magic wand I don't see that we have much choice,' she said crisply.

She moved away and began scrubbing her side of the floor. After a moment Midge wandered off to her side and slowly lowered herself to her knees. Frankie watched her for a moment.

'You'll have to put a bit more elbow grease into it than that. All you're doing is spreading the muck around.'

'Well, of course, you're an expert,' Midge returned cuttingly. 'Personally, I've never been reduced to scrubbing floors.'

Frankie bit her lip and got on with her work. Midge scrubbed listlessly for a few minutes, then straightened up with a sudden moan.

'Oh, I've got the curse!' she exclaimed, pressing a hand to the pit of her stomach. ''Fraid I'll have to make a dash for the loo.'

Frankie glared after her but there was nothing she could say. She scrubbed away, working her way across the floor. Five minutes passed . . . ten . . . more. Then she heard voices outside.

'Hello, Midge! Finished already?'

'Just stopped for a fag. Want one?'

'I shouldn't really but . . . oh, hell, why not? Thanks.'

A match scraped. Then, 'Where's your partner?'

'In there.'

'On her own?'

'Well, she's doing a great job. I thought I'd let her get on with it. After all, she's probably used to this kind of work.'

'That's true. Funny little thing. Not quite what one expects.'

'You can say that again!'

Frankie threw down her brush and marched to the door. 'I may be funny but at least I don't leave other people to do all the work! And I don't know what you expect, but I expect the sergeant will expect this floor to be clean by the end of the afternoon. And I'm not doing it all myself.'

The two other girls turned and looked at her and she had a vision of herself as they saw her, flushed and untidy and scowling with anger. Midge turned to her friend with an amused smile and shrugged.

'OK, OK! Keep your wool on. No need to let that Italian temperament run away with you.'

They finished the floor in stony silence and Frankie ended up doing far more than her share.

Frankie lowered herself onto the edge of her bed and began to ease off her boots. She had not put on the light in the dormitory because she did not want to advertise her presence. In a few minutes the other girls would be up to get ready for bed, but she needed these precious minutes to herself. In the dim light from the corridor variations in colour were indistinguishable, but she could tell from the feel of it that her sock was stiff with blood from a blister that had burst on her heel. She whimpered softly to herself as she pulled it away from her foot. She had been at Overthorpe for less than a week and every muscle in her body ached and she felt light headed from exhaustion.

Voices approached along the passage and Frankie heard Midge's detested aristocratic drawl.

'My dear, that accent! Really, we must be scraping the bottom of the barrel if we're recruiting girls of that class. I always understood that the advantage of joining the FANYs was that you knew whom you were going to be mixing with.'

Steve's voice answered. 'But you must admit she's gorgeous looking. All that dark hair, and those enormous eyes. With a bit of make-up she'd be absolutely . . .'

The light clicked on and Steve stopped in mid-sentence. Frankie huddled on her bed, her face turned away from them.

Steve said, 'Frankie! I didn't realise there was anyone here. What are you doing sitting all by yourself in the dark?'

'Nothing,' Frankie returned gruffly.

The bed gave as Steve sat down beside her and laid a hand on her shoulder. 'Are you all right?'

''Course I am.' She paused, then plunged on, 'I've got blisters on my feet from marching and housemaid's knee from scrubbing floors all day, but apart from that I'm fine!'

Steve gave a rueful chuckle. 'Well, in that case you're in good company. We're all suffering.'

Frankie looked at her. Her face was tanned, in contrast to the careful pallor cultivated by many of the other girls, and her blue-green eyes were warm and sympathetic. Impulsively Frankie said, 'It wouldn't be so bad if I could sleep properly at night. I'm not used to sharing a room. And I'm hungry all the time. Isn't the food awful?'

'It is pretty grim, isn't it,' Steve agreed. 'I suppose that's one of the benefits of a boarding-school education. You learn to sleep through anything and eat whatever's put in front of you.'

Frankie turned her face away. 'It's all right for you. We didn't all have your advantages.'

Steve said gently. 'This your first time away from home?'

'Yes.'

'I thought so. Cheer up. It does get better. I cried myself to sleep every night for weeks when I started school.'

The other three girls who shared the dormitory had come in and Frankie heard Midge call to one, 'Lend us some of that hand cream, Bruin. Mine look like an old charwoman's.'

'Just don't use it all,' replied Julia Bearing. 'We're all in the same boat.'

Midge groaned. 'Look at my nails! How can I go out dancing with hands like this?'

Steve gave a brief laugh. 'You won't be going dancing with anyone for the next few weeks, so I should stop worrying. You know we don't get any leave until we've finished our basic training.'

'If I'd known I was going to spend my days as a skivvy,' Midge said, 'I'd never have joined. When I think, if it wasn't for the war I'd be doing the Season now! Henley, Ascot, all the balls and the parties! I'd got it all planned out. Come out, be presented, do the Season and then marry some gorgeous chap with loads of money. And now look at me! I've got hands like a scullery maid!'

'Well, you're not the only one who had plans,' Steve told her. 'I was all set to marry Roddy and settle down. You know, a house in the country, horses, dogs, kids . . .'

'Heaven preserve me from that!' Midge exclaimed. 'That wasn't what I had in mind at all. Give me a nice place in town, handy for all the latest nightclubs. And kids? No thanks!'

'What I don't understand,' said someone else, 'is why they're making us do all this. I thought this was supposed to be an elite corps. Why have they got us all scrubbing floors?'

Steve got up and began to undress. 'I reckon it's some kind of test. They want to make sure we're prepared to knuckle down and get our hands dirty if the occasion requires.'

'How did you come to join up, Steve?' asked Bruin.

'I wanted to do something useful and a friend told me to go to a vicarage in Knightsbridge and say she'd sent me. All very mysterious! It turned out to be the FANY HQ.' She pulled on a dressing gown and sat down again by Frankie. 'Who recruited you, Frankie?'

Frankie looked at her shyly. 'A really dreamy-looking captain called Nick Harper. I met him during an air raid. I only joined up because I thought it would be a way of meeting him again.'

'Oh dear! Not much chance of that here, I'm afraid,' Steve said.

Frankie sighed. 'No. I might as well have gone on helping out in my father's shop.'

Midge stopped putting curlers in her hair and turned sharply to Frankie. 'Shop? Did you say shop? Do you mean your people are in trade?'

Frankie met her gaze and felt the familiar stab of anger. 'I suppose so, if that's what you want to call it.'

'My God!' The words were spoken under her breath as she turned away, but there was no mistaking the contempt in them.

Before Frankie could answer Steve cut in. 'Shut up, Midge! Take no notice, Frankie.'

'Well, at least I'm not too proud to get my hands dirty!' Frankie's voice was hoarse with a combination of fury and humiliation.

'Good for you! That makes two of us.' Steve laid her arm protectively round Frankie's shoulders.

'I don't know why you're so damned cheerful,' Midge retorted, peevishly.

Steve's tone was conciliatory. 'I suppose it's easier for me. I'm probably more used to hard physical work than most of you. My people farm and we've always kept horses. When I was at home I had to help with the mucking out, and since all the men were called up I've had to lend a hand with the farm work too. When we were haymaking I discovered muscles I didn't know I possessed!'

Frankie looked at her in surprise. 'I thought you debs just swanned around from one party to another.'

Steve grinned. 'Oh, I did that for one season. I'll let you into a secret. I was bored to death after a couple of weeks.'

Midge grunted. 'Well, anyway, here we all are. So now what are they going to do with us?'

'Heaven knows!' Steve responded. 'But I suppose we'll find out in due course. Until then, the best thing we can do is buckle down and show them we can take whatever they throw at us.'

She turned to Frankie. 'Better get ready for bed, old thing. It'll be lights out in a minute.'

Frankie looked at her kindly face and almost burst into tears, but she controlled the impulse and forced a smile. 'OK. Thanks, Steve.'

'What for?'

'Standing up for me.'

Chapter Three

After the first couple of weeks the training regime began to change. It seemed that Steve had been right and the hard, menial tasks they had been given to start with were just a means of licking them into shape. One morning they were all ordered to go to the lecture room and given a series of intelligence tests. Frankie had met this kind of puzzle before and sailed through the tests with comparative ease. When the results were announced the following day she and a Cadet Nightingale shared the top score. Later the same day, when they were all sitting around in the common room during recreation time, Frankie was roused from her book by a voice remarking, 'Well, it seems we two have a lot in common.'

She looked up to see a tall, large-boned girl with straight dark hair cut in a severe bob and recognised her as the girl who had equalled her score in the test.

'Nightingale,' her companion announced. 'Dickie to you.'

'Dickie?' Frankie queried. She was used to being called by the shortener version of her own surname but the prohibition against the use of first names in the corps and the prolifera-tion of nicknames it produced still surprised her.

'Nightingale – bird – dickie bird. Get it?'

'Oh, I see. Why not Florence – Flo?'

Dickie gave her a level stare. 'I have been known to punch people who called me that.'

Frankie found herself grinning. Dickie's forthright manner was appealing. 'Pleased to meet you. I'm Frankie.'

'Oh, I know who you are.' The other girl flopped onto the sofa beside her. 'I've been wondering what you were doing mixed up with this lot, until today.'

'How do you mean?'

'Well, you have to admit you don't quite fit the mould, anymore than I do. But now I see. We're both here on the strength of this.' She tapped her forehead.

'Well,' Frankie said, 'there hasn't been much of that involved in what we've done so far.'

'Ah well. You just wait. I know I'm not here for my pretty face and my social graces.'

'What did you mean about not fitting the mould – you, I mean?' Frankie asked.

'Background, old thing. Neither of us is exactly out of the top drawer. My father owns a factory in Stockport.'

'Mine owns a barber's shop in Liverpool. It's not quite the same thing.'

'But it's all trade, as far as this lot are concerned. You're a bit young for all this, aren't you?'

'I'm nearly eighteen. How about you.'

'Twenty-two. What were you doing before you came here?'

'Working in my father's shop. You?'

'Just come down from Oxford.'

Frankie drew in a sharp breath. She could not have been more impressed if Dickie had told her she had just come down from heaven. 'Oxford University?'

'Lady Margaret Hall.'

'What did you read?'

'Classics.'

'Golly! How on earth did you finish up here?'

'It's all my bloody brother's fault. Just because I happened to say I was bored and wanted to help the war effort. Next thing I know he's been on the phone to some friend in the Inter-Services Liaison Bureau, whatever that may be, and I'm instructed to catch the eight thirty to Paddington and look out for a tall man wearing a pink carnation. These men and their cloak-and-dagger games!'

That day marked a watershed in Frankie's life at Overthorpe. Since the evening in the dormitory Steve had made a point of drawing Frankie into her circle of friends. She had the knack of effortless popularity and a talent for bringing out the best in other people, and Frankie found herself accepted by most of the other girls. It was true that she still felt excluded when they spoke of their lives outside the confines of Overthorpe. It was a world she recognised only from popular story books, a world of boarding schools and ponies, riding to hounds and sophisticated parties; but increasingly the routine of training took over their lives and conversations centred on the common experiences of hard discipline and physical exhaustion.

Now she had another friend in Dickie. In spite of the difference in their ages they had many interests in common and they spent a good deal of time discussing books, politics and society in general – discussions that widened Frankie's horizons considerably. There was only one topic that they found it better to ignore and that was religion. Dickie was a convinced atheist and her arguments were too disturbing to Frankie's already wavering faith for her comfort. After one or two discussions, which left Frankie unable to sleep, they agreed to let the subject drop.

One aspect of the new regime proved more of a challenge than she had anticipated. One morning they were all marched out to an improvised firing range and presented with a rifle. Frankie had always loved cowboy films and had often imagined herself galloping over the range, firing her revolver with a deadly aim. Now she discovered that she was terrified of firearms. Having watched some of the others firing, hearing the noise and seeing the recoil of the weapon, it took all her will-power to pull the trigger. For some of the girls, who had been brought up with the annual ritual of shooting parties and were used to handling a shotgun, the transition to rifles was easy. Frankie got on a little better when they were introduced to pistols, but she was never able to imagine herself using a gun against a live target.

As more and more time was devoted to intelligence tests and problem-solving exercises it became clear that Frankie and Dickie Nightingale had a rival for the top marks. Midge, piqued by their success, roused herself from her usual languor to prove that she, too, had a good brain.

'Golly!' Steve remarked one evening. 'I guessed from the start you were a clever girl, Frankie. You and Midge and Dickie make me feel really stupid sometimes.'

'Oh, come on,' Frankie protested. 'You're not stupid. Far from it.'

'Oh, I don't fool myself,' Steve said. 'I've never been the brainy type. Midge was way ahead of me at school.'

'I bet you were a prefect, though, and good at games,' Frankie commented.

Steve blushed slightly. 'Head girl, actually – and captain of hockey. But I don't see what use that's going to be to me here. I keep wondering why I was asked to join.'

'I wonder that about all of us,' Frankie agreed. 'We're all so different and we were all recruited in such funny, hush-hush ways. Are you any good at crosswords?'

'No, hopeless. Why?'

'That seemed to be what Nick – Captain Harper – was inter-ested in with me, and it came up again in my interview.'

'The only thing that seemed to make an impression on the woman who interviewed me was the fact that I can speak French and cook.'

'How come?' Frankie regarded her friend with surprise.

'Well, I went to a finishing school in Switzerland where we weren't allowed to speak anything but French, and then I did a cordon bleu course in Paris.'

'So, you speak French and I speak Italian. I wonder if that's the common factor.'

'Bruin speaks French too, like a native. She lived in Bordeaux when she was little.'

'What about Midge?'

'No, not really. Well, schoolgirl French like most people, but she's not fluent.'

'Hmm. It's not that, then.' Frankie raised her hands in a gesture of surrender. 'I give up. I suppose someone, some-where, has a use for us all. We'll just have to wait and see, I suppose.'

The following evening Steve was called away to take a tele-phone call, and when she returned it was obvious that she was upset.

'What's up, Steve?' Frankie asked, feeling her own stomach cramp up with anxiety. Tragedy was only a phone call away from everyone, these days.

Steve sat down and blew her nose. 'Oh, it's nothing, really. That was Roddy on the phone. He's on embarkation leave.'

'Embarkation? He's being sent overseas?'

'Malta – next week.'

There was a silence at the table. Roddy was a fighter pilot and they had all heard on the news about the desperate struggle being waged by the RAF to prevent the island from falling to the Nazis. Now that the Battle of Britain was over, the defence of Malta was probably the most hazardous assignment available.

'The worst part is,' Steve went on, 'he's come down specially and taken a room at the pub in the village and I had to tell him I can't get out to see him.'

'Oh, surely!' Frankie exclaimed. 'If you spoke to the CO and told her the situation she'd let you have a couple of hours off.'

Steve shook her head. 'I've just been to see her. She said she couldn't make any exceptions to the rule.'

'The rotten cow!'

'No, I can see her point,' Steve said. 'I can't be the only person who's got a boyfriend in one of the services. If she let me go there would be half a dozen others with just as good an excuse.'

'You're just too damn reasonable!' Midge told her. 'Listen, you don't have to get her permission. Get back on the phone to Roddy and tell him to wait for you outside the gates about half an hour after lights out. There's a fire escape just down the passage. You can nip down that and be away without anyone being any the wiser. I'll close the door behind you.'

'And how will I get back in?' Steve asked.

'I'll wait up and let you in. You can have an hour or two with Roddy. That's better than nothing, isn't it?'

'Of course it is. But I can't let you do it. If we were found out we'd both be sacked, you know that.'

'So what? It wouldn't break my heart. I've had enough of this place anyway.'

Steve twisted her handkerchief. 'Oh, I don't know. It doesn't seem right.'

'Oh, don't be so wet!' Midge's tone was scathing. 'You always were such a goody-goody. Listen, Roddy deserves an hour or two with you before he goes off to fight, doesn't he?

How will you feel if . . .' She stopped in response to a sharp look from Frankie. 'Well, you know what I mean.'

Steve looked at Frankie. 'What do you think?'

'I think you should go,' Frankie said. 'Midge is right. You owe it to Roddy and I think the CO's being unreasonable.'

'You're sure you don't mind waiting up, Midge?' Steve queried.

'I shan't actually wait up. It'd look pretty suspicious if someone saw me hanging around by the fire escape, wouldn't it? Make sure you're back by midnight and I'll be there to open up for you.'

Half an hour after lights out Frankie watched as Steve slipped, fully dressed, out of bed and tiptoed out of the dormitory, followed by Midge. She was wishing that she had had the inspiration about the fire escape and that she possessed Midge's insouciant disregard for authority. A few minutes later Midge returned.

'Did she get off all right?' Frankie whispered.

'No, I left her dangling from the fire escape by her suspenders!' Midge retorted. 'Go to sleep.'

In spite of this injunction, Frankie found sleep impossible. Midge, in contrast, burrowed down into her blankets and seemed to fall asleep immediately. Frankie wondered how she could be sure of waking in time to let Steve back in. Eventually she dozed off, only to wake with a start some time later. With the blackout curtains tightly closed the dormitory was in pitch darkness. Frankie felt under her pillow for her torch and shone it cautiously onto Steve's bed. It was empty. In the bed beyond, Midge's humped form was visible. Frankie scrabbled for her watch. It showed 12.25.

Frankie slid out of bed and wrapped herself in her dressing gown. Although it was now well into March, winter was reluctant to give up its grip and the air in the unheated dormitory was icy. She padded over to Midge's bed and leaned down to her. She was breathing deeply and evenly, obviously fast asleep. Frankie contemplated waking her, then changed her mind and let herself quietly out into the corridor. The fire-escape door yielded easily, letting in a gust of damp night air, but there was no one on the small metal platform outside. Frankie walked out onto it and leaned over. There was no one sheltering below, either. She called Steve's name, softly, twice, but received no response. With a deepening sense of anxiety, she went back inside and pulled to door to behind her.

Perched on the edge of the window sill, her dressing gown huddled round her, she considered the situation. The most likely explanation was that Steve and Midge had agreed a last-minute change in the arrangements. Probably Midge would be along in another half-hour or so to fulfil her part of the bargain – but Frankie could not feel certain that the other girl would be any wider awake then than she was now. The sensible thing to do, she told herself, would be to go back and wake her, but she had no wish to lay herself open to another sarcastic put-down. On the other hand, she could not go back to bed knowing that Steve was out there, waiting. She wriggled farther onto the window sill, pulled her feet up under her and settled down to wait.

She did not fall asleep, her position was far too uncomfortable for that, but the cold and her own weariness induced a kind of trance-like state in which she lost all sense of time. Intermittently, she roused herself enough to lift the blackout curtain and peer out onto the fire escape, but although there was enough light from a three-quarter moon to make out the outline of the platform and the stairs leading up to it, there was no sign of Steve. Eventually, she drifted into a state of semi-consciousness in which dreams and reality became indistinguishable.

She was woken by a deafening clang that shocked her from her cramped perch onto her feet before she was fully awake. For a moment she registered the noise as an air-raid alert, but then she realised that it was the fire alarm. The powers-that-be had chosen that night, of all nights, to conduct a fire drill. She lifted the blind and looked out. To her amazement, the first light of dawn had turned the frosted landscape silver grey. She hobbled to the door and opened it. Behind her she could hear footsteps and a babble of voices as the other girls stumbled, half asleep, out of their dormitories. The garden below her was empty.

'Steve!' Frankie called. Then more loudly, 'Steve!'

There was no response. From behind her a voice said brusquely, 'Well, don't just stand there! We all want to get out, you know.'

Frankie looked round. The corridor was thronged with girls. She had no choice but to lead the way down, feeling the metal treads of the stairs strike cold through her thin slippers. Once on the ground the girls headed for their pre-arranged assembly points. This was not the first fire drill they had had and even fogged with sleep they moved with purposeful efficiency. Frankie let the crowd pass her, gazing around her at the trees and ornamental shrubs surrounding the house. Was Steve out there somewhere, afraid to show herself? Or was it possible that she had found some other way in and had been safely tucked up in bed all this time? Frankie searched the crowd for Midge and caught sight of her blonde head moving towards the assembly point allotted to their platoon. She hurried after her.

'Where's Steve?' she whispered, catching up.

'For God's sake, how should I know?'

'You were supposed to let her in.'

'Oh, grow up, Frankie! You don't really think she meant to come back before morning, do you?'

'What do you mean?' Frankie forgot to keep her voice down. 'I've been waiting up for her all night.'

'Shut up, can't you? Do you want everyone to hear you?'

They had reached the assembly point. Girls were milling around, clutching dressing gowns or overcoats around them, individual forms and faces indistinguishable in the grey dawn light. Frankie gazed around her, hoping to see Steve lurking somewhere among the bushes that edged the driveway. Fully dressed among the pyjama-clad crowd, it would be obvious to everyone that she had not come straight from her bed, but Frankie still hoped that she might be near enough to answer her name when the roll was called. Officers with clipboards were trying to marshal their charges into distinct groups, but in the half-light there was still some confusion. The sergeant in charge of Frankie's platoon began calling out names.

'Bearing?'

Julia's voice, croaky with sleep. 'Here, Sarge.'

'Curtis?'

Another voice out of the gloom. 'Yes, Sarge.'

'Escott-Stevens?'

'Here, Sarge.' Frankie pitched her voice several tones lower than normal and used her best elocution-lesson vowels. Beside her Midge turned her head with a sharp, astounded look but she was already ducking away, moving behind some of the other girls, so that when the sergeant called, 'Franconi?' her answer, with a stronger tinge of Liverpool than usual, came from a different position.

'Here, Sarge.'

The roll-call completed, they were kept standing for a while longer, while Frankie jogged from foot to foot, shivering not only with cold but with anxiety as the light grew ever stronger. At last, the order to dismiss came and the girls trooped towards the entrance of the house, but Frankie tugged at Midge's sleeve and muttered, 'This way!'

They returned to the fire escape and, as they reached it, a figure detached itself from the shadows beneath it.

'Steve! Thank God!' Frankie breathed.

Steve caught Midge's arm. 'Midge, I'm so sorry! I must have given you an awful scare! Was I missed at roll-call? I didn't dare show myself.'

'No, it's all right, you weren't missed,' Midge said. 'Now get inside before someone sees us.'

Frankie followed them up the fire escape, her throat burning with resentful tears. Steve was babbling excuses and thanks to Midge's back. She did not appear to have noticed Frankie at all.

Back in the house, Midge opened the door to a bathroom and said, 'In here, quick. Give people a chance to get dressed, so you won't be so conspicuous.'

Frankie followed them in. Steve said, 'Look, I am really, *really* sorry. Did you stay up for hours waiting for me?'

Midge looked faintly amused. 'Not me,' she said with a shrug. 'I knew you wouldn't be back till dawn.'

'You knew? How?'

'Oh, come on, darling! I'm not stupid. It was your last possible chance to be with Roddy. Of course you stayed the night.'

Frankie saw the colour flame up in Steve's cheeks.

'Midge! It wasn't like that at all. What do you think of me?'

'For goodness' sake! You're flesh and blood, like the rest of us, aren't you?'

'Yes, but I wouldn't . . . I mean . . . not before we were married. Nor would Roddy. It wasn't that at all. He was bringing me back, just as we arranged, and the wretched car broke down. We had to walk back about three miles to find a garage and then Roddy had a frightful job waking the mechanic and persuading him to come out and help us. When he finally did agree it took him ages to get ready and then even more ages to find out what was wrong with the car and put it right. I got back here just in time to see everyone pouring down the fire escapes. Just my luck! Why did they have to have a fire drill today of all days?'

There was a brief silence as Steve looked from Midge to Frankie and back again. Midge shrugged, a gesture that tried to look casual but succeeded only in being defensive.

Steve said, 'Do you mean to say you didn't wait up to let me back in?'

Frankie glared at Midge but the other girl said merely, 'I didn't think you'd be there.'

'I did,' Frankie said, her voice harsh with anger and weariness. 'I waited up.'

Steve turned to her. 'You did, Frankie?'

'I saw Midge was fast asleep, so I came to let you in. When you weren't there I waited.'

'All night?'

'Till the alarm went off.'

'Oh, Frankie!' Steve reached out and grasped her hand. Then she looked round at Midge. 'How come I wasn't missed at roll-call?'

Midge had taken a packet of cigarettes out of her pocket and was in the process of lighting up. 'Frankie answered up for you,' she said indistinctly.

Steve regarded her for a moment in silence, then turned to Frankie. 'Well, there's one thing to be said for a night like this. You certainly find out who your real friends are. Frankie, I don't know how to thank you.'

'It's all right,' Frankie muttered.

Steve put her arms round her. 'You poor thing! You're

absolutely freezing. It'll be all my fault if you go down with double pneumonia. Come on, let's get some clothes on you. The others will be dressed by now.'

She shepherded Frankie back to the dormitory, leaving Midge without another word. Glancing back over her shoulder, Frankie caught a gaze of smouldering resentment, only partly masked by an exhaled cloud of cigarette smoke.

Morning post was delivered at breakfast time and the girls took it in turns to hand the letters out. One day, soon after Steve's escapade, Frankie was performing this duty. She noticed that Midge's letters were addressed to The Hon. Marjorie Granville. She had no idea what one had to do to earn the title of Honourable but she was quite sure Midge did not deserve it.

One morning, she discovered a small pile of letters by her plate. She recognised her mother's writing and Maria's, and then her grandmother's and several friends'. It was only when she opened the first envelope and took out a card that she remembered that it was her birthday.

Steve saw the card before Frankie could slip it back into the envelope. 'Frankie? It's not your birthday, is it?'

'Yes, it is, actually.'

'Why on earth didn't you say? We could have organised a party.'

'I'd forgotten. No, really! There's been so much to think about I'd simply lost count of the date.'

'Well, many happy returns! How old are you? Nineteen?'

'Eighteen.'

'Bless you! Is that all? Congratulations anyway. But what a way to spend your birthday! It's a shame.'

'Oh, it doesn't matter. There are more important things going on than birthdays.'

At teatime Frankie was astounded to find Steve and Dickie and a group of her new friends sitting round a cake on which eight candles burned. As soon as they saw her enter the room they all broke into 'Happy Birthday to You', and most of the other girls joined in. Blushing furiously, Frankie took her place and blew out the candles.

'It's only an ordinary sponge cake, I'm afraid,' Steve said, 'and we could only find eight candles instead of eighteen. But we couldn't let your birthday go by without something.'

'It's terribly sweet of you,' Frankie answered. 'But how did you manage it?'

'I cycled to the farm down the road in the lunch hour and managed to sweet-talk the farmer's wife into to selling me a couple of eggs. Then I got Sarge to give me half an hour off so I could sneak into the kitchen and the cooks let me have the other ingredients.'

Frankie reached out and squeezed her hand. 'Thanks, Steve. You really shouldn't have gone to all that trouble, but I do appreciate it. It's the best birthday cake I've ever had.'

She cut the cake and distributed it round the group. Looking up as she did so, she became aware of Midge watching her from another table and was surprised to see an expression of pain instead of her usual hostility. On an impulse, she cut an extra slice and took it over to her.

'Here you are, Midge, have a piece of cake.'

For a moment she thought Midge would refuse. Then she mumbled, 'Thanks,' and Frankie had the satisfaction of seeing her blush.

Since the night of the fire drill there had been an obvious coolness between Steve and her old school friend. On the surface Midge maintained an air of aloof detachment, but Frankie was aware that her initial contempt had turned into a burning resentment. Midge had her own little coterie of friends, and before long Frankie began to notice barbed remarks disguised as helpful comments or concerned enquiries.

'Frankie, we don't say serviette. We say table napkin.'

'Frankie, call it a lavatory. Toilet is so terribly common.'

'By the way, do you have an inside lav at home? It must be a frightful nuisance having to go down the garden every time. Whatever do you do in the middle of the night?'

Frankie knew the remarks were intended to hurt but she hid her feelings and stored the corrections in her memory. She never made the same mistake twice.

When it became apparent that this tactic was not having the desired effect, Midge steered her friends onto a different track. Frankie's Italian origins presented a more vulnerable target. It began innocently enough one mealtime. They had been presented with a grey mess calling itself Lancashire hotpot, but the meat consisted mainly of bone and gristle and most of the girls pushed their plates aside unfinished.

'I expect you'd rather have a nice plate of spaghetti,' Midge said, with a sympathetic smile.

Frankie was still hungry, as she almost always was, and the memory of her gran's steaming bowls of pasta, with its rich, aromatic sauce, almost brought tears to her eyes.

'Actually,' she said, deliberately coarsening her accent, 'I'd rather go down the corner shop for two penn'orth o' chips.'

'Personally,' put in one of Midge's toadies, 'I can't stand that ghastly foreign muck. It's all so oily. And as for anything with garlic in it! Well, it makes your breath smell so dreadfully, doesn't it.'

'Oh, I know what you mean,' Midge agreed. 'My parents took me to Naples once. My dear, it was awful! Full of horrible greasy little wops who'd pick your pocket as soon as look at you. And it stank! What with the smell from the drains and the garlic on everyone's breath, I could hardly breathe.' She turned to Frankie. 'Where did you say your grandfather came from?'

Frankie knew what Midge was trying to do so she bit her lip and said nothing, but the following evening her self-control was stretched to breaking point. She was reading in the common room during the recreation period and was dimly aware of a group of people settling themselves in chairs just behind her. Then Midge's nasal drawl pierced her concentration.

'What I simply don't understand is why the powers that be have seen fit to recruit someone from an enemy country. After all, we are fighting the Italians, aren't we?'

'Well, quite. If you ask me it's a bit of an insult to the rest of us.'

'Mind you, they wouldn't know what to do with any information if they got it. My brother's in North Africa and he says the Italian army is an absolute shambles. He says they'd rather run a mile than fight, and the only reason they haven't turned tail and gone home is that they're more frightened of the Germans than they are of us.'

'Careful!' It was Midge's voice again. 'You want to watch what you say. Remember the posters. Walls have ears!'

There was a crash as Frankie's chair was overturned. The rest of the girls in the room stopped their conversations and looked up. Frankie flung herself on Midge, seized her by her collar and dragged her to her feet.

'You bitch! You stupid, vicious cow! How dare you suggest I'm a spy? I was born in this country. I'm as patriotic as you are. Nobody's got any right to suggest otherwise. I've had enough of you and your snide remarks, so just fuck off! D'you hear me? *Fuck off!*'

It was not a word she had ever uttered before and it would have earned her a slap from either of her parents, but she had heard the drunks outside the pubs at turning-out time use it and she knew what it meant. There was an instant of shocked silence and then Frankie saw a smirk of triumph on Midge's face. She grasped her by the hair and began to shake her.

'Don't you grin at me, you . . .'

'*Franconi!*'

The single word cut across her furious diatribe like a bullet. Slowly she dropped her hands and turned, and then she knew why Midge had smiled. The CO, Captain Markham, was standing in the doorway.

'My office, now!' Markham turned on her heel and disappeared. Midge chuckled softly.

'Oh dear, now you've done it. You really will have to learn to control that Latin temper, you know.'

Steve had crossed the room and now laid a hand on Frankie's arm. 'I'll come with you. I'll tell the captain . . .'

Frankie shook her hand off. 'I can tell her myself.'

She turned away and followed Markham down the corridor.

'Well?' the CO enquired, when she was seated at her desk with Frankie at attention in front of her. 'What was all that about?'

'We had a difference of opinion, ma'am.'

'That much was obvious. What about?'

Frankie swallowed. It was tempting to pour out the whole story but she knew that to a detached listener it would sound trivial and childish. 'Nothing important, ma'am.'

'Franconi, I was passing in the corridor and I heard you screaming like a fishwife. And you tell me it was about nothing important?'

'Yes, ma'am.'

The captain folded her hands on her desk and leaned towards Frankie. 'Is that the way you normally settle arguments?'

'No, ma'am.'

'I'm relieved to hear it.' She paused. 'I realise that it is not easy for you here. Your background is very different from most of the other girls and perhaps standards of speech and behaviour at home are not quite what we expect from our young ladies. But you must remember that we have certain standards here to which you are expected to adhere. I will not tolerate the kind of outburst, and the kind of language, to which I was a witness just now.'

'That's all right, ma'am.' Frankie found her voice. 'You won't have to. Of course you're right. I don't belong here. My family don't have much money and I didn't go to a posh school. You think I'm common but my dad would have belted me if he'd heard me use that word. We may not have all your fine manners but we don't talk behind other people's backs, either, and I was brought up to believe that you never make assumptions about someone or look down on them just because they aren't as well off as you.' She paused to catch a breath and then rushed on before the captain could speak. 'So I'll just pack my things and go. I shouldn't ever have been asked to come here. I don't fit and I never shall.'

She turned on her heel and was halfway to the door before the CO's voice stopped her.

'Stand still! Don't you dare walk out on me!'

Frankie's first impulse was to keep going but common sense told her that she would probably be physically prevented from leaving if she tried. She turned slowly back.

'Come here.'

Frankie moved back to the desk. To her surprise, in spite of her tone of voice, the captain looked quite calm.

'Now, let us get one or two things straight, shall we? First of all, it is not up to you to decide whether you stay or go. You have signed up for this and you will only leave if I decide to dismiss you. And, in spite of your little outburst, I am not of a mind to do that at the moment. Understood?'

'Yes, ma'am.'

'Secondly, I take your point about making unjustified assumptions on the basis of a person's social background. I have been guilty of that and I apologise.'

Frankie opened her mouth and took in a gulp of air. She felt as if the floor had dissolved under her feet. 'Oh no, ma'am! I didn't mean you.'

'You didn't? Then someone else has been casting aspersions on your upbringing. Who?'

Frankie started to speak, then closed her lips. Whatever Midge's offence, she knew that to complain to the CO would be the one unforgivable sin.

'Granville?' The captain suggested. Then, as Frankie remained silent, she went on, 'I'm not blind, you know. I shall be talking to Granville when I've finished with you. Meanwhile, your little outburst cannot go unpunished. You will be on extra fatigues for the rest of the week. That's all. Dismiss!'

Frankie stumbled up the stairs to her dormitory in a daze and sat down on the edge of her bed. For a few moments she had been convinced that she was going home, and the prospect of being back with her family was so tempting that she almost wept with frustration. On the other hand, the thought of the shame of admitting that her great adventure had turned out a failure was too painful to contemplate. Between the two, she did not know whether to be relieved or disappointed.

The door opened and closed again softly and Steve came to sit beside her.

'How did it go?'

'Oh, she gave me a ticking off and put me on extra fatigues for the rest of the week.'

'Poor you! But I suppose it could be worse. It's not fair, though. Midge ought to be on extra fatigues, too.'

'Oh no!' Frankie exclaimed. 'That would mean we'd have to do them together. That would be awful!'

'Yes, it would, wouldn't it? You'd be at each other's throats in no time.'

They looked at each other and laughed, the shaky laughter of relief that is close to tears.

Steve took Frankie's hand and said, 'Listen. I know Midge is behaving very badly but you mustn't take too much notice. It isn't entirely her fault. She's had a pretty tough life.'

'Tough! With her money? She doesn't know what tough is.'

Steve shook her head. 'There are other ways for life to be tough, apart from being short of money, you know.'

'What do you mean?'

'It's not my place to talk about Midge's private life. But take it from me, she's never had a proper family. Don't let on I told you. I've told her I think she's behaved disgracefully, so perhaps she'll take it to heart.'

'I think the CO's going to speak to her, too. I didn't say anything, but she guessed.'

'Of course. Markham's not stupid. It takes two to make a quarrel. Well, let's hope that's the end of it.'

'Tell me one thing. Why is Midge the Honourable Marjorie? I saw it on her letters.'

'Just because her father's Lord Farnham. It's one of those silly hereditary titles. It doesn't mean a thing.'

'You can say that again!' Frankie muttered.

It did seem for a while as if Midge had repented of her cruelty. She didn't apologise but she began to treat Frankie with conspicuous friendliness. It took Frankie a while to realise that this was a change of tactics, not a change of heart. It began with small requests.

'Frankie, darling, there's a button off my tunic and I'm absolutely hopeless with a needle. I've seen you sewing things and you're so neat. Could you possibly do it for me?'

Frankie, anxious to show that she was prepared to let bygones be bygones, did as she was asked.

Next evening it was, 'Frankie, if you're going to wash out your smalls could you just rinse through these stockings for me? It saves using two lots of hot water.'

Then it was, 'Oh God, my feet are killing me! And I've left my book in the refectory. Frankie, would you be a dear?'

It was then that Frankie caught a swift, secret smile passing between Midge and one of her pals and realised that she was being groomed to act as a personal servant. She fetched the book and waited for the next request. It came that evening in the dormitory.

Midge was combing her hair. 'Do you know, I'm really fed up with my hair. It's such a drag having to put it up every day. I think I'd prefer it short.' She turned to Frankie as if a thought had only just struck her. 'Frankie, sweetie, you're a hair-dresser, aren't you? You could trim it for me, couldn't you?'

It was on the tip of Frankie's tongue to point out that she had cut only men's hair. Then a thought came to her that was so tempting in its mischief that she could not resist it.

'OK, I'll have a go, if you like.'

She had brought a good pair of scissors with her, thinking that they were bound to come in useful. Midge sat down and wrapped a towel round her shoulders and Frankie saw her wink at Bruin, who was one of her set. Just you wait, she thought.

There was no mirror in the room, except for a small one above the washbasin, so Midge had no way of seeing what

Frankie was doing. Bruin had gone off, smirking, to the bath-room, and the only other person paying any attention was Steve. She saw Frankie make the first cut and opened her mouth, then shut it again and grinned. Frankie sliced into the sleek, peroxided waves. It went against her instincts to do a bad job but she hardened her heart. In a few minutes Midge's immaculate coiffure had been reduced to a ragged crop. Frankie swept the towel off her shoulders and shook the blonde locks into the wastepaper basket.

'There you are. You won't have to pin that up anymore.'

Midge got up and went to look at herself in the mirror. For a moment no one spoke. When Midge turned to face them again her face was white, her mouth distorted with fury.

'You little bitch! How could you? Look what you've done!'

'Sorry, Midge,' Frankie said meekly. 'My dad's a barber. I've never had to do a lady's hair. I thought you knew.'

Midge took a few steps towards her, her hands forming claws, but Steve stepped quickly between them.

'Serves you right, Midge. You've been treating Frankie like a skivvy for days. You know you only asked her to cut your hair to make her look cheap. You're lucky she didn't scalp you. I would have done.'

Midge glared from one of them to the other, then turned away and threw herself down on her bed and burst into a storm of tears. Frankie looked at Steve in alarm but the other girl shrugged and turned away.

'Leave her be. She'll get over it.'

Next day, Midge's new hairstyle was the subject of much hilarity, but she was stuck with it until the end of basic training.

As that period drew to a close Frankie received a summons to the CO's office. Also called were Steve and Midge, Dickie and Julia Bearing. On arrival, they found the commanding officer's desk occupied by Phyllis Bingham, who greeted them with her usual gentle, almost maternal manner. As she came to attention and threw up a salute, Frankie had a vivid mental image of herself at their first interview, shaking with nerves and uncertain how to behave. The recollection brought with it a realisation of how far she had progressed in the last, tough weeks.

Bingham smiled benignly. 'Sit down, my dears. I'm delighted to see you all looking so fit and I must say that I have received excellent reports on all of you from your commanding officer. Now' – she picked up a sheaf of papers from the desk – 'before we proceed any further I must ask you all to read what is written on these documents and then sign at the bottom if you agree to abide by the conditions.'

'What is this?' Midge asked suspiciously.

'That is a copy of the Official Secrets Act. I must ask you to think most carefully before you sign, because afterwards, if you reveal anything that I am about to tell you, or that you may learn in future, you could, not to put too fine a point on it, be put up against a wall and shot.'

'And suppose we refuse to sign?'

'Then you will leave this room at once and accept whatever duties your CO sees fit to assign you to. But – and this is the crucial point – in doing so you will have deprived your country of the full use of your not inconsiderable talents.'

'I'm sorry,' Steve murmured hesitantly, 'I don't really understand. In what way would we be depriving the country of our talents?'

Bingham gave her a look of sympathetic understanding. 'I know it's hard for you to take this on trust, but once you have signed I shall be able to explain much more fully.'

Frankie's heart was beating fast. At last she could see some point to the drudgery of the last weeks. Whatever it was that they were not allowed to speak of, it must be something very important. She sensed that she was on the brink of the sort of adventure she had dreamed of when she had immersed herself in the novels of John Buchan. She scanned the page in front of her rapidly and reached for her pen.

'Here you are, ma'am.'

One by one the others signed and handed the papers back to Mrs Bingham. She arranged them in a neat stack in front of her and sat back in her chair.

'Right! Now we can proceed. But remember, everything I am about to tell you is top secret and you may not discuss it with any of the other girls, or with the officers, or even with your own family – however trustworthy you may think they are. Understood?'

The five girls nodded and murmured assent.

'Very well. Even now I can only give you the broad outlines of what you will be involved in. The details are confined to people much more senior than you, or even than me. This much I can tell you. When war broke out, Mr Churchill gave orders for an organisation to be set up to encourage resistance in the occupied countries and to carry out acts of sabotage and generally make life as uncomfortable as possible for the enemy. His words were that we should "set Europe ablaze". The organisation created for that purpose is called the Special Operations Executive – SOE for short – but to the general public it is known by the title of the Inter-Services Research Bureau. Its function is to drop agents behind enemy lines to organise and coordinate resistance.'

'Excuse me, ma'am!' Julia had gone very pale. 'Is that what you expect us to do?'

Bingham smiled gently. 'No, my dear. We don't send women to do that sort of work – or not as far as I am aware. But you will all realise that such an organisation requires a great deal of support on the home front. Potential agents have to be trained and accommodated and generally taken care of while they are in this country and then, when they have reached their destination, they have to keep in touch by radio. Communications are a vital part of the system. That is where all of you come in. You see, because the FANY do not come under the command of any of the other services we have a degree of independence and flexibility not granted to others. That makes us ideally suited to clandestine operations of this nature.' She reached for a small pile of envelopes. 'Now, to business. These are your postings. You, Diana – forgive me, I refuse to abide by this silly convention of not addressing girls by their first names – and you, Julia, will proceed to Gaynes Hall, which is in Huntingdonshire, about twenty miles from Cambridge. The remaining three, Gina, Marjorie and Priscilla . . . '*Priscilla?* Frankie shot a look at Dickie Nightingale, who glared back at her. '. . . will take yourselves to Grendon Underwood, near Aylesbury. You will be informed of your duties when you get there. But first, you all have two weeks' leave. Here are your rail warrants. I'm sure you can all do with a brief rest before you start your new duties.'

A thought occurred to Frankie. 'Excuse me, ma'am. If we're not allowed to tell our parents anything about what we're doing, what are we supposed to say to them?'

'Your parents will receive letters stating that you have all been accepted as drivers in the Women's Transport Corps. That, after all, is what most FANYs do.'

'That'll cause some consternation!' Dickie remarked dryly. 'The only time I got behind the wheel of a car I drove it straight into a tree.'

'And I've never driven,' Frankie added.

'Nevertheless, that is what your parents will be told,'

Bingham said severely. 'And you must say nothing to give them any other impression.' She looked around the group. 'I think that's all. Good luck to you. Dismiss!'

As the girls rose Bingham added, 'Oh, I forgot to mention one thing. Diana and Julia. Take some pretty frocks with you to Gaynes Hall. You may find you'll need them.'

Chapter Four

'Oo-er, listen to her! We are posh, aren't we!'
'Be quiet, Maria! Let your sister finish.'

The Franconi family were gathered around the kitchen table on Frankie's first evening at home. Eager to communicate her experiences of the past weeks, she had begun by describing her fellow recruits at Overthorpe.

'Well, what's she putting on airs for?' her sister demanded sullenly. 'Who does she think she is – Lady Muck?'

'Never mind her, love,' her mother put in. 'I think you sound really nice. Really refined.'

'I don't sound any different!' Frankie protested. 'I haven't changed – and I'm not putting on airs.'

''Course you are! Just listen to yourself,' her sister asserted.

'Never mind that,' their father broke in. 'Let's hear what Gina has to tell us. Go on, Gina.'

Frankie began again, but the enthusiasm of a few minutes earlier had evaporated. She was conscious of two things. One, that Maria's jibe had some truth in it. Her speech had changed. After several weeks living among girls from a different stratum of society she had begun to pick up their accents and turns of phrase. Second, she was reminded of the fact that she could not tell her family anything about the real reason for her recruitment or the work she would be doing. Rather lamely, she described the strict discipline of the training school, the poor food and the harsh physical regime.

'Sounds miserable to me,' Maria said with a sniff. 'Rather you than me!'

'It's not miserable!' Frankie said. 'It was to start with, but once I made friends it was OK.'

'Oh, you have made some nice friends, then?' her mother prompted.

Frankie described Steve, without referring to their midnight escapade. But as she spoke a knot of anguish tightened in her stomach. It had never occurred to her that she and Steve would be posted to different places at the end of their training, and the prospect of starting again somewhere new without the support of her friend was daunting – particularly as she would still have Midge to contend with. She and Steve had promised to keep in touch, but that was a poor substitute for daily contact.

'So, what will you be doing next, now that the initial training is over?' her father asked.

Frankie busied herself pouring another cup of tea. 'I'm going to be a driver in the Women's Transport Corps. I'll probably be acting as a chauffeur to some high-ranking officer.'

'Oh, that sounds nice,' her mother said.

'All that scrubbing floors and early morning runs for that!' Maria sniffed. 'Strikes me they just want you as a servant, that's all.'

'Nonsense!' their father said briskly. 'It could be a very responsible job. But it could be dangerous, too. I hope you won't be expected to carry out these duties anywhere near the firing line.'

'There isn't a firing line, unless you count North Africa,' Frankie pointed out. 'But you needn't worry. I'm not going overseas.'

'Well . . .' Her father sat back with a broad smile. 'Since we have a chauffeuse in the family, I'd better see if I can borrow

Vito Locattelli's van. You can take us all for a spin on Sunday afternoon.'

'No!' Frankie exclaimed. 'I mean, I'm not ready yet. I haven't actually learned to drive.'

'All these weeks, and they haven't taught you the one thing they want you to do?' her mother queried.

'This was just preliminary training,' Frankie explained. She could feel herself beginning to sweat. 'They don't decide what everyone's suited for until the end of that. I'll be starting the proper course when I go back.'

Frankie did not enjoy her leave. She had been looking forward to going home, seeing old friends, sleeping in a comfortable bed and eating decent meals. The bed was still the same, and her mother was still a good cook, but with rationing growing ever tighter good food was hard to come by. Many conversations now centred on nostalgic reminiscences of meals gone by, with lip-smacking descriptions of juicy steaks, bacon and eggs or even something as simple as hot buttered toast. The thing Frankie missed most of all was the Chiappe family's wonderful ice cream. It was more than two years since she had last dropped into the familiar shop for a wafer, but in her imagination she could still taste it.

The close-knit community around Scotland Road was being split apart by the war. At church on Sunday Frankie was shocked at how small the congregation was.

'What's happened to the Boschis?' she asked her mother in a whisper.

'Bombed out, last month,' her mother whispered back. 'Gone to stay with relatives up in Scotland.'

'And what about the Andreotti family?'

'They've moved away too. I think she's gone to live with her sister. Poor woman just couldn't cope with the kids and the shop and all after her husband was interned.'

The next day Frankie went round to call on some of her old school friends. At every house she drew a blank. Anne Marie Flaherty was married and living in Sefton. Lucia Pascali was at work, in an office in the city. Floria Vicenza, Frankie's closest friend, was working as a secretary at Cammel Lairds, the shipbuilders over in Birkenhead. Others had joined up and were away in the ATS or the WRNS. Frankie managed to arrange a meeting with Lucia and Floria the following evening, but it was not a success.

'Come on, Frankie!' Floria exclaimed as soon as they were settled in her mother's sitting room with cups of tea. 'Tell us all about it. What have you been up to?'

'Oh, nothing exciting,' Frankie said. She told them briefly about the routine at Overthorpe and made the mistake of mentioning the sort of background most of the other girls came from.

'Oh, that's why you're talking as if you had a plum in your gob,' Lucia said. 'You'll be too grand for the likes of us, with all your posh chums!'

Frankie protested that she would never want to drop her old friends for 'that stuck-up lot' but she could see that they were not convinced. It did not help that she could tell them so little about what she was going to do next. She tried to sound interested when the other two talked about their jobs but they struck her as being unbearably dull and somehow the chatter about boyfriends and who was going out with whom no longer fascinated her.

The following day, when Maria came home from school, she said, 'I talked to Lucia's sister today. She says Lucia reckons you're getting too big for your boots.'

Enrico, to her relief, was at sea so she did not have to face him again. She never knew how much her mother had said to her father and grandmother about his behaviour, or her feelings on the matter, but whatever had been discussed it had not dented her grandmother's greatest ambition, which was to see Frankie married to a good Italian boy. It seemed that on every visit there was a new candidate waiting to be introduced. With most of the young men away in the services Frankie found herself being paired off with boys of sixteen and men of forty and required to sit through uncomfortable afternoon tea parties with their respective families. There were one or two boys her own age home on leave and they took her dancing, or to the pictures, both of which she enjoyed, but afterwards she had a guilty feeling that she had not repaid them for their attentions in the way they expected. It distressed her to think that they might be going back to their units to face unknown dangers with the regret that they had wasted their time with a cold-hearted girl. The simple fact was that none of them attracted her and, after her experience with Enrico, she was afraid to let matters get out of control. Besides, at the back or her mind there was still the image of the only man she had ever met who had made her pulse beat faster.

The reluctant spring had finally given way to another brilliant summer, but none of the pleasures Frankie associated with the season were available now. There was no point in trips to Southport or New Brighton when the beaches were barricaded with barbed-wire entanglements and notices warning of landmines. In the city, the air raids had become less frequent but the devastation around the docks was a constant and depressing reminder that any night could bring a fresh rain of bombs. The nightly news bulletins brought little comfort. The Germans, under Rommel, had defeated the Eighth Army at Tobruk and the island of Malta was still struggling for survival.

The first contingents of American troops had arrived and the streets were full of unfamiliar uniforms and accents. Frankie saw a lot of girls walking out on the arms of these GIs, their bare legs stained with gravy browning in the absence of stockings and their lips reddened with beetroot juice. She got used to being whistled after when she went out, and one or two of the bolder spirits actually tried to start a conversation with her. She was polite but careful to keep her distance. She knew very well that the mere suggestion that she was encouraging them would cause a family row.

By halfway through her leave Frankie had to admit that she was bored and looking forward to getting back to her unit, and to whatever mysterious task awaited her.

Grendon Underwood was another substantial country house, along the same lines as Overthorpe Hall, but any romantic images it might have conjured up were immediately dispelled by the rows of Nissen huts occupying the grounds. Frankie reported in and was allocated a bed in one of them. In the summer heat the interior of the hut was sweltering, but Frankie suspected that once winter came the iron stove in the centre would prove totally inadequate. She dumped her bag and looked along the line of beds, reflecting grimly that it was a good thing she was no longer embarrassed about sharing her most intimate activities with a dozen others. A fresh pang of loneliness gripped her as she recalled that Steve would not be among them.

'Well, here we are again!' drawled a familiar voice. 'Isn't this jolly?'

Midge was leaning against the door frame, her blonde head haloed by the sunshine, a cigarette in one immaculate hand. Her hair had grown and expert hands had converted Frankie's uneven shingle into a smooth pageboy bob.

Frankie suppressed a sigh. 'Hello, Midge.'

'Nice hols?' Midge enquired, straightening up and coming to place her bag on the bed next to Frankie's.

'Not particularly.'

'Oh dear! Shop not doing well? Trade must be a bit slack these days, I suppose.'

'We're managing, thanks. But there isn't much to do if you're not working. How was your leave?'

'Exhausting! Parties every night, dancing till I thought my feet were going to drop off. You have to say one thing for these chaps when they're on leave. They certainly know how to enjoy themselves. Especially the Yanks. They really know how to give a girl a good time.' Midge looked around her. 'Can't say this place looks like a whirl of gaiety.'

'No, true,' Frankie agreed and caught Midge's eye. For a fleeting moment she saw behind the deadpan mask and realised that Steve had been right. Underneath her veneer of sophistication, Midge was just as nervous and uncertain as she was.

'Hurray, familiar faces!' Dickie Nightingale breezed into the hut, slung her bag onto the bed on Frankie's other side and burst into song. 'Here we are again, Happy as can be, All good friends and jolly good company!'

Frankie found herself laughing. 'You're a breath of fresh air, Dickie.'

'Much needed in this place!' Dickie commented. She laid a hand on each of their shoulders. 'So! We three meet again – minus the thunder and lightning. What are we, the three graces or the three wise women?'

'The Three Musketeers?' Frankie offered.

'More like Battle, Murder and Sudden Death,' Midge commented dryly, but she was smiling.

'The Three Fates!' said Dickie. 'Clotho who spins, Lachesis who weaves and Atropos who cuts the thread of life when the time comes.'

'Don't!' Frankie said, shivering suddenly in the stifling air.

A young woman in sergeant's uniform entered the hut.

'Right, you three. My name's Sergeant Wallis. And you are . . . ?'

When they had introduced themselves Wallis went on, 'If you get across to the mess in the main house you might just be in time for tea. You're on the late shift, so you won't start work until fourteen hundred hours tomorrow, which will give you a chance to settle in. But we have a very important lecture tomorrow morning at eleven hundred hours.'

'Excuse me, Sarge,' Dickie put in. 'Start work? Would you mind telling us what we're here to do?'

'You haven't been briefed? OK. Grendon is the main signals station for SOE. We receive and transmit messages to and from agents in the field. These messages are, of course, in code. You three are here to learn to encode and decode messages. The lecture tomorrow will be given by SOE's Chief Coding Officer, who is coming down specially from Baker Street. Clear? Right. Off you go, then.'

'Clear? As mud!' Midge muttered as the sergeant moved out of earshot.

Frankie said nothing. Coding was obviously important, but it was not the exciting and possibly dangerous job she had been expecting. Days of boring routine loomed ahead of her.

At eleven o'clock the next morning Frankie took her place along with a couple of dozen other girls in what had once been the ornate dining hall and was now in use as a lecture theatre. They all rose and came to attention as Captain Henderson, the commanding officer, entered accompanied by a small, dark young man in civilian clothes, scarcely older than Frankie herself.

Henderson, a good-looking Canadian in her mid-forties, greeted them briskly. 'Good morning, ladies. This is Mr Marks, who has come down from town to introduce you to the mysteries of coding.' She smiled at the guest, who was looking extremely uncomfortable. 'I'll leave you to it, Mr Marks.'

'They've sent us the office boy,' Dickie whispered. 'Talk about wet behind the ears!'

'Ssh!' Frankie responded with a giggle.

'Nasty little Jew boy, if you ask me,' Midge muttered.

Not having been told to sit, they were all still standing. Marks regarded them helplessly for a minute and finally made a kind of flapping movement with his hands, which they took to be an invitation to sit down. There was some laughter as they settled themselves. Without speaking, Marks turned his back and began writing on the blackboard. What appeared was a sequence of apparently unrelated letters, in groups of five. When he had finished he turned back to them and Frankie had the impression that he was looking straight at her.

'Can anyone . . .' He paused and cleared his throat, then began again on a slightly lower pitch. 'Can anyone tell me what that says?'

The only response was a renewed wave of giggling.

'No,' Marks went on. 'Of course you can't. It's in code. It might have come from an agent working behind enemy lines. You are all going to be trained as coders and in a minute I'm going to ask you to try to break it. But first I want to explain why it is absolutely vital that all such messages are deciphered the first time they are sent, even if the code is corrupted. No agent in the field should be asked to transmit a message twice, because that more than doubles the risk that he will be detected. The Gestapo are waiting for every transmission. They have detector vans that can pick up the location, down to the very room it is coming from. If an agent working under great stress and at speed makes a mistake in coding that is not surprising. It is up to you to decipher that message. Let me give you an example of what might happen otherwise. A few days ago a young Yugoslav partisan was captured while transmitting a message. He refused to reveal to the Gestapo the identity of the people for whom he was working. He was eventually taken to the local morgue, no longer recognisable as a human being. Now I hope you understand why there must be no such thing as an indecipherable message.'

Frankie squirmed on her chair. *No longer recognisable as a human being!* The image conjured up was too horrible to contemplate. Around her the giggles and fidgeting had died away and there was a deadly silence.

'Right,' Marks went on, 'let me begin to explain to you how this code works. Each agent is asked to memorise a poem. They usually choose something they already know well, perhaps something they learned at school. Every time the agent encodes a message he selects five words from that poem. He then gives each letter in these words a number, and then converts those numbers, by a method I will explain in a minute, into other letters, which he will transmit by Morse Code. Each of you will adopt one or two agents, so that you get to know their idiosyncrasies. You will never meet them, of course, and you will know them only by their code names, but just the same you will be their closest contacts with home – their lifeline. Now, the poem from which this message on the board is derived begins like this. *Be near me when my light is low, When the blood creeps, and the nerves prick And tingle.* Can anyone tell me where that comes from?'

Frankie's hand was up almost before she knew it. Marks caught her eye and smiled. 'Yes?'

'It's Tennyson, sir. From "In Memoriam".'

'Well done. But this illustrates another point. The Gestapo code breakers are every bit as well versed in English literature as you appear to be. So, if they can break a few words of the code, enough to identify the poem, they will then have the key to decoding all further transmissions from that agent. That is the weakness of the poem code, but at present that is all we have so we must make the best of it. So, let us see how that poem has been used to encode this message . . .'

For the next hour the group wrestled with the complexities of indicator groups and double transposition and eventually the letters on the blackboard resolved themselves into words. *There must be no such thing as an indecipherable message.* When this was finally written out in clear there was a general whoop of triumph and Frankie realised that she had been absorbed in one of the most fascinating puzzles she had ever come across. Marks smiled at them.

'Yes, you have every reason to feel pleased with yourselves. But let me bring you down to earth a little. That poem was chosen by one of the first agents I briefed before he went overseas. Let me quote it in its entirety, to give you some idea of the mental state of that man.

> *Be near me when my light is low,*
> *When the blood creeps, and the nerves prick*
> *And tingle; and the heart is sick,*
> *And all the wheels of Being slow.*
>
> *Be near me when the sensuous frame*
> *Is rack'd with pangs that conquer trust*
> *And Time, a maniac scattering dust,*
> *And Life, a Fury slinging flame.*
>
> *Be near me, when my faith is dry,*
> *And men the flies of latter spring,*
> *That lay their eggs, and sting and sing*
> *And weave their petty cells and die.*

> *Be near me when I fade away,*
> *To point the term of human strife,*
> *And on the low dark verge of life*
> *The twilight of eternal day.*

When the group was dismissed, they left the hall in almost complete silence, and in that silence Frankie vowed to herself that no agent should ever suffer capture because of her inability to decode his message.

Frankie soon became aware that there was a strict division of labour in operation at Grendon. There were the signallers and the coders. The signallers' job was to receive and transcribe from Morse Code the unintelligible five-letter groups which the coders then deciphered into plain English. There was very little socialising between the two groups and the coders considered themselves superior to the signallers, whose job seemed to them purely mechanical. There was also, she discovered, a similar division among agents in the field. They did not work alone, but normally in teams of three – a principal officer, a radio operator and a courier, whose job was to carry messages between the two or to members of the Resistance cell with whom they were in contact. This meant that a message encoded by one agent was transmitted by another, then received over an often weak radio link by a signaller, before being passed to Frankie or one of her colleagues. The opportunities for the message to be corrupted were numerous.

Over the next weeks Frankie and the others settled into an unvarying routine. They worked eight-hour shifts, either from 6 a.m. to 2 p.m. or from then until ten at night. The intensity of concentration required left them drained and without energy for much in the way of recreation, which was just as well, since the opportunities were limited, to say the least. Grendon was miles from anywhere and there was no public transport. The only social centre of any sort was the pub in the village, where the locals regarded them with as much suspicion as if they had been German spies. The nearest cinema was miles away in Bedford, and without transport might just as well have been on the far side of the galaxy. In their off-duty hours they lay around in the grounds, reading, writing letters home or simply snoozing.

Steve wrote from time to time but her letters were, of necessity, uninformative, until at last Frankie was delighted to read, *I've got so much to tell you, and so much I want to ask, but we can't put it in writing. Can we meet somewhere? I've got my car here and it's not far to Aylesbury. I'm free on Sunday until the evening so perhaps we could have lunch somewhere. I suppose we should ask Midge and Dickie, too. Let me know what you think.*

Frankie consulted the schedule and discovered that they were on the late shift, so she wrote back suggesting that Steve should meet them at the pub in the nearby village. The prospect of the meeting lifted her spirits, though she had misgivings about Midge's reaction. She had been unusually subdued recently, but Frankie sensed that she still resented her friendship with Steve.

On Sunday morning they found Steve sitting on the bonnet of a neat little two-seater sports car outside the pub. She greeted Frankie with a hug and Dickie, who recoiled from any displays of emotion, with a handshake. Midge held back and merely nodded a casual 'hello'.

'Listen, the pub's not open yet. Anyway, we can't really talk there,' Steve said. 'You know, walls have ears and all that. Shall we go for a walk before lunch? There's a public footpath over there, into the woods.'

As they strolled down a towering aisle of beech trees

Frankie felt an unaccustomed sense of freedom. Since arriving at Grendon she had had neither the time nor the energy to explore. Brought up in the city, she had been used to expeditions to the seaside or across to the sandy heaths of the Wirral, but these majestic beech woods were new to her. It was high summer now, and out in the fields the farmers and the land girls who had been drafted in to help them toiled in the blazing heat from first light to nightfall to bring in the harvest. In the crowded rooms at Grendon they suffered the heat without the corresponding benefit of the sunshine. Here among the trees the light filtered through the lofty canopy, the air was cool and the senses were lulled by the cooing of wood pigeons.

Dickie obviously felt as she did. 'Thank God!' she remarked, stretching her arms, 'There is still a world outside Grendon.'

'Well, come on,' Steve urged. 'What are you all up to?'

By the time they had finished explaining, Steve was shaking her head in confusion.

'Rather you than me! I see now why they were recruiting brainy types like you three. It must be terribly demanding.'

'Most of it's pretty routine, really,' Frankie confessed, 'until you get an indecipherable. We've had a couple of those. If the girl dealing with it can't break it, the whole team goes at it, and there's no question of anyone going to bed until it's broken. The first one took us nearly all night. We must have made hundreds of attempts at it. But the cheer that went up when we finally cracked it must have been heard in the village, I should think. We were so cock-a-hoop that we sent Mr Marks a coded message saying "we have just broken our first indecipherable".'

'Who's Mr Marks?' Steve asked.

'Head of coding at Baker Street,' Dickie told her. 'Not much older than us, but an incredible brain.'

'Amazing!' Frankie agreed.

'I don't know what you both see in him,' Midge said. 'He's just a jumped-up little Jew boy who's managed to skive out of the call-up.'

'He's not!' Frankie exclaimed. 'The work he's doing is terribly important and no one else could do it half as well.'

'Midge! I don't know how you can say such things,' Steve said. 'Haven't you heard the rumours? Terrible things are happening to the Jews in occupied countries.'

'Propaganda.' Midge shrugged dismissively.

'It's not,' Dickie put in. 'My father has business interests all over Europe – or had before the war. We've been helping Jewish refugees to escape from Poland and Austria and Germany itself for the last year. They have terrible stories to tell.'

'Have it your own way,' Midge said sulkily. 'Sorry I spoke!'

They walked on in silence for a while, until Steve asked, 'Is your Mr Marks anything to do with Marks and Spencer?'

'I don't think so. I heard his father has a bookshop in the Charing Cross Road,' Dickie told her. 'Rare first editions and that sort of thing.'

'Anyway,' Frankie put in, 'it's your turn, Steve. What are you up to these days?'

'Nothing as glamorous as you three. I'm just a kind of glorified housekeeper, really.'

'How come?'

'You remember Julia and I were sent to Gaynes Hall? Well, it's being used as a holding centre for agents waiting to be sent on missions.'

'Is that another country mansion, like Overthorpe and Grendon?' Frankie enquired. 'Seems like we've taken over every grand house in England.'

Steve grinned. 'Well, you know what they say SOE stands for – Stately 'Omes of England.'

'Go on,' Dickie prompted as the laughter faded. 'The agents come to Gaynes – then what?'

'They stay, usually just for a few days, and then when the conditions are right we drive them to Tempsford aerodrome and hand them over to the RAF.'

'When conditions are right?' Dickie queried.

'They can only be dropped a few days before or after the full moon. There has to be enough light for the pilot to see the dropping ground but not so much that the Germans spot them coming down. Sometimes those vital few nights are no good because of low cloud or mist, and then they have to wait for another three weeks or so until the next full moon.'

'That must be hard for them,' Frankie commented.

'Yes, it is, poor lambs. But we do our best to make it as enjoyable as possible for them.'

'So what, exactly, is your job?' Dickie asked.

'Mainly cooking. You remember I told you I did a cordon bleu course in Paris?'

'Cordon bleu!' Midge cut in. 'I didn't think meals like that existed anymore. You should see the muck they serve up at Grendon.'

'It can't be worse than Overthorpe, surely,' Steve remarked.

'It is!' responded her three companions with one voice.

'Well, it's true that the men I look after get the best of everything – but that's just as it should be, isn't it?'

'No one's disputing that,' Frankie said. 'We're just jealous, that's all.'

'Actually, there's a bit more to the job than cooking,' Steve went on. 'Most of the joes, the agents – joes is what the RAF chaps call them – are heading for France and they are all fluent

French speakers, of course. But they have to be more than that. It has to be second nature. They have to think in French, so that even if they talk in their sleep it's still in French. So all through their training they are forbidden to speak anything else. That's where Julia and I and some of the other girls come in. We're able to chat to them. Do you remember that Bingham told us to pack some pretty frocks? Every evening we change into mufti and join the men for cocktails before dinner. Then after the meal we roll back the carpet and dance to a gramophone.'

'Good lord! It sounds like a pre-war house party,' Midge commented.

'Well, that's the sort of atmosphere we're trying to create,' Steve agreed. 'Something as normal and relaxing as possible.'

'At least you get to know your agents,' Frankie said wistfully. 'We try to make our contact with ours as personal as we can, sending little bits of news from home and that sort of thing, but in the end they're just a code name and a little collection of idiosyncrasies in the way they encode their messages.'

'We meet them, but we don't really know them,' Steve said. 'We never learn their real names, for one thing, only the French *noms de guerre* they've adopted. Sometimes, if they're with us for a while, they drop a few hints about what they did in civilian life or their families but we're not supposed to know who they are or where they're going – though we can guess that, of course. In the end, we just have to take them to the airfield and wave them goodbye, and know that we'll never find out what happened to them.'

Frankie cast a look at her friend's expression. 'It must be hard not to get involved.'

'Yes,' Steve admitted, 'it is.'

'Well, at least you get a bit of male company,' Midge said.

'We might as well have taken a vow of chastity. I'm fed up with being cooped up with a lot of women.'

Frankie said nothing but she sighed inwardly. All her romantic dreams had suffocated in the stuffy rooms of Grendon.

'Heard from Roddy lately?' Midge asked.

'Oh yes, he writes whenever he can. It sounds pretty grim. He says rations are so short even for the pilots that he's lost nearly a stone. But he's full of admiration for the Maltese, who are suffering even worse under the blockade. And he says the camaraderie in the mess is wonderful.'

'All this talk of food is making me hungry,' Dickie said. 'Let's turn back, shall we?'

Frankie sat back and eased her tense shoulders. For the past three hours she had been wrestling with an indecipherable from an agent whose erratic coding was a constant source of exasperation. Finally she had discovered that he had misspelt one of the words in his original code poem, rendering the whole message meaningless gobbledegook. Brave and resourceful these men might be, but in many of them their grasp of English left much to be desired – and that did not apply only to those for whom it was not their native language.

Outside, it was dark and the blackout curtains were securely fastened over the windows. Summer was over and in less than two months it would be Christmas. Frankie looked at the clock above the supervisor's desk. Still nearly an hour to go before the end of the shift and there was a small pile of messages in front of her, waiting for her attention. With a sigh, she reached for the topmost and bent her head over it.

The door crashed open to admit a breathless girl.

'I say, chaps, have you heard the news? There's been a huge battle somewhere in the desert – some place called El Alamein

– and we won! Winnie's broadcasting on the nine o'clock news. If you're quick you might catch him.'

Half-decoded messages were abandoned as they all raced downstairs to the mess, where the other shift were clustered around the wireless set. Frankie was just in time to hear the final words in the familiar growl of the Prime Minister.

'This is not the end. It is not even the beginning of the end. It may, perhaps, be the end of the beginning.'

The broadcast ended with the National Anthem and everyone in the room stood to attention. Frankie found her cheeks wet with tears and, glancing around her, saw that she was not the only one. After the disaster of Dunkirk, the loss of Singapore and Crete, the apparently endless succession of defeats, had the tide turned at last? Was it possible that they were actually going to win this war?

The following Sunday Frankie, with Dickie and Midge as usual, went to meet Steve. They had managed to make these reunions a regular feature, occurring about once a month and giving them an opportunity to exchange gossip. That day, for the first time since the outbreak of war, the church bells in the village were being rung, in celebration of the victory at El Alamein.

When there was no more to say about that and the future course of the war, Steve said, 'Do you know what? We've had our first woman agent at Gaynes.'

'I didn't think they recruited women for that sort of work,' Dickie said.

'Well, they do now. And she's not at all what you'd expect. For a start, she must be forty if she's a day. She's an incredibly gutsy, vivacious little French woman and apparently she's been through all the training they have to do, including unarmed combat and using explosives and goodness knows what else, and come through it all with flying colours.'

'And she's going to parachute into occupied France?' Frankie said.

'Well, actually I think they've sent her by boat, in case she breaks a leg or something. But what courage! Nothing seemed to daunt her. I've never met anyone so determined.'

At roll-call the next morning Captain Henderson made an announcement.

'I've had a request from Mr Marks. As you know, he has been worried for some time about the security of the code poems chosen by agents. Many of them tend to be very well known and therefore familiar to the German cryptographers. He feels that it would be much better if the agents had original works to base their codes on – something that would be known only to themselves and one or two people over here. He has asked if any of you could write some simple verses that might be used in that way. So, if any of you feel that you may be a budding poet, this is your chance. Hand your efforts to me and I'll see that they are passed on to Mr Marks.'

That afternoon, during the recreation period, the mess was unusually quiet. Small groups or isolated individuals hunched over notepads, chewing pencils or scribbling busily. The shifts had changed over so Frankie, Midge and Dickie were free and agreed to pool their ideas. In the months that had passed there had been a slow but unmistakable change in Midge's relationship with the other two. Isolated from her normal environment and without her little clique of supporters she had come to depend on them and, although her manner could still be acerbic, she was no longer deliberately unkind.

'It's got to be something easy to remember,' Dickie said. 'Think of that chap who uses the National Anthem because he maintains it's the only piece of verse he can memorise.'

'Something humorous, perhaps,' Frankie suggested. 'And maybe something to do with the war. We could use the names of people they all know – Marlene Dietrich, Vera Lynn, Hitler, Churchill . . .'

'Mussolini,' Midge put in slyly.

'If you like.'

'Of course, you know the sort of verses chaps never seem to have trouble remembering,' Midge went on. 'The sort of things they sing in the changing room after rugger matches . . .'

'Blue, you mean.' Dickie grinned. 'OK. Go on. I dare you!'

Midge sat back and drew on her cigarette. 'OK. How's this for a first line. *Benito Mussolini Has a prick that is teeny . . .*'

In response to the challenge in her eyes, Frankie's brain moved into top gear. *'And poor little Hitler Has one even littler . . .'* she supplied.

'Terrific! Write it down, Frankie!' Dickie encouraged. 'What about Winnie?'

Frankie thought, then wrote rapidly. 'How's this?'

She handed the paper to Midge, who read out, *'As for Churchill, of course, He's hung like a horse!'* She snorted with laughter and handed the paper back. 'Franconi, you have hidden depths!'

The mess door swung open with a bang that made everyone look up. Wallis stood in the doorway.

'Watch out, girls! The brig's here on a tour of inspection.'

'Quick, hide it!' hissed Dickie.

But before Frankie could dispose of the paper Henderson marched into the room, accompanied by the stern figure of Brigadier Gamwell. As the girls came to attention, the brigadier looked around the room.

'Well, ladies, I understood this was a recreation period. I'm surprised to find you all so quiet. What is it that is absorbing so much of your attention?'

There was a silence, and then someone offered, 'We're writing poetry, ma'am.'

'Mr Marks has asked the girls to compose verses to act as code poems for agents, ma'am,' Henderson explained.

Gamwell's austere features softened. 'Poetry? How very charming. May I see some of your efforts?'

The response was an uneasy shuffling. Gamwell's eyes alighted upon Frankie.

'You! Let me see what you've written.'

There was no way out. Slowly Frankie moved forward and handed the piece of paper to the brigadier. Gamwell scanned it briefly and her expression of benign indulgence changed to one of scandalised contempt.

'You are responsible for this . . . this disgusting doggerel?'

For a moment Frankie said nothing. Then she answered meekly, 'Yes, ma'am.'

'And your name is?'

'Franconi, ma'am.'

'I see.' Gamwell's gaze swept the room. 'It seems I had better read all the rest of your so-called poems. In due course I shall be having a word with Mr Marks's superior officers. I will not have him encouraging my young ladies to indulge in such scatological efforts. Franconi, collect the rest of the work and give it to me.'

In silence Frankie collected up the papers and handed them over and, with a final glare and a snort of disgust, the brigadier swept out of the room. Frankie rejoined Midge and Dickie at their table. She wanted to burst into tears and only her pride prevented her. Dickie was flushed with anger.

'Midge, how could you? Why didn't you speak up? It's not fair to let Frankie carry the can.'

Midge lit another cigarette. 'Why didn't you, for that matter? We were all in it together.'

'I didn't write any of it,' Dickie protested. She turned to

Frankie. 'Don't worry. It'll all blow over. I bet the brig's seen a lot worse than that in her time.'

'She'll sack me,' Frankie predicted. 'She'll make an example of me. I could see it in her eyes.'

'Rubbish!' Dickie said, without conviction. 'Anyway, if there's any comeback I'll speak up and tell her we were all responsible. Midge is right about that. I encouraged you, so I'm just as much at fault. Midge?'

Midge was gazing into the smoke from her cigarette and for a moment her usual hard-bitten manner had deserted her. 'Dickie's right. I should have spoken up. You're a brick, Frankie. I guess the truth is . . .' She stubbed out the half-smoked cigarette. 'The truth is I'm a bit of a coward. Sorry!'

She got up clumsily, rattling the teacups on the table, and hurried out of the room. Dickie and Frankie exchanged looks of amazement.

'Well, well!' Dickie remarked. 'What's that saying about leopards and spots?'

Three days later – days during which Frankie toyed with her food and jumped every time the door opened – the summons finally came. Frankie, Midge and Dickie were all to present themselves at the CO's office.

'How does she know?' Midge hissed as they made their way along the corridor. 'How does she know we were all in it?'

'Don't look at me,' Dickie responded.

'Frankie? Did you . . . ?'

'No! I haven't said a word. What do you take me for?'

Minutes later they were standing at attention in front of Henderson's desk. The CO looked up from a pile of papers.

'Yes?'

'You sent for us, ma'am.'

'Oh yes, of course. Just a moment . . .'

As Henderson shuffled through the files on her desk Frankie

blurted out, 'Ma'am, it was just a joke. We weren't going to give it in.'

'Joke?' Henderson looked perplexed.

'The poem. It was just a bit of fun.'

'And I started it,' Midge broke in. 'It was my idea.'

Henderson's mouth twitched. 'Ah, the poem! No wonder you all look so worried. Well, you can relax. That's not why I sent for you.'

'It's not?'

'I think the brigadier visited her wrath on poor Mr Marks instead of on you.'

'We didn't mean to make trouble for him,' Frankie said remorsefully.

Henderson's smile broadened. 'I shouldn't worry. He may look fragile but I think his shoulders are broader than they appear. And, if it's any comfort to you, yours was not the worst example – not by a long chalk. Now, let's get down to business. At ease, all of you.'

The three girls relaxed and exchanged looks of relief. Henderson continued, 'I've been looking at your records and all your supervisors speak very highly of you. Particularly of you, Franconi. They say you have an almost uncanny knack for breaking corrupted codes.' She sat back and looked from one to the other. 'How would you all feel about an overseas posting?'

Frankie's pulse rate, which had just begun to steady, leapt to a frenetic level. At last! An opportunity to escape the claustrophobic confines of Grendon and do something exciting.

'Where?' The word was out of her mouth before she could check herself.

Henderson clicked her tongue. 'You should know better than to ask that. If you decide to go, you won't know where you are being posted until you arrive there. That is, assuming your parents agree to your going. You, Nightingale, being over twenty-one, can make your own decision. For you two, I shall need written permission from your parents. Will they give it, do you think?'

'Oh yes.' Midge was carelessly confident.

'I . . . I think so.' Frankie wished she could be as sure.

'Do you want to go, all of you?'

'Yes, please, ma'am!' There was no doubt in any of their voices.

'Very well. I shall write to your parents, Granville, and yours, Franconi. If they agree your orders should come through in a week or so. That's all. Dismiss.'

The three girls turned towards the door, to be halted by Henderson's voice.

'Oh, one more thing. If this goes ahead, you'll all be commissioned as Cadet Ensigns so that you can use the officers' mess.'

Cadet Ensign Franconi! Frankie savoured the words silently as she left the room. And the chance to go abroad! To see some of the places she had only read about! Her parents had to let her go!

Chapter Five

'Gina, love, it's wonderful to have you home for Christmas. It's really nice of them to let you have the time off, isn't it, Father?'

'You talk as if the army had done us a special favour, Mother,' Frankie's father returned. 'I don't suppose it's anything of the sort. Just the luck of the draw, eh, Gina?'

'Well, in a way,' Frankie hedged. It was her first evening at home and she did not want to spoil it with the row she knew must come sooner or later. Now it seemed the moment was upon her, whether she was ready for it or not. 'Actually,' she added, 'it's a bit more than just luck. This isn't just normal leave, it's embarkation leave.'

'Embarkation?' her mother queried.

'Embarkation!' her father echoed. 'And just what the hell does that mean?'

'Father, language!' her mother protested automatically.

'Never mind language.' He was beginning to lose his temper already. 'What do you mean – 'embarkation leave'? Where do you think you're embarking for?'

'I don't know,' Frankie said. 'They never tell you where you're going. You just have to wait and see.'

'I can tell you where you're going. You're going nowhere! You can't be posted abroad without my written consent. It says so in the papers I signed when you joined up.'

'I know, Dad. That's why I've come home. To ask you to give your permission.'

'But why, Gina?' her mother asked. 'Why do they want to send you abroad?'

'I expect they've got fed up with her snotty ways where she is now,' her sister put in spitefully.

'It's not that at all!' Frankie retorted. 'As a matter of fact, I've been offered the posting because I'm particularly good at what I do.'

'What? Particularly good at driving? What makes you so special?' her father asked.

'No . . .' Frankie said and then brought herself up sharply. She had almost forgotten the lie she had been forced to tell to cover her real activities. 'It's not that I'm specially good as a driver,' she went on carefully, thinking her story out as she went along, 'it's just that the officer I drive for wants to keep me. We get on well together. He knows I'm . . . you know, reliable and that sort of thing.'

She knew as soon as the words were out of her mouth that she had made a mistake. Her father's face hardened into a mask of cynical disbelief.

'Oh yes? What's his name, this officer?'

'Atkins,' Frankie said, using the first name that came into her head. 'Captain . . . I mean Colonel Atkins.'

'And his first name's Tommy, I suppose,' her father sneered. He stood up and leaned across the kitchen table towards her. 'Don't try to pull the wool over my eyes, Gina. You haven't been able to lie to me and get away with it since you were a little kid. What makes you think you can start now? Who is this man? Are you having an affair with him? Is that why he wants you with him?'

'No!' Frankie began to protest. There was a burning sensation in her throat, a combination of equal parts of distress and anger. It was her invariable response to these rows with her father.

Mr Franconi slammed his fist on the table. 'Tell me the truth! What is going on between you and this man?'

Suddenly the burning subsided and Frankie felt completely calm. She leaned back in her chair and met her father's eyes. 'I can't tell you the truth, Dad, because I've sworn not to tell it to anyone. But I can tell you this. There's no man involved. I made him up because I can't tell you what I really do. I'm not a driver. I never have been. But if I tell you anymore than that I could be shot. I'm not making it up. I've signed the Official Secrets Act.'

Her father sank back into his chair. 'The Official Secrets Act?'

'You mean,' her mother asked unsteadily, 'you're involved with something that's so hush-hush you can't even tell your own parents about it?'

'I'm afraid so, Mum.'

'She's a spy!' Maria giggled. 'My sister, Mata Hari!'

Frankie leaned towards her. 'Now you listen. I wasn't joking just now. I'm not a spy but if you so much as hint to anyone outside this room that I'm not doing what I said I was doing you could get me shot. Understand?'

'She understands.' Her father's voice was level and calm. Both Frankie and her sister knew that there was no arguing with that tone of voice. 'Maria, you will say nothing. If I hear that you have given the slightest hint of all this to anyone I shall disown you as a disgrace to this family.'

Maria lowered her eyes. 'Yes, Papa.'

Frankie looked at her father, unable to decide how her revelation had affected her case.

'You give me your word that you are not involved with some man?'

'Yes, Father. In actual fact, I've hardly seen a man for the last six months.'

'And this job you are doing – it is important to the war effort?'

'Yes, in a small way. I'm not the only one doing it, but it's true that lives do depend on it.'

'And you have been chosen for this posting because you are the best?'

'One of the best. There are three of us.'

'But you have no idea where you will be sent?'

'No. The army never gives out that sort of information. But it won't be anywhere near the front line. I'm strictly a back-room girl.'

There was a pause. Frankie held her breath. Then her father nodded.

'If the war effort needs our daughter, Mother, we have no right to refuse. Bring me the papers, Gina, and I will sign them.'

An hour or so later Frankie passed her sister's door and saw that she was slumped on her bed with an expression of sulky disgust on her face.

'What's up with you?' she asked.

'It's not fair!' Maria complained.

'What's not fair?'

'You get all the fun. Living away from home, doing exciting things. Now you're going off abroad and I'm stuck here.'

Frankie sat down on the bed beside her. 'You'll get your chance when you leave school.'

'If the war's still on. I bet it'll be over by then.'

'I wish I thought you were right.'

'I don't!'

'Maria, that's a terrible thing to say. You can't want all this death and destruction to go on any longer than it has to, can you?'

Her sister turned an anguished face towards her. 'No, of course not. But if it's over by next year, when I leave school, I'll never have the chance to get away like you. I'll end up helping out in the shop or working in a factory.'

'It doesn't have to be like that. You could stay at school, get some qualifications, maybe be a secretary.'

'No, thanks! I can't wait to get out. I'm joining the Wrens as soon as I'm old enough. I don't care what Dad says. Or do you think they'd have me in the FANYs?'

'I don't know,' Frankie said. Maria had never been a high achiever at school. She had not won a scholarship to Notre Dame as Frankie had and Frankie was uncomfortably aware that her sister would have even more difficulty fitting into the rarefied atmosphere of Overthorpe Hall than she had done.

'I suppose you think I'm not good enough for your snobby friends!' Maria spat.

'No, it's not that,' Frankie lied. 'But I honestly don't think you'd enjoy it. I'll let you into a secret. I sleep in a Nissen hut that's boiling in summer and freezing in winter, with a dozen other girls. The food's awful, the nearest cinema's miles away and most of the time the work's really boring. Oh, and I wasn't lying when I told Dad I hadn't seen a man for months.'

Maria looked at her and for a moment sisterly hostility was replaced by naked honesty. 'But you can't see yourself. You can't see how you've changed. The way you talk, the way you walk. The way you stood up to Dad just now. You've gone up in the world, Frankie. You'll never be happy to settle down here when the war's over. You'll go off somewhere and have a glamorous life and I'll be stuck here for ever.'

Frankie put her arm round her shoulders. 'Don't be silly! You're my family. I'll always come back to you. Blood's thicker than water, you know.'

But even as she spoke, the truth of her sister's words struck home. Would she ever be able to return to the life she had grown up with? What could the future hold for her once the war was over?

It was a strange Christmas. There had been no air raids for some time but there were few streets that had escaped and the gaping craters where houses had once stood were a constant reminder that the destruction could start again at any minute. Because of the blackout the streets were dark and there were no Christmas decorations. Frankie helped her mother and sister hang paper chains in the shop and the flat above but against the general dreariness they looked tawdry. It was the fourth Christmas of the war and everyone was exhausted and dispirited. The weather was bitter and coal was rationed and of poor quality. In the evenings they huddled around a fire that smoked and spat and refused to draw. Mrs Franconi had hoarded ration points to buy dried fruit for a Christmas cake but the Christmas pudding consisted mainly of grated carrot and dinner was a scrawny chicken.

'We should be used to it by now,' she said with a sigh. 'But every year it seems to get a bit more difficult.'

Presents were a problem, too. With all clothing rationed and luxuries such as cosmetics, cigarettes and alcohol almost unobtainable, it was hard to know what to give. Here, at least, Frankie felt she had an advantage. Many of the girls at Grendon seemed to have access to all sorts of little luxuries, items that had been carefully hoarded since before the war or acquired through well-connected friends, and in the run-up to Christmas there had been a lively bartering of goods and favours. 'This nail varnish for that pair of stockings.' 'I'll give you this tin of talcum powder if you do my ironing.' And there were things on sale in the NAAFI that had disappeared from the ordinary shops. In this way Frankie had amassed a small treasure trove of scent and bath salts and chocolate and cigarettes that she was able to distribute to her family.

In spite of all the attempts at festive cheer she could not rid herself of a sense of impermanence. It was not that she no longer loved her family, but she felt all the time that the Christmas leave was just an interruption to the real business of her life. Now that the papers were signed she was impatient to be off to whatever distant destination fate, or the War Office, had in store for her.

As soon as the shop reopened after the holiday her father remarked, 'If it's not beneath you these days, I could do with a hand. Business has picked up again lately.'

Frankie sighed inwardly but she knew that this was the price for his consent to her going abroad and she knuckled down with good grace. Two days later she was sweeping the floor when the door opened to admit a telegraph boy. Frankie's heart did a little flip. There was no reason for it, except that she had seen enough of the tragedies that had befallen her neighbours to know that a telegram usually meant bad news. She was even more disturbed when she saw that it was addressed to her. She took it into the back room to open it.

Got 3 days leave from Jan. 2. Any chance you come stay? Love to see you. Telephone reply. Steve.

Frankie gazed at the words, her pulse quickening. Three days with Steve! A chance to see the farm where her friend lived and which she talked about with such fondness. A chance to get away from the grimy streets and the drudgery of the shop. But could she possibly leave her family when she saw so little of them and would soon see even less? On the other hand, if she went to Steve's she would still be at home for New Year. She carried the telegram upstairs to her mother.

'And this Steve's a girl, is she?' Mrs Franconi asked dubiously.

'Yes, she is, really. It's just this silly rule they have in the FANYs that you can't call people by their first name, so everyone has a nickname. Her proper name is Diana Escott-Stevens.'

'Ooh, sounds very posh!'

'Her father's a gentleman farmer. Steve's quite upper class but she's not a snob. She was really nice to me during our basic training, but I don't see much of her since we were posted to different places.'

Mrs Franconi handed the telegram back. 'You go, love. You deserve a bit of a holiday instead of working in the shop. Don't worry, I'll talk your father round.'

Frankie arrived at Princes Risborough station just after dark on the second. She was stiff and chilled after the journey. She had had to change trains twice and there had been endless delays. A cold rain swept the unlighted platform of the little station and she seemed to be the only person getting off there and for a moment she almost wished she had stayed at home. Then a familiar figure appeared from the shadows and ran to meet her.

'Frankie! You made it. I'm so glad you could come. Have you had an awful journey?' Steve gave her a swift hug and grabbed her suitcase. 'You poor thing, you're frozen! Come on, we'll be inside in the warm in ten minutes.'

In the station yard stood a vehicle that Frankie could dimly make out as some kind of truck.

'Sorry about the transport,' Steve said as she opened the passenger door for her. 'This is the only vehicle that had any fuel in it. It's what we use for delivering the milk.'

The truck smelt faintly of sour milk and cow dung but at least they were out of the rain and Frankie was happy to exchange gossip with her friend as they wound up through narrow lanes onto the slopes of the Chiltern hills. She told Steve about her posting and they speculated excitedly about where she might be sent. Steve chattered away merrily, except when Frankie asked after Roddy. Then she detected a note of constraint in her friend's voice.

'He's OK, so far as I know.'

'So far as you know? Is something wrong?'

'Wrong? No, of course not. But it takes time for letters to get back and anything could have happened in the meantime.'

'Is he still in Malta?'

'Yes, poor lamb.'

'He must be due for some home leave by now, surely?'

'Overdue. But it's not easy to get away when the place is under siege. Although the pressure has been lifted since the Allied landings in North Africa.'

'He'll probably be back soon, then.'

'Yes, probably. Here we are, Hillfoot Farm.'

Steve swung the truck into a driveway and brought it to a standstill outside a pillared porch. As with every other building in the country, not a glimmer of light showed from any of the windows, and all Frankie could make out was the outline of a square house, rather smaller than she had imagined, set within a protective circle of hills. Then the front door opened and she was swept into a different world.

'Come in! You must be Frankie. I'm so glad you were able to come. Come in out of the cold before some wandering Jerry bomber sees the light and decides to unload his bombs on us.'

She stepped into a large, square hall from which an oak staircase rose to a galleried landing, the banisters of which were garlanded with swags of holly and evergreens. On a polished circular table in the centre stood an arrangement of gilded fir cones and scarlet candles, and in one corner was a huge Christmas tree, decked with scarlet and gold baubles and bearing at the tips of its branches real, lighted candles.

Frankie caught her breath. 'Oh, isn't it all beautiful!'

Mrs Escott-Stevens laughed. 'I'm glad you like it. I know the candles are a bit of a risk. My husband's always telling me we should give them up and have electric lights instead. But Diana and I love it so much we can't bear to change.'

'I think it's just perfect,' Frankie said. She looked at her hostess. Steve had been murmuring introductions but even without one Frankie would have known who she was. She had Steve's broad forehead and laughing blue eyes and the same slightly unruly auburn curls.

'Now,' Mrs Escott-Stevens went on, 'I expect you're ravenous and dying for a hot drink. I've made high tea instead of dinner because we weren't sure what time you'd arrive. Diana will show you up to your room and then as soon as you're ready we can eat.'

For a split second Frankie could not think who this 'Diana' was and, as if the same thought had gone through her own mind, Mrs Escott-Stevens said, 'Oh, by the way, should I call you Frankie or do you prefer Gina?'

'Frankie, please. If that's all right with you.'

'Of course it is,' Steve cut in. 'And you mustn't be surprised, Mummy, if she refers to me as Steve. The service seems determined to turn us all into chaps! Come on, Frankie. Your room's up here.'

The room she led Frankie into had a flowered chintz bedspread and curtains to match. In one corner stood a small kidney-shaped dressing table with a skirt of the same fabric and, wonder of wonders to Frankie's eyes, a fire burned in the grate.

'Oh, what luxury!' she exclaimed. 'A fire in the bedroom!'

'We're lucky,' Steve agreed. 'That's one good thing about living in the country. Coal may be rationed but no one can stop you going out and collecting as much wood as you can carry. And wood warms you twice, you know.'

Twice?'

'Once when you chop it up and once when you burn it.' They laughed and Steve went on, 'The bathroom's next door. I'll show you. My parents have their own, so it's just you and me sharing this one.' She led Frankie to the next room. 'I'm afraid Father's had a plimsoll line painted round all the baths, just like the government told us. Three inches of hot water only! Unfortunately the boiler won't run on wood so we have to stick to the coke ration.'

Frankie saw that there was indeed a thin black line round the inside of the bath. 'Don't worry,' she said, 'I'll stick to the limit.' She did not add that at home the boiler provided only enough hot water for one bath per night and, with the requirements of the weekly wash and the need to launder the towels from the hairdressing salon, that meant only one bath a week each. The rest of the time they had to manage with a stand-up wash.

'I expect you want to have a wash and brush-up,' Steve said. 'Come down when you're ready.' She turned away and then looked back. 'Oh, don't worry about changing. We gave up dressing for dinner when war broke out.'

Frankie stared after her. *Dressing for dinner!* What would she have done if she had been expected to? She had travelled in uniform, as any service personnel were required to do. Apart from that she had one woollen skirt and a pair of slacks and a couple of jerseys. She was relieved to see that Steve was wearing trousers and a Fair Isle pullover. She unpacked, washed her hands and face, brushed her hair and went downstairs.

In the sitting room she was introduced to Steve's father, a large, broad-shouldered man with a weather-beaten face and a deep, infectious laugh, and then Mrs Escott-Stevens announced that the meal was ready. Frankie's eyes widened at the sight of the dining table. There was a joint of boiled ham, homemade bread fresh from the oven with real butter, potato salad and a tall vase of celery, with a Victoria sponge filled with homemade jam to follow. It was the best meal she had tasted for a long time and it took a lot of self-discipline not to wolf it down with unseemly speed.

'What a wonderful spread!' she exclaimed, and then blushed because she had been told that it was bad manners to comment on food.

Her hostess looked almost apologetic. 'We're so lucky, having our own land. I can't imagine how people who live in the cities manage on the ration. Of course, we have to hand over most of what we produce to the Ministry of Food but they do let us keep a certain amount – when we kill a pig, for example. And there is always milk and butter and eggs from the hens, and we grow all our own vegetables and fruit.'

'And you make your own jam,' Frankie commented. 'How do you manage about the sugar?'

'Well, we keep bees and in the winter bees have to be fed, so we get an extra ration of sugar for that.' She gave a mock-guilty grin. 'I'm afraid the bees go a bit short, but they seem to survive.'

Frankie said nothing but she thought of how her mother and their neighbours struggled to make the food go round. It seemed unfair, yet she could not blame the Escott-Stevenses for making the most of what was available. Life was not fair, and that was the end of it.

After the meal they settled down in the sitting room by a blazing log fire and Steve's mother sat down at the piano and began to play Chopin. Frankie watched her admiringly, but she was once again reminded of the contrast between their lifestyles. She would have liked to learn to play herself but there was no prospect of having a piano at home and it had seemed pointless having lessons if she could never practise. She looked around the well-proportioned, comfortably furnished room and noticed that the curtains were faded and some of the furniture needed recovering, and it occurred to her that the Escott-Stevenses were not really rich, in the wider scheme of things. Nevertheless, they inhabited a different world from the one she had grown up in and, she had to admit to herself with a sense of guilt, it was one to which she would like to belong.

Frankie woke the next morning as the first grey winter light was creeping under the curtains. The fire had gone out hours ago and the room was icy. She got out of bed, wrapped herself in a dressing gown and went to look out of the window, finding she had to scrape away a delicate layer of ice before she could see out. Under a clear, almost colourless sky the countryside lay white with frost. Beyond the garden was a stand of tall beech trees, on which every separate twig was furred with crystals of ice. Tall grasses stood like silver spears around the edge of a frozen pond, and the very air itself seemed to shimmer with a delicate mist of frost. As Frankie gazed she heard voices and the crunch of boots on frozen gravel and, peering down, she saw Steve and her mother come round the corner of the house and pass under her window. They were wrapped to the ears in heavy coats and Steve carried a pail. They moved briskly, and it was obvious to Frankie that they had been up for hours and were returning from some chore or other around the farm. Feeling guilty at having overslept, she dressed quickly and hurried downstairs.

She found everyone in the kitchen. In addition to the family there was an old man with a grey moustache and a face so wrinkled that his eyes were almost invisible, and two girls of about Frankie's age in the uniforms of the Women's Land Army. Mrs Escott-Stevens was pouring tea from a huge brown pot and Steve was stirring a large pan on the kitchen range. They brushed aside her apologies, declaring that as a guest she had the right to sleep as long as she liked, and introduced her to the others. The old chap was the cowman who had looked after the dairy herd since 'before Noah was a lad', in Mr Escott-Stevens's words. The two girls were Londoners who had volunteered to work on the land in preference to employment in a munitions factory and who, by their own admission, had never seen a cow until six months ago.

'Sit down, Frankie,' Mrs Escott-Stevens instructed. 'Breakfast is almost ready.'

Frankie found herself faced with a large bowl of porridge. It was something she had always turned up her nose at previously, but today there was honey to sweeten it and milk fresh from the cow and thick with cream to pour over it, and she soon began to enjoy it. There were boiled eggs to follow with more homemade bread, and while they ate the two girls regaled Frankie with tales of their misadventures with the cows in their early days at the farm. They had Frankie almost choking with laughter, but she did not like to admit that she was just as ignorant as they had been.

When the meal was over the farm workers and Mr Escott-Stevens left to get on with their chores and Mrs Escott-Stevens set off on her bicycle for the village, leaving Steve and Frankie to wash up.

'Well,' Steve asked with a sideways grin, 'is this the way you imagined things?'

'Not really,' Frankie confessed. 'It's lovely but I suppose I thought your people would be much grander. I thought you'd have servants and all that.'

'Sorry to disappoint you,' Steve said wryly.

'Oh no! I don't mean it like that. I wouldn't know how to behave with servants and I don't mind helping out at all. I'm just surprised.'

'As a matter of fact, we did have help before the war,' Steve said. 'There were four men employed on the farm, for a start. They've all gone into the forces except old Will. And we had a married couple who lived in. Mrs Bagley did all the cooking and Mr Bagley was a sort of butler-cum-handyman. But he was killed at Dunkirk and she left to live with a sister who had also lost her husband. So now we just have a girl who comes in from the village every day to clean.'

'Your mum and dad must find it hard,' Frankie commented.

'You would think so, wouldn't you?' Steve agreed. 'But actually I think they are quite enjoying it. Mummy was only saying the other day that she's glad to have a real job of work to do, rather than organising the village fête and hosting sherry parties for the local bigwigs. Mind you, she still finds time to run bring-and-buy sales to raise money to buy Spitfires and such like. And Daddy does his stint with the Observer Corps.'

'What were you doing this morning, before breakfast?' Frankie asked. 'I saw you and your mum come in.'

'Milking,' said Steve. 'That's something that never goes away, summer and winter, seven days a week. I give a hand when I'm at home.'

'Are there things you have to do now? Because I don't mind helping, if I can.'

Steve dried her hands. 'No, don't worry. The rest of the day's our own. Come on, I'll show you round.'

Frankie discovered that the house, which had appeared rather dour and featureless the night before, was in fact an elegant Georgian manor house. Before the war it had been surrounded by sweeping lawns and flower beds but now the whole area had been ploughed up and planted with potatoes, cabbages, Brussels sprouts and other vegetables. Steve led her to the farmyard, where she was introduced to the two dogs and an apparently numberless colony of cats and kittens. She nearly jumped out of her skin when a large sow stood up on her hind legs as they passed and grunted at them over the edge of her sty. In the meadow beyond, Steve pointed out the herd of black-and-white Friesian cows, all of whom she seemed to know by name. Then, leading the way round the corner of a barn, she said, 'And now, my pride and joy!'

A pretty chestnut mare looked over the edge of a loose-box and whinnied a welcome as Steve appeared.

'This is Scheherezade,' Steve said, producing a carrot from her pocket and giving it to the horse. 'She's half Arab. Don't you think she's beautiful?'

'Yes, very,' Frankie agreed, keeping her distance. 'Is she yours?'

'Yes. I had her for my sixteenth birthday and I used to ride her every day in the school holidays, until I went to Switzerland to be "finished". It nearly broke my heart leaving her. But now . . .' she broke off with a shrug. 'Now it's hardly worth having her shod. I haven't ridden for months.'

'You could now, while you're home. I don't mind if you want to go off for an hour or two,' Frankie said, but Steve turned away, shaking her head.

'It's not worth starting again.'

Frankie followed her, puzzled. There had been something about her sudden change of mood that was uncharacteristic. She had never known her friend to be less than optimistic.

Steve seemed to throw off her mood within minutes and suggested a walk. They set off along a track that led through the beech wood, where the fallen leaves crackled under their feet, and out onto the open hilltop from where they could look out to where the Vale of Oxford disappeared into the winter haze. They returned, glowing, for lunch and spent a lazy after-noon by the fire, playing Monopoly and listening to records. They were both fans of Bing Crosby and Steve had just bought his latest hit, 'White Christmas'. They played it over and over, until they knew all the words and could sing along with Bing. By teatime Frankie felt relaxed and disinclined to move, but when Steve announced that it was time for the evening milking she felt bound to offer to help.

'You can come and watch if you like,' Steve agreed. 'The actual milking isn't as easy as it looks.'

By the time the cows had been brought in from the field and the milking had started Frankie was beginning to feel that she would never want to drink milk again. The beasts themselves, with their heavy udders and dung-streaked backsides, at once frightened and disgusted her. She was impressed by the spot-less cleanliness of the milking parlour and the care taken to disinfect everything, but the smell of the warm milk together with the faint odour of cow dung nauseated her. She hung back as Steve and the two land girls settled down with their heads against the cows' sides, crooning gently to the animals as the milk hissed into the pails. At length Steve called to her.

'Come on, you can have a go. This old girl's quiet enough. She won't kick out at you.'

'No, thanks,' Frankie replied. 'I don't think I'd be any good at it.'

'She's chicken!' one of the girls called out and, twisting one of the teats in Frankie's direction, sent a squirt of milk splashing over the cobbles at her feet.

They all laughed at that, so Frankie had to have a go just to prove her wrong. But however she pulled and squeezed she could not extract more than a pitiful trickle of milk from the udder.

'Never mind,' Steve consoled her. 'They know when you're

inexperienced and they just won't let down. It takes time. Come on, I'll finish it off.'

By the time she had helped with the clearing up Frankie's back was aching, her feet were frozen and her hands were sore and chapped from scrubbing out buckets in icy water. She decided that life on the farm was not all it was cracked up to be, after all.

A good dinner of roast pheasant, a delicacy Frankie had never sampled, went a long way to making up for her discomfort, and by bedtime her eyelids were drooping pleasantly. She had just got into bed when Steve tapped on her door.

'Frankie, I want to talk to you. Do you mind?'

''Course not. Come in.'

Frankie sat up and Steve perched on the edge of the bed, drawing her bare feet up under her. She looked tense and troubled.

'I've got to talk to someone and you're the only person I can talk to, because we're both sworn to secrecy.'

'It's about work, then?'

'Yes. You know what I've been doing, looking after the joes before they leave for France. Sometimes they only stay for a couple of nights but occasionally they are with us for two or three weeks, if conditions are bad. And they're so brave, Frankie! So incredibly brave. Of course, some of them don't seem to worry. It's all just a big adventure to them. But there are others . . . They never let on, of course, but you can tell they're absolutely terrified about what might happen to them. Well, you know better than I do what they're facing. You read their messages.'

Frankie nodded. She knew only too well. She had decoded messages reporting that X had been captured by the Gestapo; that it was feared Y had broken under interrogation and a whole network might be in danger. Worst of all were the messages that broke off in mid-transmission, never to be resumed.

'Go on,' she encouraged her friend.

'And it's not just men. I told you we had our first woman agent through a few months back – Jacqueline. There have been others since – Andrée, Odette . . . they're only code names, of course. I don't know who they are in civvy life. But they're as brave as the men. I keep thinking, why should I be sitting here in safety, living off the fat of the land – because it's only the best for the agents, quite rightly, and we share with them – when they are going to be risking their lives in a day or two. What right have I to have things so easy, when I speak French like a native. I've lived in France and I can pass for a Frenchwoman easily.'

Frankie caught her breath. 'Steve, what are you trying to say?'

'I've applied to be trained as an agent.'

'No!' Frankie's immediate instinct was to take Steve in her arms. 'No, Steve, you can't!'

Steve detached herself gently. 'Why not?'

Frankie looked at her in silence. She could think of no good answer.

'I may not pass the selection process, of course,' Steve said. 'Or I could flunk the preliminary training. But I'm fit and healthy. It's just a question of whether I've got the guts.'

'But what about your parents?' Frankie asked.

'I can't tell them anything, of course. But then, I can't tell them anything about what I'm doing now, so there's no difference there. Baker Street will come up with some kind of cover story, I suppose.'

'But suppose something happens to you.'

'There are hundreds of families with sons fighting in the war. It's no different, just because I'm a girl.'

'And what about Roddy? Suppose he comes home on leave, expecting to find you waiting for him, and you're not here.'

Steve looked away. 'I'll have to write to Roddy and tell him it's over.'

'Over? Why? What's happened? Have you met someone else?'

'No. Sort of.' Steve would not meet her gaze.

'What do you mean, sort of?'

'There was a boy who had to wait several weeks because the weather was so filthy – well, a young man, but he seemed like a boy to me. He was called Philippe but I don't know what his real name was . . . is. He's a musician, a violinist. He'd been studying at the Paris Conservatoire before the war, so he'd volunteered because he spoke good French. He was such a gentle boy, quite wrong for the kind of work he was going to do. But he'd come through all the training by sheer grim determination and he was waiting to go over. He never said anything, of course, but I could tell he was really scared. We got . . . quite close and one evening he told me that he'd never slept with a woman and he was afraid that he might die without ever having done. So I . . . so we . . .'

'You went to bed with him.'

'Yes.'

'Are you in love with him?'

'No. He was sweet and I'm not sorry I did it, but I was never in love with him.'

'Then what's the problem?'

'Frankie, I can't marry Roddy now! How can I?'

'I don't see why not.'

'Because we promised we'd wait for each other. And if he's kept his word and I haven't . . .'

'Does he have to know?'

'But men can tell, can't they. If you're not . . . not . . .'

'Not a virgin. So they say. So tell him what you did. Do you really think he'd blame you?'

'I don't know.' Steve was weeping now. 'I just couldn't bear it if he came back and I told him and then he decided to chuck me because I'd been unfaithful.'

Frankie pulled her back into her arms. 'Oh, Steve, love! Are you sure you're doing this for the right reasons?'

'I don't know. I just know I've got to do it.'

Frankie relaxed her grip and looked into her friend's eyes. 'OK. Do it, if you must. But don't tell Roddy it's over. Write to him and say you've been posted abroad, or whatever story you give your parents. Then, when the war's over, if – when – you both come home you can decide what to say to him. And if he loves you he won't care a damn that you took pity on some poor lonely boy. He'll just be glad to have you safe. Agreed?'

Steve sniffed and forced a smile. 'Agreed. Thanks, Frankie. I knew it would help to talk to you.'

Frankie sighed. 'I wish you weren't going to do it. But I do admire you, Steve. I think you're very brave. You make me feel ashamed.'

'Why should you?' Steve asked. 'You're doing something really important. People's lives depend on you.'

'But I'm doing it in safety, just like you were.'

'Up to now. But you're about to go abroad. Who knows where you might end up?'

'That's true,' Frankie said with a sigh. 'But wherever it is, it's not going to be occupied France.'

Chapter Six

'Africa! Do you really think that's where we're going?' Frankie leaned on the ship's rail and turned her face towards Dickie.

Her friend shrugged. 'All I said was, we're heading south so that could mean Africa. But it could be lots of other places. Maybe we're going to the Far East – India, Burma. Who knows?'

'Isn't it exciting!' Frankie breathed. 'I never imagined in a million years I'd get to see places like that.'

'I shouldn't get too carried away,' Dickie said. 'From what I gather from my brothers one army base is much like another, give or take a few thousand flies and mosquitoes.' She shivered and pulled her coat collar up round her face. 'At least it's got to be warmer than here.'

'Well, we knew that,' Frankie pointed out. 'We were issued with tropical kit.'

'And you thought that meant we were heading for the tropics? You poor innocent! The way the army works, we were just as likely to find ourselves in Greenland.'

'Oh, get away! It's not that bad.'

Frankie turned round to gaze out to sea again. The winter dusk was closing in and it was almost impossible to see where the heavy grey sky ended and the ocean began. There was a dead calm, and the waves rolled towards them in an endless procession of slick, glassy ridges that hardly seemed to disturb the equilibrium of the deck beneath their feet. Wisps of low mist had formed over the surface of the water, and through them the other ships of the convoy appeared and disappeared like ghosts, grey, darkened forms on a grey sea. Only the destroyers, fussing up and down along the edges of the convoy like anxious sheepdogs, threw up a white spume of bow wave. She looked down at the surface of the water. In this atmosphere it was not hard to imagine that a U-boat might be lurking somewhere beneath its opaque surface, waiting to strike.

To distract herself she said, 'Where's Midge?'

Dickie snorted. 'Where do you think? In the wardroom, flirting with all comers and letting poor Charlie Curtis buy her drinks and make sheep's eyes at her.'

Frankie chuckled. 'Yes, of course. Silly question. Why 'poor' Charlie Curtis?'

'Because the fool thinks he's in love with her. Can't you tell?'

'He's only known her a few days.'

'Don't you believe in love at first sight?' Dickie's voice was heavy with irony. 'I'm sure he does.'

'Well, perhaps he is in love with her. So what?'

'So nothing, as far as he's concerned. Midge will suck him dry and spit him out.'

'Dickie! That's a horrible thing to say.'

'Is it? Sorry, I always forget you're an incurable romantic.'

Frankie looked at her. 'You're not, are you? You don't seem to think much of men.'

Dickie gave her a lopsided smile. 'I was brought up with two elder brothers. It tends to cure you of romantic ideas. Believe me, men are entirely motivated by balls. Either the ones between their legs or the ones they chase around muddy fields.'

Frankie felt herself blush and was glad that it was nearly

dark. In spite of that, she could not suppress a laugh. 'Dickie, really!'

'Come on.' Dickie straightened up and turned aft. 'Let's go and get warm.'

The lighted wardroom, with its blackouts securely in place, was a different world. Half a dozen off-duty officers were enjoying pre-dinner drinks and entertaining themselves in various ways. In the middle of them Midge sat on a high bar stool, one silk-stockinged leg crossed over the other, a cocktail glass poised in one immaculately manicured hand. Three of the younger officers, Lieutenant Curtis among them, were positioned around her, paying ardent court.

Frankie hung back just inside the door. The abrupt transition from the cloistered atmosphere of Grendon Underwood to this predominantly masculine setting was something she found hard to adjust to. The three girls were the only women on the ship and, since their promotion had now come through, they were entitled to share the officers' mess, where they had been welcomed, almost literally, with open arms. Admittedly, there were one or two older officers who let it be known that they felt a fighting ship was no place for young women, but even they had behaved with unfailing courtesy. The younger officers, deprived of feminine company for months on end, had no such reservations, and from the moment they appeared all three girls had been showered with compliments, bought drinks and invited to dance, in so far as the cramped confines of the wardroom permitted dancing.

Midge, of course, was in her element, and the men were drawn to her like moths to the proverbial flame. Dickie, used to the rough and tumble of a house full of her brothers' rugger-playing friends, dealt with the situation by adopting a brusque cheerfulness which indicated as clearly as words that she expected to be treated as a chum, not a potential girlfriend.

Frankie had no useful experience to draw on. Her relations with the opposite sex had been circumscribed by her father's protectiveness and largely unsuccessful. To find herself in the company of men several years older and far more sophisticated had rendered her shy and tongue-tied.

'Frankie! What can I get you to drink?'

It was Fitz – Midshipman George Fitzwilliam – at her elbow. The most attractive officers had found Frankie's awkwardness unappealing and had turned their attentions to Midge, but Fitz had stuck to her like glue from the moment she stepped aboard. Not that there was anything wrong with him. He was not bad looking and had very nice manners, but he was only just eighteen, younger even than she was, and his only topic of conversation seemed to be ships, their various sizes and capabilities.

Frankie suppressed a sigh. 'I'll have a gin and orange, please.'

The regular offers of alcoholic drinks had been another problem. At home she had been allowed a glass of wine only at Christmas or on special occasions such as a wedding, or sometimes when it was felt that she might be a bit run down and in need of a tonic. The only spirits in the house had been her father's carefully hoarded bottle of strega. During her time at Grendon there had been no alcohol available in the mess and on their rare forays to the pub in the village she had stuck to cider. Here, on board ship, there seemed to be no limit to the variety of cocktails on offer. On her first evening she had followed Midge's example and asked for a dry martini, but she had disliked the taste of it so much that it had remained more or less untouched all night. The next day a sympathetic older officer had introduced her to gin and orange. She had found that so easy to drink that she had woken the next morning feeling sick and with an uneasy sense that the previous evening

she had giggled too much and behaved in a manner that
Brigadier Gamwell would not have regarded as ladylike. Now
she was careful to make one drink last a very long time.

The first lieutenant came into the room and paused beside
her. 'Hope you've got your sea legs, Frankie. Looks like we're
in for a bit of a blow tomorrow, according to the Met Office.'

Later, preparing for bed in the cabin the three of them
shared, Frankie watched Midge painting her nails. Dickie had
gone up on deck for a last breath of air, but her comments
about Midge's attitude to her admirers were still nagging at
Frankie's brain. She liked Lieutenant Curtis. In fact, she had
experienced a pang of jealousy when he started paying court
to Midge, and now she had to admit that her concern was not
entirely disinterested. All the same, she could not resist the
temptation to probe.

'Are you in love with Charlie?'

'What? Don't be silly!'

'He's mad about you.'

'Has he said so?'

'No. Anyone can see it.'

'Poor lamb.' Midge stretched out an arm and examined her
nails.

'What will you say if he proposes?'

'I shall say no, of course.'

'Then you shouldn't lead him on.'

Midge sighed and screwed the cap back onto her bottle of
nail varnish. 'Frankie, I think it's time someone told you the
facts of life.'

Frankie felt the blood rising in her face. 'I know all about
that, thanks. I'm not a complete idiot.'

'Not the birds and the bees, darling. The real facts, about
men and marriage.'

'Which are?'

'That there are two kinds of men – the ones who are fun to flirt with and the ones you marry.'

'Why can't you marry the ones you flirt with?'

'Because, my child, the ones who are fun to have around are never the same as the ones who can keep a girl in the manner to which she wishes to become accustomed.'

'That's horribly cynical.'

'Nevertheless, it's true.'

'So what's wrong with Charlie Curtis?'

'Darling, he's the son of the headmaster of some minor prep school and his greatest ambition is to follow in Papa's footsteps. Can you see me married to a provincial schoolmaster?'

'No,' Frankie admitted, 'I can't. So what does the sort of man you would marry have to offer you?'

'Oh, let's see!' Midge leaned back dreamily. 'A house in town, obviously. A country place would be nice for weekends but I couldn't bear to live there permanently. A good allowance, which will let me buy my clothes from the best couturiers. Social position – invitations to all the top parties. My own car. And independence! That's very important. I don't want to have to account for every minute of my day or every pound I spend.'

Frankie looked at her, unable to decide whether this cold-hearted materialism was genuine or just a façade. 'And what does he get in return?'

'Me, darling! A nice-looking woman who knows how to conduct herself in society and will be a good hostess at home and a decorative partner when he goes out.'

'And love?' Frankie asked.

'Love doesn't come into it. If you mean romance, that's a different thing altogether. Charlie Curtis is very romantic, but he is definitely not husband material.'

Frankie picked up her sponge bag and headed for the door.

'Midge, I think you're the coldest fish I've ever met. You don't deserve a nice chap like Charlie.'

Midge waved a dismissive hand. 'Well, if that's the way you feel, you're welcome to him, sweetheart. If you can get him . . .'

By the next morning the first lieutenant's forecast had been proved correct. The dead calm of the previous day had been replaced by a gale and the girls woke with a start as the ship plunged into a wave with a crash that set every plate and rivet juddering. For a moment Frankie thought they had been hit by a torpedo but the alarm did not sound and as the bunk tilted under her and then righted itself she realised what was happening.

'Hey up!' Dickie exclaimed. 'Looks like we're in for a rough ride.'

The response from Midge's bunk was a prolonged groan. Then her face appeared from under the blankets, pale and haggard.

'Frankie, be a love! There are some little blue pills in my make-up case. Give them to me, will you?'

'You can't be seasick already,' Dickie objected. 'It's only just started.'

'Oh yes I can,' Midge replied. 'I went on somebody's yacht once and I was sick in the first five minutes. I thought I was going to die before we got back to shore. I'm not going through that again. Anyway, it's been getting worse for the past hour, while you two were snoring. Pass me the pills, Frankie, please!'

By the time the other two were dressed Midge appeared to be asleep. At any rate, she did not respond to their suggestions that she should get up and have some breakfast. As they made their way to the mess they found themselves being thrown from side to side of the narrow corridor, bouncing off first one bulkhead and then the other as the ship rolled. They arrived breathless and giggling and were greeted with cheers by the off-duty officers. Frankie noticed that Dickie ate very little, however, and grew steadily quieter as the meal progressed, and afterwards, in response to Frankie's suggestion that they go up on deck, she announced that she had urgent letters to write and headed back to the cabin. So Frankie went on deck alone. To her delight and secret pride she found that she was quite unaffected by the motion of the ship. Instead, she experienced a sense of elation. Clinging to a stanchion with the wind whipping her face, she rode the violent plunging and bucking of the deck beneath her feet and laughed aloud with excitement.

'Good to see someone enjoying herself!'

It was Charlie Curtis who had come up behind her, his footsteps inaudible against the roaring of the wind and the crash of the waves as the ship slammed into them. She turned to face him.

'It's great! It's better than the rides at Southport funfair.'

He laughed. 'Good for you! You're obviously a born sailor. Just make sure you hang on tight. We don't want you swept overboard.'

Midge stayed in bed all day. Frankie was not sure how many of the little blue pills she had taken but she seemed to be only semi-conscious each time she looked in on her. By nightfall the gale showed no sign of abating and the word in the officers' mess was that the forecast was not good. Suddenly Frankie found herself the centre of attention. Men who had previously had eyes only for Midge now queued up to buy her drinks and ask her to dance. Elated by her discovery that she was immune to seasickness, she responded with greater confidence than before and experienced for the first time the heady delight of being the object of masculine competition. Once or twice she caught sight of the reproachful face of Fitz on the fringes of the group but she refused to respond. After all, she told herself, she had been nice to him out of courtesy, nothing more.

One of her most eager suitors was, to her surprise, Charlie Curtis. She was flattered, since he was, as Midge had obviously decided, the pick of the bunch. She wondered, briefly, whether she was wrong to encourage him, but then reminded herself that Midge was only toying with him. She was doing him a favour by rescuing him from her clutches. So when he suggested that they go up on deck for some fresh air she agreed.

As they stepped out into the open the wind almost knocked Frankie off her feet. Curtis grabbed her round the waist and shouted in her ear, 'Over there! We'll be sheltered in the lee of the bridge.'

With her back to the wall and out of the worst of the gale Frankie regained her equilibrium, but Curtis kept his arm round her.

'You're a great girl, Frankie! Bags of guts!'

'I'm not frightened. Should I be?'

'No, of course not. This old lady's been through heavier seas than this. And it makes us less of a sitting duck for Jerry.'

Frankie found his closeness at once exciting and embarrassing. She felt she ought to move away but could not see how to disengage herself without seeming rude.

'Are you cold?' he asked.

'No, I'm fine.'

'Here, snuggle up to me.'

He drew her closer, as if he had not heard her reply. She smelt salt and sweat and felt a cold metal button from his uniform pressing into her cheek. He put up a hand to push the hair out of her eyes and gold braid on his sleeve chafed her neck. Then his lips found hers. It was the first time she had been kissed properly, by someone who knew what he was doing, and she was excited and repelled in the same instant.

The pressure of his mouth on hers increased, forcing her lips apart, and she felt his tongue, moist and chill from the cold air. Strange things were happening in the lower part of her body, and for a moment she let her senses take over. Then came the thought that the night before he had probably been kissing Midge in exactly the same way. She drew back abruptly.

'Hey!' He looked puzzled. 'What's up, kid? I'm not going to hurt you.'

'You're supposed to be in love with Midge,' she said breathlessly.

'Who says?'

'Well, I thought . . .'

'Forget Midge. Who cares about her, now I've got to know you?'

He kissed her again, and once more she let physical sensation overpower thought. His hands moved over her back, pressing her hips against him so that she could feel the swelling in his groin. Her mouth felt engorged and there was wetness between her legs. When he unfastened her coat and felt for her breast through the thin material of her shirt her head swam with the intensity of her desire. But some still-rational corner of her brain protested. She freed her mouth.

'No, Charlie, we mustn't. This is all wrong.'

He pressed her closer, squeezing her nipple. 'Come on, sweetheart. I only want a kiss and a cuddle.'

'No!' she said suddenly. 'Last night you were doing this with Midge. You don't care which of us it is, as long as you get what you want. You and Midge deserve each other.'

'Frankie . . .' he protested, but she freed herself and moved away from him.

'Sorry, Charlie. I'm not like that. It's not what I want.'

'Kiss me again,' he said, 'and then tell me it's not what you want.'

For a moment she was tempted but then she shook her head. 'No. I'm sorry if you got the wrong idea. I shouldn't have come up here with you. I'm going now. Goodnight.'

She choked on the last word, turned and battled her way back across the deck to the entrance of the companionway.

The next day Frankie was almost ashamed to show her face in the wardroom, convinced that Curtis would have told his fellow officers what had happened between them. It soon became obvious, however, that nothing had been said, and he, for his part, behaved as if the misunderstanding had never occurred until he chanced to meet her in the narrow passageway leading to the cabins.

'Look, Frankie, I just wanted to say sorry about last night. I guess I'd had a bit too much to drink.'

She could feel the colour rising in her face. Even now his close proximity did something she could not define to her body chemistry.

'That's all right. I suppose I got it wrong, too.'

'No hard feelings?'

'No, no.'

'Good.'

He touched her arm briefly and passed on.

The gale continued through the days that followed, as the ships of the convoy rolled and plunged across the Bay of Biscay and down the coast of Spain. Midge stayed in her bunk. Frankie was not sure how many of the little blue pills she was taking but she seemed to be comatose most of the time. If it had not been for her two companions' bullying she would not have eaten and scarcely even drunk.

'I'm worried about her,' Frankie said. 'What are those pills she keeps taking?'

Dickie shrugged. 'Search me. But one thing's for sure. They're not just simple anti-seasickness pills.'

Mile by mile the convoy, limited by the speed of its slowest members, buffeted its way southward. Its exact position and destination were known only to the senior officers and, deprived of any indication other than the circle of angry sea circumscribed by a grey horizon, Frankie and her friends had no way of knowing how long the voyage might last. The only compensation for the bad weather was the fact that, so far, they had escaped the attentions of the U-boat wolf packs. Then, one morning, Frankie woke to a strange stillness. Her bunk was no longer rolling her from one side to the other and the creaking and jolting that had been a regular background to every activity had ceased. She sat up. Sunlight was pouring in through the porthole.

Frankie jumped out of bed and craned her neck to see out but the porthole was only just above the waterline and all she could see was blue, sparkling sea.

'Dickie, wake up! The storm's over. The sun's shining. Come on, Midge! It's not rough anymore. You'll be all right now.'

She was pulling on her clothes as she spoke. Midge responded only with an irritable grunt, but Dickie tumbled out of the top bunk and followed suit. Within minutes the two of them had erupted from the companionway. They stopped dead, gasping. Not only had the storm abated but the convoy was now in a wide bay, and ahead of them they could see the white houses and minarets of a large city. The sun was hot on their faces, although it was still early, and shards of light glanced off the waves, forcing them to screw up their eyes.

Frankie turned and caught the sleeve of a passing seaman. 'Where are we?'

The man checked his stride and grinned. 'North Africa, miss. And unless I'm much mistaken that there is Algiers.' He winked. 'But don't you say as I told you.'

'Algiers!' Frankie repeated in a whisper. If the man had said Xanadu it could not have sounded more exotic. 'Do you think we're staying here, Dickie. Or is this just a refuelling stop?'

'Who knows?' her friend responded. 'But now that the Yanks have taken over Algiers and Monty's pushed Rommel out of North Africa I shouldn't be surprised if SOE's got some kind of establishment in the area. After all . . .'

Her words were cut off by a reverberating crash that seemed to originate somewhere below the deck on which they stood. Frankie's first thought was that the storm had returned and they had been hit by a freak wave, but the sea was as calm as ever. The ship seemed to stagger and at the same instant the siren began to sound the alarm. Feet thundered across the deck as the crew rushed to action stations.

In the midst of the noise Dickie said, in a small, flat voice, 'My God, we've been torpedoed.'

An officer came past at the double. 'What are you two doing standing around?' he demanded. 'Get to your boat station. You know the drill.'

They knew it well enough. Lifeboat drill had been a regular part of their daily routine since coming aboard. Automatically they both began to run towards their allotted position. As they passed the head of the companionway Frankie skidded to a halt.

'Midge!' she yelled. 'She's still asleep. We'll have to fetch her.'

'Don't be daft!' Dickie returned. 'No one could sleep through this lot. She'll be at the boat station. Come on!'

Frankie stood her ground. 'She won't. You know what she's been like since she started taking those pills. The Last Trump wouldn't wake her. I'm going down.'

'Don't be a fool!' Dickie tugged at her arm. 'Suppose she's

there and you're running around the ship looking for her. You'll be the one who gets it in the neck. Besides . . .'

She left the sentence unfinished. Frankie was already heading down the stairs. 'You check the boat station. I'll check the cabin,' she shouted back, and clattered down the steep companionway.

As she reached the next deck she began to smell smoke, an acrid tang that caught the back of her throat and made her cough. The deck beneath her feet was beginning to tilt, so that she kept sliding into the wall. The cabin was on the deck below. She reached the head of the next staircase and plunged downward. In the passageway the smoke was thicker, curling in oily wreaths along the ceiling. Frankie clasped her handkerchief over her mouth and ducked down to where the air was clearer. It had begun to occur to her that what she was doing was extremely foolish. The thickening smoke and the alarming angle of the deck left her in no doubt that she was risking her life – probably quite unnecessarily. Midge might well have woken or been roused by another member of the crew. Running doubled up and gasping for air, she headed down the long passageway towards the cabin.

She had just reached it when all the lights went out. The door crashed open at her touch and she half stumbled, half slid into the little room. It was scarcely any lighter here, because the list of the ship had plunged the porthole under water. For a moment she thought the cabin was empty and she was about to turn away when there was a low moan from Midge's bunk. Frankie threw herself across the space and grabbed the other girl by the arm, shaking her violently.

'Midge, come on! Wake up! The ship's sinking. We've got to get out.'

'Help me! Help me!' Midge sobbed. 'What's happening? I don't know what's going on.'

'Never mind that. Just come on!' Frankie tugged at her and she dragged herself unsteadily to her feet. 'This way. Hurry!'

Frankie started towards the door, up what was now a considerable slope, but Midge pulled free of her grasp and turned back.

'Got to get dressed,' she mumbled. 'Can't find my clothes.'

'Never mind clothes.' Frankie almost screamed the words. Her hand encountered something soft on the back of the door and she recognised a dressing gown. She yanked at it and felt the hanging tab rip away. 'Here, put this on.'

She flung the gown round Midge's shoulders and began to drag and push her towards the door. In the passageway Midge began to cough and tried to duck back into the apparent safety of the cabin but Frankie hung onto her.

'Keep your head down. The quicker we move the sooner we'll be in the fresh air. Go!'

Midge seemed to come to and begin to realise the urgency of the situation. At any rate, she stopped struggling and allowed Frankie to pull her towards the stairway. When they reached it they found that what had been a steep ascent was now an easy gradient as the ship leaned farther and farther to port. Coughing and panting, the two girls scrambled up. The air was clearer at the top but Frankie was terrified that at any moment the ship would turn turtle and take them down with her. She wondered if the lifeboats had been launched and if anyone had waited behind for them. They clambered up the last companionway and burst out into the sunlight.

To Frankie's surprise the scene on deck was much more orderly than she had imagined. The ship was listing sharply but ropes had been rigged to grab hold of and the crew were moving purposefully about, engaged in various tasks.

'Where the hell do you think you're going?' a furious voice demanded.

'Boat stations,' Frankie responded meekly. 'Come on, Midge.'

She hurried the still-confused Midge across the deck to where Dickie was waiting with a small group of sailors under the charge of a petty officer.

'Thank God!' she cried. 'I've been going out of my mind here. I wanted to come after you but they wouldn't let me.'

'Nice of you to join us, ladies,' the petty officer remarked with heavy irony. Then, taking in Midge's appearance, he added, 'She all right?'

'She'll be OK,' Frankie said. 'She's been seasick for days. But you're OK now, aren't you, Midge?'

She helped Midge over to a bollard and sat her down, pulling the dressing gown around her to cover her scanty silk night-dress. Dickie crouched beside them.

'Frankie, I feel awful. I should have come with you. I guess I was in a blue funk.'

'No you weren't,' Frankie said. 'You were being sensible. Someone had to check the boat station.'

'No, I should have come with you. I'd never have forgiven myself if . . . if anything had happened. Are you all right?'

'Yes, I'm fine, now I'm out in the open air again.' Frankie straightened up and looked around her. 'What's happening?'

'I don't really know. But it seems we're not going to sink – not at once, anyway.'

'Thank God for that.'

Frankie realised that the tilt of the deck was not getting worse. If anything, it seemed to have stabilised. The engines were still running and the ship was making slow progress through the water. A destroyer was holding station a short way off on the port side, ready, she assumed, to take them on board if it became necessary to abandon ship. Craning round, Frankie saw that farther out in the bay two other destroyers were quartering the area in search of the U-boat that had delivered the torpedo. As she watched, two fountains of water spurted up in the wake of one of them and a sailor nearby said, 'Depth charges!'

'Hope they got the bastard!' his companion grunted, then looked at Frankie with a half-apologetic grin. 'Saving your presence, miss.'

'I hope they got him, too,' Frankie returned.

'Look!' Dickie touched her arm and pointed. Turning, Frankie saw that they were slipping past the end of the harbour wall. 'We're going to make it,' Dickie said triumphantly. 'Algiers, here we come!'

'Good afternoon, ladies, and welcome to Inter-Service Signal Unit Six, otherwise known as Operation Massingham. My name is Corbett and I am the Chief Signals Officer so you will all report to me.'

Frankie was sitting with a dozen other girls in a large, airy room in what had once been a first-class hotel perched at the end of Cap Matifou. She and her two companions had been transported the ten miles from Algiers by truck to join the others, who seemed to have been assembled from a variety of different outfits. Most were in FANY uniform, though there were one or two WRNS and WAAFs. Frankie recognised one or two faces from basic training at Overthorpe Hall, and in conversation over lunch she had learned that others had been based in Cairo or had been seconded from various active-service units. They had one thing in common. They were all either radio operators or coders.

Corbett went on, 'I understand one or two of you have had a somewhat eventful voyage out from the UK.'

'You can say that again!' Dickie muttered.

'However, I hope you are now recovered from your ordeal

and beginning to get used to the heat, because we have a great deal of work to do. The purpose of this unit is to keep in touch with agents working in the South of France and ultimately, we hope, with others in other parts of Southern Europe. You are all experienced coders and signallers, so you understand what is involved. You will be working long shifts and I'm sure I have no need to remind you that if a message is garbled no one goes off duty until it is decoded. However, we can offer you some compensation for the hard work. We have taken over the Club des Pins on the beach as an officers' club and you are welcome to use its facilities during your off-duty time.' He waited for the murmur of appreciation to subside. 'The duty roster is on the noticeboard over there and you will be operational from oh eight hundred hours tomorrow. That is all for now. You have the remainder of the day to rest and get acclimatised. Dismiss!'

As soon as the door closed behind Corbett a din of voices broke out.

'The officers' club!' chortled the girl next to Frankie. 'Hey, girls! I reckon we're in for a good time!'

Midge pushed her way through the crowd from where she had been sitting, a little apart from the rest. She had said very little since the ship docked and Frankie had wondered if she was still under the influence of the little blue pills. Now, however, as she faced them, her eyes were clear and steady.

'Frankie, can I have a word?'

'Yes, Midge. Of course.'

Midge glanced over her shoulder. 'Shall we go out onto the terrace?'

'OK.'

Frankie followed her out into the sunshine, feeling vaguely embarrassed. Once they were alone, Midge turned to face her.

'Look, I've got something to say. I've been a bitch to you

ever since we met and I want to apologise.' Frankie made to
interrupt but Midge was not to be stopped. 'Yes, I have. I've
condescended to your face and sniped at you behind your
back. Steve and I quarrelled about you more than once. She
thought I was just being a snob, and I suppose I was to begin
with. I can't help it. I was brought up that way. But later I hated
you because you stayed awake and watched out for Steve that
night and I fell asleep. And because you're brighter than me.
And then, after the way I've behaved, you risked your life to
save me.'

'But I didn't!' Frankie broke in. 'I thought the ship was
sinking, but it wasn't. We weren't in any real danger.'

'But you thought we were, and you still came looking for me.
Anyway, if I'd stayed in that cabin I'd probably have been
suffocated by the smoke, so I believe you did save me. And I
just want to say thanks – and . . . and sorry!'

Frankie looked at her and wondered which of their faces was
the redder. 'It's all right,' she mumbled.

'So . . . pax, OK?'

Midge held out her hand.

Frankie laughed, the tension released by the schoolgirl
expression. She took the outstretched hand. 'Yes, OK, Midge.
Pax!'

'And can we be friends now?'

''Course we can.' She pulled Midge to her and put her arms
around her. The other girl's shoulders were bony and her
whole body seemed so stiff and brittle that it appeared it might
snap instead of bending but she laid her cheek briefly against
Frankie's and Frankie decided that this was probably about as
close as she would get to a hug. She let her go and smiled at
her. 'Come on. Let's make the most of the rest of today. We
may not get much chance to sunbathe from now on.'

At the evening meal the only topic of conversation was the

officers' club. The rumour had gone round that it was also used by agents in training.

'Do you reckon that means we shall actually be able to meet the men whose traffic we handle?' Frankie said, turning to Dickie.

'Sounds possible,' Dickie agreed. 'But even if we do, we probably won't know who we're dealing with once they're operational. We shall only have code names to go on.'

'That's true,' Frankie agreed. 'But all the same, it'll be a thrill just to get to know some of them, won't it?'

'Well, don't get your hopes up too high. You know how hush-hush it all is. They'll probably tell you they're doing some really boring desk job.'

Most of the girls were planning to go down to the bar and there was eager speculation about how they might be received.

'Do you fancy going?' Frankie asked Midge.

'Just try and stop me!' was the response. 'Coming, Dickie?'

'No, thanks. I had enough of that sort of thing on board ship. I'm going to have a quiet evening with a book and an early night.'

So Frankie and Midge brushed their uniforms, put on clean shirts and prepared to go out.

'Oh for a glamorous evening gown!' Midge sighed. 'I envy Steve being able to get dressed up every night.'

It was on the tip of Frankie's tongue to say that it was probable that Steve no longer needed her evening dresses. Instead she said, 'Well, I haven't got a glamorous evening gown, so it's just as well we aren't expected to.'

Midge looked at her for a moment. 'You'd look stunning in something by Schiaparelli. But you don't make the most of yourself, you know. Come here and let me do your make-up for you.'

Frankie submitted to Midge's efforts, and when she was

finally allowed to look in the mirror she was at once shocked and delighted. She had never used more than a dab of powder and a hint of lipstick. Any more than that at home would have had her father ordering her back upstairs to wash her face, and at Grendon there had been no incentive to change her habits. Now, Midge had applied mascara to her eyelashes and rouge to her cheeks and her mouth was a vivid scarlet bow. It made her feel as if she were about to go on stage. She would never have dared show her face like this at home, but she had to admit that the effect was striking and the more she looked at her reflection the bolder and more confident she felt.

'My God, what have I done?' Midge drawled. 'No one will look at me twice now.'

Frankie laughed. 'Don't be daft. Come on, let's go before all the dishiest men have been spoken for.'

Frankie hesitated at the entrance to the bar of the Club des Pins. It was a large room, brilliantly lit by chandeliers that were reflected in long mirrors behind the bar itself. It was crowded with men in every service uniform Frankie had ever seen and some she did not recognise. There were a few women but they were very much in the minority. The air was noisy with chatter and thick with the scented smoke of Turkish cigarettes. Midge took her by the arm.

'Come on. What are you having to drink?'

'I don't know. It's awfully posh, isn't it? I've never been in a place like this before.'

'Don't be silly, it's just a bar. And you look posh enough for anywhere. Look, grab a table and I'll get the drinks. Gin and orange for you?'

'Yes, please.'

Frankie edged through the crowd, feeling herself the object

of many interested glances. One or two of the officers greeted her, their approach varying from a polite 'Good evening' to a subdued wolf whistle and a murmured 'Hey, good lookin'!'. She found an empty table and perched tensely on the edge of her chair, wishing Midge would hurry up and join her. Midge, however, was already in conversation with a young man in RAF uniform.

A voice behind her spoke in the husky tones of Humphrey Bogart. 'Of all the gin joints in all the world, you have to walk into this one.'

Frankie twisted round in her chair. 'Sorry! What?'

The man who had spoken was in the uniform of an army major and had a full, dark beard, unusual for a soldier. He grinned at her and his hazel eyes glinted with mischief.

'Don't you remember me? I remember you, Frankie Franconi, though you've grown up a bit since we last met.'

Frankie stared at him and suddenly recognition hit her with a force that took her breath away.

'It's you! Nick!' Then she remembered the army discipline that had been drummed into her for the past year. 'I'm sorry, sir. I didn't recognise you.'

He laughed. 'It's the beard. Don't worry, it's coming off tomorrow. And it's still Nick. There's no need to be formal. I hope you appreciated my Bogart imitation.'

'Oh, yes.' She was struggling to sound composed although she felt dizzy with joy. '*Casablanca!* I loved that film. This place makes me feel as if I was in it.'

He was looking at her, his eyes appraising her behind the smile. 'Ingrid Bergman had better watch out! She's got serious competition. You're not on your own, are you?'

'No, I'm with a friend. She's over there at the bar.'

'The blonde girl heavily engaged with that large RAF type?'

'Yes, that's her.'

'May I join you?'

'Yes, please do.' Frankie watched as he pulled out a chair and sat down. She could hardly believe that at last, after all these months, she was face to face with Nick Harper again.

'Can I get you a drink?'

'No, thanks. My friend's buying me one.'

'So.' He took out a cigarette case and offered it. 'You decided to join the FANYs.'

She took a cigarette, although she hardly ever smoked. This seemed to be a day for breaking out of the old mould. 'Bet you never thought I would.'

'On the contrary.' His eyes teased her as he leant forward with his lighter. 'I've been expecting you. I heard on the grapevine that Baker Street had recruited a gorgeous, raven-haired Italian girl all the way from Liverpool. I was sure you'd turn up here sooner or later.'

'Are you based here?' she asked.

'I'm not sure at the moment. I have to report to London as soon as I can get a flight. I only got back yesterday.'

'Back from where?'

He lifted his eyebrows. 'Where do you think? You know what we are all here for.'

She caught her breath. 'You've been working behind enemy lines? In France?'

He chuckled. 'No, even the army's not as daft as that. It's Italian I speak, not French.'

'I didn't know we had agents in Italy.'

He wagged a finger at her. 'Ssh! We don't, officially.'

'So you're not staying here?' She could not keep the disappointment out of her voice.

'I'll probably be back quite soon. London won't want to keep me hanging about doing nothing.'

'So will you have to go back to . . . to wherever you've been?'

'It's unlikely, at present. I'll probably do a stint as what they call a Conducting Officer, passing on the fruits of my experience to the new recruits.' His gaze became more intent. 'So we may have time to get to know each other properly.'

Frankie felt that her face had turned the same shade as her lipstick. 'I'd like that very much.'

Midge shouldered her way through the crowd, followed by her solidly built escort carrying a tray of drinks. She greeted Frankie with raised eyebrows.

'My, my. You haven't wasted much time, have you?'

Frankie glared at her. 'This is Nick,' she said, mustering her best manners. 'Captain . . . sorry, Major Harper. Nick, this is my friend the Honourable Marjorie Granville.' There was a barely perceptible edge of irony on the word 'honourable'.

She watched Nick's face as the two shook hands but to her relief he showed no sign of the usual masculine reaction to Midge's beauty.

'Frankie and I are old friends,' he said. 'We met in an air-raid shelter in Liverpool.'

The large young airman, who Frankie now saw had the badges of rank of a flying officer and a pilot's wings on his tunic, thrust out his hand.

'James Lampeter – commonly known as Jumbo,' he announced.

Frankie grinned as her hand was enveloped in a huge paw. She had never met anyone who so perfectly suited his nickname. 'Gina Franconi – commonly known as Frankie.'

'Is it OK if I join you?' the young pilot asked. 'I don't want to barge in.'

'It's fine by me,' Nick returned. 'In fact, I've got a suggestion. A friend of mine is having a party. He's just heard that his wife has given birth so he's invited everyone for a knees-up. Why don't we all go?'

'Great!' said Midge. 'It's months since I've been to a party.'

'Frankie?'

'I'd love to. There's just one thing – we've got another friend. She stayed in the billet but I wouldn't want to go without inviting her. Can we take her too?'

Nick grinned. 'If she's as decorative as you two I'm sure she'll be more than welcome.' Then, seeing Frankie's momentary look of doubt, he added, 'Of course she can come. The more the merrier. I've got a jeep outside. We'll stop by and pick her up on the way.'

'Right!' Midge downed her drink in one. 'Come on, Jumbo. Don't hang about.'

'Oh, right. Coming.' Jumbo swallowed his beer and followed her towards the door.

Nick slipped his arm under Frankie's and chuckled. 'No doubt about who's the ringmaster in that circus. She'll have him standing on his hind legs in no time.'

Frankie laughed and hung onto his arm as he manoeuvred her through the crowd. It was going to be a wonderful evening!

Chapter Seven

The party was held in another hotel, one that had escaped being requisitioned. There were tables around a dance floor with a three-piece band and long windows led out onto a moonlit terrace overlooking the sea. To Frankie, it looked like the set for a romantic film. Nick took her arm again as they entered and she thrilled to the feeling that he was claiming her as 'his girl'. He was obviously popular and they were soon the centre of a large group, but Frankie felt she was immediately accepted because she was with him. He danced once with Midge and twice, despite her protests, with Dickie, but the rest of the evening he danced with Frankie.

She had learned to dance at Saturday morning classes, but there had never been enough boys to go round so she had usually found herself partnering another girl or a boy several years younger and several inches shorter than herself. On board ship they had danced but in the crowded confines of the wardroom there had been room to do no more than jog from foot to foot. Now, for the first time, she found herself in the arms of an expert. Nick had the grace of a born athlete and a natural sense of rhythm. She felt clumsy beside him and when her foot caught his for the second time she gasped, 'I'm sorry. I'm afraid I'm not very good at this.'

'Rubbish,' he replied, 'you're a natural. Just let yourself relax.'

So she relaxed and let herself feel the way his body moved

to the beat of the music. By the time they reached the third foxtrot their movements were flowing together as if their two bodies were commanded by a single nervous system. Frankie felt dizzy with happiness, and when the band played a slow waltz and he drew her closer in his arms she let her head rest against his shoulder and decided there could be no greater bliss than this.

At the end of the dance he suggested a walk on the terrace. She remembered her encounter with Charlie Curtis and hesitated, but only for a second. He took her arm and they strolled to the end of the terrace, away from the lighted windows of the ballroom. There they stopped and leaned on the balustrade, looking out over the sea. The moon had gone down but above them the stars hung huge and gently luminous, not like the icy, glittering pinpoints of northern skies. The air was so warm Frankie felt she could bathe in it and heavy with a perfume she could not recognise.

'Isn't it perfect?' Frankie said. 'And there's no blackout! It seems really strange seeing all the houses lit up like this.'

'Jerry's bombers can't reach this far,' he answered.

'Thank heavens!'

He turned towards her and smiled. 'You're not sorry I persuaded you to join up, then?'

'Of course not! It's the best thing that ever happened to me.'

'Is it?' He lifted a hand and brushed a wisp of hair from her face. 'When I first met you in that shelter, I had a feeling something special had happened. Now I know I was right.'

He bent his head and kissed her, very gently. This time there was no sense of being invaded and no panic-stricken urge to pull away. When his tongue found hers she felt as if her whole body had liquefied, as if the two of them were flowing into each other like two streams joining to form a river. After a long moment he released her and murmured,

'You don't mind being kissed by a chap with a beard, then?'

'No,' she replied, looking at him more closely than she had dared to do before. 'But I think you looked nicer without one.'

'Then I'll shave it off tomorrow.'

'Why did you grow it?'

'Not much opportunity to shave where I've been,' he said, and the clipped tone indicated to her that this was not a subject to be pursued.

Instead she said, 'How long will you have, before you go back to London?'

'No knowing. It's all in the lap of the gods, or rather of the RAF. There are not many flights going back to the UK with spare seats and I'm afraid they don't regard agents as very high-priority. Could be tomorrow, could be next week.'

'Tomorrow!'

He drew her close again. 'I'm afraid so, but let's hope not. I don't want to go, now I've found you.'

She leaned against him. 'You will be coming back, won't you – definitely.'

'I wish I could promise but I can't. I have to go where the powers that be decide to send me. You know that. But I can make a strong case for being sent back here and I'll certainly do my best.'

He kissed her again and then they stood quietly, folded in each other's arms. Frankie closed her eyes and realised that she was very tired. The moment when she had woken up to the sunshine that morning seemed half a lifetime ago. In spite of herself she yawned. The yawn was stifled immediately but he had sensed it.

'Come along. It's time I took you home.'

'Sorry,' she murmured. 'It's been a long day.'

'Do you have to work tomorrow?'

'Not in the morning. My sked starts at two.'

'How about meeting me in the morning?'

'I'd love to – as long as it's not too early.'

'Do you fancy a swim?'

'Oh yes! That sounds wonderful.'

'I'll meet you at the club house. About eleven?'

'Fine.'

'Right. Home, James!'

He led her back along the terrace and into the lighted room. Midge was not ready to leave and Jumbo promised to see her back safely, so they collected Dickie and drove back to base. Dickie tactfully hopped out of the jeep as soon as they arrived and disappeared inside and Nick put his arm round Frankie's shoulders.

'Goodnight, my sweet. See you in the morning.'

'Yes. Thanks for a lovely evening.'

'No, I should thank you. You know, I haven't been able to get you out of my mind since that first meeting. I'm so glad you eventually found your way here.' He kissed her once more and whispered, *'Buona notte, cara mia,'*

'Buona notte,' she breathed in return, and reluctantly climbed out of the car.

In the billet she was relieved to find that Dickie seemed in no mood to talk. She slid into bed, intending to relive in her mind everything that had happened that evening. She had got no farther than the door of the bar when she fell into sleep as if dropping off the edge of a diving board.

While Dickie remained more than usually taciturn Midge had no such inhibitions and pestered Frankie from the moment they woke up with questions about how she and Nick had first met and what had passed between them the previous evening. Frankie, meanwhile, was rummaging in her luggage for her bathing costume and being thankful that Steve had advised her to take it, just on the off-chance.

When she produced it, however, Midge gave a low groan.

'Frankie, you are not going on a date with that gorgeous man in that!'

Frankie looked at the costume. It was the one she had had for school swimming lessons and she had to admit it was a sad-looking object, made of sagging navy wool and darned in a couple of places.

'It's all I've got,' she said miserably.

'Oh, wait a minute. Let's see what I can find,' Midge said in long-suffering tones. She hunted in her bag and produced a deep red confection that looked as if it had never been worn. 'Here, try this for size.'

When Frankie arrived at the club, carrying the red costume wrapped in a towel, she almost failed to recognise Nick for the second time. He had shaved his beard, as promised, and looked ten years younger. He was sitting with a group of friends but jumped up as soon as he saw her and came to meet her.

'Good morning! How are you?'

'Very well, thank you.'

Several of the other girls from her section were sitting around, waiting for their escorts or hoping to catch the eye of one of the officers who used the bar, and Frankie could feel them watching her. She felt a glow of pleasure at being so warmly greeted by the best-looking man around.

Nick rubbed his chin. 'Well, what do you think? An improvement?'

'Definitely. You don't look so . . . so. . .' She searched for a word. '. . . so fierce without it?'

'Is that the impression I gave? Talk about a lamb in wolf's clothing! Come on. Are you ready for that swim?'

He showed her where to change and then led her through the sand dunes to a sheltered cove where turquoise waves lapped onto white sand. Frankie's only experience of sea bathing had been in the chilly waters of the Irish Sea off Southport, where even on a warm day it required an act of courage to immerse yourself. She hesitated on the water's edge and Nick, who had run straight in and dived under the waves, came to the surface and waved at her.

'Come on! You're not scared, are you?'

'Is it cold?' she called back.

He laughed and waded back towards her. 'Of course it's not cold! Come on, chicken!'

He took her hand and pulled into the water. To her delight it was just cool enough to be refreshing but no more. She had never been a strong swimmer but she let him lead her out until she was waist deep, gasping and laughing as the small waves splashed up into her face. He let her go and struck out strongly for a small raft moored some yards out into the bay. Then, seeing that she was not following, he came back.

'Don't tell me you can't swim!'

'Oh yes! I can swim,' she responded, 'but I don't like getting out of my depth.'

He lifted a hand and brushed her cheek with wet fingers. 'You'll be safe with me. Turn on your back and float.'

She did as he told her, feeling the water more buoyant than the sea at home.

'OK. Now, just relax.'

She felt him take her head between his hands and then the powerful thrust of his legs as he kicked out, towing her out into deeper water. For a moment she panicked, then the proximity of his strong, lithe body overcame her fear and she let him take her. A moment later he swung her round so that she could grasp the edge of the raft and boosted her up onto it.

There! OK?'

'Yes, fine.'

He pulled himself up to sit beside her. She looked at him, suddenly shy. He was not a large man but she could see that he was solid muscle with not an ounce of spare flesh.

'You swim very well,' she said.

'I grew up by the sea.'

'So did I, in a way. But you can't count the Mersey as seaside.'

He stood poised for a moment and then dived. She watched him as he swum, sleek as a seal, beneath the water. He climbed back onto the raft and repeated the dive two or three times, while she sat and basked in the unaccustomed heat.

Next time he returned he said, 'Time I got you back to the shore. You must get into the shade before you burn.'

'Oh, I'm all right,' she insisted. 'I love the sun.'

'Just the same,' he returned, 'you mustn't sit out in it too long. You have no concept of how strong the sun is out here. I've seen chaps get hideously sunburnt in a matter of hours. I don't want that to happen to you. Come on, we'll go and get dressed and then have a drink before we get a bite of lunch.'

He helped her off the raft and lowered himself in beside her. 'Now, are you OK to swim back, if I stay close by you?'

She nodded and struck out for the shore, while he kept pace with a lazy sidestroke. When they reached the shallows and stood up he caught her hand and pulled her to him. His lips tasted of salt and she could feel the warmth of his flesh through the coolness of the water on his skin. He kissed her briefly, then turned and led her up the beach.

When Frankie came back from the changing rooms she saw Nick sitting at the bar, deep in conversation with Midge, and a stab of jealousy went through her.

Damn Midge! she thought. She's already got Jumbo under her thumb. Can't she leave any man alone?

Nick got up as she came over and took both her hands. His face was serious.

'Frankie, why didn't you tell me?'

'Tell you what?'

'About the torpedo yesterday morning. Midge has just been telling me how you saved her life.'

'But I didn't. The ship wasn't sinking after all.'

'It could have been, for all you knew. You took a real risk, going below to find Midge. I had no idea you'd been through all that. And then I wanted you to come dancing with me! You must have been exhausted.'

The concern on his face brought a lump to Frankie's throat. She smiled up at him. 'I wanted to come dancing. I had a wonderful time.'

'Well, you're a brave girl. But then, I knew that already.'

Midge slipped off her bar stool and winked at Frankie. 'Well, that's my good deed for the day so I'll toddle off now. Toodle-oo!'

Nick watched her go. 'You know, I thought last night she was a bit of a vamp but she seems to be a nice kid after all.'

Frankie was tempted to tell him that his first impression had been correct but instead she said, 'She has her good side.'

'Ah!' he said, nodding. 'But it's not always on show, eh?'

For three days Frankie lived with an intensity she had never known before. She worked her 'sked' from two o'clock onward, often until late in the evening, coping with an ever-increasing flow of messages. Then she went to bed and slept the moment her head touched the pillow, to wake the next morning with a feeling of excitement rising inside her like the bubbles in a glass of champagne. The mornings were spent with Nick, swimming or strolling along the beach and talking, talking. She told him about her early experiences with the FANY, about Midge's hostility and Steve's kindness, and made him laugh at the tale of how she had cut Midge's hair and the poem that Brigadier Gamwell had intercepted. She talked about her family and how hard it had been to persuade her father to let her join up.

Then she asked shyly, 'What about you? I know your mother died when you were little but that's all. Where did you grow up?'

'A little village called West Dean in Sussex. My father's the local doctor.'

'And where did you go to school?'

'A minor public school – Hurstpierpoint.'

'I might have guessed. Then what?'

'Oxford to read history. Then when I graduated I went out to Italy for a holiday job during the summer and fell in love with the place. I was living with the family of a silk merchant in Milan, teaching his two boys English, and when he offered to take me on on a two-year contract it seemed too good a chance to miss. I was still there in the summer of '39, until it became obvious that the war was coming and Italy was going to be on the wrong side. So I came home to join up.'

'Did you go straight into SOE?'

'No, but after Dunkirk, when we were all sitting around wondering what on earth was going to happen next, the word went round that some outfit up in London was looking for men who were fluent in other languages, so I put my name forward.'

Frankie wanted to ask him what he had been doing there in the last few months, but when she mentioned the subject his replies were uninformative and, knowing the prohibitions that hedged them both about, she did not press him.

On the fourth day, as they were walking up from the beach, an army corporal approached and saluted.

'Message from the Transport Officer, sir. There's a plane leaving this afternoon at two pip emma with a spare seat.'

Nick thanked him and watched as he spun on his heel and marched away. Then he turned to Frankie.

'Sorry, darling. Looks like this is it. I can't pass up the chance of a flight back to Blighty.'

'I know,' she said, her throat tight. She put her arms round his neck. 'You will come back as soon as you can, won't you?'

'I'll do my best. You know I can't promise.'

'But if they do send you somewhere else, you'll write to me. Promise me that!'

'Of course I will.' He took her face between his hands. 'Darling Frankie! These last few days have been very precious to me. You know that, don't you? I've never felt like this about anyone before. I'm not going to lose touch with you, now I've found you again.' He kissed her. 'I'll have to go now. I've got to pack my kit and get out to the airfield. Take care, my darling.'

'I'll be fine. Don't worry about me. You're the one who needs to take care.'

'I will.'

They kissed once more and then he let her go and she watched him walk away through the sand dunes. He had promised to take care but she knew that there was very little he could do. Any plane flying across the Bay of Biscay was in danger of attack from enemy fighters based in occupied France and he would have no control over that, anymore than he would have over the bombers that still pounded London from time to time. His safe return depended on much more than the whims of the senior officers in Baker Street. As he disappeared behind the last sand dune she was gripped by a terrible fear that she might never see him again.

Routine life continued without him but Frankie felt that she was somehow suspended outside time. Nothing could happen that had any significance until Nick returned. For the first time she began to find her work as a decoder boring. Also, she realised that she had been neglecting her friends and they had turned elsewhere for company. Midge was spending every spare minute with Jumbo and Dickie had struck up a friend-ship with a slender, fair-haired girl called Felicity Vane, whose company nickname was Flick. She was spared from having to spend her mornings alone, however, by the fact that Jumbo's flying duties rarely coincided with Midge's hours, so very often she and Frankie went down to the beach together. Algiers was out of bounds so there was little to do other than swim and sunbathe. Frankie worried about Midge and Jumbo. He was obviously besotted with her and she seemed happy in his company, but Frankie could not forget the conversation she had had with Midge on board ship. She liked Jumbo. He was always good natured and there was a straightforward solidity about him that made her feel he was a man who could be trusted. She did not want to see him hurt.

One morning about a week later she was sitting among the sand dunes with Midge in the shade of a large sun umbrella. Midge stretched and yawned luxuriously.

'Aren't we lucky? Just think of all those poor souls at Grendon, cowering round that one oil stove in the Nissen hut.'

Frankie was writing to her parents. She put down her pen and looked around. 'Yes, we are. It's hard to believe that it's still only February, isn't it?'

'Finished your letter?' Midge asked.

'Nearly.'

Midge sat up and began to rub oil into her legs. 'Get on well with your people, do you?' she asked casually.

Frankie stopped writing again. 'Well, yes. I suppose so. Dad can be a bit difficult at times but it's only because he wants to look after us.' She paused, remembering what Steve had said months ago at Overthorpe. 'You don't talk much about your family. Do you get on well with them?'

Midge shrugged. 'Hardly know them. I think they found having a kid cramped their style. I was brought up by nannies until I was old enough to be packed off to boarding school.'

'How old was that?'

'Seven.'

'You were sent away from home at seven?' Frankie was incredulous.

'Yep. After that I only saw my parents in the holidays. Not always then.'

'Why?'

'They were away very often. My father's mad about fast cars. He travels round the world from one race meeting to another. Well, he did before the war.'

'As a driver?'

'He used to drive. When he got past it he went to watch.'

'And did your mother go with him?'

'No, she has her own interests, which largely involve keeping up with the social scene. In summer she'd be cruising the Med on somebody's yacht and in the winter it was skiing at Klosters or shooting in Scotland, or wherever the smart set happened to be.'

'What about now?'

'Oh, Mother went back to the States as soon as the bombing started. She's American. And he's got some cushy number at the Ministry of Information.'

Frankie looked at her. She could not imagine a life where your parents regarded you as nothing more than an inconvenience. It explained a good deal. 'Your father's a lord, isn't he?'

'Lord Farnham. Actually, that's part of the trouble. He came through the first war without a scratch but his father was drowned when the *Lusitania* went down, so he inherited the title – and the family debts. So when the war finished he did the classic thing and married an American heiress. I think . . .' Midge was frowning, and Frankie had the feeling that she was using the conversation to try to make sense of things she had never allowed herself to think deeply about before. 'I think he felt guilty because he had survived when so many other young men had died. So he decided that as he had he might as well make the most of it and enjoy himself. Or perhaps he thought the fast cars would finish the job where Jerry hadn't succeeded. I don't know. All I can say is, I hardly ever saw him until I turned sixteen. At that point I think he and Mother realised that I might be an asset and they had better take me in hand and make sure I was presentable.'

'What sort of an asset?'

'Matrimonially, darling. Father is determined I shall marry money and mother is equally determined I shall marry class.'

'So that's why . . .'

The sound of a plane, flying quite low over the dunes, made Frankie stop and sit up. She could distinguish at once between the buzz of a fighter and the low drone of a bomber and this was definitely not a fighter plane. The sound recalled nights in the shelter back home.

'Listen!'

'Relax,' said Midge. 'It's probably Jumbo or one of his pals.'

She got up and stood clear of the umbrella and Frankie joined her. The plane was low enough for them to read its identification letters.

'There he is. It is Jumbo!' Midge waved cheerfully in the direction of the plane.

'What's he doing?' Frankie asked.

'Watch!'

The plane circled and climbed and then Frankie saw a string

of dark shapes appear below it, shapes that blossomed after a moment into the white mushrooms of parachutes.

'Training drop,' Midge said. 'That's what his squadron is here for.'

'To train the agents?'

'Not just to train them.'

'What do you mean?'

'When the moon's full they fly them over to France and drop them.'

'That sounds pretty risky.'

'Jumbo says it's a piece of cake, but of course he would. They go in very low and just hope no one spots them.'

Frankie watched the parachutes floating downward. They would land in the dunes some distance away. She wished it was nearer so she could talk to one of the men.

'That must be a fantastic feeling,' she mused. 'Like being a bird for a few minutes. Don't you think so?'

Midge turned back to stretch out on her towel again. 'No, I do not! No power on earth would persuade me to jump out of an aeroplane. I can't imagine anything more terrifying.'

'Oh, I don't know,' Frankie persisted. 'It would be scary the first time, but once you got used to it . . .'

'No, thanks! Thank God we're not required to do anything like that.'

One day a brief letter arrived from Steve. *This is just to let you know that Aunt Mary has been taken ill and I am going to stay with her for a while.* It was a code they had agreed on before Frankie left Hillfoot Farm and meant that Steve had been accepted for training as an agent. The letter went on, *As you know, she is quite a demanding old lady so I may not have time to write but if you send letters to my home address I'm sure I shall get a chance to pick them up sooner or later. Do keep in touch!* Frankie sat gazing at the letter for several minutes. She could not imagine what the training would be like or how Steve would cope with it. All she could think of was those interrupted messages from agents in the field and Leo Marks's warnings about the possible fate of agents caught in the act of transmitting. She considered briefly telling Midge or Dickie about Steve's plans but she knew that she should not confide in anyone, even if they were all working for the same organisation. Strictly speaking, Steve should not even have told her. It was a heavy secret, and one she had to carry alone.

Nick reappeared almost a month after he had left. They met almost exactly where they had parted, on the path from the beach, and Frankie saw him a second before he saw her. She gave a cry of delight and started to run towards him, then checked herself and was suddenly afraid. They had had three days together and now they had been apart for more than three weeks. Would he still feel the same? An instant later he broke into a run and she threw herself into his arms. He held her tight and covered her face with kisses.

'Oh, Nick,' she gasped. 'I'm so glad to see you. It's been such a long time!'

'I know, I know,' he answered. 'I'm sorry I couldn't make it sooner. They kept me hanging around in London for days, debriefing me. Then they gave me two weeks' leave and I felt I had to go home and see the old man.'

'Of course you did. He must miss you dreadfully. How is he?'

'Oh, fine. Overworked, of course. With all the young men called up he's having to deal with twice as many patients as usual. But he's coping.' He held her a little way off and looked at her. 'I've missed you so much. How are you?' He laughed. 'I can see you haven't been paying attention to my advice. Your nose is peeling.'

Frankie rubbed her nose self-consciously and decided not to tell him that a week after he left she had been in real pain from blisters on her back.

'Are you here to stay now?' she asked.

'For a while, at any rate. They've done as I expected and given me a stint as a Conducting Officer. So I'll be here working with the new recruits for the next few months.'

'Months! How many?'

'Could be as much as six. It depends on circumstances.'

She hugged him. 'Oh, Nick, that's wonderful!'

'Yes, it is, isn't it,' he responded, his voice muffled in her hair. 'Let's make the most of every minute.'

Time ceased to drag. Frankie was now working the morning shift, which meant less time for the beach but more to spend with Nick, who was on duty during the day. They went dancing and to parties, which seemed to happen on the slightest pretext, and Frankie found herself part of a group of friends, consisting of Nick's fellow instructors and girls from the FANY detachment. Sometimes they were joined for a few days or weeks by other young men, from different branches of the services and of varying nationalities, who never discussed their reasons for being at Cap Matifou and who disappeared as mysteriously as they arrived. They were a cheerful crowd, all determined to make the most of the fact that they were out of the firing line and enjoying better food and conditions than they could have expected at home. They never talked about what might be round the corner.

When they were alone, however, Nick showed a more serious side to his character. As before, he and Frankie talked endlessly. To start with they discussed neutral subjects – books, films, music. He introduced her to jazz and she persuaded him that Crosby and Sinatra were as worthy of attention in their own field as Gigli and Caruso. They discovered a mutual love of poetry and he told her about Oxford and talked about his special interest, which was the history of the Roman Empire. As they became more at ease with each other they moved on to more sensitive subjects, such as religion. Nick had been brought up in the Church of England and still adhered to it, although his loyalty was founded more on a respect for tradition and a love of the poetry of the King James Bible than on a serious consideration of theology. Frankie talked about her Catholic upbringing and admitted that in the last year or so she had come to question her faith more and more frequently.

But it was when they turned to politics that Nick really caught fire.

Once she asked him what he planned to do after the war. He gave her a sideways look. 'What's this? Are you checking up on me to see if I'm a good prospect?'

Frankie felt herself blush. 'No! Of course I'm not. I'm just interested, that's all.'

He slid his hand under her arm. 'Sorry. I was only kidding. The fact is, I can't think beyond the end of the war. I found some time back that the best way of getting through it is not to think about the future.'

'I'm sorry,' she said in her turn. 'I didn't mean to poke my nose in.'

He turned to her. 'I don't mind. It's such a pretty nose,' and he kissed the tip of it.

They kissed properly then and after a while he said, 'Actually, I do have plans. If I'm still around when this bloody war is over I rather fancy going into Parliament.'

'Parliament?' Frankie said, stunned.

'Yes. I know it sounds a bit over-ambitious for a country doctor's son but I've learned a lot in the last few years. I've met people from all sorts of backgrounds and I can see that a lot of things have got to change after the war. The old forelock-tugging, cap-raising culture is going to vanish. People are going to want more equality – and they're quite right.'

'I'll go along with that,' Frankie agreed. 'I've seen enough of the so-called upper classes to know that they are no different from the rest of us.'

'Exactly. Ordinary people have put up with too much for too long. Take the folk my father deals with. I've grown up listening to him complaining that some of them won't send for the doctor until they're practically at death's door, because they're terrified that they won't be able to pay his bill. Many's the time he's accepted a rabbit or a brace of pheasants in lieu of payment – poached, of course, but he doesn't ask questions. It's not right that people should have to live like that.'

'I know what you mean,' Frankie agreed. 'There are plenty of families round where I live who wouldn't call a doctor except as a last resort. But doctors have got to live, haven't they? If they didn't charge they couldn't survive.'

'Yes, but there must be other ways!' He spoke with an intensity she had not heard before. 'There should be some way people can save for when they need treatment. I don't mean pennies in an old teapot or something like that. A properly organised scheme that everyone belongs to. And the better off should jolly well have to subsidise the poorer folk. What's the point of fighting this war if we are just going to sink back into the bad old ways when it's over?'

They were silent for a moment and then he sighed. 'Sorry, I didn't mean to get on my soapbox. All we can do now is concentrate on winning the war – and at least now it looks as if there is some prospect of that.'

In bed that night Frankie went over and over their conversation in her mind. It was the first time Nick had spoken of the future, but it seemed to be a future that had no place for her. In the first weeks after meeting him again she had been carried along by the euphoria of finding that he preferred her to any of the other girls. It had been sufficient simply to be 'Nick's girl'. But now she was beginning to wonder why he appeared content to let the relationship drift. That she was in love with him was never in doubt and she thought he was in love with her, but she could not understand why he had never mentioned marriage. Only a day or two earlier one of the other girls had announced her engagement and Frankie had felt a sharp pang of envy. Still, she reminded herself, he had not tried to seduce her and that ought to be a comfort. She knew that several of the other girls were sleeping with their boyfriends – girls who would never have dreamed before the war of going to bed with a man without a ring on their finger. She had been brought up to believe that to do so was not only unwise from a practical point of view but also a mortal sin; and though she found herself increasingly out of sympathy with many of the Church's teachings she still believed in God and feared his disapproval. At least, she feared the disapproval of some authority figure, though whether that was God or her father she was never quite sure.

The fact was, in spite of her doubts about the morality of such actions, Nick's self-restraint in this area was beginning to worry her. Whenever they were together he would find some opportunity to be alone with her and they would kiss and hold each other close until she was lost and afloat on a warm tide of desire. Yet he was always the first to draw back and to lead her back to the company of their friends. She often asked herself what she would do if he tried to persuade her to sleep with him. Sometimes, half asleep, she dreamed of all sorts of delicious activities that made her blush when she remembered them in the cold light of day. She recognised, guiltily, that where she should be grateful for his gentlemanly restraint she was, in fact, frustrated by it.

The weeks passed and the weather grew hotter. The sand scorched their bare feet when they ran down to bathe and in the coding room the girls sweated over their work, in spite of the introduction of electric fans. At night, it became harder and harder to sleep. News came from home, via the BBC and weeks-old papers. Air raids continued, though they were less intensive than in earlier years. One hundred and seventy-eight people had died in a Tube station at Bethnal Green. A woman had slipped on the stairs in the rush to take shelter, knocking down those ahead of her. Others, coming behind, had fallen over them, crushing them. The pianist Rachmaninov was dead. The RAF's new Lancaster bombers had wreaked retribution on Berlin. The combined forces of Britain and America had finally driven Rommel and his men out of Africa and, at home, Churchill announced that now that all fear of invasion was over church bells might be rung for services again.

One evening Nick arrived for their date brandishing a copy of *The Times*.

'Look! Remember what I was saying about medical services? The government is actually doing something about it. See?'

Frankie looked at the paper. The headline read 'Government accepts Beveridge plan for a National Health Service'.

'How is it going to work?' she asked.

'It seems they envisage a kind of universal insurance scheme. Everyone pays in each week and then, if they need treatment, they just go to the local GP or the hospital.'

'And they don't have to pay?'

'Not a penny! The government pays the doctors and nurses out of the money from the insurance.'

Frankie thought of some of the people she knew back in Liverpool.

'That will be the most wonderful relief to so many people,' she murmured.

'And,' Nick said triumphantly, 'it's been thought up and passed in the middle of a ghastly war. Now that is the sort of politics I want to be part of!'

Frankie forgot her doubts about the future for a moment and smiled at him tenderly. 'And you will be! I'll bet you anything you like.'

He put his hands on her shoulders and looked into her eyes and for a moment she thought he was going to say the words she longed to hear, but all he said was, 'Dear Frankie!'

As the days passed Frankie became increasingly restless. Life was very pleasant, if you discounted the daily drudgery of coding and decoding messages, but it was this pleasantness which made her uncomfortable. She felt that they were in a backwater, away from the real war and having everything much too easy. The pleasures offered by the officers' club were limited in scope, and after a while even the frequent parties began to seem flat. In May there was some distraction from the regular routine when the King came to Algiers to congratulate the troops, and for a day or two they all felt they were the centre of attention, but the excitement was short lived. More concrete encouragement came with the news that Allied aircraft were now attacking Italian airfields and that the Allies had invaded the Mediterranean islands of Pantelleria and Lampedusa. The beginning of July brought better news still. Allied forces had landed on Sicily.

One morning Frankie and Nick were lounging on the beach. The shifts had changed again and Nick had managed to snatch an hour or two from his duties to spend with her. The deep throb of aircraft engines made them look up and they watched as a string of parachutes unfurled behind the plane.

'Have you ever done that?' Frankie asked.

'Of course. It's all part of the job.'

'What's it like? I think it must be a wonderful feeling.'

'Do you?' He looked amused. 'Well, I suppose it is, when you're jumping on a beautiful clear day like this, knowing that you're going to be picked up by friends when you hit the ground. Not so good on a dark night over enemy territory, though.'

'Of course not,' she said. 'I'm sorry, I didn't mean to make it sound as if you did it for fun. I think you're terribly brave to do that. But what's the actual parachuting like? Are you scared?'

'I certainly was the first time. I suppose the moment of leaving the plane is always scary – stepping off into nothing. But once you're out there and the 'chute's open – yes, it is a good feeling. You should try it.'

'Oh, I wish I could!' she exclaimed. 'I would love to have a go.'

'Well, why not? There's a new course starting in a couple of days. I'll have a word with Johnny Pearson, the man in charge, if you like.'

'You mean, I could actually join in? Would I be allowed to?'

'I don't see why not. One more or less won't make any difference to Johnny.'

'But I mean – will it matter, me being a girl?'

He looked at her. 'Girls are doing all sorts of unladylike things these days. I've met some women doing jobs that would make a strong man think twice. Why not try, if that's what you want. Only don't tell your CO. She might feel she had to stop you.'

Frankie thought of Steve and wondered whether she was learning to parachute. Or had she already been dropped into the darkness over occupied France?

'OK,' she said. 'I'll do it, if you can fix it.'

Next morning Nick greeted her with the words, 'Right, you're on. Are you sure you still want to do it?'

'Yes,' Frankie answered firmly, her pulse racing.

He grinned approvingly. 'Good for you! I'll pick you up tomorrow morning at eight o'clock.'

Frankie had assumed that you learned to parachute by jumping out of an aeroplane. She soon discovered otherwise. Johnny Pearson was a small, wiry RAF sergeant with a voice that could stop a tank in its tracks. He treated her respectfully for the first few minutes and called her 'miss' or, when he remembered she was an officer, 'ma'am'. After that he called her 'girlie' with either furious reproach or grudging approval, depending on her performance.

'If you don't keep your legs together, like your mother taught you, girlie,' he would shout, 'you're going to split yourself in half!'

They began training in an improvised gymnasium, learning to jump off boxes and roll with the impact. When they had mastered that they were made to jump from the back of a moving truck. Then came the most frightening part yet. They had to climb a tall scaffold and jump, wearing a harness counter-weighted with sandbags to simulate the drag of a parachute. Frankie being so slight, the aircraftsman in charge of attaching the sandbags miscalculated her weight so that, instead of experiencing a rapid descent, she floated gracefully down and hovered a few inches above the ground. One of the men in the group commented that it reminded him of being taken to see *Peter Pan* as a child, and from then on she was known to them all as Wendy.

The men on the course treated her with slightly doubtful chivalry to begin with, but as they got used to her she was accepted as one of them. They swore when they landed wrongly and wrenched an ankle or bruised an elbow. Frankie endured in silence, although there were times when she had to grit her teeth to stop herself from groaning aloud, and they respected her for it. She often arrived back at base bruised and aching and had barely enough time to shower and pull on her uniform before she went on duty but, surprisingly, she found her concentration sharper and the long, hot afternoon less soporific than before. She told no one what she was doing and all her friends assumed she was spending the time with Nick.

In fact, she saw less of Nick than before, since she was too tired by the time she came to the end of her shift to go out anywhere. She worried from time to time that he might get lonely and turn to someone else, but he showed up at the airfield occasionally and, although they were not alone, she sensed a new electricity in their relationship.

The day came when she was to make her first proper jump. She had hardly slept the night before and was unable to eat any breakfast. When Nick picked her up she saw that instead of his normal uniform he was wearing the same kind of overalls as the other men she was training with.

'I'm going to jump with you,' he said. 'It's time I had a refresher.'

She did not answer because she was fighting back tears of gratitude, but she felt for his hand and squeezed it hard.

Waiting in the hut for the order to go out to the plane was almost the hardest part. It was hotter than ever, but they had been instructed to dress warmly under their overalls because it would be cold when the plane reached the necessary altitude. Frankie could feel the sweat running down her back and between her breasts, and she longed to strip off the layers of stifling garments. The walk to the plane, with her unwieldy parachute bumping against her legs, almost exhausted her. Eventually they were all on board, sitting in a line along the side of the fuselage, in the order in which they would jump.

She was glad to see that Nick would jump immediately ahead of her. At least if she lost her nerve at the last minute he would not be there to see her humiliation.

The engines started and then rose to a howl that made Frankie want to clasp her hands over her ears. She tensed and felt herself begin to shake. Nick, sitting beside her, took her hand and squeezed it. She put her mouth close to his ear and yelled, 'Why are they making so much noise?'

He looked puzzled. 'Just running the engines up to go through the usual checks,' he shouted back.

The plane jerked into motion, bouncing over the uneven ground of the makeshift runway. Frankie could feel that they were accelerating but there were no portholes in the cabin and she could see nothing of the outside. Faster and faster they went, with the engines roaring, and she began to wonder whether there was something wrong. Then she felt a lurch in her stomach and the vibration of the wheels on the ground ceased and she realised they were airborne. For a moment she forgot her nerves and thought only of how much she longed to see out. Then the plane tilted alarmingly, almost throwing her forward off the bench. In spite of herself she gave a little cry of alarm.

Nick grabbed her arm and smiled at her. 'Relax!'

She leaned towards him and asked, 'Why is it tipping over?'

'Banking to turn,' he answered. Then he gave her a sharp, incredulous look. 'You've never been up in a plane before, have you?'

'No,' she admitted.

He shook his head, marvelling at her. 'Bloody hell! Never been up in a plane and the very first time she's going to jump out. What a girl!'

The plane droned on and Frankie felt her hands and feet grow cold. The wait seemed interminable and she longed to be free of this dark, noisy box in which they were imprisoned. At last the dispatcher got up and opened the big door in the side of the fuselage. A blast of cold air hit her in the face and at last she could see out, but the doorway framed nothing but empty air. A red light went on above the door and the dispatcher gestured to them to get up. Frankie rose and clipped the ripcord of her parachute to the running line along the side of the plane. Nick reached up and gave it a tug to make sure it was secure. Then he smiled at her reassuringly. She knew that one of the main reasons for a parachute failing to open was that the cord had not been securely fastened. The line of men shuffled forward until the first one was standing in the open doorway, the dispatcher's hand on his shoulder.

Nick twisted round to look at Frankie and put his mouth to her ear. 'I'll be waiting for you when you get down.'

Frankie nodded and in that instant knew that she would jump. It was unthinkable to do otherwise.

The light changed from red to green and the dispatcher gave the leading man a shove. He disappeared into the void, followed immediately by the next and then the next. Before Frankie had time to think Nick was in the doorway; then he was gone and the dispatcher's hand was on her back, propelling her forward into nothingness. The slipstream of the aircraft caught her, knocking the breath out of her body and sending her tumbling over and over. Then she felt a jerk on her shoulders and she was hanging suspended in mid-air. She looked up and saw the canopy of the parachute above her head. To her right and below were the parachutes of those who had jumped before. She guessed the one nearest must be Nick's but she could not see him beneath the billowing silk. She craned her neck, trying to see the men who had followed her, but the 'chute hid them from view. Then she looked down. The earth seemed impossibly far below. She could see the coast stretching away into the heat haze in both directions and the white line of the breakers and for the first time she had a proper view of the mountains that reared up inland.

There was no sensation of falling. She felt that she could hang there between earth and sky indefinitely, and she was so busy gazing around that it came as a shock to realise that the ground was rushing up towards her uncomfortably fast. She looked down. Where was she going to land? Were there any obstructions? That thorn bush looked nasty! She must remember to keep her feet together and roll. In the event it was the conditioned reflexes produced by her training that took over. She hit the ground, rolled over twice and sat up, breathless but uninjured.

Immediately she struggled out of her harness and fought to master the billowing folds of the parachute, which caught the sea breeze and threatened to drag her along the sand.

A voice behind her said, 'Here, let me give you a hand,' and she turned to see Nick trudging up the slope of the sand dune. Together they threw themselves on the parachute to control it and in the process Frankie found herself wrapped in Nick's arms.

'My darling, wonderful girl! Are you all right?'

'Yes,' she gasped. 'I'm fine.'

He kissed her hungrily, and for the first time she felt that the urgency of his desire might overpower his self-control. Through the thickness of the clumsy overalls his hands moved over her body, and her only wish was to be free of the clothes that encumbered them. Then, from the far side of the dune, they heard voices calling and the grinding engine of the truck that would take them back to base.

Nick let her go and sat up. 'Sorry, old thing. We'll have to move.'

She was not sure whether he was apologising for his

passionate embrace or for the fact that they were not free to follow it through to its logical conclusion. Together they rolled up the parachute and scrambled across the dune to the waiting truck.

Frankie reached the base, sweaty and bruised but triumphant, to be greeted by two bits of news. Mussolini, the Italian dictator, had fallen from power and Colonel Dodds Parker, the Head of Station, wanted to see her in his office before her shift began.

Chapter Eight

As she scrubbed herself under the inadequate trickle of water that passed for a shower and scrambled into her uniform, the same questions were going round and round in Frankie's mind. How had the CO found out what she had been up to? She had told no one except Midge. Had Midge shopped her? If so, why? What would the colonel's reaction be? Had she, in fact, broken any army regulations? What was her best line of defence?

When she reached Colonel Dodds Parker's office she found two other girls already there. One was Dickie and the other was Mary MacIntyre, the coder in charge of Frankie's section. Had Dickie somehow found out and told Mary, who had reported her to Dodds Parker? As she came to attention and saluted, Frankie studied the CO's face. He looked serious but not apparently angry.

'At ease, Franconi. Sit down.'

Frankie sat and Dodds Parker looked from her to the other two girls. 'I'm going to start by emphasising that nothing of what you are about to hear must ever go beyond this room. I know you have all signed the Official Secrets Act and that you are used to being discreet, but what I am about to tell you is not to be discussed or even hinted at to anyone else – not to other coders, however trustworthy you may think they are, not to boyfriends, nobody. Am I making myself clear?'

'Yes, sir.'

The response was almost automatic. Frankie was struggling to readjust her thoughts. She was not in trouble. This was something else altogether.

'Very well,' Dodds Parker went on. 'You are about to be part of what may turn out to be one of the most crucial negotiations of the war. I have chosen you because you are three of the best coders and also because I judge that you are all reliable and level headed enough to deal with this very great responsibility.'

It crossed Frankie's mind to wonder whether he would have said the same if he had seen her earlier that morning.

'First of all, I must give you a bit of history. Last autumn an agent named Richard Mallaby was dropped into northern Italy to make contact with local partisan leaders and test the strength of possible resistance to Mussolini. Unfortunately something went wrong and his radio set was never used. We assumed that he had probably been killed or arrested immediately he arrived – until two days ago, when we suddenly received a message on his wavelength. It seems that he has been a prisoner all this time but that the Germans eventually handed him over to the Italians. Now certain elements of the Italian government wish to make contact with us. For this reason Mallaby's radio has been restored to him and he has been asked to act as a go-between.'

'I don't understand, sir,' Mary put in. 'Why not use the normal diplomatic channels?'

'Because it is vital that these contacts remain secret. Now that Mussolini has fallen the government has been taken over by King Victor Emmanuel and Marshal Badoglio. Badoglio wishes to find out what terms he can negotiate for a surrender.'

'Surrender!' All three girls echoed the word in amazement.

'And if Italy surrenders,' Dodds Parker went on, 'there will be nothing to stop our troops from marching straight up to the

Alps to attack what Mr Churchill calls "the soft underbelly of Europe". It could shorten the war by months, if not years. But if the Germans were to get wind of such a possibility they would undoubtedly march into Italy and take control, and I imagine Badoglio and even King Victor would find themselves facing a firing squad. So you see why absolute secrecy is so essential. The negotiations will be code-named Operation Monkey.'

'But where do we come in, sir?' asked Mary.

'You three are going to handle all Mallaby's traffic from now on. You will work in a separate room and the decoded transcripts will be handed directly to me and to nobody else. There is one complication. As I said, Mallaby has been in enemy hands for several months and we must assume that before they passed him on to the Italians the Gestapo interrogators have had plenty of opportunity to work on him. No one resists their methods for long. Mallaby must have given them something and the chances are that he has given them his code poem. After all, he would have assumed that he was never going to get a chance to use it so it would not have been a security risk. Now, however, it is being used, and we must pray that the German cryptographers have not yet picked up his transmissions and started to work on them. The first priority is to transmit to Mallaby a completely new poem. Leo Marks in London is working on that now, composing something that will have special significance for Mallaby but will mean nothing to any cryptographer who happens to decipher the odd word or two. Your job, initially, will be to encode that poem, using Mallaby's current code, and transmit it to him. Understood?'

'Yes, sir.'

'It's going to be hard work. You will need to be listening out round the clock, so the three of you will have to work out a shift pattern between you. You start tonight. I'll show you where you will be working.'

Left to themselves, the three girls turned to each other, wide eyed.

'It's a tremendous compliment,' Dickie said.

'And an awesome responsibility,' Mary added.

'If the Italians surrender . . .' Frankie repeated, but Mary raised a warning hand.

'I don't think we should talk about it, even amongst ourselves. You know what they say – walls have ears. Let's get these shifts sorted out.'

They agreed that there would always be two of them on duty during the day but only one at night. It meant that they would all have to work twelve hours out of every twenty-four, but they felt that it would be easier to share the burden of responsibility rather than shoulder it alone. Frankie and Mary would work from 8 a.m. to midday and then Dickie would relieve Frankie. Frankie in turn would take over from Mary at four o'clock and she and Dickie would work together until eight. Then Frankie would take the first night shift alone, until midnight. Mary would take the dog watch from midnight to 4 a.m. and Dickie would follow her from four until eight. At the end of a week they would swap round so that each in turn would suffer the broken nights.

The weeks that followed were some of the hardest and yet some of the most exciting of Frankie's life. Her field of vision narrowed to the scope of that one room, where she and the others worked feverishly to encode the new poem that had been sent from London and then waited anxiously for the first messages from Mallaby. Incredibly, they arrived perfectly encoded. In time they learned that a secret delegation had visited London to open talks and that negotiations were continuing. Then, one morning, Dodds Parker sent for them again.

'There is an extra job I want you to take on. The Italians want another face-to-face meeting to thrash out some of the details and they are coming here tomorrow. Of course, the visit is top secret and they have insisted that no one else is present but myself. However, I wish to have a record of the discussions so I am arranging to have hidden microphones placed in this room. You three will be able to listen in and make notes of exactly what is said. Franconi, I believe you speak fluent Italian. Is that correct?'

'Yes, sir.'

'I want you to pay special attention to any exchanges between the members of the delegation. They know I don't speak the language and they have resisted the idea of having an interpreter present, so they may feel they can speak freely. I want to know everything they say.'

'Very good, sir.'

Frankie left the office glowing with pride. She had wanted to make a contribution but she had never imagined that she might find herself at the centre of such vital negotiations. She wished ardently that she could tell Nick, but these days she hardly saw him. When she was off duty he was usually working and when he was free she was either closeted in the coders' room or sleeping. She had explained to him that her shifts had been changed but he could obviously see that most of the other girls were still working normal hours. She had been afraid that he might press her for an explanation but he was far too well trained for that. He gave her a keen look and nodded.

'OK. The job comes first. We'll have to grab what time we can.'

Frankie was working what was regarded as the worst shift – eight till four during the day and then the midnight watch until 4 a.m. It left her exhausted because she could rarely get to sleep before going on watch at midnight, but at least it had the advantage that she was able to spend some time with Nick when he came off duty. She knew that every moment was precious because he was coming to the end of his six-month assignment as a conducting officer and there was every possibility that he might be sent back behind enemy lines. She had a very personal stake in the ongoing negotiations. If Italy surrendered there would be no need to send undercover agents to work there. She knew that Nick would almost certainly be posted somewhere but she hoped that it would be as some kind of liaison officer with the advancing army. Working in a friendly and peaceful Italy, he would be out of immediate danger.

The day after the interview with Dodds Parker the three girls were in position well before the Italian delegation arrived. Frankie never saw any of the officers involved, though friends spoke of a convoy of cars with darkened windows sweeping into the grounds from the direction of the airfield. To her they were only disembodied voices, one slow and deep, weighing each word before it was spoken, the other lighter, more excitable. To begin with there was the usual exchange of pleasantries, then Dodds Parker and the two Italians got down to business. With headphones clamped to their ears the girls listened as the details of the surrender were worked out. There was some argument about the handing over of equipment. The Allies were demanding that their one-time enemies hand over tanks and aircraft, so that they did not fall into the hands of the Germans. Frankie listened intently as the two Italians murmured together in their own language and finally agreed. The most important element was the timing. It was vital that the Allied troops should be within hours of landing before the surrender was announced, so that the Germans would have no time to react. Bit by bit a delicate filament of mutual trust was being spun until the delegation declared themselves satisfied and announced that they would report what had been agreed to Marshall Badoglio. It would be for him to give the final go-ahead.

The next evening they were strolling along the beach when Nick said, 'Have you spoken to Midge lately?'

'Only to say good morning and goodnight,' Frankie admitted. 'Our paths don't seem to cross very often at the moment.'

'Did you know she's broken up with Jumbo?'

'No! When did that happen?'

'A couple of days ago, as far as I can make out. Jumbo won't talk about it.'

'Do you know what went wrong?'

'No idea. As I said, he won't say and I can't very well ask Midge.'

'Well, I can,' Frankie said. 'Midge is such a fool! Sometimes I could shake her!'

After she had said goodnight to Nick, Frankie went to the club. The bar was noisier than ever. Some sort of mad game was in progress, with a dozen young men charging about with girls riding piggyback on their shoulders, trying to knock each other off with pillows. The air was full of flying feathers and Midge was in the thick of it, laughing like a mad thing. Frankie waited until they all collapsed with exhaustion and then picked her way across to Midge.

'Come outside. I want a word with you.'

Midge rolled her eyes at her escort. 'Hark at her! Talk about her mistress's voice!'

Nevertheless, she got up and followed Frankie out onto the veranda. Frankie was in no mood to beat about the bush.

'Midge, what's all this about you breaking it off with Jumbo?'

Midge turned away and lit a cigarette. 'None of your business.'

'Yes it is. You and Jumbo are my friends. I'm concerned about you.'

'Well, don't be. I'm fine.'

'Jumbo isn't.'

'That's his hard luck.'

Midge shrugged her shoulders and Frankie saw that there were bite marks on her neck.

'Have you found someone else?'

'Not really.'

'Then what went wrong? Come on, Midge. You and Jumbo were so good together.'

There was a silence. Then Midge said, in a different tone, 'We were, until he ruined it.'

'How?'

'The poor sap only asked me to marry him.'

'What's wrong with that? I thought you really loved him.'

'So did I, until he started going on about his background and his so-called prospects. I think the poor fool thought he was offering me something really appealing! He couldn't understand why I turned him down.'

'Why did you?'

'Do you realise his father works in a car factory in Solihull, or some such God-forsaken hole?'

'Are you sure?' Frankie queried. 'I had the impression he was quite well off. Jumbo went to public school, didn't he?'

'So what? He's a . . . an artisan. And what's more Jumbo's going into the same business after the war. If he thinks I'm going to bury myself in the Midlands, waiting for him to come home every evening covered in grease and stinking of petrol, he must be crazy.'

Frankie looked at Midge for a moment, then she turned away.

'You're a cold bitch, Midge. Jumbo's well rid of you. You don't deserve a nice chap like him.'

'Listen!' Midge spat back at her. 'You told me once to fuck off, remember?'

'I've apologised for that.'

'Well, now I'm returning the compliment. Fuck off, Frankie, and mind your own business.'

She turned on her heel and went back into the club. Looking through the open doors, Frankie saw her take a glass out of a young officer's hand and down the contents in one.

It was Mary MacIntyre who decoded the crucial message and carried it triumphantly to Colonel Dodds Parker.

'We've done it, sir! Marshal Badoglio has agreed to the surrender terms.'

Even then Frankie and her two companions had to hide their jubilation. No word of the surrender must leak out until the Allies were ready to invade. But their work decoding Mallaby's messages was done and they were returned to normal duties. Frankie was in the bar at the Club des Pins with Nick when someone shouted above the chatter.

'Shut up, you lot! There's something coming through on the news.'

They crowded round the set and heard the newsreader announce that the Allies had landed at Salerno and Marshal Badoglio had declared the Italian surrender. As soon as the words were spoken the whole club erupted into cheers. At last victory seemed inevitable. With Allied troops on the borders of Austria and occupied France they would be able to divert German forces from guarding the Channel ports and launch a Second Front in western Europe. With the Russians advancing from the east the Third Reich was doomed.

Nick looked at Frankie in the middle of the cheering and said, 'You knew something about this, didn't you?'

She nodded gleefully. There was no need now for secrecy.

He took her arm. 'Let's go outside, where we can hear ourselves think.'

Out on the veranda she told him what she had been working on for the past weeks and he hugged her.

'My clever little darling! I knew that encounter in the air-raid shelter was important for me. I didn't know it was going to be so important for the war effort, too.'

'Oh, if I wasn't here someone else would have done my job,' Frankie said. 'But isn't it wonderful? Now there won't be any need for you to go back under cover.'

His face became grave. 'I don't think it's going to be quite as straightforward as that lot in there think.'

'What do you mean?'

'Do you really think the Germans are going to stand by and let us march our armies through Italy unimpeded?'

'But Italy is an independent country. If they decide they're on our side . . .' Frankie began.

'That isn't going to stop the Nazis. Did it stop them going into Poland? Believe me, even now they will be rushing all the troops they can spare to the south of Italy to confront our chaps. And if the Italians get in the way they will be swept aside like any other enemy.'

Frankie looked at him. Tears welled up in her eyes. After the weeks of hard work and lack of sleep, when she had been buoyed up by the thought that the end of the war might be close, this hard reality was difficult to bear.

Nick took her in his arms. 'I'm sorry, my darling. I know what you must have been hoping. But I'm afraid we're not out of the woods yet – not by a long way.'

The very next day they heard news that bore out what he had said. The Germans had occupied Rome and begun disarming the Italian army.

Frankie had hardly spoken to Midge since their late night argument. They continued to share a room, but until recently Frankie's unusual hours had made it easy for them to ignore each other. Now that they were working the same shifts again, however, they had settled for an armed truce. Midge was getting a reputation as one of the fastest girls in the camp and treated Frankie with silent contempt, and Frankie had no intention of apologising for what she had said.

One evening she noticed that Midge was not present for the evening meal. She was not at the club, either, though several of her recent escorts were there, but when Frankie enquired none of them had seen her. Frankie noticed that the atmosphere in the club was quieter than usual and a group of pilots, who were usually the rowdiest lot, were drinking morosely in one corner. On the table between them, placed upside down, was an empty glass.

Towards the end of the evening, she and Nick went for a stroll along the beach as usual and cresting a sand dune they saw ahead of them a single, crouched figure.

'That looks like Midge!' Frankie said. 'I had a feeling something was wrong.'

She looked up at the sky. The moon was almost full. She met Nick's eyes and they both spoke at the same instant.

'Jumbo!'

Frankie started down the dune and then turned back to Nick. 'Better let me talk to her on my own.'

He nodded agreement. 'Take care. I'll wait at the club but if you don't come back I'll know you're with her. See you tomorrow.'

She kissed him briefly and then made her way down to where Midge was huddled just above the waterline. She sat down beside her and said tentatively, 'Midge?'

'Bugger off!' came the reply in a tight, hard voice.

'Has something happened? Is it Jumbo?'

'Leave me alone, can't you?'

'Midge, talk to me. What's wrong?'

There was a silence. Then Midge said, 'You're right. I am a cold-hearted bitch and I deserve everything that's coming to me.' Then her voice cracked. 'But he didn't! Poor Jumbo. He didn't deserve what I did to him.'

'Has something happened to him?'

'He's been reported missing. He went on an op last night and he didn't come back.'

'Oh, Midge, I'm sorry!' Frankie put her arms round Midge's narrow shoulders, forgetting her anger. 'Do they know what happened?'

Midge shook her head. 'Ralph Dawson, one of his squadron, came to tell me. I think he wanted to make me squirm! I don't blame him. There's been no contact. They have to keep radio silence on these undercover ops, of course, so no one knew anything was wrong until he failed to return.'

'So that doesn't mean he's dead,' Frankie said. 'He may have baled out over France and be hiding from the Nazis. There are Resistance groups who look after downed airmen and get them home, you know. Or he could have ditched in the sea and been picked up by a fishing boat or something. Don't give up hope. He could turn up like the proverbial bad penny in a day or two.'

Midge sniffed. 'You may be right. But I'm not going to pin my hopes on it. I don't deserve him to come back. I treated him abominably. I saw him the other day, with some of his friends. He looked like a kicked puppy!' She was weeping now. 'And I let him go, feeling like that.'

'You really do love him, don't you?' Frankie asked.

'From the top of his stupid head down to the bottom of his size-twelve feet!' Midge affirmed. 'And now I'll never have a chance to tell him.'

'Yes you will! You'll see. He'll be back. Chaps like Jumbo are indestructible.'

As she spoke Frankie wondered whether she was doing the right thing in encouraging Midge to hope. She knew that the likelihood was that Jumbo's plane had been shot down and it was quite probable that he was dead, but she could not bear the agony in her friend's voice. Let her cling to hope for a while, she thought, until she has a chance to get over the shock.

After a while she persuaded Midge to walk back to the billet with her and to take two of her little blue pills to help her sleep. Then she went to bed herself. The euphoria of the past weeks had evaporated and she felt tired and depressed.

The next morning there were letters from home, a rare treat that always caused great excitement. Frankie had a letter from her mother, one from her grandmother and one from her sister and a postcard with a picture of the Pyramids. She turned it over and read, *Guess where I am! Having a wonderful time. Hope you and Nick are both well. Love, Steve.*

Frankie puzzled over the card in her spare moments all morning. What was Steve doing in Egypt? Had she changed her mind about becoming an agent or failed some aspect of the training? Why was the message so brief and cryptic? She longed to discuss the questions with someone, and it occurred to her that the one person she could speak freely to was Nick. Once the idea had come to her she could not understand why she had not thought of it before, and as soon as they met at the club she said, 'Come out onto the terrace. I want to talk to you about something.'

He followed her out and slipped his arm through hers.

'What's up? You look worried.'

'You remember I've talked about my friend Steve, the girl who was so kind to me at Overthorpe?'

'Yes. Has something happened to her?'

'I'm not sure.' Frankie told him about Steve's decision to apply for training as an agent and her last letter, telling her in coded terms that she had been accepted. 'I haven't heard from her since and I assumed she was somewhere in France by now. Then, this morning, I got this. I don't know what to make of it.'

Nick took the postcard and scanned it quickly then gave a small, grim smile. 'Standard procedure. Family and friends are bound to start asking questions if they don't hear from someone for months on end, so the agent is given a story about where they are being sent – somewhere innocuous and miles away from the real location. Then, before he or she leaves, they write a series of postcards provided by Baker Street with appropriate pictures and those are posted from the agreed location at intervals all the time they're away.'

'So Steve has never been near Egypt?'

'No.'

'Have you had to do that, for your father?'

'Yes. I was supposed to be in Canada. Had to answer a heck of a lot of difficult questions last time I went home, I can tell you.'

He smiled at her and she managed a small laugh in return. But the explanation was small comfort. 'So she probably is in France.'

'It seems likely, yes.'

Frankie sighed. 'I keep thinking about her. When I was at Grendon we used to get messages that suddenly broke off in mid-transmission. Then later we'd hear that such and such an agent was 'no longer operational'. I can't forget what Leo Marks told us about what happens to agents caught in the middle of transmitting a message. I can't bear the idea of Steve being tortured.'

He put his arms round her. 'Try not to imagine the worst. I've met chaps who've operated in France for months without arousing the least suspicion and have been brought home for a rest. And a girl is less likely to be suspected than a man, I'm sure. Steve will be all right.' He held her in silence for a moment, then he said, 'Frankie, love, I'm terribly sorry to hit you with this on top of everything else but there's no help for it. I'm leaving tonight.'

She stared at him. 'Tonight! Where? Where are you going?'

'You know I can't tell you that.'

'Don't be stupid!' She almost spat the words at him. 'I handle messages from agents all the time. I could be handling yours. Do you think I can't guess?'

'I'm sorry. You're right, there's no point in keeping secrets from you.'

'Is it Italy?'

'Where else? It seems that since the Huns started disarming the Italian troops some of them have chosen to go missing rather than give up their weapons. They are heading up into the hills, where there are already small groups of partisans who were opposed to Mussolini. If those groups can be reinforced and persuaded to work together they could be a serious irritant behind the German lines. If they can make enough of a nuisance of themselves the Huns may have to withdraw troops from the battlefield to deal with them, making life easier for our boys.'

Frankie nodded, trying to be calm and think sensibly. 'That makes sense.'

'The trouble is, there are at least two different factions out there. There are the Fiamme Verde – that's the Christian organisation. Then there are the Garibaldini. They're communists. And the two groups hate each other's guts. That's what I mean by getting them to work together.'

Frankie was losing the battle to control herself. She flung herself against him. 'I don't want you to go!'

'My darling, I have to. You know that. And it isn't as bad as you're imagining. I'm not going under cover, for one thing. I'll be dropping in uniform, as a British liaison officer. That way, if I'm caught I can't be shot as a spy. And I'm dropping to friends, contacts I made on my last trip. They're only a small outfit at the moment but they are armed and well led. They're the ones who will be doing the fighting. I shall just be there to advise.'

She let herself be reassured. 'Are you going alone?'

'No, I'm taking Joe Prentiss as my radio operator.'

'I'm glad you'll have someone there with you,' she murmured. She had met Prentiss once or twice, though since he was only a sergeant the rigid distinctions of rank debarred him from the officers' club. He was a tough little Yorkshireman, and she had a feeling that he had many of the same qualities as the terriers that came from the same county.

'Do you have to go tonight?' she asked in a last act of rebellion against fate.

He glanced upward. 'Yes. Conditions are good and the flight is all laid on.'

'I'll miss you so much.'

As he kissed her they heard laughter behind them and three young men came out of the club and chased each other past them and off into the darkness. Nick said, 'Let's go somewhere quieter, shall we?'

They walked with their arms around each other down the path that led through the sand dunes to the beach. There they stopped and gazed across the quiet waters and up at the moonlit sky.

'I hate that moon!' Frankie exclaimed. 'I wish I could put it out!'

'You don't want me to have to drop in complete darkness, do you?' he asked.

'I don't want you to drop at all,' she responded.

He held her close. 'I don't want to go, my love. Believe me, I would infinitely rather stay here with you.' Then he drew back a little and looked into her face. 'Frankie, you do know I'm in love with you, don't you?'

'You've never said,' she whispered.

'I know, and I meant not to even now. If this was peacetime I'd have asked you to marry me weeks ago. But I can't, in these circumstances.'

'What do you mean? Why not?' She was trembling.

'How can I? It wouldn't be fair to ask you to tie yourself to me, when I could be away for months – when I don't know if I'll ever come back. You should be free to find someone else, someone who can give you the security I can't.'

'I'd never want anyone else,' she said urgently. 'Don't you know that? Ever since that first evening in Liverpool there's never been anyone else for me.'

He pulled her to him. 'Oh, my darling! Do you mean that?'

'Of course I do.'

'What an idiot I've been! If I'd asked you before we could have had all these last weeks together. The padre would have married us. Now it's too late.'

'No it's not.'

He forced a laugh. 'My sweet, we can hardly get the poor man out of bed and demand to be married on the spot.'

'That's not what I meant.'

In the moonlight his eyes had lost their laughter. They were wide and liquid. 'Are you saying what I think you're saying?'

For a moment Frankie was poised between love for him and the wrath of God. Then an inner voice reminded her that God, if He existed, was Love.

'What time do you have to fly?'

'I have to be at the airfield by midnight.'

She glanced at her watch. 'We've got a couple of hours, then.'

She turned and took his hand, leading him back from the sea up into the seclusion of the dunes.

Frankie had always thought that when the moment came she would be shy – that the whole process would be awkward and perhaps painful. It was none of those things. She was aware only of an all-consuming hunger, a need that must be satisfied. And when at last she had him inside her she longed to keep him there, safe and protected for the rest of their lives.

After a long time he rolled away and drew her against his shoulder. 'My sweet love! I just pray you will never regret this.'

'I never shall,' she told him. 'Whatever happens from now on.'

After a while she said, 'I might be handling your messages but I shan't be able to tell unless I know your code name.'

He gave a low laugh. 'Some joker at HQ has decided we're all going to be called after different types of fish. I'm Salmon.'

'That's good,' she approved. 'Salmon are slippery. Hard to catch. I'll find out who is scheduled to deal with your traffic and persuade her to swap with me. And when I reply I'll put in a special personal message for you. We used to do that at Grendon, so the joes didn't feel quite so cut off.'

'You'll need a code name too,' he said, 'so I can be sure it's from you.'

'Yes!' She lifted her head and looked down into his face. 'And I know what it'll be. I shall be Red Herring.'

He laughed. 'A red herring leads you astray. Is that what you've done to me?'

'Yes,' she said. 'And I'll lead you home again, too.'

He kissed her, then sighed and looked at his watch. 'I've got to be moving.'

They got up and brushed the sand off each other's bodies as best they could, and Frankie thought how strange it was to feel so at ease with another person's naked flesh. When they were dressed they walked slowly back to where Nick's jeep was parked outside the club.

She said, 'Can I come and see you off?'

He shook his head. 'No, better not. There will be too many people about, too much going on. Better to say goodbye here, where it's quiet.'

There were tears on her cheeks but she managed to keep them out of her voice. 'How long will you be away?'

'There's no knowing. It depends on how long it takes our boys to fight their way up to where I'm going. But things aren't looking good. The Germans are digging in and winter's coming. I don't think there will be much movement until the spring. I'm afraid I'm not likely to be back much before this time next year.'

Frankie swallowed hard. 'I'll be here, waiting. That's a promise. You mustn't ever doubt that.'

'I shan't. And anyway, I'll have your messages. My own personal Red Herring.'

They kissed again and whispered last goodbyes. Then Nick got into the jeep and drove away into the darkness.

Chapter Nine

Once again, time seemed to have lost its meaning for Frankie. She lived from day to day, refusing to let her mind stray beyond the present instant. She would not let herself think about Nick. It would have been easy to lose herself in memories of their time together or dreams of the future, but some instinct told her that in the end this would only increase her loneliness. She was worried about Steve, too. That postcard must mean that she was somewhere in France by now. It was hard to imagine the honest, open-hearted Steve living a life of deception. Sometimes Frankie thought that it was hard that the two people she cared for most, outside of her family, were both in danger. She concentrated on her work, and it was work that saved her. With more and more agents being sent to Italy and the growth of resistance movements in southern France the volume of radio traffic grew almost beyond the capacity of the FANY detachment to handle it. Regular shifts had to be abandoned and everyone worked all day and long into the night. Social life was reduced to an occasional snatched half-hour when there was a temporary slackening of the pressure.

One anxiety, at least, was lifted from her mind. For the first week after Nick's departure she was haunted by the thought that they had taken no precautions when they had made love. The possibility that she might be pregnant terrified her. She knew Nick would stand by her, but he had said he might be gone for up to a year. She presumed that if she was found to be pregnant she would be dismissed from the service and she was certain that her father would disown her. When her period arrived on time she almost wept with relief.

Frankie had no difficulty in discovering which of her colleagues had been assigned to deal with signals from the agent code-named Salmon and persuading her to do a swap. After an anxious two days Nick's first message came through at the scheduled time. He and Joe had landed safely and succeeded in linking up with the Fiamme Verde partisan band that was their objective. The message concluded 'Love to the Red Herring'.

When Frankie handed the decoded message to her supervisor the older woman glanced through it and snapped, 'Who might this Red Herring be, may I ask?'

'No idea, ma'am,' Frankie lied.

'Doesn't Major Harper know that every extra sentence transmitted makes it easier for the enemy to get a fix on his position? Send back 'message received and understood' and tell him not to waste valuable air time.'

'Yes, ma'am.'

Frankie encoded the required message and added 'Red Herring understands. No need to repeat'. Nick took the hint and reduced his personal addition, but he still managed to include a word or two for her. 'Missing RH.' 'Hope RH well.' 'RH, love, S.' Frankie decoded them but from then on did not include them in the text she handed over to her superiors. In return she slipped in her own words of love and encouragement. She had no need to worry that any of the signallers who transmitted her messages would draw attention to them. Once encoded, the messages were unintelligible to anyone who did not hold the key.

As Nick had foretold, the news from the front was

depressing. The Allies, instead of a triumphal march up to the Alps, were being forced to fight every inch of the way. They had occupied Brindisi and Naples but were forced to fight a terrible battle in order to force the crossing of the River Volturno. The weather was appalling, and as winter began the Allied forces found themselves brought to a standstill by the Gustav Line, a strongly fortified line of defences that the Germans had thrown across the width of the Italian peninsula.

Because she had closed in on herself to such an extent, Frankie ignored what was happening to Midge. It was Dickie who remarked, 'Midge is going to get herself sacked if she doesn't watch out.'

Ashamed of her self-absorption, Frankie began to take notice and saw that Midge had reacted to Jumbo's disappearance very differently. She flung herself into whatever distraction was offered, which usually meant alcohol. Whenever she could get away from the decoding room she headed for the club, where her reputation was becoming a joke. There were plenty of young officers who were happy to dance and drink with her but none of them took her seriously or cared much what lay behind her wild gaiety. She was drinking too much and burning the candle at both ends and, as a result, her work was suffering. Frankie worried about her, but she had no emotional resources to spare for her friend's troubles.

One evening, in a rare hour of leisure, Frankie was sipping a gin and orange and chatting to Ralph Dawson, one of the pilots from Jumbo's squadron. Midge was on the far side of the room, flirting madly with three young men. Ralph nodded in her direction.

'You know, I used to quite like that girl when she was going out with Jumbo. What's wrong with her?'

'I'm afraid she's gone off the rails since Jumbo went missing,' Frankie responded.

'But why? I thought they had broken up long before that.'

'It's true. Midge only realised how much she cared for him when it was too late.'

'Do you know what went wrong? Jumbo was – is – a chum of mine, and I know he really cared for her. He was terribly cut up when she dropped him, but he would never tell me why she did it.'

Frankie sighed. 'I'm afraid he made the mistake of telling her about his family and his ambitions for the future.'

'What's wrong with that?'

'Apparently his father works in a factory in the Midlands and Jumbo intends to go into the same business. Midge is a terrible snob. She just couldn't see herself marrying into that sort of environment.'

'Works in a factory? How did you get hold of that idea?'

'It's what Midge told me. Isn't it true?'

'Well, I suppose it is, in a sense. Jumbo's dad just happens to be one of the biggest motor manufacturers in the country, that's all. Oh, I think he started off in a pretty humble way, mending motorbikes in a shed in the back garden or something similar. But that was at the time when the motor trade was just taking off and in a few years he'd moved into making cars and built his own factory. Since then, the business has grown and grown.'

'But why on earth didn't Jumbo tell Midge that?' Frankie exclaimed.

'Oh, that's Jumbo all over. He hates blowing his own trumpet. The fact is, his old man is probably one of the richest men in England. And now he's building trucks for the army he's probably getting richer still.'

'Oh?' Frankie queried dubiously.

'I don't mean he's profiteering. Far from it. I believe he's actually donated enough money from his personal fortune to pay for two Spitfires. And he's so well thought of that the War Ministry have taken him on as an adviser on procurement.'

'How do you know all this?' Frankie asked.

'Partly because I was at school with Jumbo and I've met the family socially. And partly because my father is a civil servant working for the ministry. In fact, he introduced Mr Lampeter to the minister. Don't, for God's sake, say anything, because it's all unofficial at the moment, but it's highly likely that Mr L will get a peerage after the war for his contribution to the war effort.'

Frankie stared at him. 'You mean, one day Jumbo would have been Lord Birmingham, or something?'

'Something like that. And he still might. I refuse to believe the old so-and-so's bought it.'

'And Midge would have been Lady Whatever.'

'If she hadn't turned him down, yes.'

Frankie shook her head. 'I still can't see her living in Solihull.'

'She wouldn't be. Old Man Lampeter has built himself a beautiful mansion in the Warwickshire countryside. I gather he's quite a hit with the local county set.'

Frankie looked across at Midge, who was knocking back a dry martini and shrieking with laughter. 'Don't tell her, Ralph. I think she hates herself badly enough already. She wouldn't be able to bear it if she knew she'd thrown him over just because he was too modest to tell her the real facts.'

The next morning Frankie received a summons to the CO's office. Colonel Dodds Parker greeted her with a brief smile and told her to take a seat.

'I've sent for you, Franconi, because a posting has come up that I think should be right up your street.'

Frankie's breath caught in her throat. *A posting!* Where to? Did she want to go anywhere else? Aloud she said simply, 'Sir?'

'You will be aware that recently we have been dropping more and more agents into Italy. Now that our forces have got themselves established it has been decided to set up a forward station nearer to the front line – at Monopoli, to be exact. It will be known by the code name Maryland. Obviously, it will need to have its own signals unit. I have been impressed by the work you did on Operation Monkey and, of course, you speak fluent Italian. You seem to be the ideal person to head up that unit.'

'Head up, sir? You mean, take charge?'

'Exactly. It will mean promotion, of course. Do you think you can handle that sort of responsibility?'

Frankie hesitated for barely a second. Promotion would be good, the new challenge was exciting, but all that was irrelevant beside the thought that in Italy she would be nearer to Nick. 'Yes, sir,' she said firmly.

Dodds Parker nodded approvingly. 'Good. Now, I must warn you that conditions in Monopoli are not likely to be nearly as pleasant as they are here. Apart from the climate, and I'm told that is enough to put anyone off at the moment, the facilities will be primitive. I don't know what sort of accommodation they'll find for you but there certainly won't be anything like the Club des Pins. Does that bother you?'

'No, sir.'

'There's one other thing. We can't afford the personnel to provide signallers as well as coders. You and your team will have to do both. That means you will be posted back to the UK to undertake an intensive course in Morse Code. You'll get a week's leave, so you will be able to spend Christmas with your family. Then eight weeks at Fawley Court doing signals training. After that you'll be transferred to Monopoli. OK?'

'Yes, sir.'

'There will be six of you. You can select your own team. You know the girls better than I do and it's going to be important that you all get on. Anyone you like except MacIntyre. I need her here. Any questions?'

Frankie tried to steady her whirling brain. 'I don't think so, sir. Oh, when do we leave?'

'As soon as I can arrange transport. It may take a few days.'

Outside the room Frankie leaned against the wall and waited for her heart to stop pounding. It dawned on her slowly that being at a forward station in Italy would not in any practical sense bring her nearer to Nick. In fact, when his work with the partisans was over he would probably be sent back to Algiers, where he would expect to find her. There was one comfort. She would still be dealing with his radio traffic, presumably, so she could let him know where she was. Beyond that, there were other thoughts crowding into her mind. She was proud of the fact that Dodds Parker had chosen her from among all the others, and she knew her parents would be thrilled at her promotion. It would be wonderful, too, to be home for Christmas. But did she really want to leave? She would miss her friends, miss the evenings in the bar at the club, miss the dances and the parties. She had accepted the posting now, however, and there was no going back.

She began to consider who she would ask to go with her. Dickie, of course. And if she took Dickie that meant taking Flick, too. That was OK. Flick was as bright as Dickie and they would make a good team. There were two or three others she got on well with, and knew could be relied upon. The question was, should she take Midge? A few weeks ago the answer would have been an unhesitating 'yes'. But recently Midge's behaviour had been so erratic Frankie was not sure she could be trusted. Besides which, she might not want to leave Algiers. If Jumbo was still alive and managed to escape he would be posted back here. On the other hand, Frankie had a feeling that taking Midge away from the temptations of the officers' club might be the saving of her. In the end, she decided to discuss the possibility with her before she spoke to any of the others.

Midge's reaction surprised her.

'Oh, Frankie, please! Please take me with you! I'm going mad here. I know I can be a bitch and I know I've been drinking too much, but it's just because everything here reminds me of Jumbo. I can't get over how badly I treated him and I can't bear it. If you let me come I swear I'll reform. I won't let you down. Promise!'

Frankie looked at her doubtfully. 'You do realise that I'm going to be in command? You'll have to take orders from me. Can you cope with that?'

Midge nodded slowly. 'Yes. You deserve the promotion. You've always been brighter than me, and you work harder. I'm just not 'officer material', as they say. Congratulations, Frankie. You're the right girl for the job.'

Dickie and Flick accepted Frankie's invitation to join the team without hesitation. They had never been part of the drinking and dancing culture of the club and were happy to have a change of scene. To make up the numbers Frankie chose Patricia Milne, who was nicknamed Tigger, partly as a reference to the author of *Winnie the Pooh*, to whom she was distantly related, and partly because of her irrepressible good humour. The sixth girl was Maureen 'Mouse' Rattray, who had been with them ever since Overthorpe.

Three days later, all six of them took off in a Lancaster bomber for Gibraltar, en route for home.

Frankie looked forward to being home for Christmas but the reality turned out to be disappointing. It was good to see her family again but she could not shake off a sense of dislocation.

Sometimes she felt as though time had folded in on itself so she was back exactly where she had been a year ago. Everything was so much the same as on her last home leave – the same icy wind off the Mersey, the same drab streets pock-marked with bomb craters, the same struggle to produce an illusion of festivity within the limits of the available rations. At others, it seemed that she had been away for half a lifetime. She had seen and done so much and she knew she had changed. She tried to be the daughter her parents remem-bered, the sometimes wilful but otherwise obedient seventeen-year-old, but she had grown up and grown away and there was no going back. They were proud of her, they made that clear. She grinned to herself and wished she had a shilling for every time she heard her mother say 'Our Gina's been promoted again, you know'. But she caught them looking at her sometimes as if she were a stranger.

Worst of all was being out of touch with Nick. In Algiers she had at least had the comfort of decoding his regular messages and knowing that he was still safe. She had left her address with the girl who had taken over from her and begged her to let her know if anything went wrong but a letter could take many days to reach her and she was tormented by the idea that Nick could be dead or wounded without her being aware of it. Her last action before leaving had been to encode a message to him. *Posted UK for course. Back in nine weeks. Contact you then. All love R.H.* So at least he would understand why her personal messages had ceased, but that was small comfort.

It did not help that the atmosphere in the house over Christmas was tense for another reason. Maria had left school and had found a job in a local shipyard. She was learning to be a welder, which horrified her parents, who regarded it as a most unsuitable job for a girl. It was useless to point out to them that, all over the country, women were taking over jobs normally reserved for men. What worried them was the company she was keeping. To make matters worse she had taken up with an American sailor whose ship was in the yard for repairs. Two days before the beginning of Frankie's leave, she was seen out dancing with him and the fact was reported to her father. He had reacted furiously and forbidden her to see the young man again. Maria had raged and wept, to no avail, and by the time Frankie arrived home she had relapsed into a sulk that cast a gloom over the whole house.

The situation was explained to Frankie over tea on her first evening.

'I bet *she* goes out dancing,' Maria said, throwing her sister a bitter look. 'You can't stop her.'

Her father looked at her. 'Well, Gina?'

'Yes, I do sometimes,' Frankie said carefully. 'We are allowed to use the officers' club and there is dancing there quite often.'

'See?' said her sister triumphantly.

Frankie looked at her father and felt a sudden twinge of pity. She knew that his only desire was to protect Maria and recognised that he was right. Maria was too young and too headstrong to be allowed unlimited freedom. At the same time, Frankie could see that he felt his position as head of the family was under threat. She guessed that he would like to be able to forbid her to associate with men he did not know but she was now beyond his control and that undermined his authority with Maria.

Trying to help, she added, 'But most days we are all much too tired to go out dancing after we have finished work.'

'Huh!' said Maria disbelievingly and then fell silent, quelled by a look from her father.

'What Gina does is not the question here,' he said. 'She is nearly twenty and you are not sixteen yet. Also, she is under the authority of the army and I'm sure they have strict rules about these matters.'

'Oh yes, very strict,' Frankie agreed. She thought of the parties she had been to – the couples dancing cheek to cheek and then slipping off into the surrounding darkness.

'Nice crowd, are they?' Her mother was eager to relieve the tension. 'Your officer friends?'

'Very nice.'

'Is there anyone special?'

Frankie met her mother's bright, encouraging look and knew that she was hoping that the answer would be yes. Her mother was a romantic but her idea of romance began and ended with the desire to see her daughters married and 'settled down'.

'No, not at the moment.'

The lie came unbidden and for a moment she was surprised at herself. At the back of her mind was the memory of that hot night in the sand dunes, with Nick's naked body pressing against her own and the nearly full moon above them. She realised that she was afraid even to speak his name in case she somehow gave herself away. There was nothing her father could do to prevent her from seeing Nick again, if he ever returned from his mission, but she knew he would never forgive her if he found out that she had slept with a man outside of wedlock.

'Who is this American boy, anyway?' she asked, to change the subject.

'His name's Nathan.'

'How old is he?'

'Eighteen.'

Frankie remembered Fitz, the midshipman who had followed her around with such dog-like appeal on the voyage to Algiers. 'I expect he's lonely, so far from home,' she said. 'Couldn't we invite him to tea or something?'

Her father opened his mouth and then shut it again and her mother said, 'Yes, why not? Can't do any harm, can it?'

So Nathan came to tea on Christmas afternoon. He was a red-haired, freckled lad from the Deep South with an accent almost too broad for them to understand. He was painfully shy but had impeccable manners. He called Mr Franconi 'sir' and Mrs Franconi 'ma'am' and brought gifts of chocolate and cigarettes and – undreamed of luxury – silk stockings for Maria. At the end of the day Mr Franconi announced that he would be welcome to call on them whenever he had shore leave but, if he wanted to see Maria, it must be under their roof. Maria pouted but had to be content.

Frankie made a point of spending as much time as possible with her grandmother over that leave in order to speak Italian as often as she could. It meant putting up with another batch of 'eligible' suitors but she found herself better able to deal with them than on her previous leave and took the opportunity to practise her Italian on them as well. The old lady was delighted to get so much attention and Frankie felt guilty because she could not explain her real motive but she convinced herself that the small deception was justifiable, under the circumstances. It was this inability to explain herself that weighed heaviest on her all through the holiday. Friends and relations wanted to hear all about her adventures and she longed to tell them that she had played a small part in negotiating the Italian surrender; that she had jumped out of an aeroplane with a parachute; above all, that she was in love. Instead, she fell back on the formula that she was not allowed to talk about what she did but it didn't matter because most of the time it was really boring.

One thing there was no way of hiding was the fact that she had been somewhere hot. With her tanned skin she felt as though she stood out against the pallor of her companions like

some exotic bird among a flock of hens. At least she was able
to offer something unusual in the way of Christmas presents.
She and the other five girls had persuaded their commander
to give them passes to go into Algiers, chaperoned by three
off-duty officers, and they had spent a fascinating afternoon
in the souk. Frankie had bought silver jewellery for her mother
and Maria and soft leather slippers that turned up at the toes
for her father. There was a beautifully embroidered shawl for
her grandmother and trinkets of all sorts for friends. She
enjoyed watching the presents being opened and felt that she
had at least been able to bring a hint of the warmth and colour
she had been enjoying into their wartime lives.

Fawley Court was another of the stately homes that had been
taken over by SOE for the duration. It had the same institu-
tional smell as Overthorpe and Grendon Underwood, the
same chilly rooms and the same poor food. Frankie had little
time to think about her surrounding, however. From the
moment they arrived the six girls were plunged into an intensive course that soon had the dots and dashes of the Morse
Code running through their brains even when they were
asleep.

   Initially Frankie did not find it too difficult. She had a good
memory and it was not hard to learn the different com-
binations of dots and dashes that stood for each letter. But
when it came to operating the Morse key to send a message or
picking out individual letters from the stream of bleeps that
came through her headphones she began to struggle. For a few
days she really feared that she might not pass the course – and
that would mean an end to her promotion and to her posting
to Italy.

   She knew from her experience as a coder that each segment
of a coded message contained five letters and because these

letters did not make words it was impossible to guess. One wrongly transcribed letter could turn a message into gobble-degook and have a team of coders tearing their hair over yet another 'indecipherable'. When her tutor told the group that to pass they would have to be able to transcribe twenty-five words a minute, in other words 125 letters, she almost burst into tears.

She and the other girls rapped out messages with the handles of their knives at meal times and tapped them with their fingers on the arms of their chairs during recreation periods. They lived, ate, slept and dreamed in Morse and, miraculously it seemed to Frankie, at the end of the course they all passed.

They had one day's leave to celebrate and at Midge's insistence they spent it in London. They stayed at the Strand Palace Hotel, which seemed to Frankie the last word in sophistication. She had expected that Midge would want to go home but when she mentioned the idea Midge replied tersely that the London house had been requisitioned by some ministry or other and her father was living in a bachelor flat with no spare bedroom. Frankie was about to suggest that surely she would want to go and see him but the look on Midge's face warned her to let the subject drop.

Everyone wanted to see a show and after a couple of mysterious phone calls Midge announced that she had got them tickets for *Show Boat*. It was Frankie's first big London show and she came away dazzled, her mind a riot of music and colour. The others were equally overwhelmed and they came out of the theatre singing 'Old Man River' and 'Just My Bill'.

On the pavement outside Tigger stopped and looked around her. 'I'm much too excited to go to sleep. Can't we go on some-where? Somewhere there's music and dancing?'

Frankie was about to remind her that they had to be up promptly in the morning when Midge cut in with a grin. ' 'Course we can – and I know just the place!'

'Do we have to?' asked little Mouse. 'It's late and I'm sleepy.'

'You're always sleepy!' retorted Tigger. 'We ought to call you Dormouse.'

'That's OK. We'll put her in the teapot,' said Dickie. Then, in response to puzzled looks, '*Alice in Wonderland*? The Mad Hatter's tea party? Anyway, I'm game – as long as no one expects me to dance.'

'Come on, let's find a taxi.' Midge began to move away.

Frankie caught her arm. 'Midge, are you sure about this? I mean, is it safe?'

Midge burst out laughing. 'Bless you, I'm not going to take you to a den of vice or get you kidnapped as white slaves! The Blue Parrot is a perfectly respectable nightclub. Trust me!'

'All right, then,' Frankie agreed. She was too excited to sleep as well and the idea of dancing into the small hours was very tempting.

'It's impossible to get a taxi when you want one these days,' Midge complained. 'Come on, we'll walk down to Charing Cross Road. We might pick one up there.'

They set off with Mouse clinging tightly to Frankie's arm. She had grown up in the Scottish Borders and it was her first visit to London. Tigger pranced ahead. Because of the blackout the street was dark, though thronged with people coming out of the various theatres and restaurants.

'Whee! Isn't this exciting!' Tigger executed a pirouette, and her extended arms caught a passing American airman a sharp smack on the nose.

There was a flurry of apologies on both sides. Then his companion, a tall, dark-haired man with a pilot's wings on his tunic, said politely, 'Say, you ladies wouldn't be able to tell a couple of lonely airmen where they could get a drink and maybe a bit of company, would you? We're strangers in town.'

Frankie was about to make an excuse and shepherd the other girls away but Midge got in first.

'As it happens we're on our way to just such a place now. If you can find us a couple of taxis, we'll take you.'

The airman saluted. 'Consider it done, ma'am! Just you wait right there.'

The two men disappeared into the throng and Frankie turned to Midge. 'What are you thinking of? We don't know anything about them.'

'Oh, come on, darling! They're officers and presumably gentlemen. You heard how polite he was. And they're lonely. What harm can it do? Besides' – she winked broadly – 'they're far more likely to get a taxi than we are. All the taxi drivers know that the Yanks are big tippers.'

She was proved right. Within minutes two taxis drew up beside them with a broadly grinning American in each. The girls piled in and Frankie found herself with Midge and Mouse and the tall American. He introduced himself as Duane Chalmers from North Carolina and they all shook hands but it was obvious from the start that he had eyes only for Midge. Frankie watched Midge uneasily. Was this the start of a new affair? Had she forgotten Jumbo? But then she realised that to flirt was as natural as breathing to Midge, that it was all a game and that the American was fully aware of the fact. She relaxed and let herself admire the skill of the two performers, noticing the subtle flicker of eyelashes as Midge looked away and then back, the tilt of her chin, the grace with which she leant forward to allow him to light her cigarette. Frankie knew it was a game she could never play herself but she had to admire Midge's mastery of it.

The Blue Parrot was located in a basement in Jermyn Street and as they descended the steps Frankie had a flash of her former misgivings but once inside she saw that Midge had spoken the truth. The furnishings and decoration succeeded in establishing an atmosphere that combined luxury and light-hearted gaiety and the service was polished and attentive. Blue-clothed tables on which candles burned surrounded a dance floor and on one side a band in dinner jackets was playing 'Moonlight Serenade'. Already the floor was crowded with dancers, some in evening dress but many, both men and women, in uniform.

Midge was obviously well known and was greeted effusively by the manager, who pointed out that normally a member was only allowed to sign in a maximum of four guests but that, since it was the Honourable Marjorie, he would make an exception. Two tables were pushed together and as they settled themselves a waiter appeared with glasses and two bottles of champagne. Frankie was seized by a sudden panic. How much was all this going to cost? She had quite a bit of pay saved up, since there was little to spend it on at Cap Matifou, but she was carrying only five pounds. It was a relief when Duane raised his glass and proclaimed, 'Drinks are on us, ladies. Least we can do to thank you for your hospitality.'

After that Frankie began to enjoy herself. Two young men in the uniform of the Grenadier Guards came over and greeted Midge with delight. She invited them to join the party and introduced them as Johnny and Will. Frankie began to see another side to her character. She remembered their conversation on board ship on the way out to Algiers, when she had asked Midge what her imaginary husband would gain from the marriage. Midge had replied, 'Me, darling! A nice-looking woman who knows how to conduct herself in society and will be a good hostess at home and a decorative partner when he goes out.' Midge was in her element here, introducing people, arranging the seating so that the men and women were evenly distributed, making sure that everyone who wanted to dance had a partner. She encouraged Mouse and calmed the exuberant Tigger and laughingly steered one of the young Guardsmen away when he tried to insist that Dickie should dance with him. Frankie had to admit that she would make a very good wife to a man who needed those skills and reflected for a moment on what an excellent complement she would have been to Jumbo.

She was distracted from these reflections by an invitation to dance. She danced the foxtrot with Johnny and the quickstep with Will. She was just getting her breath back when the band struck up a number with a different and much wilder rhythm. The other American, whose name was Jack, leaned over to her.

'This is my kind of music! May I have the pleasure?'

Frankie looked at the gyrations of the couples on the dance floor. 'I'm sorry. I've never danced this dance before. I wouldn't know where to start.'

'Never danced the jitterbug! Well, ma'am, let me tell you, you haven't lived! C'mon, I'll teach you.'

He grabbed her hand and pulled her, protesting laughingly, onto the floor. It took her a few minutes to get the hang of the rapid footwork but Jack was clearly an expert and she soon found herself being whirled around the floor and swept off her feet. Out of the corner of her eye she caught sight of Midge, her face flushed and her hair coming loose, and realised that it was the first time she had seen her look really happy since the news came that Jumbo was missing.

Eventually, after several more dances, Frankie remembered her responsibilities and looked at her watch. It was 2 a.m. Mouse was asleep with her head on the table. Dickie and Flick, who had resolutely refused all attempts to get them on the floor, were crooning softly to the band's rendition of 'Blue Moon'. Even Tigger seemed to have danced herself to a stand-still. Frankie gathered herself and got up.

'Come on, kids! We've got a plane to catch in the morning. Time to call it a day.'

The Americans escorted them back to their hotel and thanked them politely for a wonderful evening. Hardly able to drag one foot after the other, they stumbled into the lift and along the corridor to their rooms. Frankie's last thought as she fell asleep was that she was going to have a terrible hangover in the morning but it would be worth it.

Next day they were airborne en route for Gibraltar and then Italy.

Chapter Ten

Conditions at Monopoli were every bit as bad as Dodds Parker had threatened. Italy was in the grip of one of the coldest winters in living memory. It had rained for weeks and the perimeter of the airfield, where SOE had set up their forward station, was a sea of mud. The signals section was accommodated in two wooden huts, in which the girls lived, slept and worked and each of which was heated, very inadequately, by a small oil heater. There was a shortage of everything – especially heating oil. The only thing that was not in short supply was work. They worked in pairs, in four-hour shifts, around the clock. In between, they slept or scrounged whatever small luxuries were available or huddled around the heater talking.

'We must be mad,' Dickie remarked gloomily. 'Just think. We could have been basking in the sun back at Cap Matifou.'

'Yeah,' Flick agreed. 'You know what they say in the army. Never volunteer! We should have remembered that.'

'Why us, that's what I'd like to know,' Dickie enquired. 'What's Dodds Parker got against us?'

Frankie knew she ought to say something encouraging. As the senior officer it was her job to maintain morale but she was beginning to realise that promotion meant more than the extra stripe. But all she could think of was, 'Well, someone has to do it. And I picked you, not him – because I thought you were the people I'd most like to work with.'

To her surprise it was Midge who chipped in. 'And we're jolly glad you did. I think it's a terrific compliment.'

'Of course it is,' Dickie said with a grin. 'Take no notice of us, Frankie. We're just belly-aching for something to do.'

The news from the front was as dispiriting as the conditions at the base. The advance, which everyone had expected to be so rapid, had come to a standstill and terrible losses were being reported from the battle for Monte Cassino. The messages coming in from Nick and his fellow British liaison officers were equally downbeat. Nick reported that conditions in the mountain village where he was based with a small group of partisans were so bad that men who had volunteered eagerly a few months ago, when the Germans started disarming the Italian army, were now deserting in ever greater numbers. Those who remained were short of food, weapons and even warm clothing. Shortly after this message came another. The Germans, relieved of the immediate pressure of the Allied advance, had turned their attention to the minor irritation of the partisans and were conducting what the Italians called *rastrellamenti,* sweeps designed to gather up resisters and intimidate those patriotic Italians who might be tempted to aid them. One such sweep had been conducted in Nick's area and the partisans had been forced to leave the village and take refuge in a cave high up in the mountains. The Nazis, who had been tipped off by a traitor, took reprisals against the villagers. They chose ten men at random, lined them up in the village square and shot them.

Cannot risk innocent civilians, Nick's message read, *so must stay where we are. Essential supplies desperately short and morale very low. Airdrop of food and weapons urgently needed to prevent further desertions.*

Frankie decoded the message and passed it on to her superiors with an aching sense of despair. She knew only too well how short they were of supplies themselves and how small the chances were of Nick's request being fulfilled.

His next message was more desperate in tone. *Conditions here now appalling. Food very short. Deep snow and freezing temperatures. Many men have no warm footwear and we have several cases of frostbite. If we want these men to fight for us we must give them some support. Supply drop now imperative.*

This time Frankie took the message in person to her Commanding Officer, a Colonel MacIntosh.

'Can't we do something, sir?'

MacIntosh looked up wearily. 'Franconi, you know what the situation here is like. You decode messages from all our BLOs. They are all crying out for supplies. The simple fact is we don't have the *matériel* or the aircraft to drop it.'

'But, sir, what's the point of sending men like Salmon in if we can't support them?' Frankie knew she was out of order but she felt compelled to make an effort on Nick's behalf.

MacIntosh gave her a shrewd look. 'Got some special interest in Salmon, have you?'

Frankie felt herself blush. 'I've met him, sir. At Cap Matifou.' She plunged on. 'I know everyone is having difficulties but he does sound particularly desperate. And the partisans must be very brave men. It doesn't seem fair to expect them to go on fighting for us if we can't even send them some warm socks!'

'War isn't fair, Franconi. The sooner you get that into your head the better,' MacIntosh said grimly.

'Yes, sir.'

'Now, get back to your duties and leave the logistics to those who understand the full picture.'

'Yes, sir.'

Frankie saluted and left, feeling more despondent than ever. Five days later she was given a message to encode, telling

Nick to organise a dropping zone and set out signal fires to guide the pilot. The drop was scheduled for two nights later. She sent the message and then, as soon as she was off duty, headed first for the NAAFI, where she used up her entire sweet ration for the month, and then for the local village. There was a small corner shop she had been into once or twice. It had hardly anything on the shelves but she had noticed that the woman who owned it passed her days knitting a variety of rainbow-coloured garments. She had asked her once where she obtained the wool and the woman had explained, with a smile and a shrug, that people brought her worn-out sweaters and she unravelled them and used the best bits of the wool to knit up into socks and scarves. Frankie haggled briefly and handed over half the chocolate and some cash in return for a pair of blue and brown socks and a scarf in vivid tones of red and purple and green. Returning to the base, she managed to scrounge some waxed paper from the stores to wrap the garments, together with the rest of the chocolate. She added a long letter, telling Nick how much she loved him and missed him and giving him all the little items of gossip that she could not include in the brief personal messages she added to her radio communications. She addressed the package PERSONAL - MAJOR HARPER and set off for the RAF base on the other side of the airfield. A few enquiries led her to the hangar where the stores were being packed and she was shown a container that would be labelled specifically for Nick. An aircraftsman took her package with a sympathetic grin and let her see that it was safely stowed with the other items. It was only a small gesture, but Frankie made her way back to her hut feeling that she had at least done something to make Nick's life a little better.

Nick duly sent back the map coordinates for the drop and everything seemed to be in place. But on the morning after the drop had been due to take place Frankie decoded a new message.

Waited all night in icy conditions to light fires but no sign of plane.

With tears of anger and disappointment burning the back of her throat Frankie headed for the CO's office.

'What happened, sir? Why weren't the supplies dropped?'

MacIntosh looked up with a mixture of irritation and amusement. 'Franconi, I'm running this show, not you. Are you intending to be insubordinate?'

'No, sir. Sorry, sir. I just wondered . . .'

'You're not here to wonder – or to ask questions,' the CO responded with exasperation. Then his face relaxed. 'Oh, all right. The plane was required for an urgent operation elsewhere. OK?'

'So when will the drop take place?' Frankie persisted.

MacIntosh laughed out loud. 'Well, you don't give up. I'll give you that! I'll let you know. But just remember. Salmon is not the only fish in the sea.'

Frankie had to be content with that, but two days later she received another message to encode, setting a new date for the airdrop. This time Nick's message was very different.

Supply drop successful and gratefully received. Special thanks for the consignment of socks and gloves. Tell Red Herring I am rationing the chocolate but wear the rainbow scarf every day.

Spring came quite suddenly. The sea of mud around the huts turned to dust that got into their clothes and even into the food. The scent of orange blossom wafted down from the orchard on the hill and the sun was warm on the girls' backs as they walked to and from their sessions in the signal hut. One morning Frankie went over to the mess to discover that one of the infrequent deliveries of mail had arrived. She collected her letters and those for the other girls and sorted through them as she walked back. There were two letters from her mother and one from Maria and another whose writing she did not recognise. Eager to read all the news, Frankie perched herself on the step of a parked truck and opened Maria's letter. It had been a long time getting to her and was full of woe. Nathan's ship had sailed and she missed him terribly. He had promised to write but she had not heard from him for weeks. She was convinced that either his ship had sunk or he had forgotten her. Either way, her heart was broken.

Her mother's first letter carried the usual family news and local gossip but the second, written some time after the other two, sounded quite desperate.

We are at our wits' end with your sister. After Nathan sailed she moped around as if the end of the world had come but then last week she suddenly announced that she was going to stay a couple of nights with one of the girls she works with at the yard. The girl's mum had been taken into hospital and she was frightened of being alone in the house, what with the blackout and the possibility of an air raid. It seemed quite reasonable, so we let her go. Then, a day or two later, Luigi Brettone told your father that his son, who is home on leave, had seen Maria at the Palais dancing with an American airman. When we spoke to her about it she turned really defiant and told us she was old enough to choose her own friends and she didn't see anything wrong in going to a dance. Your dad was furious, of course, and even threatened to throw her out of the house, but she just stuck her chin in the air and said that she could go and live with her friend Lily any day and they would have a really good time on their own with no one to order them about. Of course, we couldn't stop her. She's sixteen and earning good money. So I persuaded Dad that it would be better to swallow our pride and keep her at home, where at least we'll have some idea of what she's up to. Things have settled down a bit now but I'm really worried about her. You hear such terrible things about these Yankee servicemen getting our girls into trouble. I've had a good talk with her and warned her to be careful but she's such a head-strong kid. I wish you were here to talk to her. She looks up to you and I'm sure she'd take more notice of you than she does of me and her dad.

Frankie sighed deeply. There was nothing she could do at this distance. She would write to Maria, of course, and try to reason with her but in her heart of hearts she couldn't help sympathising with her. What right did she, Frankie, have to moralise about going dancing and having relations with men who had not been approved by her father? To distract her mind from the problem she picked up the fourth letter. Turning it over, she saw that it was from Jumbo's friend, Ralph Dawson. Puzzled, she slit it open.

Dear Frankie,
I'm writing to you because I have a bit of news that I think you will be glad to hear. Jumbo is alive and well and back with us! He walked in, large as life, yesterday afternoon, looking as though nothing had happened. Apparently, the plane was hit by ack-ack fire and Jumbo had to bale out over enemy-occupied territory. Fortunately, he was picked up by a local farmer who was in contact with the Resistance. He hid him for a couple of days and then passed him on to an organisation that had set up an escape line over the Pyrenees. He had a pretty bad time hiding from the Gestapo in a tiny flat for days, afraid to make a sound in case someone gave him away, and then trekking over the mountains in the dark. And

then to cap it all he was interned by the Spanish, but the British embassy got him out and eventually he made it back to Blighty! The penguins (RAF-speak for top brass – birds that don't actually fly. Get it?) at HQ kept him for a while, debriefing him, etc., then gave him a spot of leave and posted him back to the squadron. Of course, we are all delighted to have him back. The question is, do we tell Midge? I suppose she has a right to know, but after the way she treated Jumbo I'm not so sure it's the best thing to do. Anyway, I'll leave you to be the judge of that. Personally, I think he deserves someone much better but I think the poor sap is still carrying a torch for her.

I hope things are not too grim over there and that you and the other girls are keeping well. We carry on with the same old routine here.

All the best,

Ralph

Frankie folded the letter and jumped up. There was no doubt in her mind. Of course Midge must be told. Ralph had not seen the change in her since the news of Jumbo's supposed death was received. She almost ran back to the huts. Midge was sitting in the doorway of the sleeping-hut, making the most of the sunshine and darning a stocking. Dickie and Flick were on duty and the other two were fast asleep inside. Midge looked up as Frankie approached and raised her eyebrows.

'What's got into you? Has peace broken out or something?'

'Not quite as good as that,' Frankie replied. Midge's faintly supercilious expression had quelled the bubbling excitement inside her and for a moment she was tempted not to pass on her news. Then she reminded herself that Midge's manner was a relic of her old self and concealed a much more vulnerable person. She crouched down beside her chair.

'Actually, it is as good as that – well, almost. At least you may think so.'

'What on earth are you talking about?' Midge enquired.

'He's alive, Midge.'

'Who? Nick? I didn't know there was a problem.'

'No, not Nick! Jumbo! Jumbo's alive and back with his squadron.'

'Bugger!' Midge stabbed herself with the darning needle and put her finger in her mouth. Over her hand her eyes stared into Frankie's. 'You're not having me on, are you?' Her voice was muffled. 'How do you know?'

'I've just got a letter from Ralph Dawson – you remember Ralph?'

''Course I do. Why did he write to you, not me?'

'Oh well, we talked about you and Jumbo once. He thought I could break the news better, I suppose.'

Midge lowered her hand to the darning in her lap and Frankie saw that it was trembling. 'And Jumbo's OK?'

'Right as rain, apparently.' Frankie gave her friend a résumé of Ralph's letter and Midge sat with her eyes lowered until she finished. Then, without looking up, she said, 'What shall I do, Frankie?'

'Well, write to him, of course.'

'But he may not want to hear from me. I was so foul to him. How can he ever forgive me?'

Frankie thought of her last conversation with Ralph and wondered for a moment if she should tell Midge what she had learned about Jumbo's background. She decided against it.

'Write to him, Midge. Tell him you love him and that you made a terrible mistake turning him down. Tell him it doesn't matter to you what his father does or what he plans to do after the war – that all that matters is that you and he should be together. If he really loves you – and I'm sure he does – that will be all he needs.'

'Do you think so?' Midge looked up. 'I'm such a stupid bitch, Frankie. I don't deserve a wonderful chap like Jumbo. I think it would be kinder if I just let him forget me.'

'No it wouldn't!' Frankie said energetically. 'It would just be cruel to both of you. He loves you and you love him. All it needs is for you to swallow your pride and write to him.'

'It's not pride!'

'Well, whatever it is. You made a silly mistake. Now you've got a chance to put it right.'

Midge looked at her for a moment, then nodded. 'OK. I'll write. But I'll make it clear he's under no obligation. I don't want him to think he's committed himself in any way.'

'Oh, Midge, for God's sake!' Frankie erupted. 'Just tell him you love him. That's all it needs.'

Midge went back into the hut and fetched her writing case and Frankie left her alone. Midge never told her what she put in the letter but a week or so later she came to her with shining eyes.

'He's written back, Frankie. He says if I'm prepared to put up with living in the provinces and being married to a man who comes home with oil on his hands then his proposal still stands.'

Frankie suppressed a grin. Was that Jumbo's idea, she wondered, or had Ralph put him up to it? She thought about the manor house in the country and the potential peerage and wondered how long it would be before Midge found out the truth.

'And are you?' she asked.

'Of course I am! I'd live in a mud hut to be with Jumbo!'

'Then write back and tell him so.'

*   *   *

With the warmer weather came more encouraging news from the front. The British together with the Poles had finally succeeded in taking Monte Cassino and the combined Allied forces had broken out of the beachhead at Anzio, where they had been contained all winter, and the two armies had joined up across the width of the Italian peninsula.

Nick's communications became more optimistic, too. Using the extra weapons they had received in the airdrop, the partisans, who were commanded by a man whose *nom de guerre* was Luciano, had attacked a police post manned by the Brigata Nera, the Blackshirts who had remained loyal to Mussolini. They had succeeded in capturing a store of ammunition, including grenades and explosives, and freeing a number of prisoners. These were mostly young men who had refused the German order to report for forced labour and who were only too happy to join forces with Luciano's men.

Nick's next message told how they had been joined by three escaped POWs who had been hiding out in the mountains. *Two Russians, one French pilot. The Russkies will stay and fight with us but the Frenchman is desperate to rejoin his squadron so I will endeavour to exfiltrate him with one of our couriers.*

Frankie had heard of these couriers before. They were Italian montagnards, wild men who lived outside the law in the mountains and knew every goat path. They could pass through the German lines like wraiths of mist and often carried messages where radio communication was impossible.

A few days later came another message, and even through the dry, clipped language Frankie could sense Nick's exaltation. *Wish to report another successful operation. Enemy communications post at N.43°20"; W11°16" attacked and blown up. Five enemy killed. No casualties on our side.*

A steady stream of further messages followed. News of the group's success had brought more recruits flocking to join them. They had ambushed a German convoy and captured supplies of food and more armaments. Together with these reports of military successes came information that Frankie knew was even more valuable. Nick had recruited local people, many of them women, simply to observe troop movements in their area and report back to him. From these piecemeal sightings, reported by BLOs in various areas, Allied Military Intelligence was able to put together an invaluable picture of German dispositions.

Women excellent for this job, Nick signalled. *Clear heads and good memories – also extremely brave.*

Frankie felt a glow of pride as she decoded these messages. At last women were being allowed to play their full part and getting credit for it. She thought of the girls she worked with, and of Steve, and of her little sister working as a welder in the shipyard. Her father's world of obedient and protected girls was never going to be the same again. She was immensely proud of Nick, too, but at the same time, she lived in a perpetual state of anxiety. Nick was not supposed to fight, merely to co-ordinate and advise, but she knew him well enough to be sure that he could not sit back and let others take all the risks.

On 4 June the Americans marched into Rome. Two days later Dickie came tumbling into the signals hut where Frankie and Midge were on duty, red faced with excitement.

'I say, you chaps, wonderful news! I've just been listening to the Forces network and they interrupted the programme to tell us. We've launched a massive attack on the French coast.'

'Where? Who?' Frankie demanded. For months now people had been talking about the need to attack the Germans on the Western Front as well as from the south. There had been a general feeling among those who were involved in the Italian campaign that they were being left to do all the hard work while the High Command dithered.

'Normandy. A huge Allied invasion,' Dickie said breathlessly. 'General Eisenhower's HQ has just announced it.'

'It's the real thing?' Midge enquired. 'Not just a diversion?'

'No, it's the real thing, all right. They broadcast an eye-witness account by Richard Dimbleby. He said the Channel was covered with ships as far as the eye could see in all directions, with massive air support and thousands of gliders carrying paratroops. We're back in France at last!'

'Yippee!' Frankie pulled off her headphones, jumped to her feet and threw her arms round Dickie. Together they executed a mad polka around the tiny hut until they were forced to stop from lack of breath.

'Oh, isn't it fantastic!' Frankie panted. 'All these years we've had to grit our teeth and take whatever Hitler chose to throw at us and now at last we're getting our own back. With our chaps here advancing from the south and the this new invasion in France, he can't hold out much longer, can he?'

'And don't forget the Russians,' Dickie said. 'Hitler's going to have to fight on three fronts now. The chaps in the mess reckon it'll all be over by Christmas.'

'All over!' Frankie said. 'I can hardly believe it.'

'Yes,' Midge put in. 'And then what?'

She had sat quietly while the other two cavorted and now Frankie dropped back into the chair beside her.

'What's up, Midge? It's good news. What's wrong?'

Midge gave her a pale smile and a shrug. 'I don't know. It's just . . . well, this war's made such a difference to me – to the way I think, the way I see things. I know it's been awful for most people, but for me it's been the best time of my life. I don't quite know what I shall do with myself afterwards.'

'You'll marry Jumbo and settle down, of course,' Frankie said.

'And you'll marry Nick, I suppose. And then what?'

'Well, kids, family life – the usual sort of thing.' But Frankie spoke without the certainty she had felt before.

'Exactly,' Midge replied. 'The usual sort of thing. Is that going to be enough?'

'I don't know. It'll have to be, I suppose.'

'No it won't!' Dickie broke in. 'You don't have to go back to the old ways. We women have shown the chaps what we can do. We're not going to take a back seat after this.'

'So what are we supposed to do?' Frankie asked.

'Anything you like! Politics, the law, the civil service. There's no reason why women can't do the top jobs – be diplomats, ambassadors, government ministers even.'

Frankie laughed. 'Oh, come off it, Dickie!'

'No, I'm serious. The sky's the limit now.'

'Maybe for you. You've got a degree. I've only got Matric.'

'Then get a degree! You're perfectly capable. Believe me, the country's going to be crying out for able men and women to rebuild our society when all this is over. Think about it, that's all I'm saying. Just don't settle for marriage and mother-hood as if they're the only option.'

'Well, marriage will do for me,' Frankie said. 'That is if Nick's still . . . if Nick still wants me.'

Nick was not scheduled to come on air that evening so Frankie had to wait until the next day to give him the news. That night, lying in bed, she worked out what she was going to say and mentally encoded it. She knew his code so well by now that she hardly needed the code book to work from. With any luck, she told herself, by the end of the summer the Allied forces would have overrun the area where he and his partisans were operating and he would no longer be needed. Then, if past form was anything to go by, he would be given some leave and then a six-month stint as a conducting officer. That should keep him safe until the end of the war. She hugged the thought to herself and even allowed her imagination to begin to create images of their wedding and the life they would lead afterwards – a thing she had never permitted herself to do before. But these thoughts brought her back to what Dickie had said. What would life as Nick's wife be like? He had talked about going into politics. She had no idea what was expected of a politician's wife. She had never met Nick's father, or any of his family, and she had never imagined living south of the Mersey, let alone down in Sussex, where he came from. And she had to admit to herself that, like Midge, she would miss the companionship and the sense of purpose that had filled her life for the last two years. Peace, in its way, was going to be as big a challenge as war had been. On that thought, she fell asleep.

The next evening she tuned in to Nick's wavelength with an extra thrill of excitement. She had come to recognise that every wireless operator had an individual touch on the Morse key and she would have known Joe Prentiss's 'fist' even without his call sign. Although she knew that it was Joe who transmitted Nick's carefully encoded words it still felt as if she were listening to Nick's own voice. She waited for the hands of the clock to arrive at the appointed time. Joe was always very punctual with his transmissions. At the correct moment she transmitted the call sign but instead of a response there was only silence. Frankie waited, watching the clock, repeating the call sign at intervals. There was a window of ten minutes during which she was scheduled to be listening out. The seconds ticked away. At the end of the time she was due to tune in for another transmission. She dreaded changing the frequency, imagining Joe hurrying to his set only to find no response, but when the moment came she turned the dial with a hollow sense of betrayal.

At a pause in their work Midge looked across at her. 'What's up? Are you OK?'

'Salmon didn't come up on air.'

Midge reached across and laid a hand on Frankie's arm. 'Not to worry! There could be all sorts of reasons. Maybe his battery's flat. Or there's too much German activity in the area to risk transmitting. Or perhaps they're on the move. He'll come through tomorrow.'

'Yes, I expect he will,' Frankie agreed but she could not shake off a sense of foreboding.

There was no response to her call sign the following evening or the next. As soon as her shift was over Frankie made her way to the CO's office.

'Salmon hasn't come up on air for three consecutive transmissions, sir.'

MacIntosh looked at her with a frown. 'So? You know as well as I do that there could be any number of reasons for that.'

'He's always been so regular, sir. I'm worried that something may have happened to him.'

'Well, if it has there's nothing we can do about it. Just keep listening out and let me know if you hear anything.'

For the next three nights Frankie hardly slept. At every opportunity she tuned to Nick's frequency and sent out her call sign, in case he was desperately trying to get in touch, but there was only silence. Then on the fourth day she was summoned to the CO's office. His aide-de-camp, a willowy lieutenant called Viney, was with him and also a short, dark man with a huge moustache dressed in rough peasant clothes and looking as if he had not washed in a long time.

'This man has been sent back from the front line,' MacIntosh said. 'It seems he's got some information about Salmon but he doesn't speak any English and neither Viney nor I can understand his accent. See what you can make of it.'

Frankie turned to the man. Her heart was thudding and her

throat felt so constricted that she could barely speak. 'What do you know about Major Harper?' she asked in Italian.

The answer came in a torrent of words, heavily accented with the dialect of Emilia. Frankie had to struggle to follow them but the gist was clear and struck her like blows to the stomach. Feeling sick, she turned back to MacIntosh.

'The Germans caught them in the middle of an operation. There was a battle. Sergeant Prentiss was killed and Nick – Major Harper – was badly wounded. They managed to get him away but he needs urgent medical attention.'

'Is there no local doctor who could be trusted?'

Frankie translated and conveyed the reply. 'A doctor has seen him but he needs surgery. They don't have the facilities.'

'Where is he?'

Again she translated. Her sickness had been replaced by a deadly calm.

'They've taken him to a camp somewhere in the mountains. He doesn't know exactly where.'

'Could he be brought out by the same route this man used?'

'No. He says it is a difficult path. Impossible for men carrying a stretcher.'

MacIntosh was silent for a moment, then he called for the corporal on duty outside the door. 'Take this man to the canteen and see he gets a good meal. Thank him, Franconi, and tell him we may want to speak to him again later.'

When the man had gone Frankie said, 'What can we do, sir?'

'Very little until we know exactly where he is. We need to establish radio contact.'

'But Sergeant Prentiss was his radio operator. Nick – Major Harper – doesn't know Morse.'

MacIntosh sat in silence again, drumming his fingertips together. Unable to bear it, Frankie broke in, 'There must be something we can do, sir?'

The CO looked up as if he had forgotten her presence. 'That's all, Franconi. Thank you.'

Frankie stood still, bewildered. It was unthinkable that she could leave the room without knowing what was going to be done. MacIntosh repeated, 'I said that's all. Dismiss!'

Frankie shook her head. 'I can't, sir. Not until I know. What's going to happen?'

For a moment she thought MacIntosh was going to shout at her. Then he leaned back in his chair. 'Well, what would you suggest?' There was a bitter irony in his voice.

'Can't we get a plane in to fly him out?'

'Well, let us suppose that we could find a suitable aircraft and a pilot mad enough to attempt a landing in the mountains. How would we know where to send him?' Frankie could think of no answer and MacIntosh went on, as if talking to himself, 'As it happens, there is such a man. A crazy Italian called Lauri who flies a Nardi 305. It's only a two-seater but it can land on a sixpence. But before we could send him in we would have to know the exact location and we would have to contact Luciano's men and tell them to prepare a landing strip and light signal fires to guide him in. And for that we need radio contact.'

Viney spoke for the first time. 'Couldn't we drop a new radio operator to him, sir?'

MacIntosh looked up at him. 'Michael, you know as well as I do that competent radio operators prepared to volunteer for this kind of assignment are about as rare as hens' teeth. We've no one to spare.'

'I'll do it.' Frankie heard herself say the words before she was aware of having taken a conscious decision to utter them. She rushed on. 'I'm a trained radio operator and I know Salmon's code back to front and inside out. You can drop me to him.'

MacIntosh looked at her as if seeing her for the first time. For a moment he appeared to consider the idea, then he shook his head. 'I appreciate your desire to help but I'm afraid it's out of the question. For one thing, you would have to be trained to parachute and by the time you'd gone through the course it might be . . .'

'But I've done it!' Frankie broke in. 'I learned to parachute while I was at Cap Matifou.'

'You learned? How come?'

'Major Harper fixed it for me. I wanted to try it so he arranged for me to go through the course with Sergeant Pearson.'

'And you completed it? You actually jumped?'

'Yes.'

'How many times?'

'Only once – but I'm sure I could it again.'

'Why did you do it?'

'For fun.'

The CO raised his eyes to his aide. 'She did it for fun!' he repeated. Then he looked back at Frankie. 'That's all very well but it's one thing to jump on a nice clear day when you know that there are going to be friends waiting for you on the ground. It's a very different thing to jump in the dark over enemy-occupied territory. Do you think you could do that?'

Frankie took a deep breath. 'Yes, sir. I'm sure I could – if someone gave me a bit of a push.'

For the first time the faint hint of a smile that she had thought she detected in the corners of the CO's eyes became a reality but it vanished as soon as it appeared. He shook his head again. 'No, it's not on. We'd have to drop you blind. There'd be no reception committee waiting for you, no one to show you where Harper is. How would you find your way to him?'

'I could ask.'

'Ask whom? How would you know who you could trust? The first person you spoke to might hand you over to the Nazis.'

Frankie's brain was working overtime. 'I speak fluent Italian.

I can pass for a local. We can work out a cover story for me. No one need know why I'm really there. Then when I'm sure I can trust someone . . .'

'No, Franconi!' MacIntosh interrupted her rush of words. 'It won't do. Even if it worked, by the time you got to him Harper could be dead.'

Frankie stared at him in silence, struck dumb by the sound of the words she had been trying to avoid thinking of.

Viney leaned down to his superior's ear. 'Just a thought, sir. Couldn't we drop her to Swordfish? His territory borders Salmon's. His people may know where Luciano's lot are hiding out. Or if not, they could probably find out.'

MacIntosh frowned. 'It's a good idea, Michael. There's just one snag. The group Swordfish is working with are Garibaldini – communists. Salmon's men are Fiamme Verde – Catholics. They are rivals, not friends.'

'But surely they have agreed to work together to get rid of the Germans,' Viney protested.

'In theory, yes. In practice it seems to be a matter of how any individual is feeling at any given moment. However' – he paused, considering – 'it's the best idea we've come up with so far. Right!' He looked at Frankie. 'Make a signal to Swordfish asking if he is prepared to receive you and if his men know where Harper is to be found. Meanwhile, I'll arrange for you to do a couple of practice jumps with Major Nicholson. If he is satisfied with your level of proficiency and if we get a positive response from Swordfish, you're on. I don't like it, but it's the best we can do under the circumstances. OK, off you go.'

'Yes, sir! Thank you, sir!' Frankie was halfway to the door before she remembered to turn back and salute. As she closed the door behind her she heard a low whistle followed by a chuckle, quickly suppressed.

Frankie made her way straight to the signals office, where

Dickie and Flick were on duty. Without speaking she sat at a spare desk and composed a signal. When she was satisfied with it she took it over to Dickie.

'You handle Swordfish's traffic, don't you? When is he next scheduled to make contact?'

Dickie glanced at the clock. 'In just over an hour.'

'Right.' Frankie put the piece of paper down in front of her. 'Encode this and send it as top priority. Let me know as soon as you get a reply.'

Dickie read the signal aloud. *Urgent. Salmon wounded, requires immediate exfiltration. RT operator killed. Can you establish whereabouts of Salmon? If so, will you accept drop of new operator and arrange conduct to Salmon's location? Immediate reply required.*

Dickie dropped the paper and stared at Frankie. 'Salmon? That's Nick, isn't it? Oh, Frankie!'

'Yes,' Frankie said, 'it's Nick.' The mood of deadly calm still gripped her. 'Just get that encoded, will you?'

'Who are they going to drop as his new RT operator?' Dickie wondered.

'Me,' Frankie responded crisply and left the room before anyone could speak. She was not sure why she could not discuss what had happened with her friends. She just knew that she had to focus on what lay ahead of her and think as little as possible about its likely outcome.

Fortunately she did not have to wait long for the order instructing her to report to Major Nicholson at the parachute training centre on the far side of the airfield. Nicholson, a large, fair, mild-mannered man, looked her up and down and remarked, 'Well, we're not going to need a very big 'chute for you, are we?'

Frankie did not know if he had been told of her planned mission, but he made no reference to it and the only questions he asked were about her earlier training at Cap Matifou. He made her go through a number of the exercises she had learned and she became painfully aware that she had lost a good deal of the muscle tone she had built up then. Nicholson seemed satisfied, however.

'OK. I'll get a plane organised to take you up. We're between courses so fortunately I've got some spare manpower.'

Panic gripped Frankie at the pit of her stomach. For the first time that morning she remembered that she had her regular duties to perform. She looked at her watch.

'My shift starts in twenty minutes, sir. Can I come back about four thirty?'

'Fine by me,' Nicholson replied. 'See you then.'

There was no time for a meal. Frankie grabbed a chocolate bar from the NAAFI and hurried to the signals hut. She found the other five girls all waiting for her.

'Frankie, where have you been?' Midge demanded. 'We've been worried sick. Is it true about Nick being wounded and you being dropped to him?'

For the first time Frankie was forced to stop and confront what was happening. She sank down into a chair and put her head in her hands. The image of Nick lying in agony in some remote mountain hideout filled her mind.

'Yes, it's true,' she whispered.

Midge put an arm round her shoulders. 'Have you had anything to eat or drink? Where have you been all morning? Get her a cup of tea, Mouse.'

'What, exactly, are you planning to do?' Dickie wanted to know. 'Have you cleared this with the CO?'

In disjointed phrases Frankie explained the plans that had been drawn up.

'You're mad!' Dickie said. 'Stark, staring, raving bonkers. But, by golly, I admire you for it!'

'Have you had any reply from Swordfish?' Frankie asked.

'An acknowledgement, that's all. He promised to get back to me this evening.'

'They won't let me go unless he agrees,' Frankie said. 'I don't know what I'll do if he says no. I can't sit here and do nothing.'

'Swordfish will want to help,' Dickie pointed out. 'After all, it could be him needing to be got out.'

Somehow Frankie got through her shift and headed back to the airfield. A plane was waiting with its engines ticking over and a corporal helped her into her parachute harness. She was grateful that there was no time to think before she scrambled aboard. The dispatcher, a lanky Australian with a face so weathered by sun and wind that his eyes almost disappeared among the creases when he smiled, greeted her with a cheerful grin.

'Done this before, ma'am?'

'Once.'

'You'll be right. No worries!'

He offered her a cigarette and when she refused replaced it with a stick of chewing gum. The plane taxied out across the airfield and this time Frankie was not afraid when the engines roared as the pilot ran them up for his last-minute checks. In a few minutes they were airborne. The plane was a lumbering old bomber that had been handed over by the Italian air force as part of the surrender terms. As they began to circle, gaining height above the airfield, the dispatcher settled himself opposite Frankie.

'Name's Lou.'

Frankie reached out a hand. 'Frankie.'

'Pleased to meet you, Frankie. Where're you from?'

'Liverpool. You?'

'Little town called Wodonga. Bet you've never heard of it!'

It was difficult to talk against the roar of the engines but Lou chattered on about his home on a sheep farm and Frankie was glad of the distraction. Last time she had been with a large group and Nick had been beside her. Now, all alone except for Lou, her stomach was crawling with cold fear. At last the red light behind the cockpit came on and Lou got to his feet. To Frankie's consternation, instead of opening a door in the side of the aircraft he heaved open a hatch in the floor. She would have to drop through that into thin air. Obeying his gesture, she worked her way along the bench and lowered herself to the floor, so that her legs were hanging into the void. Lou reached up and clipped her ripcord to the line running along the fuselage, giving it a reassuring tug. Then he crouched beside her.

'No worries!' he repeated. 'Easy as falling off a log.'

Then the light turned green and she felt a firm push in the small of her back and the next instant she was out and falling. Then came the tug on her shoulders and the crack of the parachute opening and the few minutes of blessed silence as she hung suspended above the world. She landed harder than the first time, the hard-baked earth of the airfield perimeter much less yielding than the sand dunes of Cap Matifou, but she rolled with the impact and scrambled to her feet with nothing worse than a few bruises. Already a jeep was racing towards her. As they reached the hangar where Nicholson was waiting, the plane that had carried her landed behind them.

Nicholson nodded, his teeth clamped around the stem of his pipe. 'OK? No problems? Right, up you go again.'

This time it was easier and she was actually able to enjoy the view. When they got back to the hangar again Nicholson said, 'You'll do. I'll let your CO know I'm happy with you.'

Back at the signals hut Dickie greeted her with the words, 'You're on! Swordfish says he'll see you get to Nick somehow. You're to report to the boss.'

MacIntosh leaned back in his chair and looked her up and down. 'Well, it seems you're quite a remarkable young lady. Major Nicholson is a hard man to impress but you appear to have done it.'

'When can I drop, sir?' Frankie said. She was no longer interested in what her superiors thought of her.

'Hold your horses!' MacIntosh exclaimed. 'We have to give Swordfish a chance to establish a dropping zone and send us the coordinates. You know how these things work. Fortunately, we're in about the right phase of the moon and the weather forecast is reasonable. With any luck we can drop you a couple of nights from now.'

'Two nights!' Frankie protested. 'But . . .'

'No buts!' her CO interrupted. 'You really are the most insubordinate officer I've ever had to deal with! Meanwhile, you have some homework to do. Come and look at this map.'

He led her over to a large wall map peppered with coloured pins, each representing the location of one of their agents. 'This is Salmon's last reported position. Luciano's men operate in roughly this area.' He circled an area of mountainous terrain south of Parma. 'Swordfish's people are here,' indicating an area to the east. 'You will have quite a long journey to get to Salmon and I've no idea what form of transport he can provide. I hope you're a good walker.'

He paused and looked at Frankie. She was struggling to concentrate but her knees felt weak and she was longing to sit down. Only the fear that MacIntosh would change his mind about sending her kept her on her feet.

'You've had enough for one day,' he said, in a softer tone than she had ever heard him use before. 'Go and get something to eat and then get a good night's sleep. Get the MO to give you something if you think you'll have difficulty sleeping.'

Frankie spoke through a haze. 'I'm on duty again at two a.m. sir.'

'No you're not,' he said. 'I've had a word with your squad. Nightingale will be in charge while you're away and they are going to cover your shifts between them. Now, get off and get some rest.'

Amazingly, Frankie slept the moment she fell into bed and did not wake till the following morning. The others fussed round her with cups of tea and bacon sandwiches and then she reported again to Major MacIntosh. All morning she pored over maps, trying to memorise landmarks and major routes. Around midday Dickie appeared with a sheet of paper.

'Coordinates for the DZ from Swordfish, sir. He says he can be ready any time from tonight.'

'Tonight?' MacIntosh repeated. Then he looked at Frankie. 'Well?'

'Yes, sir. I'm ready. The sooner the better.'

In the afternoon she was sent to see the MO for a check-up and when he had finished examining her he produced a medical kit.

'It seems we have no idea of where Major Harper is wounded or what the nature of problem is. But if he needs surgery there will obviously be very little you can do until we get him out. However, there are sterile dressings here, which could be important, and morphine, which is probably the most essential. Have you ever given an injection before?'

'Yes, once.' Frankie had a sudden sense that everything that had ever happened to her had been in preparation for what she was about to do.

The doctor went over the use of the various items in the medical kit with her and then sent her back to MacIntosh. In his office she found a staff sergeant with the rest of her kit.

'We're giving you a new radio set, in case Prentiss's set has gone missing or is US. You're familiar with this model?' Frankie checked the equipment and nodded. 'There are emergency rations and money in local currency. Maps, torch, batteries. Oh, and this.' He held out a tin.

'What is it?'

'Anti-louse powder. With any luck you may not need it, as you're going in and out fairly quickly, but conditions can be pretty rough over there. And you'll want this. I take it you did do basic firearms training at Overthorpe?'

Frankie looked at the pistol. 'Yes, but I don't think I could shoot anyone,' she said.

'Let's hope you don't need to. But in an emergency just the threat of this could be useful. Let's see you load it.'

Frankie did as she was ordered. The pistol was heavy and felt unwieldy in her small hand. The idea that she could frighten anyone with it seemed ridiculous.

'Do you have good boots?' MacIntosh put in. 'Ones you can walk in for long distances?'

Frankie nodded, then added, 'But I won't be in uniform, will I?'

'Oh yes you will,' he said. 'If you should happen to be picked up we don't want you getting shot as a spy. This way, the worst that can happen to you is a spell in a POW camp.'

Frankie did not argue, but as soon as she was dismissed she borrowed a bicycle and rode into the village. There she spent some time with the young woman who owned the little shop and came out with a bundle under her arm. She found the man who was packing the canister to be dropped with her and asked him to include it among her kit. Then she went to say goodbye to Midge and Dickie and the others.

Chapter Eleven

Major MacIntosh drove her personally to the hangar just before eleven that night. He introduced her to the three-man crew of the aircraft and she was grateful to discover that Lou was to be her dispatcher.

'Couldn't let you go off with a stranger, now, could I?' he said with a grin when she told him so.

She was glad, too, of the casual manner of the pilot and co-pilot. They knew that flying deep into enemy-held territory was a hazardous business but they treated it as if it were, in RAF parlance, 'a piece of cake'. Frankie tried very hard to appear as relaxed as they did but her legs were shaking and her hands were clammy. She had been afraid that the other girls would make an emotional scene when she said goodbye, which would have been the end of her precarious self-control, but they had had the sense to keep the atmosphere light-hearted.

'Give Nick our love,' Midge had said. 'And no hanging around when you've found him. We're not covering your shifts for you indefinitely, you know.'

MacIntosh waited while she was strapped into her parachute harness and walked out to the plane with her.

'No heroics, now,' he warned her. 'If the situation starts to look dicey radio in and we'll make arrangements to get you out. Whatever happens, I want you back here within ten days, whether or not you've located Harper. Understood?'

Frankie nodded and had to swallow hard before she could say, 'Yes, sir.'

'Right, off you go. Good luck.' MacIntosh held out his hand and she took it, hoping that he would not feel how hers was shaking.

Lou helped her up into the plane and the engines began to roar. When they were airborne Lou leaned across to her.

'Tell me about Liverpool. I did my training at Moreton-in-Marsh. Never got farther north than that.'

Frankie knew he was trying to take her mind off the danger. She began to chatter about her home and family and found herself telling him about Maria's latest escapades and her father's losing battle for control.

'Daughters, eh?' said Lou. 'Who'd be a dad? I don't know how I'll cope when my little girl gets to that age.'

'You've got a daughter?'

'Yep. Five years old when I last saw her. Guess she's eight now.'

'Such a long time to be away!' Frankie said.

As they talked on other thoughts were running in her mind, refusing to be suppressed. What if the pilot couldn't find the dropping zone? What if she came down in the wrong place? What if there was no one to meet her, or she was injured in the drop? What if Nick was already dead?

After what seemed a very long time the co-pilot put his head round the door to the cockpit.

'Skipper's spotted the signal fires. We're just turning now to make a run over the area to check it out. Stand by.'

Lou opened the hatch in the floor of the aircraft, revealing a rushing darkness. Frankie clipped her ripcord to the line along the side of the fuselage and tugged it to make sure that it was firm, then moved to sit on the edge of the hole. Far below her she made out a single orange glow, then another and another. The red light was on and she fixed her eyes on it. Beside her, Lou prepared the parachute attached to the canister containing her kit, which he would throw out immediately after her. Then he knelt beside her and she felt his hand in the small of her back.

'Good luck! No worries. You'll be right.'

For a moment Frankie thought she was not going to be able to go through with it.

Then the light turned green and she was out and falling almost before she felt Lou's gentle shove.

The few seconds of chaotic tumbling ended with the now familiar jerk as the parachute cracked open above her head. Then came an unreal stillness and quiet. She could hear the plane's engines fading into the distance and the wind in the shrouds of the parachute but because it was dark she had no sense of her position in space. She had the impression of floating, disembodied, above the world. Below her the ground was only a deeper darkness, devoid of any features, and the only division between it and the sky was the shadowy line of a distant range of mountains. Then a light breeze caused her parachute to revolve and she saw again the pattern of signal fires, brighter now and rapidly growing larger. As the ground came closer she was able to make out that the fires were laid out in the floor of a narrow valley, the steep sides of which were clothed in dense forest. She recognised that the pilot had done a good job and dropped her right on target, so precisely in fact that for a moment she was afraid that she might land in the middle of the nearest fire. She tugged on one of the shrouds and the chute jinked to one side, out of danger. She could see men, now, in the light of the fires, running towards the spot where she was going to come down. It crossed her mind that they could be German soldiers. If Swordfish's code had been broken the reception committee might not be the one she was expecting. She had known it happen before. Then there was no more time for speculation as the ground rushed towards her.

It was difficult to judge distances in the dark and she landed sooner than she expected, coming down with a jolt that rattled every joint in her body, but she rolled with the impact and scrambled to her feet unhurt. Feet pounded towards her and voices greeted her in Italian. Helping hands mastered her parachute and folded it, others assisted her to struggle out of the harness. There were three young men, eager faced, grinning broadly, though she thought she caught some curious glances passing between them.

'My equipment?' she asked. 'There should be another parachute with a container.'

'*Si, si, signorina!*' one responded. 'We have seen it. It will be brought to you. Come, this way.'

He led her down a rocky path to meet another small group. As they approached, a taller figure than the rest detached itself and came towards her. Frankie recognised the uniform of a British army captain. He stopped a few feet away and peered at her.

'I'm Devenish. Who the hell are you?'

'Franconi, sir. Reporting for duty. I'm the replacement radio operator for Salmon.'

'You're Franconi? But we were expecting a man.'

Frankie felt a spasm of irritation. 'Sorry about that, sir. I'm afraid I'm the best HQ could come up with at short notice.'

There was a brief pause. Then Devenish said, in a different tone, 'God, I'm sorry! How incredibly rude of me. I'm afraid you took us all by surprise. Can we start again? Peter Devenish. Pleased to meet you.'

Frankie took his extended hand. 'Gina Franconi, sir. Everyone calls me Frankie.'

'Are you all right? No injuries?'

'Only a few bruises. Nothing important. Have you seen the canister with my gear in it?'

'Yes, don't worry. A couple of our chaps have just brought it in. All intact, as far as I could see.'

A second man stepped forward, shorter and thicker set than Devenish.

'*Signorina, benvenuta in Italia! Mi chiamo Mario.*'

'Mario's the leader of this company of Garibaldini,' Devenish said, reverting to Italian but with a strong English accent.

Frankie shook hands and greeted the smaller man in the same language.

'But surely you are an Italian!' he exclaimed.

'No,' Frankie told him. 'I'm English but my grandparents were Italian.'

'Shall we go?' Devenish put in. 'There's some transport a bit farther down.'

He led the way to a small clearing where two jeeps stood. Frankie was relieved to see that two men were already loading the canister containing all her equipment into one. She and Devenish climbed into the other with Mario at the wheel, and they set off over the rocky track at a speed that showed no mercy to Frankie's bruises. The ride was, however, mercifully brief, and soon they drove into the courtyard of what appeared to be a large farm. There was a long, low stone-built house and a number of large buildings she took to be barns, but the impression of rural peace was immediately dispelled by the two armed sentries guarding the gate. Other men came trooping in behind the two jeeps and Frankie saw that they all carried rifles.

Mario led her into the kitchen of the farmhouse, where a very fat woman was stirring a large pot on an open range.

'Sit!' he said, gesturing to a bench alongside the scrubbed deal table that took up the centre of the room. 'Paola, bring some wine! We have a guest!'

Frankie sank onto the bench gratefully. Now that the adrenalin had ceased to flow she felt deathly tired. A young girl appeared from another room with a pitcher and poured red wine into a collection of chipped glasses. Devenish sat opposite Frankie and half a dozen other men, whom she took to be Mario's lieutenants, arranged themselves around the edges of the room, watching curiously. Now that she could see him in the light of the oil lamp, Frankie decided that Devenish was exactly her idea of the quintessential Englishman – tall and fair, with regular features and pale blue eyes. But there was something about his mouth, a softness that was almost a pout, which prevented him from being attractive. Spoilt, she thought. Too used to getting his own way.

'*Salute!*' Mario called. 'Here's to victory!'

The contrast between him and Devenish could not have been greater. The Italian was short and squat with thick dark hair and a heavy moustache. In spite of his affability there was a look in his eyes and a sharpness in his movements that made her feel he would not be a good man to cross. She sipped her drink. She had very little experience of wine but this one tasted to her like vinegar combined with red ink and she had difficulty restraining a grimace.

Mario slapped the fat woman resoundingly on her behind. 'Luisa, this is Frankie! Frankie, this is my wife, the best cook in Italy. Are you hungry?'

Frankie realised that she was. She had hardly been able to eat anything before the flight. As Luisa doled out bowls of steaming pasta the smell of the ragu brought back such sharp memories of her grandmother's kitchen that they were almost painful. She turned her attention to Devenish.

'Have you managed to make contact with Major Harper?'

'Not directly. But Mario sent two of his men on a recce and they met up with some of his chaps. So we've got a pretty good idea where he's hiding out.'

'Is he . . .' Frankie stopped and then rephrased the question. 'He is still alive, then?'

'So far as we know, yes.'

'When will I be able to get to him?'

'One of Mario's men will drive you to the village nearest to where he is tomorrow. We're pretty sure that the village priest is a supporter of Luciano's Fiamme Verde, if not an actual member. He should be able to take you to where Harper is.'

'I could be there tomorrow, then?'

'With any luck, yes.'

Frankie bent her head over her bowl to hide her emotions. It would not do to show how personally involved she was. Tomorrow she would be with Nick. She had never dreamed it could be so easy. Perhaps as early as the following night the plane would come that would take him to hospital. Soon he would be safe and in good hands.

Devenish was looking uncomfortable. 'There's just one problem . . .'

Feet clattered on the wooden staircase leading from the courtyard to the upper storey and the door opened to admit a slight, sandy-haired young man in the uniform of a sergeant in the Argyll and Sutherland Highlanders. He looked around the room, focused on Frankie and broke into a broad grin.

'Well, well!' he remarked in a broad Scots accent. 'There is a God after all.'

'This is Ginger Galbraith, my radio operator,' Devenish said. 'Ginger, this is Lieutenant Franconi.'

Galbraith saluted, still grinning. 'You're more than welcome, ma'am.'

'Thank you,' Frankie replied, puzzled.

'That's what I was about to explain,' Devenish said. 'I'm afraid we're a bit short of accommodation so, assuming you were a chap, I've arranged for you to bunk in with Ginger here.'

'I've no objection if the lady hasn't,' the Scot said.

'You watch your lip,' Devenish reproved him without rancour.

Frankie was saved from embarrassment by Luisa, who broke in to enquire what was being said. Devenish explained and she nodded, as if she had guessed what the conversation was about.

'She can sleep with Paola. I'll put another mattress in her room.'

Ginger, who obviously understood Italian, sighed philosophically. 'Aye, well. There's no harm in dreaming.'

At Devenish's invitation he sat down and poured himself a glass of wine.

'I'm sorry I wasnae here to greet you, ma'am, but I'd a sked to keep to. You'll understand that. I was up on the roof. It's the only place where I can get any reception. Anyway, I've told HQ that you've arrived safely.'

'Thank you.'

He leaned forward. 'Mind you, it's a miracle I can get through at all. The battery on my set's on its last legs. Did you bring the replacement?'

'Replacement?' Frankie queried. 'No, I'm afraid not. No one mentioned anything like that.'

'They've dropped you and not sent a battery for us?' he asked incredulously. 'When we've been at them for weeks for a new one?'

'No. I've got my own radio set, but that's all.'

Devenish swore and apologised. 'God knows what Mario's

going to make of this.' He glanced at the Italian commander, who was chatting to one of his men at the end of the table. 'I've been promising him a supply drop for weeks to keep him sweet. Doesn't HQ have any idea of what we're trying to do here?'

'I'm sorry,' Frankie said. 'But you must understand that you're not alone. I read messages every day begging for guns and ammunition and extra clothing from all the BLOs. The trouble is, we just don't have the stuff to send. Everything is in short supply.'

'What a way to run a bloody war!' Devenish said petulantly. 'Oh well, I'll just have to keep telling him it's only a matter of time.'

Luisa tapped her on the arm and gestured towards the door, and Frankie excused herself gratefully and followed her outside. Luisa led her to a privy on the far side of the yard, which seemed to be the only form of sanitation for the inhabitants of the farmhouse. What the men quartered in the surrounding barns did Frankie could only imagine. As it was, she had to hold her breath and perform her necessary functions as rapidly as possible to control her nausea. When she emerged, Luisa led her up the outside staircase to Paola's room, which was a tiny cubby-hole under the roof, scarcely bigger than the narrow single bed. Paola herself was already asleep, breathing with a regular catarrhal snuffle. A straw mattress had been laid out on the floor in the remaining space and covered with a couple of none-too-clean blankets. Frankie, who was feeling that she would be happy to sleep in a pigsty as long as she could lie down, pulled off her outer clothing, crawled under the blanket and slept at once.

She was woken by Paola crawling over her to get to the door and lay for a while with her face buried in the crook of her arm, trying to convince herself that it was still the middle of the night. Very soon two facts forced themselves on her attention. One was that it was broad daylight and in the yard below men were calling to each other, boots were clattering on the cobbles and water was being pumped with a rhythmic squeak and splash. The other was that the tin of anti-louse powder had not been included in her kit as a joke. She struggled to her feet, scratching and pulling bits of straw out of her underwear. Her flesh was patterned with red weals and she could smell her own body odour. She wanted, above everything else, a bath.

There seemed to be nowhere to wash on the upper storey so she reluctantly pulled on her uniform slacks and battledress tunic and made her way down the stairs. Ginger was sitting on the bottom step, cleaning his pistol, and he jumped up at the sound of her footsteps.

'Is there somewhere I can get a wash?' Frankie asked, when they had exchanged good mornings.

Ginger jerked his thumb ruefully towards the pump in the middle of the yard. 'I'm afraid the ablutions leave a lot to be desired. But I can find you a bucket if you like.'

Frankie looked around the yard. Mario's men were sitting around in small groups, cleaning weapons and chatting, and many of their eyes were fixed on her. Clearly there was no possibility of a proper wash under the pump. She smiled at the Scotsman.

'Thanks. I'd be grateful.'

With Ginger's help she lugged a bucket of cold water up to her room and then found the canister containing her kitbag and managed to have a more or less adequate wash. With a change of underclothes and a liberal dusting of anti-louse powder she felt ready to face the day, though nothing stopped the itching. She tried to close her mind to it. All that mattered was that today she would be taken to Nick.

There was no sign of Devenish in the kitchen but Luisa said he would be in shortly. She and Paola were hard at work baking batches of loaves. It seemed that they were responsible for feeding the entire company. Frankie sat at the table and ate coarse, freshly baked bread with some goat's cheese and drank a bitter brew that masqueraded as coffee but was made, Luisa told her, from roasted acorns. When she had finished there was still no sign of Devenish so she set out to look for him. She found him behind one of the barns, in urgent and apparently angry conversation with Mario. When they saw her approaching both men stopped speaking and glared at her.

'I'm sorry to interrupt, sir,' Frankie said. 'I was wondering when I can start for the village where Major Harper's group is based.'

Devenish looked at her in silence for a moment, biting his lip. Then he strode forward and took her by the arm.

'Come inside.'

Alarmed, Frankie followed him back to the kitchen.

'I'm afraid we've got a problem,' he said in English when they reached it.

'What sort of problem?'

'If only HQ had had the sense to send some of the stuff I've been begging for for weeks this wouldn't have happened,' he exclaimed. 'As it is, Mario is cutting up rough. He wants to hold you here until they come up with the goods.'

'But he can't!' Frankie protested. 'I have to get to Major Harper as a matter of life and death.'

'I've told him that. Unfortunately, there's no love lost between Mario and Luciano, who leads Harper's outfit. Mario reckons the Fiamme Verde are getting more than their fair share of the supplies because we don't like the communists. If only you'd brought the spare battery, that would have helped. Now he's saying that if he keeps you here at least we'll have your radio set if ours goes on the blink. But he wants to use you as a bargaining counter for a lot more than that.'

'You mean, he's holding me hostage?'

'I suppose that's about it.'

'What can we do? I have to get to Major Harper.'

'I don't see what we can do. The jeeps are under Mario's control. There's no chance of getting hold of one of them – or of getting one of his men to guide you.'

'So what are we going to do?' Frankie repeated.

Devenish shrugged. 'Nothing I can do at the moment. I'll signal HQ telling them the situation and ask them to drop a new battery and the other gear asap. With any luck it should be here in a day or two.'

'In a day or two Nick Harper could be dead!' Frankie's voice was cracking with frustration. 'You've got to make Mario see sense.'

'Look,' he said, and she saw the weak mouth working, 'I've got a job to do here. If I get on the wrong side of Mario I shan't be able to do it.'

'You mean you're afraid of him.'

'No! But if I cross him he won't trust me anymore.'

'You undertook to get me to Major Harper.' Frankie had abandoned all respect for rank in her fury. 'I'll signal HQ myself and tell them that you're prepared to let a fellow officer die rather than risk annoying a jumped-up little communist.'

'It's not that.' He was beginning to look desperate. 'What do you expect me to do? I've told you, there's no transport.'

'I'll walk if I have to. How do I get there?'

Devenish looked at her for a moment and she saw him struggling to weigh up the risks of defying the orders of his distant superiors against the more immediate ones of defying Mario. Then she saw a change come over his expression. 'OK. If you're determined, we'll have to find a way to get you out of here without Mario or his men spotting you.' He glanced towards Luisa and Paola at the other end of the room but they had their backs to them and were busy kneading a new batch of dough. 'It's all right,' he went on, 'neither of them speak English.' He paused for a moment and Frankie could see that he was beginning to enjoy the challenge. 'We'll have to wait until after dark. There's a window in one of the storerooms that looks outward instead of into the yard. If we can get out of that without being seen we've got a chance. There's a farmer in the next valley. He doesn't like the communists because he's a devout Catholic, but he owes me a favour. If we can get to him I think I can persuade him to take you to Montefiorino, that's Harper's village. It'll be a long walk in the dark. Are you up for it?'

'Yes! Yes, of course.' Frankie did not wait to consider the implications of the question. 'Where is this window?'

'I'll show you.'

Devenish glanced again at the two women, who still had their backs to them, and then led her into a stone-flagged passage with several doors leading off it. He opened one at the far end and she followed him into a small, dusty room with a single window high up in one wall. From the layer of husks on the floor Frankie deduced that it had once been used for storing grain, though it now contained nothing except some empty sacks.

Devenish looked up at the window and murmured, 'Wait here.'

In a minute or two he was back, rolling a barrel that, from its smell, had once contained olive oil. He set it under the window and climbed up. Frankie watched him wrestling with the casement, afraid that it would prove to be too firmly welded shut by age and disuse to open, but at last there was a crack and a sound of splintering wood and the window opened. Devenish peered out for a moment and then dropped back to stand beside her.

'Yes, it's OK. We'll be out of sight of the sentries at the gate, at least until we move away from the house. Anyway, they will be watching out for someone trying to get in, not out. Meet me here at midnight. People tend to settle down for the night pretty early so everyone should be sound asleep by then. Can you get out of your room without waking Paola?'

'Well, she didn't stir when I went to bed last night. What about my kit?'

'How much is there?'

'The radio set, that's the vital thing. And a first-aid box. That's important. Apart from that it's just personal items.'

'How is the set packed?'

'In a box that looks like an ordinary suitcase.'

'Standard issue, then. That's good. Leave that to me. I'll tell Mario I've taken it into safekeeping if he asks. You collect the rest of what you need together. No one will be surprised if you want your personal stuff. Pack it so you can carry it easily and bring it with you. OK?'

Frankie made her way back to the kitchen and went to the canister that contained her equipment. A rucksack had been included and she put into it the first-aid kit, a few essential personal items and the bundle she had obtained from the woman at the corner shop. At the bottom of the canister she found the pistol in its oiled silk wrappings. She picked it up and balanced it in her hands. The rucksack was heavy already and she was tempted to leave the gun behind, but then she remembered MacIntosh's comment that the mere threat of it might get her out of a difficult situation. She pushed the weapon into the bottom of the rucksack. Neither Luisa nor Paola seemed to notice when she carried it out and took it up to her room.

When she came down Mario was waiting at the bottom of the stairs with Devenish behind him. Frankie realised it was time to put on an act.

'Signore, is it true that you will not let me go to Major Harper? Surely you cannot be so cruel!'

Mario smiled ingratiatingly. 'But of course I shall let you go. Just as soon as your people provide me with the things I need to carry on the struggle. Captain Peter will send a message and I am sure your commander will see the urgency of the situation.'

Frankie normally kept the temper she had inherited from her Italian family under strict control, but on this occasion a display of histrionics seemed not only justified but desirable. For several minutes she screamed at Mario, calling him a heartless traitor, a man without a soul, a cruel devil. By the time she had finished Devenish was looking distinctly alarmed but the Italian was unmoved.

'*Si, si, signora*,' he said dismissively, 'I am probably all of those things, but the fact remains you do not leave here until I receive the supplies I have asked for.'

Frankie threw one last, very rude Italian expletive in his direction and bolted up the staircase. From there she saw him shrug and turn away, followed by Devenish. She found that she was trembling and sat down on the top step. Her outburst had been contrived to convince Mario that she had no thought of escape but it had tapped a genuine anguish, which she had been thrusting to the back of her mind. She envisaged Nick, lying in pain, perhaps dying when, if everything had gone according to plan, she could have brought him relief by that evening. She remembered the previous night – how frightened she had been, how hard it had been to force herself to jump – and now all her efforts were being thwarted by the self-importance of one man. Tears of anger and weariness dropped onto the worn wooden step below her.

After a few minutes she pulled herself together, aware that curious eyes were watching from the courtyard. Her distress was perfectly in keeping with the deception she was trying to sustain, but at the same time her pride would not allow her to show weakness in front of strangers. She wiped her eyes and began to look about her. Nick had impressed on her how useful an intelligent observer could be and, although these men were ostensibly on the same side, she guessed that he would want to know as much about them as possible. They were a mixed bunch. Some wore army uniform, though it was shabby and unkempt. Others were in civilian clothes with the addition of the odd item of army equipment. There were boys who looked as if they might just have left their flock of goats and others who were still dressed for the city. All carried weapons of some sort, but among the modern army-issue rifles there were some that appeared to date from the previous war, and even one or two shotguns.

As she watched, Mario and some of his lieutenants began shouting orders and the men gathered their gear together, somewhat reluctantly, Frankie thought, and headed off in various directions. She went down the stairs and wandered casually after one group. No one seemed to be bothered by her presence and over the next hour or two she watched new recruits being drilled, others practising at an improvised firing range and a third group being taught unarmed combat by Captain Devenish.

The day dragged by. Bored with military activities, Frankie offered her help in the kitchen. The food was basic but there seemed to be enough to go round. After the midday meal she decided that she should try to get some rest, as it seemed unlikely that she would sleep much that night. She went up to her room and shook out the mattress and blankets, then sprinkled them liberally with anti-louse powder, but even so the attentions of their inmates gave her little chance to sleep. She dozed uneasily until voices in the yard below and the smell of cooking told her that evening had come. She went down and, ignoring the eyes that followed her, put her head under the pump.

The evening meal seemed to go on forever and was made more tedious by the fact that Mario chose to taunt her by pretending concern that there had been no response so far to his request for supplies. Devenish had been right, however, when he said that people went to bed early. Frankie helped with the clearing up, partly out of a sense of solidarity with Luisa and Paola and partly to reinforce the impression that she had accepted her incarceration. Then she followed Paola up to bed.

As on the previous evening, the other girl fell asleep almost instantly. Frankie fidgeted on her straw mattress, afraid that her restlessness would disturb her companion but unable to relax. She kept remembering the night at Overthorpe when Steve had gone to meet Roddy. What if she fell asleep, as Midge had done, and missed her rendezvous with Devenish? Ironically, now that sleep was forbidden her, she was so tired that even the biting of the bedbugs would not have kept her awake.

At last her watch showed ten minutes to midnight. Frankie crawled to the end of the bed and gathered up her outer clothes and her rucksack, then crept out onto the balcony that ran the length of the upper storey. The yard was deserted but she kept well back in the shadow of the overhanging roof while she pulled on her clothes. Then, with her rucksack on one shoulder and her boots in the other hand, she stole down the stairs and made her way to the kitchen door.

As she stepped inside a sound froze her to the spot – a sonorous, male snore. Frankie stood, feeling her whole body shaken by the pounding of her heart, and strained her eyes into the gloom. The kitchen range was still just alight and in its glow she made out half a dozen shrouded figures, stretched out on the floor or on the benches alongside the table. She clenched her teeth. Why had Devenish not warned her that some of Mario's men slept in the kitchen? Had he not known? Scarcely breathing, she tiptoed across the room and reached the farther door. To her relief it was slightly ajar and the lightest push swung it soundlessly open. Had Devenish oiled the hinges? She slipped through and almost ran down the passage. Outside the door to the storeroom she hesitated. Was Devenish waiting for her inside – or might she find Mario with a pistol in his hand? As she opened the door there was a scurrying sound and she almost cried aloud. Then she realised that the noise was made by mice – or perhaps rats. The thought made her skin creep but at least the room was empty apart from them. She pulled the door to behind her and waited in the faint moonlight from the dusty window.

She looked at her watch. Three minutes past midnight. She wondered what she would do if Devenish had overslept. She had no idea where his quarters were, so there was no possibility of waking him. A minute passed, then another. Then she jumped violently as the door swung open. She had not heard anyone approach.

Devenish came in carrying a torch, its light almost obliterated by his fingers. He nodded at her but she could not read his expression. Then she noticed that, apart from the torch, he was empty handed.

'My radio set?' she whispered.

For answer he lifted a sack in one corner and showed her the brown leather suitcase that contained the set.

'OK?' he whispered, and she nodded. 'Right, let's get going.'

Devenish climbed on the barrel and opened the window. Like the door, it gave easily and she realised that he must have found time when no one was about to oil these hinges too. He pointed to the suitcase and indicated that she should hand it up to him. As she did so, she saw that he had tied a piece of rope to the handle. He pushed the case through the window and lowered it gently to the ground. Then he held out his hand for the rucksack and dropped that after the case. He got down from the barrel and put his lips close to her ear.

'It's going to be difficult for you to get up to that window. You go first and I'll give you a boost from behind.'

Frankie nodded and climbed onto the barrel. Devenish was right. The window sill was about level with her shoulders. She gripped hold of it and felt his hands on her waist.

'On three,' he whispered. 'One, two . . .'

She jumped, pulling herself up and feeling him lifting her from below. She managed to get her head and shoulders out of the window, then felt his hand shift to her bottom. The thought flashed through her mind that her father would be furious if he could see her. She wriggled upward until she was lying across the window sill. The window was narrow and it was a struggle to squeeze her legs through but she succeeded and twisted her body so that she was hanging by her hands. The ground was about ten feet below her but that held no terrors after her parachute training. She let go and dropped with scarcely a thud onto thick grass. A moment later Devenish's head appeared above her, followed by his torso. There was no way he could twist a leg through, so he gripped the sill with both hands, pushed himself out head first and somersaulted to land beside her.

For a few minutes they stood silent, listening intensely to the sounds of the night. Crickets chirred and somewhere beyond the farm an owl called, but there were no noises of alarm. Frankie looked along the wall of the house towards the main gate and saw that, as Devenish had said, they were hidden from the sentries by the angle. Devenish touched her arm and pointed to a tumbledown stone wall running away from the building.

'This way,' he breathed. 'Keep down.'

He picked up the suitcase and Frankie shouldered her rucksack and followed him, bent double, across the grass to the shadow of the wall. Glancing back, she saw that from here the sentries could see them if they stood up. Devenish led the way forward, keeping close to the wall, until they dropped into a dip in the ground. There he straightened up and Frankie, gratefully, did likewise.

He caught her eye and nodded. There was a gleam in his eyes that suggested to her that the excitement of the adventure had overruled his doubts. 'Well done. It should be plain sailing from here on.'

Devenish climbed over the wall and Frankie, following, found herself on a stony track that led downhill through the forest. Fortunately the moon was almost full now and the trees were set far enough back from the path to allow its light to illuminate the uneven ground. Nevertheless, Frankie found herself stumbling more often than was comfortable. Devenish set a steady pace that made no concessions to her shorter legs and she was soon breathing hard with the effort of keeping up. He did not seem inclined to speak and for her part she was glad not to have to make conversation. The weight of the rucksack made her shoulders ache and spasms of pain ran up the muscles of her calves. From time to time she glanced at her watch. An hour passed, then another ten, fifteen, twenty minutes. She reminded herself of the books she had enjoyed as a teenager, the stories of John Buchan and Rider Haggard, and how often she had dreamed of having similar adventures. Well, she told herself, now you're having an adventure of your own. So stop whinging!

At length the path joined another, wider track running at right angles, and Devenish turned left along it. Here the ground was more level and Frankie saw that they were following the course of a river along a broader valley. The going was a little easier here, but before long Devenish veered off again, on to a smaller path that climbed steeply towards the shoulder of a hill. Frankie struggled upward, almost weeping with pain and exhaustion, but in spite of her efforts Devenish was getting farther and farther ahead. At last he seemed to realise that she was no longer just behind him and stopped to wait until she caught up.

'Sorry,' he said curtly. 'Forgot you're not used to this sort of thing. Here, give me that.' He took the rucksack from her and added, more gently, 'Not far now.'

A few minutes later they crested the shoulder and Devenish pointed ahead. 'Down there. See?'

They were above the trees now and on open ground covered in rocks and rough grass. Frankie strained her eyes and made out the dark shape of a house a few hundred yards below them. She breathed a silent prayer of gratitude.

As they approached a dog began to bark furiously and Devenish said, 'Keep back. Let me do the talking.'

A window was thrown open on the upper storey and a guttural voice shouted, 'Stand still, whoever you are. I warn you, I am armed. Come any closer and I'll shoot.'

Devenish called back in his English-accented Italian. 'It's me, Luigi, Captain Peter. I need your help. Don't worry. There's no danger. Please come down and let us in.'

'You? Come closer, so I can see you.'

Devenish stepped forward and shone his torch on his own

face and the speaker muttered something unintelligible and slammed the window shut. A moment later a door opened and a heavily built man appeared carrying an oil lamp. Devenish beckoned Frankie forward and she followed him into a room with walls of undressed stone and a floor of beaten earth. The smell of hay and dung and a stirring of movement from the other side of the wall told her that the rest of the ground floor was used for stabling the beasts.

The farmer set the lamp on the table and turned towards them. There was something about his ponderous movements and the way he carried his head lowered, his jaw thrust forward, that made Frankie think of a bull. Before Devenish could speak an inner door opened and a woman came in dressed in a voluminous nightgown that had once been white, followed by a younger man.

'Who's this? What's going on?' she demanded, her voice harsh and rough with sleep.

'It's the English captain,' the farmer replied. 'You remember.'

'And who's she?' The woman fixed Frankie with a stare that accused her of being no better than she ought to be.

Devenish said, 'This is Lieutenant Franconi. She is a British officer here on a special mission and she needs your help.'

While Devenish explained Frankie's objective she was uncomfortably aware that the younger man was watching her with a fixed stare. He had his father's heavy build, but whereas the older man's movements suggested controlled strength there was something uncoordinated about the son's. He was hollow cheeked and slack jawed and his head was crowned with a thatch of dark hair that looked as if it had never seen a comb. When Frankie caught his eyes he did not look away but met her gaze with a moist-lipped leer.

Devenish glossed over their reason for leaving Mario's

encampment in the middle of the night and instead pressed the urgency of Frankie's mission and its humanitarian purpose. When he finished the farmer grunted.

'So what do you want of us?'

'I want you to take the Lieutenant to Montefiorino. Father Antonio will take charge of her from there.'

'To Montefiorino? And how am I supposed to get there? I have no motor car, no jeep. Why can't you take her?'

'Because I have to return to my duties. And because Mario is not prepared to help her.'

'Why not?'

'He is not a God-fearing man like you, Signore Luigi. We both understand the duties of a Christian. But what can you expect of a communist like Mario?'

Not just a pretty face after all, Frankie thought.

Luigi regarded Frankie in silence for a moment. Then he said, 'Very well. I will see that she gets to Montefiorino. Leave it to me.'

'Thank you. And here is some money towards any expenses.'

Devenish handed over some notes, which the farmer pocketed with a grunt, and turned to Frankie.

'I've got to get going. If I'm missing when Mario wakes up he'll know I helped you escape.'

Frankie followed him to the door. She did not particularly like Devenish, but the thought of being left alone with these strangers filled her with horror.

'Couldn't you take me?' She knew the answer before she spoke but she could not stop herself.

'You know I can't. You'll be all right with Luigi. He's a rough sort of cove, but he's honest. He'll get you to Montefiorino. When you get there, go straight to the priest's house. Father Antonio will look after you.' He reached out and touched her arm. 'Good luck. I hope you find Harper on the mend. Get HQ to send me a signal telling me how you got on. 'Bye.'

She watched him walk away into the darkness and then turned back into the house, where the family waited for her with suspicious, resentful eyes.

Chapter Twelve

A sense of imminent danger dragged Frankie unwillingly from her sleep. She stirred and groaned at the pain of stiff, cramped muscles. As soon as Devenish had left, the farmer's wife had thrust a blanket smelling strongly of dog into her hands and nodded at a broken-down easy chair in front of the kitchen range.

'You can sleep there.'

With that, she had stomped off upstairs and after a moment's hesitation the two men had followed. Frankie had been hoping for something to eat, or at least a drink, after the long walk, but since neither seemed forthcoming she had made herself as comfortable as she could and fallen into an uneasy doze that had gradually deepened into a profound sleep. Now she forced her eyes open. The farmer's son was standing a few feet away from her, his hand thrust down the front of his trousers, working vigorously.

Frankie struggled upright. 'What do you want?' she demanded. The answer was obvious but it was the first thing that came into her head.

The boy was unabashed. His face broke into a leer and he uttered a low, guttural laugh. Then he turned away and went out of the door leading to the yard. Frankie started to get to her feet and was checked by the sensation of something hard digging into her thigh. She remembered that her last action before settling down for the night had been to dig the pistol out of her rucksack and slip it into her trouser pocket. For the first time, she felt glad to have it. She looked around her. Her watch showed a few minutes after six. Pale sunlight slanted in through a dusty window pane, lighting the room, and for the first time she saw how mean and basic it was. Apart from the rusty iron stove and the chair she had slept in the only furniture was a rough wooden table and two benches. There were a couple of rush mats on the earthen floor and a few battered pans hung on hooks above the stove. The only attempt at decoration was a crude figure of the Virgin standing on a high shelf in one corner.

Frankie felt humbled. She thought she had seen poverty among her neighbours in Liverpool, but that had been nothing compared with this. No wonder they resented having her thrust on them in the middle of the night, with the demand on their time and resources required to get her to her destination.

Footsteps descended the stairs and the woman came in, dressed now in the universal dark cotton dress of the Italian peasant woman. Frankie wished her good morning and she nodded in reply.

'There's water in the well. Fill this while you're at it.'

Frankie took the bucket that was thrust at her and fetched her washing kit from her rucksack. At the door she hesitated, looking around, afraid that she might come face to face with the son. To her relief, as she watched he came out of the byre, leading a donkey and a couple of nanny goats, and disappeared round the corner of the house. Farther away, she saw the farmer, already at work hoeing a patch of stony ground between rows of straggly tomato plants. She left her bucket by the well and found the privy, which was if anything more primitive than the one at Mario's farm. Then she returned, drew a bucket of water, sluiced her face and neck and scrubbed her teeth. Remembering the woman's injunction, she refilled the bucket and carried it back into the house.

Breakfast consisted of dry bread dipped in a little olive oil and a small cup of goat's milk. Frankie had just finished eating when the farmer came in, followed by his son.

'Good morning, signore.' Frankie made an effort to be polite. 'When can we leave for Montefiorino, please?'

Luigi jerked his head in the direction of his son. 'Enzo will take you. He doesn't say much but he knows the way. You'll be there by tonight.'

Frankie swallowed hard. The thought of being alone on the hills with that lout appalled her but she could think of no way of voicing her objection.

Luigi went on, addressing the boy. 'Fetch the donkey and load the signora's baggage on him.' Then to her, 'You can leave as soon as your stuff is loaded.'

Frankie watched as the case containing the radio set and her rucksack were strapped to the donkey's back and wished that she could climb on as well. She had said to Devenish that she would walk to Montefiorino if necessary but after the previous night's trek she was painfully aware of what a foolish boast that had been. She had never walked more than a mile or two, and then usually on city streets. The early morning runs at Overthorpe had toughened her up temporarily but that had been long ago and, though she had swum and played a bit of tennis at Cap Matifou, since her transfer to Monopoli she had done little but sit in front of her radio set. Now her feet were blistered and every muscle in her body ached. She had been counting on the farmer having some means of transport but clearly this one small donkey was the limit of his resources. At least, she told herself, she didn't have to carry the rucksack.

Enzo looked across at her with his familiar loose-lipped grin. 'We go now.'

Frankie told herself that, although not very bright, he was probably quite harmless and forced herself to smile back. 'Yes, I'm ready. Let's go.'

The woman said, 'Enzo, remember. You can tell Father Antonio that you did your duty.'

Frankie thanked the farmer and his wife for their help and followed Enzo and the donkey down the rough track that led downward again towards the valley. After a while her stiff muscles began to loosen up and she was able to enjoy the scenery. It was still early and the air was clear and fresh. She had never been in the mountains before and the sight of the jagged peaks rising around her, some of them still topped with snow, their slopes covered in dark forests of pine and chestnut, made her feel like something out of the Heidi books she had devoured as a child. As long as they were going downhill the walking was easy and she reasoned that Montefiorino was probably in the valley so the chances were that it would be downhill all the way. She thought of Nick and tried to project her thoughts to him. Hold on, my darling! I'm coming. I'm nearly there!

Abruptly, Enzo turned off the main path onto a narrower track that contoured around the hillside. The donkey obviously did not agree with this change of direction and balked, causing the boy to come to a sharp halt. He swore at it and began to belabour it with a stick, while Frankie looked around. The path leading down into the valley was obviously the more used and she found herself agreeing with the donkey.

'Are you sure this is the right way?' she asked.

Enzo stopped hitting the donkey long enough to grin at her. 'Germans down there. Better this way.'

That made sense and when the donkey reluctantly gave in and set off in the new direction Frankie followed. Soon the path began to climb again. Enzo walked ahead, leading the donkey, apparently indifferent to her company. The sun grew hotter and Frankie began to sweat. It was a relief when Enzo halted under the shade of a lone thorn tree and tied the donkey to one of the branches. He glanced up at the sun, which was now directly overhead.

'We eat now.'

He undid a sack that had been tied across the donkey's back with the rest of the gear and took out a loaf of bread, a small piece of hard cheese and a few olives and tomatoes. Frankie dropped to the ground and wondered if she dared take off her boots. Her feet were throbbing but she was afraid that once she took her boots off she would never get them on again. Enzo held out a leather flask.

'Drink.'

Frankie looked around for some kind of receptacle to drink from but the boy mimed drinking from the neck of the flask. Frankie was repelled by the idea of sharing it with him but there seemed to be no other way and she was desperately thirsty. She lifted the flask and tipped some of the contents into her mouth. It was water mixed with sour red wine and tepid but she swallowed it gladly. The bread was dry and the cheese fit only for a mousetrap but she forced them down, glad of the extra moisture provided by the tomatoes. And after the first tremor of disgust, she found she no longer cared that Enzo had just had the neck of the drinking flask in his mouth.

As they ate she tried to make conversation with her companion but all her remarks were greeted either with a suspicious sideways look or the now familiar inane grin and giggle. Far too soon, Enzo returned the remains of the food to the sack and untied the donkey.

'Come!'

'Is it much farther?' Frankie asked, struggling to her feet. But he merely shrugged and turned away.

All afternoon they walked. Occasionally they passed a shepherd with his flock or a boy herding a few goats and once or twice Frankie made out the roofs of isolated cottages among the trees below them, but nothing that could possibly be a village. Once they heard a low rumbling from the valley below and Enzo pointed downward to where a section of road could be seen running alongside the river. A column of vehicles was moving slowly along it.

'Germans,' Enzo said, and tapped his forehead as if applauding his own sagacity.

At length, when the sun was almost touching the rim of the mountain range to the west, Enzo led the way down into a small valley, at the head of which a spring welled up from the base of a rock to form a pool before trickling away as a shallow stream. Beside the pool was a rough hut built from wooden hurdles interwoven with bracken. Enzo led the donkey to it and began to unload the luggage.

'Dark soon,' he said, pointing to the sky. 'We sleep here.'

'But your father said we would be in Montefiorino by night-fall,' Frankie protested.

He looked at her slyly. 'Germans down there. Too dangerous on the road.'

'Where is it?' Frankie demanded. 'Which way?'

He pointed down the valley. 'That way.'

'How far?'

'Three hours. Four.'

Frankie was ready to weep with frustration but there was obviously no point in arguing and she was too tired to go on, anyway. She turned away and went to the side of the pool. The water was icy cold and tasted of moss. After she had slaked her thirst she sluiced her face and hands and then eased off her boots and lowered her blistered feet into the water. The shock of it almost made her cry aloud but after a moment the pain eased and was replaced by a delicious numbness. She looked up and realised that Enzo was watching her, his mouth open and a trickle of spittle drooling from his bottom lip.

He turned away when he saw her looking and busied himself hauling a couple of blankets out of his sack and taking them into the hut. Then he set out the rest of the food. There was nothing apart from what they had left at midday and Frankie suspected that Enzo's mother had given him only enough for a journey she expected to be finished by nightfall. She was beginning to wonder whether there was not a much shorter route that they could have taken without encountering a German patrol. Had Enzo deliberately brought her out of the way, so that they would be forced to spend a night alone on the mountain?

It was a poor meal but Frankie was too tired and too anxious to eat much. Enzo swallowed his share and then finished off what she had left. Then he took himself off behind the hut and she heard him relieving himself as copiously, it seemed to her ears, as the donkey. It was almost dark now, and when he returned she followed his example, peering anxiously into the twilight, half expecting to see him watching her. When she reappeared he pushed open the door of the hut and beckoned her inside. In the gloom she could just make out the two blankets spread side by side. The hut was very small and too low roofed for either of them to stand upright, and at this close proximity she could smell his unwashed body. She contemplated taking her blanket outside and saying she preferred to sleep under the stars but now that the sun was down the mountain air was cold and anyway she was too frightened to sleep without the protection of a roof over her head.

Enzo nodded at the blankets. 'Sleep now.' He simpered at her and pulled off his shirt, revealing a filthy vest. After a moment Frankie lay down, fully dressed. Enzo knelt on his blanket and reached over to pull at her tunic.

'You take off.'

Frankie shook her head.

'Yes,' he reiterated. 'You take off now.'

'No!' Frankie said.

He moved closer to her, reaching for the buttons. He lowered his voice to a throaty whisper. 'You take off. We make love now.'

'No, Enzo!' she said, pushing at him. 'I'm not that sort of girl. I've got a fiancé. I'm keeping myself for him.'

'You a virgin?' he asked sceptically.

'Yes,' she lied.

He shook his head. 'No. Good girls don't do like you. Good girls stay at home, wear dresses, not trousers.' His hand tugged at her belt. 'You be nice to Enzo and Enzo take you to Montefiorino.'

'Stop it!' She tried to roll away from him but he moved on top of her, pinning her down with his weight. 'Enzo, leave me alone. What will your father say when he finds out?'

'You be nice and Enzo take you where you want to go,' he repeated. 'If not, he take you to the Germans. Tell them he caught a spy!'

Frankie stopped struggling as the force of his words hit her. She was completely at his mercy. Without him to guide her she might wander for days, and if he chose to deliver her to the Germans there was nothing she could do to stop him. He interpreted her sudden passivity as consent and began to drag at her clothing, ripping the buttons from her tunic. His breath was foul and the smell of him nauseated her. Instinctively she began to struggle again, but he was twice her weight and muscled like an ox. His rough hands found her breasts, pulling and pinching, and then shifted to the waistband of her slacks.

She felt the fabric rip and the elastic of her knickers cut into her flesh as he yanked at them. Then, as she rolled to one side in an attempt to avoid him, she felt the hard lump of her pistol against her hip. His hand was between her legs and he laughed in her ear.

'Not a virgin! Oh no! Bad girl!'

Then, for a second, he half released her to fumble with the fastenings of his own trousers. She seized her chance and brought her knee up hard into his groin. As he grunted with pain she wriggled free and pulled the gun from her pocket, thumbing off the safety catch as if this were second nature.

'Get away from me or I'll shoot you,' she panted, levelling the gun at him. He glowered at her, breathing hard, and in the momentary stalemate the question flickered across her mind as to what she should do next. Could she stay awake all night to watch him? And if she did, could she trust him to guide her to the right place the next morning?

He resolved the problem by lunging at her with an animal growl. She felt him grab at her wrist and once again his weight pressed her back against the ground. Whether she deliberately pulled the trigger or whether it happened by accident in the struggle she did not know but the report seemed to shatter her eardrums and the force pressing her down became a dead weight. For a moment she lay still, dazed and breathless. Then she felt something warm and wet trickling over her breasts. With a cry of revulsion, she wriggled free and Enzo slumped to the ground, inert.

Whimpering with shock, Frankie scrambled across the hut to where her rucksack stood in the corner and dragged out the contents until she found her torch. With hands that shook so much that she could hardly hold the beam steady, she turned the light on Enzo. He was lying prone, his trousers pulled down so that his bare buttocks gleamed obscenely in the light.

She crawled across and pulled at his arm. He was heavy and it was all she could do to turn him over. When she succeeded the sight caused her to turn away and vomit into a corner. The gun had torn a gaping hole in the side of his chest from which blood no longer pumped but welled slowly. Whether he was alive or dead was not in question.

Somehow Frankie crawled across his body to the door and escaped into the clean night air. She sank down into a crouching position, her back against the wall of the hut and her arms wrapped around her knees, whimpering and keening like an animal. For a long time she stayed there, incapable of thought, until the cold roused her. She got to her feet and saw the moonlight reflected in the little pool. The sight triggered a raging thirst and she staggered to the edge of the water and thrust her hands into it. In the faint light she could see a dark substance rising in lazy spirals from her fingers and she retched again and scrubbed at them until there was no sign of blood. Then she cupped her hands and drank draught after draught of the icy water.

By the time she had slaked her thirst she was shivering violently. She turned back to the hut but stopped at the door. Every instinct urged on her the overriding need for warmth and rest. In the last three days she had not slept for more than three or four hours each night and the long walk had taxed her endurance to the utmost. But how could she sleep with that . . . thing lying there? Gritting her teeth, she grabbed Enzo's body by the feet. It took all her remaining strength to drag him out of the hut. Crawling inside, she realised that the blanket she had lain on was soaked in blood, but Enzo's had remained relatively clean. She pulled it over to the other side of the hut, as far away as it was possible to get from the bloody mess on the ground. Her gun was lying where she had dropped it and she picked it up and closed her fingers around it. Then she wrapped herself in the blanket, pillowed her head on her ruck-sack and almost instantly lost consciousness.

A low, insistent droning woke her, a sound that rose and fell in volume but never ceased. She opened her eyes. Sunlight was coming in through the cracks in the roof and dust motes danced in the beams. She was warm and rested and for a second she experienced a sense of ease. Then she turned her head in search of the source of the noise and bile rose in her throat. The blood-soaked blanket and the pool on the floor were a solid dark mass of flies.

Frankie got to her feet, stooping under the low roof, and edged towards the door. She needed to get away from the sound and the stench but she knew that worse waited for her outside. For a moment she almost made herself believe that she would find nothing, or that Enzo would be there loading the donkey ready to continue the journey. She stepped over the bloody mess on the floor and out into the sunshine. The body was where she had left it, just outside, and the cavernous wound was also black with flies. She turned away and went to the pool, where she washed her hands again and drank. In the process she became aware that her uniform tunic was in tatters and stained with blood and her trousers were hanging around her thighs because the fastenings were ripped away. She could smell her own body odours mingled with Enzo's sweat. She looked around. The glade was empty and there was no sign of life on the hills above. She stripped off all her clothes and stepped into the pool, gasping as the water struck her skin but sluicing and scrubbing with a manic determination until she felt she had washed all traces of the previous night from her body.

There was obviously no point in trying to put on the clothes she had been wearing so she walked, naked, to the hut and forced herself to go inside once more to retrieve her rucksack and the precious radio set in its case. She dug in the sack and found the bundle she had obtained from the woman at the corner shop. Inside were a simple dark cotton dress, well worn, a headscarf and a pair of down-at-heel shoes. They were the sort of clothes any poor Italian woman might wear. Frankie found her one change of clean underwear, put on the dress, combed her hair and tied the scarf over it, knotting it at the back of her neck as she had seen the local women do. Then she pushed her raw and swollen feet into the shoes.

Her investigations in the rucksack had revealed another half-forgotten item – the emergency rations she had been issued with before the parachute drop. There were some hard biscuits, a tin of sardines, a packet of glucose sweets and a small tin of Horlicks tablets. The sight reminded Frankie that she had eaten very little the previous day. She hobbled over to where Enzo's sack lay by the wall of the hut and searched inside. He had obviously been saving some provisions for the return journey. There was another piece of cheese and some olives. She took them back to the pool and, sitting on a flat rock with her back to the hut and the body, she began to eat. Once she started it was hard to stop, but she made herself save the sardines and some of the biscuits and half the sweets.

The food made her feel better and she began to think about what to do next. Her mind was surprisingly clear and focused. At some deeper level of consciousness she was aware that a time would come when she would have to confront what she had done, but for now all that mattered were the practicalities of the situation.

Plainly, she was on her own from here. Enzo had said last night that Montefiorino was somewhere down below them and it seemed reasonable to assume that the little stream ran down to join the river in the valley. And in the valley there was a road, which must surely lead to Montefiorino. So all she had to do was follow the stream. She could take the donkey – there was no point in leaving it here – so she wouldn't have to carry her baggage. The village, she reasoned, could not be very far away.

There was one major problem. What was she to do with the body? She could not simply leave it where it lay, to be torn apart by carrion eaters. Already she could see two dark birds circling overhead and guessed that they must be vultures. The rocky ground was too hard for her to dig a grave, even if she had a spade. She thought the best thing she could do would be to drag it back inside the hut.

Looking at the hut gave her a new idea. Among her emergency supplies was a box of matches, and the timber and bracken were tinder dry. She got up, wincing at the pain in her feet, and went to one side of the building. The main uprights were too firmly fixed for her to move but the fine branches and bracken woven between them were easy to pull away. She heaped them into the interior, working until there was only a skeleton left. Then, conquering her revulsion, she dragged Enzo's body into the middle of the heap. After a moment's thought she added her own torn clothes, retaining only her boots and the identity discs she wore on a chain round her neck. She fetched the donkey, which was grazing placidly, tethered to a stunted tree on the far side of the stream, and with some difficulty fastened her baggage to the panniers slung across its back. Then she took out the box of matches, lit one and dropped it into the pile. It caught at once and began to flare up. When it was well alight she took hold of the donkey's halter and set off down the valley.

She looked back once, to see the ribs of the structure standing out against a pyramid of flame. She had no idea how much fuel was needed to consume a body, but it seemed to her that she had done all that she could. She turned her face away and plodded onward.

About midday the faint track she had been following came out onto a broad unpaved road. It was not the main road she had seen from the hill the day before, which she now realised was on the opposite side of the river, but it was obviously well used. She decided to eat before joining it and sat down in the shade to consume the sardines and the remainder of the biscuits. Then she stood and looked along the road in both directions, uncertain which way to turn. To go right would be to go back in the opposite direction to the way they had travelled yesterday, so left seemed the obvious way. But on the other hand she was now convinced that Enzo had deliberately taken her by a circuitous route, so it was possible that the village was now behind her. Finally, she decided to follow her instincts and turn left.

She had not gone very far before she heard the sound of an engine behind her. She stopped and turned eagerly towards it. Surely she would be able to flag down the driver and ask whether she was going the right way. She might even get a lift. The donkey would be able to take care of itself. The noise came closer and then the vehicle appeared round a bend in the road. It was a motorcycle and sidecar and the driver and passenger wore the uniform of German soldiers. Frankie's first instinct was to dive into the trees and hide but she knew she must already have been seen and nothing would be more likely to arouse suspicions, so she lowered her head and plodded on. She had her story ready, but what would happen if the soldiers demanded her papers? What if they decided to search her baggage?

The motorcycle slowed as it approached her and Frankie forced herself not to look round. Then a piercing wolf whistle sounded above the noise of the engine. Instinctively she glanced round and met the blue eyes of a young soldier.

'Hey!' he shouted. *'Bella bambina!'*

Then he revved his engine and accelerated away in a cloud of dust. Frankie's heart was thudding but she told herself that she had had no need to be afraid. A simple peasant girl leading a donkey. They must pass a dozen of those every day. Why should they bother with her?

With every bend in the road she hoped to see some sign of habitation but the way wound on through the forest, which restricted her view to a few hundred yards in any direction. She began to be afraid that she had chosen the wrong direction and that she might still be no nearer civilisation when night fell. To add to her problems the donkey, which had followed her docilely all morning, now seemed to feel it had gone far enough and kept stopping, unmoved by all efforts at persuasion, so that she was reduced to walloping it with a stick broken from one of the shrubs beside the path. And all the time the thought beat at the back of her mind that every hour that passed might be bringing Nick closer to death.

Eventually, she came to a place where a small stream ran through a culvert under the road. The donkey tugged obstinately towards it so she let it pick its way down the bank and followed. After she and the donkey had slaked their thirst, Frankie sat down, took off her shoes and trailed her feet in the water. They were red raw after walking so far in shoes worn down by someone else and she had contemplated changing them for her boots, but she knew that one glance at these would proclaim to anyone she met that she was not what she was trying to appear. She was still trying to pluck up the courage to put her shoes on and press on when she heard footsteps on the road behind her. A tall, sturdily built middle-aged man was coming towards her. In one hand he swung a long-handled axe and in the other a pair of dead rabbits. It was too late to take cover, so Frankie sat still and returned his *Buona sera'* with what she hoped was a suitable blend of modesty and self-assurance.

He stood above her on the road and looked down. 'Come far?'

'Yes, a long way.'

'Where from?'

Frankie waved her hand vaguely behind her. 'I can't remember the name of the village where I stayed last night.'

'Last night? You're on a long journey, then.'

'Yes.'

'Going where?'

'Is there a place near here called Montefiorino?'

'Yes. Straight ahead.'

'How far?'

'Oh, an hour, maybe a bit more. Is that where you're headed?'

'Yes.'

'Do you mind if I ask why?'

'I'm looking for my fiancé. He was in the army but I heard he deserted when the Germans ordered them north. I was told he might be here somewhere.'

The man jumped down from the road and joined her on the bank of the river. His broad, open face was creased in a frown.

'And you've come all this way to look for him. Where are you from?'

'Naples.' Frankie had been told by her grandmother that she had inherited her Neapolitan accent. 'When the British and the Americans attacked there was a lot of fighting. The Germans destroyed many houses before they left. My house was bombed. My parents were both killed. I have no one now. So I came to look for Gianni.'

'Poor girl!' he exclaimed. 'What a story! German pigs!' He turned his head away and spat. 'But what makes you think your Gianni is here?'

'A friend who was with him got home to Naples. He told me that Gianni was wounded and could not walk, so he stayed here in Montefiorino. He said Gianni told him that when he was strong enough he might join the partisans. Do you think that is possible?'

She saw a minute change in the man's expression, a faint closing of the mouth and narrowing of the eyes. He knew something about the partisans, something he was not prepared to give away. 'Maybe,' he said curtly. Then he added, 'If you're going to Montefiorino we could walk along together. My house is that way.'

Frankie hesitated, but there was something reassuring about this man that made her want to trust him. And the prospect of company, at least for part of the way, was appealing. She got up and reached for her shoes, but the pain of forcing her feet into them was too much. Her head swam and she would have fallen if the man had not caught her round the waist.

'*Povera piccina!*' she heard him murmur. 'Look at your feet! Come, you must ride the donkey. I will carry your case.'

Still barely conscious, she let him half carry her up to the road, pulling the unwilling beast after him. Then, before she could protest, he had unstrapped the suitcase, exclaiming as he felt the weight of it.

'Santa Maria! What have you got in here?'

'Everything I possess,' she said tragically. 'Everything I could salvage from the ruins of my home.'

He seemed to accept the explanation and set the case down. 'Up you go!' He lifted her as if she weighed no more than a child and set her on the donkey's back. 'Now, you will stay the night with us. My wife will look after you. You can't walk the rest of the way to Montefiorino in this state.'

'But I must!' Frankie cried. 'I must find Gianni.'

The man laughed. 'If he's waited for you this long another night isn't going to kill him.'

She wanted to say that it might do just that, but she kept silent. He slung the rabbits into one of the panniers, took hold of the donkey's halter and set off along the road, carrying the case and his axe in his free hand.

'By the way,' he went on. 'My name is Roberto. I'm a wood-cutter – as you can see.'

'My name is Gina,' she told him, and he nodded and smiled.

The relief of not having to walk anymore was so great that Frankie put all her other anxieties to the back of her mind. She was not going to have to spend the night alone in the forest and at least she was heading in the right direction. Tomorrow she would reach Montefiorino.

Before long they came to a clearing in which stood a log cabin. Smoke was rising from the chimney and in a little patch of ground beside the house vegetables and a few marigolds grew. A goat was tethered a short way off and half a dozen chickens scratched around the doorway. To Frankie it looked like something out of a children's storybook. Roberto shouted and a tiny, dark-haired woman appeared in the doorway.

'Anna, come here,' he called. 'We have a guest. She needs your help.'

The woman came towards them, clucking and cooing like one of her hens. Frankie was lifted down from the donkey's back and helped into the single room that constituted the whole of the cabin. There was an open fire in a huge stone fire-place, some basic furniture and a ladder leading up to a sleeping platform at the back. Now that she was safe, for the time being at any rate, exhaustion swept over her like a wave and she gave up trying to fight it. Water was set before her and a small glass of something that caught at her throat and made her choke but left a warm glow in the pit of her stomach. She was dimly aware of her host and hostess bustling about. Anna skinned the rabbits and placed them on a spit above the glowing embers. Roberto brought in a tin bath, which he set before the fire and filled with warm water from a huge cauldron hanging over it. As soon as he had finished Anna shooed him out of the room with the instruction to go and feed the hens. Then she came to Frankie.

'Now, *piccina*. Let me help you to undress. The bath water is ready. You will feel better after that.'

Frankie, once so bashful, allowed herself to be stripped and helped into the bath. It hurt her feet to begin with but that passed and she sat back, luxuriating in the warm water. Anna brought her a cloth and some coarse soap and helped her to wash. By the time Roberto returned, she was clean and dry and dressed in a cotton nightgown that had been washed so many times it felt as soft as silk. Before long the rabbits were cooked and there was a fragrant ragout of vegetables and herbs to go with them. Frankie would have turned up her nose at the idea of eating rabbit a year or two ago but that night she thought she had never tasted anything so delicious.

While they ate her host and hostess questioned her about the fall of Naples and her journey from there.

'You haven't walked all that way!' Anna marvelled.

'No, no. I got lifts to begin with, with the British soldiers mostly. Until we got to the front line.'

'How did you get through, past the Germans?'

'I bribed a man to show me a path through the mountains. He sold me the donkey, too.'

Much of this she had concocted in her mind during the walk, in case she needed to explain herself. But she was glad to fall back on extreme tiredness as an excuse for not going into details. As soon as they had finished eating Anna said, 'Now you must sleep. Come, I will show you where.'

She led Frankie to an alcove under the sleeping platform, which was screened off by a couple of old sacks in lieu of a curtain. In it was a bed.

'This is where our son, Tommaso, slept,' Anna said, 'until the Germans came for him.'

Frankie wanted to ask why the Germans had come and what had happened to Tommaso, but Anna murmured 'goodnight' and left her before she had the chance. Frankie pulled back the blanket and stretched out on the almost unbelievable luxury of a feather mattress. For a short while she heard Roberto and Anna talking softly and moving around the cabin. Then the ladder creaked as they mounted it and the lamplight that had filtered through cracks in the planks above her went out. She closed her eyes and let herself sink into sleep.

Chapter Thirteen

In the middle of the night Frankie woke suddenly, with an overwhelming sense of distress. Her little cubby-hole was pitch dark and she lifted the sacking aside to let in a gleam of light from the dying fire. Above her, she could hear the regular, heavy breathing of Roberto. She remembered that she had been dreaming and that the dream had something to do with Enzo and a fire. She burrowed down into her pillow, trying to force herself to think of something else, but the images would not go away. Like someone forced to watch again and again the film of a terrible event, her brain replayed the events of the previous night. She saw Enzo's face leering at her, smelt the odour of his unwashed body, felt his hands groping her. And each time the replay ended with the explosion of the gun and the sight of that gaping hole in Enzo's chest. I am a murderer, she told herself. I have taken a human life.

She thought of Enzo's parents waiting for him to come home. Would they search for him when he did not return? Did Luigi know of the shepherd's hut? She imagined him going there and finding the burnt-out hut and the charred remains of his son's body. Or would they never find him, never know what had happened to him? Would they report his disappearance to the police and would the police then come looking for her? But the police were the Brigata Nera, the Blackshirts who supported the Nazis. How could Luigi go to them without admitting that he was guilty of aiding an enemy agent? She wished she could explain what had happened, apologise and ask for forgiveness, but she could think of no way to contact them. Even if she wrote a letter, she had no idea of the address to send it to.

She asked herself if she could have acted differently. Could she have talked Enzo out of his intention? She knew that would have been useless. Then perhaps she should simply have let him have his way. At least then his blood would not have been on her hands. But her whole being revolted at the thought. And how was she to be sure that he would not have killed her afterwards, to prevent her from telling anyone what he had done? Or worse, he might still have handed her over to the Germans. She had done what she did, she told herself, in order to carry out her mission – in order to save Nick. She had wanted to preserve herself for him. How could she have given herself to him with the memory of that violation? But how could she offer herself now, with the memory of her mortal guilt?

Eventually her desperate need for sleep overcame the anguished circling of her thoughts, and when she woke again it was morning and her mood was different. She was safe, she had found friends and soon she would reach Montefiorino. After that it could only be a matter of hours before she got to Nick. She could hear Roberto and Anna talking quietly on the other side of the curtain. Her clothes were on the end of the bed and she wriggled into them, with some difficulty in the confined space, and then drew back the sacking to greet her host and hostess.

Roberto and Anna were standing on the far side of the table, looking at her. On the table between her and them were the suitcase containing her radio set and her rucksack. Both were open.

Roberto said hoarsely, 'Who are you? What do you want?'

Frankie stared at him, her mouth dry, her stomach in a knot. It had seemed that he disliked the Germans but that might have been a pose. Even if it were true, would he be prepared to risk helping a British agent? She knew that the German revenge on those they suspected of treachery was terrible. Then she recalled Anna's voice when she said that her son had slept in that bed 'until the Germans took him' and decided that she must trust her instincts.

She stood up and moved to the table. 'My name is Gina Franconi. I am a British officer.' (Even now the words seemed strange, as if she were playing a part.) 'I have to find another officer who has been working with the partisans and who has been wounded. I believe he is in this area somewhere and that Father Antonio, the village priest at Montefiorino, can take me to him.'

Roberto and Anna exchanged looks. 'Franconi?' he said. 'That is not an English name.'

'No. My grandfather came from Naples but I was born in England.'

'Can you prove that you are a British officer?'

For answer Frankie went to the rucksack and pulled out the identity discs that she had hidden in a side pocket. She handed them to Roberto, who scrutinised them with a frown. She guessed that he had no idea whether they were genuine or not. An inspiration struck her.

'Look in my boots. You'll see that they were made in England.'

Anna pulled the boots out of the rucksack and handed them to Roberto. He looked at them and nodded, then raised his eyes to Frankie.

'This officer you are looking for. What is his name?'

Frankie hesitated. Was he trying to pump her for information to pass on to the Germans? But Nick was not here under cover so what harm could it do to reveal his name?

'Major Harper,' she said. 'Major Nick Harper.'

Roberto's face broke into a grin. 'But why did you not tell us all this to start with? We all know about Major Nick! He fights with Luciano and his group.'

'You know him?' Frankie repeated breathlessly. 'He is still alive?'

'I don't know. I heard he was wounded, no more than that.'

'Are you supporters of Luciano?' Frankie asked.

'We are all supporters of Luciano here,' Roberto said. 'He got rid of the Brigata Nera and took over the police post. The mayor is one of Luciano's men and Father Antonio is with him. They run Montefiorino now, not the Nazis.'

'That's very impressive,' Frankie said. 'I knew they were doing well but I didn't realise they were in complete control. Can you take me to Father Antonio?'

He nodded. 'Yes, we will go at once. Father Antonio has a car. He can take you to where Major Nick is. Come, sit down and eat. I will harness the mule.'

Anna set bread and cheese and goat's milk on the table and Frankie ate quickly. By the time she had finished Roberto had harnessed the mule to a rough cart and loaded her belongings into it. As she left, Anna embraced her and invoked the blessing of the Holy Virgin upon her, and Frankie thanked her for her hospitality with tears in her eyes. Then Roberto helped her up into the cart, took the mule by the bridle and set off down the track.

As he had predicted, in a little over an hour the road took a sudden turn to the right and dropped down a slope to an old stone bridge over the river. Beyond it Frankie saw the village, a jumble of red roofs and white walls climbing a low hill to the church set among the bushes of oleander that had obviously given the place its name.

As they approached Frankie heard the church bell begin to toll and saw people hurrying up the narrow streets.

'Is something happening?' she asked.

Roberto looked round with a grin. 'It's Sunday. Have you forgotten? People are going to mass.'

As they made their way up the hill several people greeted him and looked curiously at Frankie.

'My wife's cousin,' he explained cheerily. 'Here for a visit.'

At the church Roberto tethered the mule and helped Frankie down. 'The Father will be saying mass. We shall have to wait until after the service.'

He led the way into the little church and they took seats in one of the rear pews. The service began and Frankie felt a painful nostalgia as the familiar litany unfolded – nostalgia for her home and her parents but also for her lost faith. When the congregation went forward to take communion she stayed seated. How could she partake of the Body of Christ when she no longer believed in Him or his Heavenly Father? And even if she had believed, she was not in a state of grace. It would be blasphemy to partake when she was burdened with the most heinous sin of all, the taking of a human life. She hid her face in her hands and felt the tears trickling between her fingers.

At the end of the service, as the congregation filed out, Roberto touched her arm.

'Come. We will find Father Antonio in the vestry.'

Father Antonio was a big man, built more like a heavyweight boxer than a priest. He greeted Roberto affably and then looked enquiringly at Frankie.

'Father,' Roberto said, 'this is Gina Franconi. She is a British officer who has been sent to help Major Nick.'

The priest's bland expression changed to one of sharp concentration.

'Why are you not in uniform?'

Once again, Frankie decided against going into detail. 'There was an accident. It got torn. And anyway I had to find my way here and I thought I would be safer like this.'

She showed him her identity discs and the radio set, which she had insisted on bringing into the church with her. He asked some searching questions about where she had been dropped and why she was alone, and when she explained about Mario's refusal to let her leave he nodded grimly.

'That does not surprise me. He is a godless man, interested in nothing but his own aggrandisement. Very well, give me a moment to change and I will take you to Luciano. There is no time to be lost.'

He pulled off his surplice and Frankie was astounded to see that under it, strapped around his waist, he wore a pistol in a holster. Seeing her surprise, he smiled.

'It is not fitting that one should celebrate the Holy Office wearing a gun. But circumstances alter cases. The Germans have left us alone for some time but one day they will return, and if they do I do not intend to let them take me alive. I know too much.'

On that grim note he led them outside to where his small car was parked. Frankie's equipment was loaded into the boot and she kissed Roberto on both cheeks in farewell. A moment later they were heading out of the village and into the hills beyond.

'We have to cross a main road,' the priest said. 'Normally it is clear but occasionally there are patrols. If we meet one let me do the talking.'

'Have we far to go?' Frankie asked.

'No, not far. We shall be there within the hour.'

Frankie asked, 'Do you know Major Harper?'

'Yes, I know him. He is a brave man and a good friend to Italy.'

'Have you seen him recently?'

'I saw him two days ago.'

'How was he?'

'Very ill. The doctor has done all he can for him but his resources are limited and all the hospitals are controlled by the Nazis.' He glanced sideways at her. 'He is more than just a fellow officer to you.'

There seemed to be no point in lying. 'We are to be married,' she answered, and was aware that it was the first time she had actually spoken the words.

The priest nodded. 'Then we must pray that we are in time.'

Frankie looked at the burly figure beside her. Could she confess to this man? And would it help if she did?

Before she could make any decision the priest said, 'We are coming to the junction with the main road now. Let us pray that we are in luck.'

The car rounded a bend and Father Antonio exclaimed under his breath, 'Santa Maria!' The junction was blocked by an armoured car and two German soldiers stood in front of it, machine guns slung on their shoulders. Frankie's stomach clenched but the priest said quickly, 'Don't worry. If they ask you, you are the daughter of Giorgio Praboni, a farmer who lives up in the hills over there.'

He slowed the car to a halt and wound down the window. One of the soldiers bent and looked in.

'Where are you going, Father?'

'On a mission of mercy, my son. One of my flock is dying and I am going to administer the last rites. In the name of the Holy Mother, do not delay us. His time is short.'

'Who's this?' the soldier asked, indicating Frankie.

'His daughter. She came to fetch me. Poor child, she is the only one left at home since her brothers went to fight for Il Duce. Let us pass, please. You would not wish the poor man to meet his reckoning unshriven and without the benefits of the Holy Church, would you?'

The soldier looked uncomfortable. He glanced round at his colleague and then surreptitiously made the sign of the cross. 'Go in peace, Father. I hope you will be in time.'

He called something to the other soldier, who got into the armoured car and moved it out of the way.

Father Antonio raised his hand in benediction. 'Bless you, my son.' He let in the clutch and in a moment they were across the road and heading up an unmade track into the hills.

'How did you know that man was a Catholic?' Frankie asked, when they were out of sight of the soldiers.

The priest smiled. 'I didn't. I just knew that the Holy Mother would take care of us.'

The track wound up into the mountains, following the course of a small river that rushed and churned over a rocky bed. At length, they rounded a bluff and the valley opened out before them into a grassy meadow, through which the river flowed more quietly. By the river was an old stone building that had obviously once been a mill, though its water wheel no longer turned. Around the mill were other buildings that might have been barns and between them were pitched several tents. Men were moving between the buildings.

'So,' Father Antonio said, 'we are here. This is Luciano's headquarters.'

As he spoke a man with a rifle stepped out from behind a rock and barred their way. The priest explained rapidly who Frankie was and her purpose and the man immediately waved them forward and stepped onto the running board to escort them into the small settlement. The car drew up outside the door of the mill and a slight, youthful figure came out to greet them. He was clean shaven but his hair was rather longer than was usual and tinted auburn by the rays of the sun.

Father Antonio heaved his bulk, with some difficulty, out of the small car and the man bent his head to receive his blessing.

'Father, we were not expecting you, but you are always welcome.' He looked at Frankie, who had just come round from the far side of the car. 'Who is this?'

'This,' said the priest, in the tone of a conjuror who had just accomplished a particularly remarkable trick, 'is what we have been praying for – a new radio operator for our friend Major Nick.' He turned to Frankie. 'My child, this is Signor Luciano – or at least that is the name by which he wishes to be known.'

Luciano's eyes widened. 'A woman!' Then he pulled himself together and held out his hand. 'Signora, you are more than welcome. What is your name?'

Frankie introduced herself and added impetuously, 'Is he . . . how is Major Harper?'

Luciano's smile faded and Frankie saw that he was not as young as she had first thought. 'In great pain. A bullet is lodged close to the base of his spine. The local doctor has done his best but he says he dare not try to remove it without the facilities of a hospital. There would be a risk of permanent paralysis. But the wound is beginning to fester and we have no more morphine. He needs an operation urgently. Will your people come for him?'

'Yes,' Frankie said. 'They'll come, as soon as I let them know where.' After everything that had happened, she could not admit to herself that there might be delays back at head-quarters. 'How did it happen?'

'We made a night raid on the airfield at Pavullo, to sabo-tage as many enemy aircraft as possible. Nick should have stayed in the background but he would never let us face risks he did not face himself. Besides' – for an instant a faint smile crossed his face and Frankie intuited the friendly teasing between the two men – 'I think he did not trust us to set the charges properly. We had laid them all and were leaving when one of the guards spotted something and raised the alarm. There was shooting and Nick fell. He couldn't walk but we managed to carry him to safety.' He lifted his shoulders. 'That's it.'

Frankie shouldered her rucksack. 'Can I see him? I have medical supplies here, including morphine.'

'Of course. This way.'

Luciano led her up a rickety staircase to the first floor. As they went he said, 'Franconi? Surely you cannot be . . . Do they call you Frankie?'

'Yes, how did you know? Has Nick mentioned me?'

'Mentioned you? He talked of nothing else. And now in his delirium he calls your name.' He paused with his hand on the handle of a door. 'You are lovers, no?'

'Yes.'

'I am afraid you will find him very weak. He may not know you at first.'

Frankie swallowed and nodded. 'All that matters now is to give him something to ease the pain.'

Luciano nodded and opened the door. The small room contained nothing but a low bed and a rough wooden table. Nick lay on his back, his lower limbs covered with a sheet and the top half of his body naked and glistening with sweat. She could just see that from the waist down he was swathed in bandages. He was unshaven and his cheeks were sunken and flushed. His eyes were closed but he turned his head restlessly from side to side and murmured incoherently.

Frankie knelt by the bed and caressed his face. 'Darling, it's me, Frankie. I've come to help you. Don't worry, my love, we're going to get you out of here. We'll get you to hospital and soon you'll be well again.'

The muttering stopped for a moment but Nick did not open his eyes or give any sign that he had heard her. She turned away to grope in her rucksack for the first-aid box and took out the hypodermic and the vials of morphine. Her hands were shaking. She forced herself to stop and breathe deeply. Then she punctured the seal of the vial and drew up the dose and expelled the air. She took some cotton wool and moistened it with alcohol and swabbed Nick's arm. It was much harder to drive the needle into the flesh of the man she loved than it had been to do it to a complete stranger all those years ago, but she held her breath and pushed it in. Slowly she depressed the plunger and withdrew the needle. When she laid the hypodermic back on its case it clattered in the silence. Her hands were shaking again.

Nick stopped muttering and lay still. For a few moments there was no change, then he heaved a deep sigh and she saw his muscles relax. Almost at once he seemed to slip into a deep sleep. Frankie looked up at Luciano and Father Antonio, who had followed them upstairs.

'We need to find a place where a small plane can land.'

'It's already done,' Luciano replied. 'Nick organised it all while he was still fully conscious. He knew we had sent a message south and that the only hope of getting him out was by air. There's a plateau a little higher up, what I think geologists would call a hanging valley. There's a steep drop at one end into the ravine but we paced out the flat area and Nick says a plane should be able to land there. We've cleared it of rocks. It's all ready.'

Frankie got up. 'Can someone fetch my radio set from the car, please? I need to contact base as soon as possible.'

'Of course,' Luciano said. 'But do you need your own set? The one Sergeant Prentiss used is still upstairs. I'll show you.'

'What happened to Sergeant Prentiss?' Frankie asked as she

followed him up to the top floor. 'Was he killed in the same action?'

'No. It was the Devil's luck,' Luciano replied. 'The day before, we were moving from here to a base nearer Pavullo. We had to cross a main road at night and we knew it was regularly patrolled. Most of us got over all right but Joe was a little behind. He had to carry the set, which slowed him down. A patrol came up just as he was going into the forest and one of them spotted him and took a shot at him. Nine times out of ten it would have missed but this one got him in the chest. He managed to struggle into cover and in the dark the Germans couldn't find him. Nick and I went back for him, of course, but we had to lie low until the Germans moved off. By the time we got to him he was dead.'

'Poor Joe,' Frankie murmured.

'Anyway, we saved his set,' Luciano said. 'If only one of us knew how to operate it! Here it is.'

He showed her into a room at the top of the building. The case containing the radio set was on a table and beside it was a box containing the grids necessary for encoding messages. Spread out over the rest of the space was a map.

'The landing site is here,' Luciano said, pointing to an area circled in pencil. 'And these are the grid references. Do you know Nick's code?'

'Like my own name,' Frankie told him. 'I was the operator who handled all his traffic.'

'Then do you need anything else?'

'No, thank you. It will just take me a little time to encode the message.'

'Then I'll go down and sit with Nick and Father Antonio.'

Frankie settled herself at the table and took paper and pencil from the box. She knew Nick's code poem by heart. He had chosen lines from Keats.

> *A thing of beauty is a joy forever:*
> *Its loveliness increases: it will never*
> *Pass into nothingness; but still will keep*
> *A bower quiet for us and a sleep*
> *Full of sweet dreams and health and quiet breathing.*

She had loved the lines when he first spoke them to her but now they seemed almost prescient in their aptness.

She selected the necessary five random words and began the tedious task of transposition by which each letter was given a number and then that number assigned to a new letter. Then she switched on the set and sent out the familiar call sign. It was not at the scheduled time but she knew that her colleagues would be keeping a round-the-clock listening watch on this wavelength. Nevertheless, she exclaimed aloud with relief when the message came back: *receiving you. Go ahead.* Who was it, she wondered, at the other end? She could recognise the 'fist' of any of the disembodied messengers whose words she transcribed every day but did not know her own friends' touch. Was it Midge, or Dickie, or one of the other girls?

She collected her thoughts and began to transmit her message, working carefully and forcing herself not to hurry. She did not want to be the author of one of the notorious inde-cipherables. *Salmon still alive. Fisherman can catch him at North 44 degrees 16 minutes; west 10 degrees 22 minutes Urgent action required. Red Herring.* There was a short wait and then the routine acknowledgement: *Message received.*

Frankie switched off the set and went down to Nick's room. He was still sleeping and Father Antonio was kneeling by the bed, telling his rosary, while Luciano stood by the window looking out.

'I've sent the message,' she said. 'Now we have to wait for an answer. The next scheduled time is six tonight.'

Father Antonio got to his feet and made way for her by the bed. She stroked Nick's face.

'He's so hot! Can't we bathe him with cool water or something?'

Luciano sighed heavily. 'The doctor is afraid that septicaemia may be setting in. But we can try.' He went to the door and called down the stairs. 'Sophia, bring some water from the well and a cloth.'

After a moment a girl of about Frankie's age appeared with a bowl. Frankie took the cloth and began to sponge Nick's face and chest. The girl hesitated for a little, then said, 'Mama says that food is ready. If you like, I can do that while you eat.'

Frankie wanted to refuse but Father Antonio said, 'You must eat, child. We all depend on you now. You need to keep your strength up.'

Frankie reluctantly allowed herself to be led downstairs to the main room, where an older woman was busy at an iron range. They ate pasta with a tomato sauce and Luciano said apologetically, 'I'm afraid supplies are limited. We only get meat if one of the men has been lucky hunting. But someone did bring us a couple of old hens the other day. They were too old to lay and there was hardly any flesh on them but we boiled them up and made broth for Nick. It was the best we could do.'

'Thank you,' Frankie said, her voice thickening. 'I know you've all done your best for him.'

She ate without tasting her food. All through the meal she was thinking about what she would say to Nick when he regained consciousness. Sometime, perhaps not today but eventually, he would want to know the story of her adventures. How could she tell him about Enzo? Yet how could she not tell him? If they were to be married, how could she go through their life together with that sin always on her conscience?

At the end of the meal Father Antonio rose and declared that he must return to the village. On an impulse Frankie rose too.

'Father, can I speak to you in private before you go?'

He gave her a thoughtful look and then said quietly, 'Of course, my child.'

Luciano offered the use of his own room, which contained a bed, a chair and a table scattered with maps and papers. Father Antonio gestured courteously towards the chair but Frankie said in a rush, 'Father, I want you to hear my confession.'

He nodded and seated himself in the chair and Frankie sank awkwardly to her knees beside him.

'Bless me, Father, for I have sinned.' The phrase came automatically, although it was years since she had last been to confession. But there she stuck, unable to find words for what had happened that night in the shepherd's hut.

The priest said gently, 'You are much troubled, my child. Take your time and remember, there is no sin so heinous that it cannot be forgiven if you truly repent.'

Frankie took a deep breath and blurted out, 'I killed a man.'

She stole a look at the priest's face and saw that he looked mildly surprised but not shocked.

'We are in the middle of a war,' he said. 'You are in the army. This is what happens in war.'

'But it wasn't an enemy soldier,' Frankie said. 'He was a civilian – an Italian.'

'Tell me exactly what happened,' Father Antonio said.

In broken sentences Frankie told him the whole story, beginning with her escape from Mario's compound and arrival at the farm, the long day's walk and finally the terrible events of that night.

When she had finished Father Antonio sighed. 'I know this family. It is not the first time Enzo has been accused of this sort of thing. A year ago there was a girl in the village who had a child out of wedlock. She claimed that Enzo had raped her but his father insisted he had been with him at the farm at the time she said the attack had taken place and it was impossible to prove anything. But there have been other cases. Several young women have come to me complaining of Enzo's behaviour towards them. I have remonstrated with Luigi but he has always refused to believe the stories. Nevertheless, he should not have entrusted you to Enzo. He knows in his heart that he cannot be relied upon. And it is clear that the boy planned the attack from the start. There were shorter routes he could have chosen, without danger of being intercepted by the Germans. You were the victim here, not the aggressor.'

'But it is a terrible sin to take a human life, isn't it?' Frankie persisted. 'I don't think I meant to kill him. I thought the gun would frighten him, that's all. But I don't know if I pulled the trigger or if it went off by accident.'

'All human life is sacred,' the priest agreed, 'but there are times when we have to do a great wrong in order to avert a greater. I believe that if Enzo had succeeded in his intentions he would have gone on to repeat the offence and my great fear has always been that one day he would kill to cover up his crime. He might have killed you. It may be that by killing him you saved your own life or perhaps that of some other innocent girl in the future.'

'So what should I do now?' Frankie asked. 'I keep thinking about his parents waiting for him to come home.'

'Is he still up there, in the hut?'

'I burnt it, with him in it. I didn't want to leave him to the wild animals.'

The priest nodded. 'You did well. I shall go and see Luigi and his wife. I will tell them what happened and that they are as much to blame as anyone for sending you off alone with him. They can retrieve his remains and see that he gets a proper burial. Be at peace, my child. I am in no doubt that you truly regret his death and that you have already done greater penance than any number of Our Fathers and Hail Marys could inflict.' He raised his hand and made the sign of the cross over Frankie. '*Ego te absolvo, in nomine Patris et Filii et Spiritus Sancti. Amen.*'

Frankie followed Father Antonio out to his car, puzzled by the fact that, although she had rejected the teachings of the Church, she still felt that a burden had been lifted from her. When the priest had departed, she went up to the room where Nick lay and found the girl Sophia still sitting by the bed.

'He is sleeping, signora,' the girl said. 'If you wish to sit with him, I will go and fetch some fresh water.'

She went out and Frankie took her place. Nick lay quiet, his breathing more regular than before, and when she took his hand it seemed less feverish. She longed to talk to him but told herself that it would be cruel to rouse him. The noises of the encampment had subsided in a deep midday somnolence and the house was quiet and cool. She sat on, emptying her mind of thought, occupied by the simple act of waiting.

Suddenly she realised that Nick's eyes were open. She leaned over him and caressed his face.

'Hello, darling!'

He gazed up at her without surprise. 'Hello, my angel. Have you come to see me again?'

'Yes, I'm here. Everything's going to be all right. There's a plane coming to take you to hospital. You'll soon be well again.'

He smiled. 'This is a lovely dream. I almost believe you're real. I like it when you come to me but I wish you could stay longer.'

Frankie leaned closer. 'Nick, darling, it's not a dream. I'm really here. Look, feel . . .' She found his hand and pressed it to her cheek. 'See? Flesh and blood. I'm here and I'm not going to leave you.'

He closed his eyes for a second and when he opened them again they focused on her with a quite different expression. 'Frankie? What on earth are you doing here?'

'I've come to get you out, my love, and take you back to where you can be properly looked after.'

'But why . . . how?' His eyes flicked around the room. 'Where am I?'

'At Luciano's camp, where you've been all the time.'

'Then how did you get here? You shouldn't be here. It's not safe.'

I didn't need you to tell me that! she thought. Aloud she said, 'I came the same way as you, by parachute.'

'You? Parachuted? In here?'

'Well, close. You arranged for me to learn, remember? I made my first jump with you.'

He frowned at her. 'But that was in Africa. Why are you here?'

'You needed a new radio operator. We couldn't get you out unless we had contact.'

'And you came, to do that?'

'Yes. Aren't you pleased to see me?'

'Oh, Frankie! My darling girl!'

He made to take her in his arms but the effort was too great for him. Seeing this, she bent closer and slid her own arms under his shoulders, holding him with her cheek pressed to his. For a long time they stayed this way, not speaking. Her tears soaked into the pillow and she could feel his trickling down the side of her neck. At length she straightened up and they looked at each other.

'I'm in a bad way, Frankie,' he said, not looking for

sympathy but merely stating a fact. 'I can't move my legs and I'm getting weaker. I may not make it.'

'Yes you will!' she assured him fiercely. 'I haven't come all this way to let you slip through my fingers now.'

'How soon will they send the plane?'

'I don't know, until tonight. There should be a message then. But I've brought morphine and fresh dressings and everything. You won't have to suffer anymore. You've got to hang on, for my sake.'

He closed his eyes and she felt his fingers close round hers. 'Guess I'll just have to try, then.'

'Yes, my darling. That's it. Try to hang on.'

The doctor from came up from the village later. He was delighted with the fresh supplies and changed the dressing on Nick's wound but outside the room he took Frankie's hand and shook his head.

'The infection is getting worse. He may have only a day or two. You must prepare yourself for the worst.'

At six o'clock Frankie was sitting by the radio set. Dead on time, she heard the call sign and sent the standard response: *Receiving you. Go ahead.* The message followed, an unintelligible jumble of letters. It was not until she had decoded it that she was able to read, *Fisherman will arrive 06.00 hours June 20*. June 20! Frankie struggled to work out that day's date. Swept along by events in the last few days, she had lost all track of time. She ran downstairs to where Luciano was sitting with some of his lieutenants in the main room.

'What date is it today?'

'June eighteenth. Why?'

'They're sending a plane for Nick the day after tomorrow. Six o'clock in the morning.'

The next thirty-six hours were the longest Frankie had ever spent. Most of the time she stayed by Nick, feeding him sips of water or broth, washing him, helping to turn him. Sometimes they talked but he drifted in and out of full consciousness and never asked her for the story of how she had found her way to him. Some of the time she talked to him, about the happy days they had spent at Cap Matifou, or about the war. Luciano had a radio set that could pick up the BBC and when she was not with Nick they hunched over it listening to the latest reports on *Radio Italia Combatte*. In France the Allied armies had broken out of the beachhead and were moving inland. At last victory seemed to be in sight.

'Everyone's talking about the war being over by Christmas,' Frankie told Nick. 'Then we'll be able to go home and do all those things we talked about.' It was the first time she had actually spoken out loud about their future together and she would not have done so if she had thought that he was actually listening to her.

Even at night she stayed in the same room, dozing on a makeshift bed and ready to wake if he stirred or groaned. She gave him the regular injections of morphine but she knew that as the time for each drew closer he began to suffer again and it was hard to resist the temptation to bring the dose forward.

Luciano sent men up to the plateau to check that there were no obstructions and to prepare the signal fires that would guide the pilot in. Apart from that there was nothing they could do but wait.

Shortly after midnight the next night Frankie injected Nick with a slightly larger dose of morphine than usual, as the doctor had instructed. Then Luciano and two of his men lifted him carefully onto a stretcher and swathed him in blankets against the night air, which at this altitude was chilly even in midsummer. It was impossible to carry the stretcher down the winding staircase, so they opened a hatch in the side of the building and lowered him down from the beam that had once been used to haul up sacks of grain. Then, with a relay of stretcher-bearers, they set off up the valley. Where the path was wide enough, Frankie walked beside the stretcher, holding Nick's hand and talking to him. When it was not, she followed close behind. By a little after five they had reached the plateau where the landing strip had been prepared. White painted rocks had been set to mark out a runway and the fires were ready to be lit but it seemed frighteningly short to Frankie. At one end was a steep moraine of tumbled rock, rising to the shoulder of the mountain. At the other was a sheer drop of several hundred feet into the river valley below. It would require a pilot of consummate skill and daring to land there.

She knelt by the stretcher and tucked the blankets more tightly round Nick's shoulders. He was coming round from the morphine and his eyes were open.

'What's going on?'

'There's a plane coming for us, darling. In an hour or two you'll be safely tucked up in hospital.'

The sky lightened to a pale, unblemished duck-egg blue and the eastern mountain crest was edged with fire. It was a perfect, still morning. Frankie looked at her watch. Twenty minutes to go. Time dragged by. Five minutes. Luciano gave his men the order to light the fires. The smoke from them rose straight up into the crystalline air. Six o'clock. Frankie strained her ears for the sound of an aircraft engine but heard nothing. Was it possible that she had made a mistake decoding the message? Or that they had the date wrong? What if the plane had come yesterday and found no one waiting?

Then one of the men exclaimed, *'Ecco la!'* and she heard the drone of the engine. Scanning the sky, she could see nothing, until suddenly the tiny plane appeared, rising up from below the level of the precipice to pass only a few feet above their heads. She realised then that the pilot had flown low along the winding valley to escape detection. He circled the plateau once and then disappeared from view and Frankie's heart sank. Had he taken one look at the area and decided that landing was impossible? An instant later, the plane came into sight so low over the edge of the precipice that its wheels were almost touching the ground. It bounced once and ran on, the propeller feathering, smoke coming from the brakes, and as it slowed half a dozen of Luciano's men ran out and seized it by the wings, bringing it to a stop just before it reached the moraine. They manhandled it in a tight circle, turning it so that it was ready to take off again, and then the hatch over the rear cockpit slid back and a lanky figure with a mane of blond hair climbed out and jumped to the ground.

Luciano went to meet him and brought him back to where Frankie waited beside the stretcher. The pilot bowed over her extended hand.

'Furio Lauri, at your service, signora! And it is true what they say! You are as beautiful as you are brave.'

Frankie blushed, at a loss for words, and Lauri turned to kneel by the stretcher. '*Eh bene, amico,* I have come to take you home.'

'Nice of you to drop in,' Nick murmured in English, and Frankie thought she saw a trace of the old mischievous grin.

Lauri straightened up. 'Can he walk?'

'No,' Frankie said. 'He can't even sit.' She had looked at the plane and realised two things. One, that there was no possibility of putting the stretcher in it and two, that there was room for only one passenger. It was designed simply to take a pilot and co-pilot, in two separate cockpits one behind the other.

'We can lower him into the cockpit and strap him in,' Luciano said.

'It might damage him,' Frankie said. 'The doctor said he should be kept still.'

'It's the only chance,' Luciano said. 'If he stays here without treatment he'll die. There is no other way of getting him out.'

Frankie looked at Nick and then at the plane. 'All right. Just wait a minute.'

She took the hypodermic from her rucksack and administered another dose of morphine. Then she bent and kissed him on the lips. 'Goodbye, my darling. It won't be long now. You're going home.'

Two men lifted the stretcher and carried it to the plane. Two others climbed up onto the fuselage and between the four of them they lifted and hauled Nick's limp body up and then turned him so that Luciano could direct his legs into the well of the cockpit. They lowered him into the seat and Luciano fastened the harness around him. Nick groaned once or twice during the process but made no complaint.

When he was in, Luciano leaned over and gripped his shoulder. 'Goodbye, my friend. We shall meet again, when the war is over.'

Lauri climbed into his cockpit and Luciano made to close the cover over Nick but Frankie called, 'Just one minute. Please!' She scrambled up and kissed Nick again.

'Goodbye, darling. See you soon.'

Nick's face was ashen and there was sweat on his forehead but his eyes were open. 'What do you mean? You're coming too.'

'I can't. There isn't room.'

'You must! I'm not going without you.'

'Don't be silly. You must go.'

'Not without you,' Nick repeated. He began to fumble with the buckles of the harness and tried to lever himself out of the seat. 'You go, if there's only room for one.'

'Stop it!' Frankie cried. 'Luciano, make him see sense.'

Luciano looked across at Lauri in the rear cockpit. 'Could she sit on his lap?'

Lauri shook his head. 'Impossible. It will be hard enough to get off before we tip over the edge. With the extra weight we'd never make it.'

'It doesn't matter,' Frankie said. 'I'll stay. I expect you can use a radio operator, Luciano.'

'No!' Nick shouted, his voice harsh with anguish.

'Perhaps we could exfiltrate you through the German lines with one of our couriers,' Luciano said doubtfully.

'Listen!' Lauri broke in. 'I will come back for her tomorrow. That will solve the problem.'

'It's too risky. I shouldn't ask you to . . .' Frankie began, but Luciano interrupted her.

'Did you hear that, Nick? Furio will bring her tomorrow. OK?'

'We must go!' Lauri called. 'The longer we are the more the chance of meeting an enemy fighter on the way home. Get down now, both of you. I will be back tomorrow. You have my word!'

Luciano closed the cockpit canopy and helped Frankie down to the ground. As they moved away Lauri shouted to the men standing by to hold on to the wings until he told them to let go. He started the engine and revved up until the little plane was quivering like a greyhound at the start of a race. Then he gestured to the men to release their hold and it shot forward, gathering pace, towards the abyss. Frankie held her breath. It seemed that the wheels would never leave the ground, but just before it reached the precipice she saw the plane's nose come up and a second later it was airborne. It dipped a wing, banking to follow the line of the valley, and disappeared from sight.

She stood in silence with Luciano until they could no longer hear the engine. Then he touched her arm.

'We'd best be getting back. There's nothing we can do now except pray.'

Frankie asked, 'Do you think he really will come back for me?'

'I'm sure he will – provided the Huns don't stop him.'

Chapter Fourteen

The airfield at Monopoli was baking under the relentless summer sun when Furio Lauri's tiny Nardi 305 landed there for the second day running. Frankie hauled herself out of the cockpit, stretching cramped limbs, and climbed down to the ground. Lauri joined her.

'You see? Furio is a man of his word.'

'I never doubted that,' Frankie said with a smile, handing him back the leather flying jacket he had lent her for the flight. Underneath she was still wearing the shabby dress and head-scarf she had bought from the woman at the corner shop.

A perspiring flight sergeant arrived pedalling an ancient bicycle. 'Back again, sir? You must like this spot,' he said with a grin. He looked at Frankie. 'Sorry, sir. The young lady can't stay. The base is out of bounds to civilians.'

Lauri grinned back. 'Careful, my friend. You are in the presence of a British officer.'

The flight sergeant peered at Frankie and grew even redder in the face than before. 'Cor blimey! It's Lieutenant Franconi, isn't it? Beg pardon, ma'am. I didn't recognise you for a minute.'

'That's all right,' Frankie said wearily. 'Just get me some transport over to Colonel MacIntosh's office, will you?'

'I'll send a jeep over right away, ma'am,' the man promised and pedalled away at top speed.

Ten minutes later Frankie presented herself in the outer

office. Viney, the colonel's aide-de-camp, looked up from some papers and asked curtly, 'What do you want? Who let you in here?'

'It's me, sir,' Frankie said. 'Franconi.'

'Good God! You got back after all! Good show!' Viney leapt up and came round his desk. 'You'd better go straight in. The old man's been like a cat on hot bricks for the last day or two.'

He knocked on the door of the inner office and announced, 'Franconi's here, sir.'

'Franconi?' came MacIntosh's voice. 'Send her in.'

Frankie came to attention in front of the CO's desk and was about to salute when she remembered that she was not properly dressed. Instead she said lamely, 'Hello, sir.'

MacIntosh looked her up and down. 'What the hell have you been up to? Why aren't you in uniform?'

Frankie hesitated. She had no intention of embarking on the full story. 'It got damaged, sir, so I burnt it.'

'You burnt it?'

'Yes, sir. It seemed the best thing to do, in the circumstances.'

'How long ago was this?'

'I'm not sure, sir. Several days.'

'So you have been wandering around in enemy-occupied territory dressed like that for several days? Do you realise you could have been shot as a spy?'

'Yes, sir. But only if they caught me.' She took a breath. 'Sir, did Major Harper get back all right?'

'Yes, Furio Lauri brought him in yesterday.'

'How is he?'

'In a bad way, I'm afraid. The MO checked him over and then sent him straight back to the hospital at Brindisi. I telephoned this morning and it seems the surgeon operated yesterday afternoon but they say it's too early to tell if he'll come through.' He studied Frankie's face for a moment. 'What is it between you and Harper?'

'We're engaged to be married, sir.'

'You realise if I'd known that I would never have sent you on that mission, don't you? You're far too emotionally involved.'

'Yes, sir. That's why I didn't tell you.'

MacIntosh leaned back in his chair and studied her. 'Franconi, you never cease to amaze me. There are times when I don't know whether to put you on a charge for insubordination or recommend you for promotion.'

'Can I go and see him, please, sir?'

Frankie suddenly felt that her legs were going to give way underneath her. MacIntosh's expression changed abruptly and he came round the desk to her.

'Look here, I think you'd better sit down.' He pulled up a chair for her and poured water from the carafe on his desk, then went to the door and shouted, 'Corporal, bring some tea for Lieutenant Franconi.' Returning, he perched on the edge of his desk and looked down at her. 'When did you last get a good night's sleep?'

Frankie thought. 'I'm not really sure, sir. The last two nights we had to leave the camp in the early hours to get to the landing strip in time and before that . . . before that I was looking after Nick and then . . .' She trailed off into silence.

MacIntosh said quietly, 'OK. You can give me a full report when you've had a chance to rest. Just tell me why it took so long for you to reach Harper. We heard from Swordfish that you'd dropped successfully days ago.'

Frankie gazed at him. The events of the past week were a blur in her mind. In the end she managed, 'Mario wouldn't let me go. Captain Devenish helped me to escape. After that I had to walk.'

The corporal came in with a mug of sweet tea and MacIntosh put it into her hand. 'OK, that'll do for now. Drink up.'

'When can I go and see Major Harper, sir?'

'You're in no fit state to go anywhere.'

'I'll be all right if I can have a shower and change my clothes,' Frankie said. 'Please, sir!'

He sighed. 'Go and do that, and get yourself a decent meal and then come back and see me and I'll decide if you're fit to travel. OK?'

Frankie swallowed the last of her tea and got up. 'Thank you, sir. I won't be long.' She left the room without waiting to be dismissed.

She had almost reached the hut that her team used as living quarters when the door crashed open and Midge came running out.

'She's here! She's here!' Midge flung her arms round Frankie, half laughing, half crying. 'We've been going crazy with worry about you. Thank God you're safe!'

'Hush,' Frankie admonished her. 'The others will be sleeping.'

The warning came too late. Dickie and Flick had followed Midge out of the hut, pulling on dressing gowns over their pyjamas.

'No chance of that,' Dickie said. 'Captain Viney just phoned across to let us know you were back.' She looked at Frankie quizzically. 'You look as if you've lost a bit of weight.'

Midge looked at her properly for the first time. 'My God, Frankie, you look terrible! What's happened to you?'

'Thanks a lot,' Frankie responded. 'Look, I'll tell you all about it sometime but right now I'm desperate for a shower and a change – and then I've got to go and see Nick in hospital. Do you mind?'

In a babble of overlapping questions and answers she was escorted into the hut. It was only then that she realised that her rucksack and all its contents had been left behind at Luciano's camp. The other three rummaged through their kit and produced between them a new toothbrush, a half-used tube of toothpaste, the dregs of a bottle of shampoo and Midge's last tin of carefully hoarded Coty talcum powder. Midge insisted on coming to the ablutions block with her and when she returned she found that Flick had pressed her second-best uniform and Dickie was cooking omelettes over a Primus stove.

'We managed to buy some fresh eggs off a local farmer,' she explained. 'Do you more good than that muck they serve up in the canteen.'

'And look what I've got,' Flick said, whisking the lid off a tin and exhibiting a fruitcake.

'Flick, your mother sent that for your birthday,' Dickie protested.

'So what? I'd rather cut it now than wait until Friday. I wish we had some champagne to go with it, so we could make it a real celebration.'

'Well, I'm afraid we'll have to make do with a nice cup of Rosie Lee,' Dickie said, exchanging the omelette pan for a battered kettle.

Frankie dressed, wolfed down the food, combed her hair and looked in briefly on Tigger and Mouse, who were on duty in the signals hut. Within the hour, she was back in MacIntosh's office. The CO looked her up and down appraisingly.

'Well, that's an improvement, at least.'

'Can I go to the hospital now, sir? I'm OK. Really!'

MacIntosh gave her one of his rare grins. 'OK, get along. I've laid on some transport for you. There's a jeep and a driver waiting for you outside. I can see I'm not going to get any sense out of you until you've seen Harper.'

Frankie wondered whether you could be put on a charge for kissing a superior officer. 'Thank you, sir! Thanks awfully!'

'Just remember, I want a full written report as soon as you get back.'

'Yes, sir. Straight away, sir.' Frankie went to the door, stopped, remembered to salute and ran to the jeep.

The receptionist at the military hospital directed her to a ward, where she was met by a sister in a uniform so well starched that it crackled when she moved.

'Are you a relative?' she demanded in response to Frankie's request to see Nick.

'I'm his fiancée,' Frankie responded.

The sister gave her a look that conveyed as clearly as words that she very much doubted the truth of this assertion but she said grudgingly, 'You'd better see Dr Harris first. He's in his office.'

Dr Harris wore a major's uniform under his white coat and looked as though he was even more in need of a good night's sleep than Frankie, but his manner was gentle.

'I'm afraid you'll find him very weak. We operated yesterday and removed the bullet but septicaemia had set in. Six months ago I wouldn't have given much for his chances but now we have this new drug, penicillin, and it does seem to be doing the trick. I have every hope that he'll pull through.'

Frankie became aware that she had been holding her breath. She let it out with a rush. 'Thank you, Doctor. That's wonderful news.'

'It's not quite all, though,' the doctor said. 'The bullet had lodged very close to the spine and at the moment Major Harper has no sensation in either leg.'

'But that will get better now, won't it?' she asked.

'It may but it's too early to tell yet. I'm afraid you should prepare yourself for a very long haul.'

'Can I see him now?'

'Yes, Sister will take you to him. But don't stay too long. He needs to rest.'

Nick was in a side ward, lying flat on his back between clean white sheets. When Frankie had last seen him his cheeks had had a hectic flush. Now they were sunken and dead white against the dark stubble of his beard. She saw that he had been shaved and his hair had been cut short and was surprised, until she remembered the lice. His eyes were shut but they opened as she approached. Her breath was fast and shallow and she could feel the pounding of her heart.

She said, 'Hello,' but her throat was constricted and she had to clear it and try again before the word was audible.

'Frankie!' he whispered. 'Furio got you out safely. Thank God!'

'Yes, this morning,' she answered. 'I came as soon as I could. How are you feeling?'

'Pretty rough. They tell me I'm lucky. I'm on some kind of miracle drug. They keep coming and sticking needles in me. I feel like a human pincushion.'

'Poor you. Never mind, I'm sure it's for your own good.'

The words sounded ridiculous. She wanted to put her arms round him and kiss him but now that he was fully conscious she felt inhibited.

He gazed up at her with a small frown between his eyebrows. 'Frankie, the last few days are all a bit hazy. I am right, aren't I? You were there, at Luciano's camp? I didn't dream it?'

'Yes, I was there.'

'How did they know where to drop you?'

'They didn't. I dropped to Swordfish – Captain Devenish.'

'But that's miles away. How did you find your way to me?'

Frankie hesitated but a look at Nick's face told her that this was no time to embark on a long narrative. 'I walked. Don't worry, I'll tell you all about it when you're stronger.'

She saw his throat work as he swallowed. 'I don't know what to say. Thank you sounds so inadequate.'

'You don't have to thank me!' Tears were starting at the back of her eyes. This was not the rapturous reunion that she had dreamed of and yet she did not know how to break out of this stilted formality. She reached for his hand. 'Let's not think about all that. Let's talk about the future. Have you heard the news? The war will be over soon.' He had closed his eyes but she stumbled on. 'Even if it's not, you're bound to be sent home as soon as you're strong enough. Maybe I can get some home leave too. Just think, my darling, we could spend Christmas together.'

He opened his eyes again and looked up at her with more pain in them than she had seen at the worst times in the partisans' camp. 'Frankie, I've got something to say to you and it's so damn difficult that there's only one way to say it. I think we should call it off.'

'Call what off? You mean, spending Christmas together?' Something that felt like a large block of ice was forming in her stomach.

'No, I mean us – the engagement.'

'You don't want to marry me anymore?'

'It's not that I don't want to. I can't.'

'There's someone else?'

'No! No, I swear there's no one else. I could never love anyone else the way I love you. I just can't marry you.'

'But why? Why, Nick?'

He looked at her for a moment without speaking and she could see the tears in his eyes too. At length he said, 'I don't know if they've told you, but the chances are I'll never be able to walk again. You're such an amazing person. You've got so much vitality and courage. You could do wonderful things. I can't let you sacrifice your life to look after a cripple.'

Frankie gazed down at him. 'Is that the only reason you want to call it off?'

He nodded, compressing his lips to stifle a sob. 'I love you, Frankie, more than I can ever put into words. But I can't marry you.'

She sat back and took his hand in both of hers. Suddenly she felt calm, as she had the first time she had stood up to her father.

'Listen to me, Nick. There's something I haven't told you.' She fixed her eyes on the hand in hers. 'I said I had to walk from Mario's camp to Montefiorino. Part of the way I had a guide, the son of a local farmer. Instead of taking me directly to Montefiorino he took me to a shepherd's hut up in the mountains and tried to rape me. He said he'd hand me over to the Germans if I didn't do what he wanted. I had a pistol with me. I tried to threaten him with it but it went off somehow and killed him. I didn't mean to shoot him and I'll live with the guilt of that for the rest of my life but if I had to do it again I would, if it was the only way of getting to you. Now, if you want to throw me over because of a lot of crap about not letting me sacrifice myself, everything I've done will all be for nothing. You're too late. I've made my sacrifice.'

With a great effort he lifted his free hand and touched her face. 'I don't know what to say.'

'Can you still love me, now you know I've got blood on my hands?'

'How could I possibly not love you, after what you've done for my sake?'

'Then marry me.'

*   *   *

The doctor was right in more ways than one when he told
Frankie to be prepared for a long haul. To begin with there
were the anxious days when Nick's life still hung by a thread
and nothing else going on around her mattered. MacIntosh
gave her a week's leave and she stayed in a little *pensione* near
the hospital so that she could spend as much time with Nick
as the nursing staff permitted. At first all conversation
exhausted him and he drifted in and out of sleep, so that all
she could do was sit silently beside him, holding his hand.
When she was not at the hospital she took a book into the little
garden behind the *pensione* and sat under the shade of a
grapevine. She intended to read but found her mind
wandering until she sank into a semi-comatose state similar to
Nick's. It took her a day or two to realise that she needed time
to heal, mentally and physically, just as he did.

On the fifth day she began to see a change in Nick. He
stayed awake longer and there was a hint of colour in his
cheeks. The doctor came into the ward while she was there
and, after feeling Nick's pulse, gave Frankie an encouraging
smile.

'I think we're winning. This penicillin stuff really is all it's
cracked up to be.'

When her leave came to an end they were just beginning to
enjoy each other's company and it seemed cruel to have to part
but at least she had the consolation of knowing that Nick was
out of danger, though he was still unable to move his legs. The
doctor told her that as soon as he was strong enough to with-
stand the journey he would be flown back to England for
specialist treatment. This meant that they would have no
chance of being together but she told herself that it was all for
the best in the long run and tried to direct her thoughts to her
work.

Tigger and Mouse were sunning themselves outside the hut when Frankie climbed out of the lorry she had thumbed a lift on from Brindisi. Mouse was asleep but Tigger leapt up with a cry of delight and hugged her.

'Hurray! You've actually arrived when we're off duty. Last time we missed all the excitement.' She prodded her companion with her toe. 'Wake up, Dormouse! Look who's here.'

Mouse roused herself with a groan that changed to a mumbled, 'Frankie, you're back. Jolly good!'

'Where are the others?' Frankie asked. 'Who's on duty?'

'Midge has just gone to relieve either Dickie or Flick,' Tigger explained. 'While you've been away we've had to double up on some shifts.'

'Sorry,' Frankie said. 'I'm really grateful for the way you've all filled in for me. I'll try to see that you all get some time off now I'm back.'

'Never mind that,' Tigger replied gleefully. 'We've got you all to ourselves for once. Now, we want the full story.'

'Not quite you haven't.' Dickie rounded the corner of the hut and nodded casually at Frankie. 'Hello. Good leave? How's Nick?'

'Making progress, thanks.'

'Come on, Frankie,' Tigger pleaded. 'Give us all the gen. You know we're itching to hear all about your adventures.'

'No, wait,' Dickie commanded. 'She doesn't want to go over it all twice. It's pretty quiet on the signals front at the moment. Come into the hut and you can tell us all.'

Reluctantly Frankie allowed herself to be marched over to the hut where Midge and Flick were sitting in front of their radio sets.

'Now,' Dickie said, when the initial greetings were over, 'start from the beginning and don't leave anything out.'

Frankie began her story but discovered that it all seemed strangely distant, as if months or even years had passed instead of the one week of her leave. She told them about the drop, about Mario's perfidy and Devenish's prevarication and their ultimate escape from the compound but her account was flat and factual and she could see that her audience was disappointed. When she came to Luigi's farm and how she had got from there to Montefiorino her manner became even more clipped and elliptical. She warmed to her story when she spoke of Luciano and Father Antonio and Furio Lauri's skill and daring but it was a relief to get to the end.

'She's tired,' Dickie pronounced. 'No wonder. I bet it was all a lot tougher than you're making out, Frankie. You go and relax. You're not back on duty until tomorrow morning.'

Frankie had prepared her written report for Colonel MacIntosh while she was on leave and she handed it in once she had had a wash and tidied her uniform. It was even briefer than the account she had given her friends but MacIntosh asked a number of probing questions that came close to disturbing her precarious emotional equilibrium. Even with him, however, she managed to avoid referring to Enzo's attack and its consequences. Next morning she returned to her desk in the signals office and tried to put the whole episode out of her mind.

Several times over the ensuing weeks she managed to get a lift into Brindisi during her time off in order to visit Nick and each time he was a little stronger and more alert. Then one day he said, 'Frankie, darling, they're sending me back to England. There's a hospital ship sailing in a couple of days so we shan't see each other for a bit.'

'A ship?' she queried. 'Wouldn't you be safer in a plane?'

'Planes aren't equipped to take stretchers,' he pointed out. 'And don't worry. The Nazi U-boats are pretty well finished and anyway even the Huns don't fire on hospital ships.'

She took his hand and rubbed her cheek against it. 'I ought to be glad. It means you're getting better and you'll soon be being looked after by specialists who can help you to walk again. But I'm going to miss you terribly.'

'I'll miss you too,' he answered tenderly. 'You're the shining light at the end of the tunnel that keeps me going. Couldn't you apply for a posting back to Blighty?'

'I don't know,' she said doubtfully. 'There's still a lot of work to do here. The other girls had to work extra shifts while I was away. I don't like to run out on them.'

'No, of course not. I shouldn't have suggested it. You're doing an important job and I mustn't be selfish. Anyway, the way things are going, you could all be home in a few months.'

'Yes.' She forced a smile. 'That's right. We must try to look on the bright side.'

Nothing had been said about marriage since her first visit. Nick had never hinted again that he wished to break off the relationship and he was as loving as he had ever been but Frankie longed to have something definite to hang onto while they were apart.

Against her better judgement she said, 'Then, when I get back, we can start thinking about a date for the wedding. I suppose I ought to write to my parents and tell them I'm engaged.'

Nick did not look at her and his hand slipped out of hers. 'I think we ought to keep it to ourselves for a bit, Frankie. I don't feel up to making long-term plans at the moment. Do you mind very much?'

She told him she did not. There was nothing else she could say. But she said goodbye to him with an aching void under her ribs.

The long, hot summer weeks dragged past. Frankie was finding it increasingly hard to keep her mind on her work. Each message she decoded brought back vivid memories of her time with the partisans and by contrast her present job seemed dull and unimportant. When she was not imagining what was happening to Luciano and his men she was dreaming of Nick and worrying that now they were apart he might go back to his previous determination not to marry. She did not doubt his love for her but she recognised the altruistic side of his nature and was afraid that unless the surgeons could hold out hope that he would walk again he might yet decide that he could not commit her to a life looking after a cripple. Uncharacteristically, she found herself making the kind of slips in transcribing or encoding messages that she had once regarded with contempt.

Letters arrived from Nick at irregular intervals and usually long after they had been written. He told her that he had been transferred to Stoke Mandeville Hospital, where there was a team of doctors who specialised in treating people who had been disabled. He wrote that he was getting stronger every day and was now out of bed and 'whizzing around' in a wheelchair. He also mentioned that his enforced idleness had given him a chance to study, and that he had been reading a lot of political theory. Everyone knew that there would be a general election as soon as the war was over and he was determined to be involved in it in some way. Frankie was glad that he was taking such a positive view but found it hard to see what he could do, in his condition. He wrote lovingly and said often how much he missed her, but there was no mention of marriage

One morning Midge came into the hut with the mail and handed Frankie a letter postmarked Princes Risborough. Her first thought was that it must be from Steve, but she did not recognise the handwriting. She slit the envelope and read:

Dear Frankie,

I probably should not be writing this letter at all but we are so worried about Diana – Steve as you would call her. She was home on leave last May, over a year ago now, and said that she was being posted abroad, but since then we have heard nothing from her except for a few very brief and un-informative postcards from Cairo. It's so unlike her not to write proper letters that we feel sure there must be something wrong. I even wrote to the War Ministry, asking if they could put me in touch with her CO or someone else who might be able to give me some concrete information. The result was a visit from a mysterious man in civilian clothes, who told us that Diana is doing very important work and that we should not expect to hear from her for a while as it is all very hush-hush. He said that he could assure us that she was alive and well but he couldn't tell us anymore.

I suppose we should be satisfied with that but I simply can't imagine what she can be doing in Cairo that is so secret she can't even write normal letters. I know you and she are close and I am wondering if you have heard from her. I know you can't tell me anything about what she is doing, even if you know, but if you can just let us know that she has been in touch it will help to set our minds at rest.

Oh dear, this is rather a rambling letter and I realise that we are probably asking you to do something impossible, but any reassurance you can give us will be so welcome. I hope all is well with you and we look forward to seeing you next time you are on leave.

Yours sincerely
Annabel Escott-Stevens

The letter weighed on Frankie's mind all day. She had been trying to put Steve's possible fate to the back of her mind, but now she could not help imagining what might be happening to her. Her own recent experiences made the pictures she conjured up more vivid than ever. She told herself that Steve was probably fine and reminded herself of Nick's reassuring words, but she kept remembering those radio messages from agents in France that had come to an abrupt end in the middle of transmission and had never been resumed. What could she write to Steve's parents that would give them any comfort? In the end, she said simply that she had had no more news from their daughter than they had but the army censors were a law unto themselves and they should not read too much into Steve's failure to write more fully. Whatever she was doing had obviously been classified as secret but as long as the postcards kept coming they should not worry.

Frankie wished that she could have shared the burden by discussing it with Midge, but she knew she had to keep Steve's secret. Anyway, Midge had other things on her mind. Jumbo wrote to say that he had forty-eight hours' leave coming and would try to wangle a seat on a plane coming over to Monopoli. Midge was on tenterhooks for days, snapping at everyone and making mistakes in her coding. Then there was a phone call from Brindisi. Jumbo had arrived there and could stay two nights.

'You can manage without me for a couple of days, can't you?' Midge begged. 'Please, Frankie!'

Frankie assured her that they could and two days later Midge returned radiant. Everything was settled and they were engaged. Midge's left hand was adorned with a rather impressive diamond solitaire. That evening they drank a bottle of Asti Spumante to celebrate.

By the end of summer it became obvious that the war was not going to be over by Christmas. After the euphoria of the Normandy landings and the liberation of Paris and then

Brussels came the debacle of Arnhem and the beginning of the long, hard slog towards the German frontier. In Italy the Allies took the city of Florence but every mile gained had to be fought for against an enemy that refused to give in. The newspapers and radio bulletins were full of the advances on the Western Front and a mood of bitterness began to percolate through the ranks of those fighting the Italian campaign. People at home, unaware of the privations and the bitter battles being waged, tended to think of them as the lucky ones who had avoided the trauma of D-Day. The troops in Italy, in response, dubbed themselves 'the forgotten army'.

All through the summer Frankie and her colleagues had transcribed triumphant messages from the agents working with the partisans. More and more volunteers were flocking to join them and by the end of the summer partisan groups ruled most of the mountainous regions of Emilia and Modena. Only the main roads and railways were under German control. Then, as autumn faded into winter, the Allied advance was brought to a halt just outside Bologna by a new German defensive line, the Gothic Line. In November the Americans abandoned their attempt to take the city and the Allies dug in for another winter. A few days later Frankie and her team were ordered to encode messages to all the British liaison officers working with the partisans, instructing them to tune in to a bulletin on Radio Italia Combatte the following evening for a special message. Intrigued, the six girls gathered round their radio set at the appointed time with Frankie as translator.

The message was from Field Marshal Alexander, C-in-C of the Italian campaign. Frankie began to translate and then stopped in horror.

'What?' Dickie demanded impatiently. 'What's he saying?'

'It's mad!' Frankie muttered. 'Absolutely stark, raving bonkers! He's telling them to cease operations for the winter.

There will be no more supply drops. He's advising them to go back to their homes and wait for the spring.'

'They can't mean that!' Dickie said. 'It's tantamount to telling them to go home and wait for the Gestapo to pick them up.'

'I know,' Frankie responded. 'It's got to be a mistake. I'll go and see Colonel Mac and ask what he makes of it.'

MacIntosh was in his office, looking more weary than Frankie had ever seen him.

She began without preamble. 'Sir, did you hear the bulletin on Radio Italia?'

'I've just switched it off.'

'It must be a mistake, sir. The field marshal can't realise what he's asking.'

'I'm sure you're right.'

'Well, can't we do something? Can't we tell him what the consequences will be?'

The colonel's lips twitched in an ironic smile. 'If only they'd let us run the war, eh, Frankie? But you know the often quoted line, "Ours not to reason why". All we can do is obey our orders and hope to God the partisans will have the sense to ignore theirs.'

From that evening on Frankie became increasingly disenchanted with her job. After a week of sleepless nights she went to see MacIntosh again and asked if she could be posted back to Britain. He looked at her sympathetically.

'You've had a basinful out here. I should have sent you home immediately you got back from that mission. I'll support your application and with any luck you should get your posting quite soon. Oh, and by the way, you might like to know I've recommended you for a decoration. It won't come through until the war's over, because of the secret nature of your work here, but I want you to know that your courage hasn't gone unnoticed.'

Frankie said nothing to the others about her request until the notification of her posting came through early in December. She was to return to Grendon Underwood. That evening she bought a bottle of wine in the village and called all her team together.

'Look, I don't quite know how to say this. I'm afraid you'll all feel I'm leaving you in the lurch, but I've asked for a posting back home and it's just come through. I hate the idea of leaving you but I'm fed up with this place and this job. Please don't be angry with me.'

Midge reached across and took her hand. 'Of course we're not angry, darling. We've all seen how tired you are, and how worried you are about Nick. We'll be sorry to see you go but I'm sure you're doing the right thing.'

'Anyway,' Dickie put in, 'the work here is coming to an end. We'll probably all be posted home soon. We'll have a massive reunion party as soon as we all get back.'

Mouse kissed her shyly on the cheek. 'You've been a brick, Frankie. I'd have hated it here without you. We'll miss you but of course you must go. Nick must be aching to see you again.'

Early in the morning four days before Christmas, Frankie stood on the deck of a troopship as the convoy crept into the Solent. She had managed to talk her way onto a plane leaving Monopoli for Gibraltar but there had been no possibility of an onward flight. There were ships in the harbour preparing to sail for England, however, and she had found a berth on one of them. It was a still, grey morning with mist lying over the water and she was reminded of the day she and Dickie and Midge had set sail for Algiers. How long ago that seemed, and yet it was not quite two years. She could hardly believe she was the same person as that naive, excited girl.

She had quite expected that the ship would dock in

Liverpool and had imagined herself sailing past the famous buildings on the waterfront, underneath the Liver Birds atop their towers. What was the joke? That the stone birds flapped their wings every time a virgin passed underneath. Well, they'd have no need to exert themselves for her! Instead, it was the Needles slipping past on the starboard bow, but Frankie had no regrets. If it had been Liverpool she would have had no choice but to go straight home but now, since she was making landfall in the south of England, she had other plans. In her pocket was Nick's last letter telling her that he had been discharged from hospital and demobbed and was going home to West Dean.

By the time the ship docked in Portsmouth harbour and Frankie was able to go ashore the working day was in full swing. In Monopoli winter had hardly taken a grip and she was used to blue skies and gentle sunshine. Here everything was grey and damp, with a steady drizzle falling, adding to the bleak atmosphere of destruction created by the shells of bombed-out warehouses and factories. But the dockside swarmed with activity. Men whistled as they worked or called out cheerfully to her as she passed and women in dungarees, with their hair tied up in scarves, greeted her with friendly nods. On every face she read the message: 'We've taken the worst Hitler could throw at us and we've come through. There's no stopping us now.' In the main street queues of women stood patiently outside every food shop but Frankie noticed that most of the shop windows had made some effort at Christmas decorations.

At the station she boarded a train crammed with soldiers and sailors going home on leave. Among them was a sprinkling of businessmen in pinstripe trousers and bowlers and women with jaunty hats and bright red lipstick, conveying the same message: 'Business as usual. We won't be ground down.'

Frankie changed trains at Lewes for a local service that took her to Seaford but there she discovered that the morning bus going to West Dean had left hours ago and there would not be another until late afternoon. Undaunted, she stationed herself at the corner of the street leading out of the town with her kitbag at her feet and began to thumb. It was not long before she got a lift in a baker's van heading in the right direction.

West Dean was the sort of village Frankie knew only from picture books – thatched cottages along narrow lanes and an air of timeless tranquillity. Only the concrete pillbox at the seaward entrance to the village reminded her that the country was still at war. At the village store she enquired where the doctor lived and was directed to a solid Georgian house with white walls and a straggling rose bush over the front door on which a few bedraggled red blooms still hung. A brass plate announced 'Dr A. W. Harper, MD and the name sent a thrill of anticipation through her stomach. She was about to ring the bell when she realised that the door was ajar. She pushed it open cautiously and found herself in a square, wood-panelled hall that smelt of beeswax polish. A Christmas tree hung with a random collection of baubles stood in one corner and paper chains were strung from the central light fitting.

There was no sign of anybody and Frankie began to wish that she had rung the bell but it seemed silly to go back outside now. She thought of calling Nick's name but felt too shy. On her left was a door labelled 'Waiting Room'. She looked in and saw rows of chairs around the walls and the usual collection of old copies of *Picture Post* and *Punch*. The room was empty and she was about to retreat when a voice called through the open door of an adjoining room,

'Sorry, surgery's over for this morning. You'll have to come back at five o'clock.'

A second later Nick wheeled himself smartly through the

door and stopped dead at the sight of her. 'Frankie? Darling, is it really you? How did you get here? Why didn't you telephone?' Then he held out his arms. 'Oh, come here!'

She threw herself across the room and fell to her knees by the chair, wrapping her arms round his neck and burying her face in his chest.

'Oh, Nick! Oh, I'm so glad to see you. I've missed you so much!'

'Me, too,' he whispered, and raised her face so he could kiss her.

For some time after that they said nothing except for a few broken exclamations but his kisses told her all she needed to know. At length he pulled her up off her knees to sit on his lap and looked into her face.

'You're more beautiful even than I remembered. How are you? Last time I saw you, you looked so tired and thin. I was worried about you.'

'Never mind me,' she replied. 'How are you?'

She examined him properly for the first time. He was wearing an open-necked shirt under a Fair Isle pullover. She had never seen him in civvies before and it seemed strange. He looked much younger and more vulnerable without the authority of his uniform and she realised that she had always been a little in awe of him, until now. More importantly, his skin was clear and his eyes bright and his face had filled out so that he was no longer the gaunt, skeletal figure she had last seen in Brindisi.

'You look wonderful,' she told him.

He hugged her. 'I feel wonderful, especially now you're here. If it wasn't for the legs I'd be back to normal.'

'No improvement there?' she asked, after a moment's hesitation.

'Yes, some. I've got some feeling back so the doctors think

there may be some regeneration of the nerves. There's definitely hope.'

'Oh, that's fantastic!' She kissed him again and then asked, 'What were you doing in there when I arrived? You haven't taken up medicine, have you?'

He laughed. 'No thanks! But I help out with some of the paper work. Dad's run off his feet so I make myself as useful as I can. He's out on his rounds at the moment but he'll be delighted to meet you. He'll be back for lunch any minute. Now, we'd better see about a room for you. You are staying, aren't you?'

'Just for a couple of days. I must get home for Christmas. I ought to have gone straight there, really, but when I discovered we were docking at Portsmouth I couldn't resist the temptation. I hope you don't mind me turning up without warning.'

'Of course I don't! It's the most wonderful surprise. When you wrote that you were coming home I assumed you'd go to Liverpool. I'd reconciled myself to not seeing you until after Christmas at the earliest. Now – he eased her off his lap – let's go and find Mrs Barrett. She's our Mrs Mop, only not so miserable. She's looked after Dad and me ever since Mum died.'

Frankie followed as he wheeled himself out into the hall and along a passage to the back of the house. Mrs Barrett was in the kitchen, a plump, grey-haired woman with a weathered face and bright blue eyes. Nick introduced Frankie and it was obvious that he had no need to explain their relationship. It seemed to be taken for granted.

'I'm sorry to turn up unannounced like this,' Frankie said. 'Especially just before lunch.'

'Bless you, you don't want to worry about that,' the woman replied in a soft country accent that enchanted Frankie. 'We can always stretch to another helping if need arises, can't we, Major Nick.'

Nick chuckled. 'You really will have to stop calling me Major, Mrs B. I'm out of the army now.'

'Oh, I'll get used to it in time, I dare say,' she replied. 'Now, let me take you up to the spare room, m'dear. It won't take a minute to put clean sheets on the bed.'

Frankie was shown into a large, rather bare room with dark mahogany furniture and curtains of brown velvet. It was obvious, she thought as she unpacked, that the house had lacked a woman's touch for a long time. No doubt Mrs Barrett kept the place spotless but she would not have much say regarding the furniture or decorations. She wondered briefly if this was Dr Harper's taste or Nick's, and for a second or two allowed herself to speculate about what their home would be like after they were married. She considered changing into mufti since uniform seemed unnecessarily formal but realised she had nothing in her kitbag that was warm enough for an English winter. So she washed her face and hands, brushed her hair, dabbed on some make-up and went downstairs.

Nick was waiting for her in the hall, and as she reached the foot of the stairs the front door opened to admit a draught of damp air and an energetic figure wearing a raincoat turned up around his ears.

'It's miserable out there,' he announced, and then stopped abruptly at the sight of Frankie. For a few seconds he gazed at her in silence and she felt her heart begin to pound. What would this respected country doctor make of the little Liverpudlian his son had fallen in love with? Then the doctor stepped forward and held out his hand with a broad smile. 'You must be Frankie. By George, I'd have known you anywhere! Nick's talked that much about you.'

'No need for introductions, then,' Nick said with a laugh. 'Frankie, this, obviously, is my father.'

'Pleased to meet you,' Frankie murmured shyly.

'And I'm delighted to meet you at last,' was the hearty response. 'When did you get here? Have you come down from Liverpool?'

While Frankie explained she watched Dr Harper take off his coat and shake it out of the door. He was thicker set than Nick and his dark hair was peppered with grey but she felt she would have recognised him in a crowd. He had the same humorous glint in his hazel eyes and the same readily smiling mouth.

Mrs Barrett came through from the kitchen. 'Oh, you're back, then, Doctor. Lunch is all ready.'

'Bring it on, Mrs Barrett,' her employer commanded. 'And bring one of those bottles of claret I've been keeping. This is an occasion for a celebration.'

Over lunch Nick asked for news of the other girls and the general progress of things in Italy, adding, 'Dad knows all about what I've been doing, so you can speak freely.'

Frankie gave him a brief summary of affairs as they were when she left and when she mentioned Alexander's orders he exclaimed in disbelief.

'The sheer stupidity of it! Don't they realise at HQ what those men have done for us? But don't worry,' he went on, 'Luciano and the others are not going to give up everything they've gained because some brass hat from London tells them to. They didn't listen to their own High Command, so why should they listen to ours?'

Later, conversation turned to Dr Harper's practice.

'It's the old, old story,' the doctor said with a sigh. 'So many of the country people round here won't call in a doctor until they're at death's door. They're so terrified of not being able to pay the bill. I keep my fees as low as possible but we've all got to live.'

'It's the same where I come from,' Frankie told him. 'There was a family round the corner from us when I was a kid. The father lost his job as a docker because he hurt his back and they had a child who suffered dreadfully from asthma. They were up to their necks in debt from doctors' bills. That poor woman nearly lived at the pawnbroker's and there was hardly a stick of furniture left in the house. My mum used to go round with a bowl of soup or an apple pie two or three times a week and the other neighbours helped out where they could, but people shouldn't have to live like that.'

'It makes my blood boil!' Nick said. 'But you wait. If Labour get in at the next election the Beveridge Report will be implemented in full and we'll have a proper National Health Service.'

'They won't get in,' his father said. 'People are never going to vote Winnie out, after all he's done for us.'

'You wait and see,' Nick predicted.

When the meal was over Dr Harper went out to finish his rounds and Frankie was left alone with Nick. He pulled her onto his lap and she stroked his hair.

'So, what have you been doing with yourself since you got home – apart from helping your dad?'

'Ah!' he said. 'That's something I've been saving up to tell you. I've done what I told you I was going to do. I've offered my services to the local Labour Party in Eastbourne.'

'Eastbourne? Do they have a Labour Party in a lah-di-dah place like that?'

'It's not one of their natural strongholds,' Nick admitted, 'but you'd be surprised how many people are coming round to our way of thinking. Everyone agrees that things have got to change.'

'So what have you been doing, exactly?'

'Helping to duplicate leaflets, writing some of them. I've even spoken at one or two meetings.'

'Really? Gosh, that's brave!'

'Oh, rot! Brave is what Luciano and Father Antonio are doing. Brave is what you did, coming to find me. Talking in public's nothing.'

She kissed him. 'And brave is what you did, fighting with Luciano. But I still think you're terribly clever, to be able to talk politics to a lot of strangers. I wouldn't know where to begin.'

'Just tell them what you told Dad just now. That would convince them better than any amount of political argument.' He broke off with a laugh. 'That's enough politics. What would you like to do? It looks as if it's stopped raining. Shall we go for a walk?'

It was on the tip of Frankie's tongue to say that for him, surely, this was an impossibility, but she bit back the words and said instead, 'I'd love that. You can show me your village.'

Minutes later she helped Nick to negotiate his chair down the wooden ramp that had been constructed over part of the front steps and they set off down the village street. She offered to push him but he insisted on wheeling himself, letting her help only on the uphill stretches. As they went he told her anecdotes about the people who lived in the various houses or related scrapes he had got into as a boy. There were a few women and old men about and she noticed that they greeted Nick with a mixture of friendliness and a slightly awkward respect.

When she commented on this he replied with a laugh, 'They don't know what to make of me yet. Most of them have known me since I was a kid but now I'm back as *Major* Harper' – his voice enclosed the words in invisible quotation marks – 'they don't know quite how to treat me.'

'To say nothing of coming back as a wounded hero,' Frankie said.

'No!' he exclaimed with a vehemence that surprised her. 'I'm no hero. After Dunkirk I didn't see a single major battle. The real heroes are the chaps who are slugging it out in the Ardennes right now.'

Back at the house they found Dr Harper sitting in front of the newly lit fire in the drawing room, drinking tea and eating scones baked specially by Mrs Barrett in honour of Frankie's arrival. It was exactly the sort of room Frankie expected, with big leather armchairs and walls lined with books. They chatted about the progress of the war until it was time for the doctor to start his evening surgery. Once they were alone, Nick hauled himself out of his chair onto the sofa and Frankie snuggled up beside him and they kissed and talked until Nick glanced at his watch and reached over to switch on the wireless. Frankie was not surprised. These days everything stopped for the six o'clock news.

Their mood changed as they listened. A few days earlier the Germans had mounted a massive counter-attack in the forests of the Ardennes in an attempt to break through the Allied lines. Now the news came that American troops were trapped in the little town of Bastogne, which commanded a crucial crossroads. The weather was appalling, with deep snow everywhere, and fog so thick that it was impossible for the Allied air forces to come to their rescue. If Bastogne fell, the Germans could sweep through Belgium into France, just as they had done in 1940.

'Is it never going to end?' Frankie wailed when Nick turned off the radio. 'A month or so ago everyone was expecting the Germans to surrender at any moment. Surely they must see now that they can't win.'

'I'm sure most of them do,' Nick responded. 'It's just Hitler who can't face defeat.'

Frankie groaned. 'If they break through it'll be like Dunkirk all over again.'

'No it won't! For one thing, we've got the Americans with us now.' He pulled her close to him. 'Cheer up. As soon as the weather clears and the planes can fly again they'll soon push the Jerries back. The Luftwaffe is finished. Our chaps have got the freedom of the skies.'

'I hope you're right,' she murmured. 'I'm so sick of this war. It's a terrible thing to say, but there was a time when I was really rather enjoying myself. Back at Cap Matifou, you know? And even in Italy, some of the time. But not anymore. Now I just want it all to be over.'

'So do I, my darling,' he said, 'and it will be soon. Trust me!'

He pushed her gently away and began to struggle back into his wheelchair. 'I've got an idea – something to cheer us up. Wait there a minute.'

He wheeled himself away and Frankie guessed he had gone to the room that had been converted into a bedroom for him on the ground floor. Very soon he was back, with a small parcel on his lap, wrapped in Christmas paper.

'You won't be here on Christmas Day, so you might as well open your present now.'

'Oh well,' she exclaimed, 'if that's what we're doing you'll have to wait for me a minute.'

She ran upstairs and came down with her own parcel. 'Here you are, my darling. Happy Christmas!' She kissed him. 'Open it!'

'No, you first.'

She tore the wrapping paper off and gave a cry of delight. 'Nylon stockings! Nick, you wizard! How on earth did you manage to get hold of them?'

'An American airman who was in Stoke Mandeville with me. These Yanks can get their hands on anything, it seems. Are they all right?'

'All right!' She held the stockings up to the light to admire their filmy texture. 'They're beautiful. See how fine they are? But they're much stronger than silk stockings. Oh, Nick, they're perfect!' She kissed him again and added, 'Now you.'

He held up his package and shook it gently. 'Well, it's a bottle of some sort, that's for sure.' He undid the paper. 'Strega! Brilliant. This will bring back memories. Luciano had a bottle he kept for special occasions. We used to sit round the camp-fire with it, after a successful mission.' He held out his hand to her. 'It brings back another memory too. Your father insisted on giving me a glass when I brought you home, the first time we met. Do you remember?'

'How could I forget? That's why I was so glad when I found someone in Monopoli who was prepared to sell me a bottle. I don't like it much myself. I hope you do.'

'I love it. Thank you, darling.' They kissed again and then he said, 'Oh, I almost forgot. I've got something else for you.'

He reached into his pocket and handed her a small parcel. Inside it was a box and inside that was a sapphire-and-diamond ring of a size and brilliance that made Frankie gasp.

'It's not new, I'm afraid,' Nick said. 'It belonged to my mother. She left it to me in her will, with the proviso that I should give it to my fiancée when I decided to get married. I hope that's all right.'

Frankie knelt by his chair and put her arms round him. 'Darling, it's the most beautiful thing I've ever seen and it makes it even more special to think that it belonged to your mother. It's a wonderful, wonderful gift.'

'And it belongs here,' he said, putting the ring on the fourth finger of her left hand. 'As long as you haven't changed your mind?'

'Never!' she whispered, her throat so choked with tears that she could hardly speak. 'It's all I've really wanted ever since that night in the air-raid shelter.'

His kiss was long and passionate but at length he drew back. 'I've got one last surprise for you.'

He wheeled himself across the room and into the hall. She followed, puzzled, as he drew the chair up to the side of the staircase and grabbed hold of the banisters. He paused for a second, as if gathering his strength, then with a great effort dragged himself to his feet. 'There!' he panted. 'I was determined to do this by the time you got here and I managed it for the first time yesterday.'

A second later his legs gave way under him and Frankie was just in time to grab him and lower him back into the wheelchair. In the process she ended up on his lap, both of them breathless and laughing.

'Frankie,' he murmured, 'dearest girl! It's going to be all right. Everything's going to be all right. The war will be over soon and we've come through. There was a time when I never expected to, but here I am. Here we both are. And we've got the rest of our lives together ahead of us. You know that song the Hitler Youth used to sing, the Horst Wessel song? "The future belongs to us". Well, they got it wrong. It doesn't belong to Hitler and his stooges. The future belongs to us and we're going to make the most of every minute!'